LEST SHE FORGET

LISA MALICE

LEST SHE FORGET

CamCat
Books

CamCat Publishing, LLC
1281 E. Magnolia St. #D1032,
Ft. Collins, CO 80524
camcatpublishing.com

Hardcover ISBN 9780744307153
Paperback ISBN 9780744307184
Large-Print Paperback ISBN 9780744307498
eBook ISBN 9780744307566
Audiobook ISBN 9780744307573

Library of Congress Cataloguing-in-Publication Data available upon request

Cover and book design by Olivia Hammerman (Indigo: Editing, Design, and More)

5   3   1   2   4

For my parents in Heaven:
Joan Bleich Wuebker,
who inspired me to write by sharing with me
her for passion for books and mysteries,
and
Dennis Wuebker,
who taught me that I could do anything
I set my mind to do.
For my family, my angels here on Earth,
Lou, Olivia, and Frank,
who bring me so much joy.

There is no refuge from memory and remorse in this world.
The spirits of our foolish deeds haunt us, with or without repentance.
—Gilbert Parker, Canadian novelist/British politician, 1862-1932

With the right music, you either forget everything,
or you remember everything.
—Author unknown

CHAPTER 1

The loud heavy beat of my heart echoes in my ears, pulsing in sync with the car's wipers as they furiously slap at the snow alighting the windshield. The frantic rhythm draws me in as I stare ahead into the darkening night and the thick snowflakes swirling in the beams of the headlights. The effect is almost mesmerizing.

My eyelids start to droop. I want nothing more than to sleep, let my mind shut off. Under slumber's spell, the ache in my heart would subside, the guilt in my soul would vanish, and, if I was lucky, I'd wake up to find that the words I heard earlier today were just part of a gruesome dream, an awful nightmare.

She's dead.

My chest tightens, my heart races as my thoughts are pulled toward our last moments together. Fraught with suspicion, accusations, anger. My eyes tear up.

It's your fault.

The words reverberate in my ears as my head starts to throb. How could I have been so stupid and naïve to fall for that man's lies, his manipulations? If I could go back in time and change everything, fix my mistakes, right a host of wrongs, I would. Things would have turned out differently. Two—*no, three*—people would still be alive. But there's no going back. Worse, I see no path forward, at least not one I can live with.

My gaze is drawn to a hazy pair of headlights reflected in the rearview mirror. A chill runs down my spine, even as a bead of sweat trickles down the side of my face. My fingers, clenched atop the steering wheel, go numb as my foot presses down on the accelerator.

"Calm down," I tell myself. I can't let fear trick me into imagining what is not there.

I squeeze my eyes shut for a second, then open them again and glance into the side mirror. They're still there, those headlights, keeping pace with me. I focus on the road in front of me, take a deep breath, and let it out slowly. "Get a grip," I tell myself. "If he wanted me dead, I wouldn't have made it this far."

Staring ahead, a forest of tall pines engulfs the road, blocking out much of the remaining daylight and casting a gloom all around that grows blacker and grimmer with each fleeting moment. But I can't go back. Not now. I'd have to face the truth, accept my own culpability, surrender myself, my life, my future. I'm not ready to do that.

I turn on the radio and press the scan button, hoping for a distraction. Music pours through the speakers in short clips—Spanish, hard rock, country, polka—and then a soft, familiar melody, its words just on the tip of my tongue.

"... *I would surrender my soul, if it would bring back yours . . .*"

My gut twists with remorse. The pain is cut short as the radio scanner moves to the next station.

"... *Could you forgive me, if I made it to Heaven . . .*"

Tears well up in my eyes as the radio, again, moves on.

"... *My name won't be on St. Peter's list . . .*"

A mournful sob erupts from deep inside me. My hands, clutching the steering wheel, suddenly go weak and start to tremble. Those songs, their lyrics—words that never held any personal meaning—now haunt me. It's as if some cosmic disc jockey knows what I've done and doesn't want—no—*won't* let me forget it.

"Please, no more!" I shout.

A woman's voice pops over the speakers, a news program. "Finally," I sigh, poking the scan button to set the station.

"... it's time for a quick station break, after which we'll go to a weather update with WCVA's meteorologist, Alec Bohanan. Our weather team says this blizzard hitting Virginia and much of the East Coast, the first significant snow event of 2017, is a bad one. It could be a killer, so sit tight at home and keep your radio dial tuned to this station ..."

She's right. The snow is coming down thicker and heavier with each passing mile. The roads will only get worse. But I need to press on. I must get home. I can think better there. Figure out what options I have left.

My attention is pulled back to the voice on the radio. "When the last segment of *The June Jeffries Show* returns, we'll join the Virginia State Police press conference with breaking news on the missing person case of—"

It's your fault.

The words echo in my ears, pulsing louder and faster with each echo, drowning out the newscaster's voice. I slam my fist down on the radio's power button.

Suddenly, flashes of light bounce off the windshield. The muscles in my jaw tighten. My neck stiffens. My hands, locked in a death grip on the steering wheel, grow cold, numb. My gaze darts to the rearview mirror. Unable to look away from the looming vehicle behind me, I throw my left arm up to block its intense beams.

The steering wheel jerks to the right, pitching the passenger-side wheels off the road. I grasp the steering wheel with both hands and pull to the left, but overcorrect. The car careens across the snow-swept blacktop, skids beyond the center line.

When I finally pull the car into the right lane, my heart is pounding, my body trembling, while my grip on the steering wheel goes weak.

Keep hiding.

I heed the warning, squeeze my eyes shut, and allow myself to drift away into a welcoming blackness.

CHAPTER 2

he roar of a powerful engine fills the void. When I open my eyes, I find myself strapped into the front passenger-side seat of a monstrous vehicle, a high-end pickup truck with a rich black interior and leather seats. As I turn to face the driver, the blood seems to drain from my body. The looming silhouette of a man is shielded in the shadows of a large, dark cloak, like the proverbial Angel of Death.

The narrow two-lane road on which we travel seems to stretch on for miles through a rolling valley. We've not passed a single other vehicle nor a building of any sort. The rays of the setting sun are blocked by a thick forest of tall hardwoods, enveloping the truck and the two of us in near darkness. My stomach roils at the gloominess of the setting.

I try to engage the driver in conversation in the hope of learning our destination, but he doesn't respond. He turns his head toward me. Though his face is hidden in the shadows, in the dim light his eyes seem to glow red with malice. He laughs, a loud, maniacal chortle that fills the truck cab. I pull away, cowering, unsure what to make of him.

The truck slows, turns onto an off-road trail. My bones jostle with each lurch of the truck as it traverses the uneven and rock-strewn terrain. The vehicle comes to a stop in a heavily wooded area.

Something awful is about to happen. My body knows it. My heart aches. I can barely breathe.

Suddenly, I'm viewing the scene from a different angle, a short distance away, like a spectator, watching as the cloaked demon bursts out of the driver's side door. He drags behind him a kicking, screaming woman. Terror seizes me. She looks very much like me. The malevolent figure throws the woman against the side of the truck. He grasps her throat with his thick, strong hands and proceeds to choke the life out of her. She struggles, thrashes about, but to no effect. His strength overpowers her.

I'm her only hope. I must stop him, do whatever it takes to save the young woman's life. Yet, I'm frozen in place, restrained by some unseen force that prevents me from moving an arm, a leg, or even closing my eyes. I cry for help, but my plea can't escape my throat, as if the same invisible power holding me in place has imprisoned my voice. Seconds later, the poor woman's body slumps to the ground, her head facing me. Her eyes—bloodshot, wide, fixed with the horror of a violent death—accuse me. Guilt forces me to look away, to focus on her killer.

Crouching over the woman's lifeless body, the figure flashes a devilish grin, then moves to the back of the truck and pulls a shovel from the bed. With a few swift and powerful strokes, he digs a shallow grave then, with a forceful push of his boot, rolls the woman's corpse into the hole. Each shovelful of dirt he dumps atop her remains seems to weigh on my own chest, until finally, when the last of the earth has covered her, I can't draw a single breath.

In a flash, the phantom disappears. His spell suddenly lifts. I gasp for air, then scramble behind a tree, where I collapse in a fit of near hysteria, gasping, sobbing, bemoaning the unspeakable violence I've witnessed and my inability—my failure—to intervene.

From out of nowhere, a voice, a woman's, speaks to me, it's tone angry, accusing, "It's your fault."

I slap my hands against my ears, but the echo of the words continues its haunting refrain inside my head.

In the next moment, the phantom is back, looming over me. His malevolent glare, his words, pierce my soul like a dagger.

"You can't hide from me."

I bolt upright wheezing for air, light-headed, flailing for something to hold onto. A hand, warm and firm, grasps my arm. A cry escapes my lips.

"Settle down now. No need to panic. You're safe. You must have had a bad dream." The voice is calm, soothing. I turn my head, flutter my eyes to adjust to the light, and discover a Black woman with graying hair and kind eyes leaning over me, smiling. Standing next to her is a thin young man with short flaming-red hair. Dressed in blue scrubs, he looks equally pleased.

A quick glance around me reveals I'm lying in a bed, shielded from the rest of the room by a thin white curtain. An IV tube runs from my left arm to a bag of clear liquid hanging from a metal post nearby. I turn my head and gasp at the unrecognizable woman staring back at me from the mirror hanging on the wall. Above her one black eye, a butterfly bandage has been applied to a small cut. A purple bruise peeks out from under the large white gauze bandage taped across her nose. Her upper lip is red and swollen.

My chest tightens as my body starts to tremble. I lunge at the bed's guardrail and pull myself toward the mirror. I raise my hand and watch in horror as the woman follows my lead. I touch my nose and wince at the pain; she does, too.

"What's happened to me?" I ask, barely squeaking out the question.

"Don't fret, honey," the young man says. "You're not seriously hurt. Just some bumps and bruises." A gentle pair of hands pulls at my shoulders, easing me back into the bed, and away from the mirror. "Nothing a good rest won't cure."

"Jimmy is right," the woman adds. "He's a nurse on staff here at Summer Oaks. I'm Dr. Malone. You were in a car accident two days ago. January fifth. According to the preliminary police report in your medical file, the car you were driving skidded off the road and into a lake. A Good Samaritan pulled you free before the car sank. He drove you to the nearest hospital. You lapsed into a coma on the way there. But you're awake now, so we can put that little problem behind us."

"A car accident?" I close my eyes, frantically trying to recall the incident but can't. "I don't remember a car accident."

"It's nothing to be worried about. Some degree of memory loss is common after such events, particularly after waking from a coma, Kay."

I open my eyes and turn to the doctor with a sense of panic rising in my chest. "Kay?" The name doesn't ring a bell, not even a tiny jingle. "Is that my name?"

"Yes. Kay Smith."

"But I . . . I don't remember that name." My throat tightens as I strain to speak. "I can't recall anything about myself. My mind's not just a blur—it's blank." I gasp for air. "Is that normal, too?"

Her smile disappears. That's all the answer I need.

"Not normal, no. But given your condition on arrival here, not totally unexpected. That's why I was called in to consult. I'm a psychiatrist."

"I . . . I don't understand."

"The hospital neurologist who treated you couldn't find any traumatic brain injury or other physiological cause for your coma. Further examination suggested your coma was psychogenic in nature—"

"Are you telling me I'm crazy?" I can feel the fear rising in my throat, strangling my words as I try to speak.

"Crazy is not the word I'd use." She gives my hand a gentle squeeze. "Take it easy."

I can't seem to breathe.

"Let's try a little relaxation exercise, one that should help calm you. Close your eyes. Focus on your breathing to my count." Her voice is soft, soothing. "Take a slow breath in through your nose, go deep, use your diaphragm, then let it out through your mouth."

I do as she says, but the air feels thick, heavy, ready to suffocate me as it fills my lungs.

"That's good. Now, let it all out. One ... two ... three ... four ...

As she runs me through the breathing exercise, it gets easier and seems familiar.

"You're doing fine, Kay. Really great. It's clear you're practiced at this technique."

Piqued by the doctor's comment, I bat open my eyes and glare at her. "What's that supposed to mean?"

"It doesn't have to mean anything other than sometime in your past you learned this relaxation technique, perhaps used it to control anxiety or stress. Or it might simply be that you practice yoga."

I heave a sigh of relief. "So, I'm not locked away in some sort of mental hospital?"

"No, not at all." She holds my hand and smiles. "Summer Oaks is a rehab and convalescent facility located here in the DC area. According to your file, you were transferred from a small rural hospital a couple of hours from here. You were inpatient there until yesterday afternoon. Seems a bad strain of flu was going around, highly contagious, and they couldn't spare a single bed. Additionally, your coma was not physiological in nature. The hospital staff felt ill-prepared to treat you, so you were released and transferred here for observation and treatment."

The doctor's explanation helps to calm my fears. "So, what caused my coma? Will I get my memory back?"

"What caused your coma? That's the big question. We don't know. Yet. As to whether your memory will return—we'll find out. It'll happen, but I can't be sure how soon. That you regained consciousness without any drugs is a good sign. Actually, it appears you were jolted awake by a nightmare."

"A nightmare? I don't—"

"Do you recall dreaming?"

I close my eyes, squeeze them shut and focus, but nothing comes from the effort. "No, I'm sorry." I open my eyes.

"No worries. People dream every night, averaging four to six episodes, but most are quickly forgotten."

"Why is this even important? I mean, I can't even remember my name. Shouldn't we start there?"

"Of course, Kay, and we'll work on that. Together. But dreams, especially the scary ones, often reflect the problems we face in our waking lives. We'll explore any dreams when we have the opportunity, but for now, you don't need to worry about anything except getting some rest. Summer Oak's staff and I will do our best to restore your health, both physically and mentally, so you can get out of here and on with your life."

Get *on* with my life? I can't remember my life, so how can I possibly get on with it?

She turns to the nurse. "We're good here, Jimmy. Let's get her more comfortable, then you can get back to your other patients."

A couple minutes later, my arm is relieved of the IV, the catheter and urine bag are gone, and so is Jimmy. All I'm left with is the doctor and a bad, or rather, *no* memory.

Lying back with the bed's headrest elevated, I should feel relaxed, but I don't. My whole body seems tense, my muscles clenched from my feet to my forehead. "What's wrong with me, doctor? Why can't I remember my own name, or anything about myself?"

"As I mentioned before, your coma was diagnosed as psychogenic, not based on any physical cause, such as a head wound, drugs, or disease. After your arrival here, I came to the same conclusion. Such comas are triggered by psychological trauma, something your unconscious self doesn't want you to face. But it seems you did face it, in your nightmare. Now that you're awake, your amnesia is serving as a cognitive defense mechanism, keeping your conscious self from having to face this traumatizing event and the stress that preceded it."

The doctor's explanation, though delivered in a soft, comforting voice, offers little relief. "What could be so traumatizing that I'd lose my memory? Would a car accident be enough to cause that?" I ask, hoping for a simple "yes."

"People often suffer partial amnesia for the events immediately preceding a serious car crash, but it usually takes something more disturbing than an accident to cause what you appear to have, which is 'global psychogenic amnesia,' also known as 'dissociative fugue.' As with your coma, the onset of this type of memory loss is caused by severe psychological trauma and often accompanied by confusion and wandering or unplanned travel."

If I wasn't confused before, I am now. "What do you mean, 'wandering or unplanned travel'?"

"Well, the most common cases of dissociative fugue involve soldiers suffering from PTSD, that is, 'post-traumatic stress disorder.' It was called 'battle fatigue' or 'shell shock' in the old days. In such cases, soldiers crack, so to speak, after experiencing excessive combat stress, such as losing a close buddy or fighting a harrowing battle. They suffer a mental breakdown and wander away confused and foggy, unable to remember who or where they are. They're often reported as AWOL or MIA. The lucky ones regain their memory and find their way back to their units, or they're found by their comrades or MPs before they are captured or killed by the enemy."

I still can't see the connection to me. "But I'm not a soldier in a war zone. Why do you think I was wandering around confused?"

"It's clear from your amnesia that you've suffered a severe psychological shock, a last straw so to speak, after experiencing sustained, debilitating stress or psychological trauma. As for 'wandering around confused,' well, according to your file, you were alone in your car, driving in a blizzard—a very dangerous situation. I see two possibilities that fit with a fugue diagnosis for such reckless behavior. First, you were already not thinking clearly, in a fugue, travelling with no specific destination in mind."

"What's the second possibility?" I ask, unsure whether I want to hear what she has to say.

"Well, most people heed the weather service's warnings to stay off the roads during dangerous blizzards. Perhaps you didn't because you felt you had no other choice. Maybe you thought it was safer than staying put."

"What? You think I was running away?"

"Could be. The outward fear you evidenced from your nightmare might suggest that."

Two words pop into my head.

Keep hiding.

Nearly every muscle in my body seems to clench. Is the command a warning from my subconscious, an effort by my forgotten self to acknowledge the truth of the doctor's theory that I'm on the run, hiding from some awful person, some threatening situation? If not, am I hearing voices? Unsure what it means, nor ready to know, I decide to keep the warning and my thoughts to myself.

"Your car accident may have pushed you over the edge, past that threshold needed to lapse into a full-blown fugue state," Dr. Malone continues. "I think this is a likely scenario. Notes in your file indicate you were awake when your rescuer pulled you from the car, at least conscious enough for you to give the man your name, 'Kay Smith.' Unfortunately, that's all he got out of you before you lost consciousness."

I take a moment to process the psychiatrist's words. "Do people suffering from this kind of amnesia ever recover their memories?" My insides quiver as a more disturbing question flashes through my mind. *Do I even want to remember?*

"Yes and no. Fugue sufferers are usually found with their previous memories intact, but with no recollection of anything that happened during their fugue episode, including what they did and who they met. The experience is usually short-lived, no more than a few days in duration."

Usually. The word hangs in the air, overshadowing every other word she uttered.

"But what if I'm not a usual case? How long could my amnesia last? Days? Weeks?"

The doctor pauses for a long moment. Her silence rattles me.

"Well, I don't want to alarm you, but there are documented missing-person cases where individuals were found after living in a fugue for months, even years. Unable to recall their past, they assumed new identities, took on jobs. Some even married and had families."

I try to speak, but can't, unsure even of what I would say in response to the doctor's revelation.

"Now, before you get yourself all wound up, let me stress one important fact that should alleviate your fears." She reaches across the bed rail and lays a gentle hand on my shoulder. "Dissociative fugue episodes that persist for weeks are rare. Those that last months, a year or longer, even more so. You started coming out of your coma only a short while ago, so be patient. I'm confident you'll have full recollection of your past soon. The odds are in your favor now that you understand the psychological basis of your condition and have access to therapy."

I avert my gaze and consider her words, uncertain how I should feel about the prospects of recovering my memory, one way or the other. As I do, I spot her smiling face on the ID tag clamped to her coat lapel. It leaves me wondering if there is someone in my forgotten life whose face would light up at my safe return.

Keep hiding.

I shiver at the chilling words my mind seems determined to force upon me. Who should I hide from—and why? The answers are locked in my memory. I need a key, something to jog my memory, to open it up.

"Is there anything I can do to stimulate my memory and move the process along? Should I contact the police and file a, what would you call it?" I stumble for the right words. "A found-person's report?"

In my mind, I can see the photo the authorities would send out to the media, one showing the battered face of a woman with shoulder-length blond hair and green eyes. The description of my situation would be no more flattering. I cringe at the headline. *Lost her mind and needs help finding it.*

"Let's wait a couple more days before going to the authorities."

The deep sense of worry I hear in her voice startles me. That fleeting moment of hope I feel disappears, leaving my stomach queasy.

She's telling me what my own subconscious keeps warning me to do.

Keep hiding.

CHAPTER 3

"**Y**ou want me to *hide* from my family, my friends, anyone and everyone who might be looking for me? People who might know me, who could tell me about my past? Why?"

Dr. Malone stiffens her back as she crosses her arms and furrows her brow. Clearly, she's considering her words carefully. Every muscle in my body seems tense. Is *she* hiding something from me?

"Hide? No. That's not it at all," she finally says. "I don't normally offer such advice, but in your case, I think it would be best if you recovered some of your memory before returning to your life. Something traumatic happened to you. Something you found so threatening that you ran away from yourself. It's a potentially dangerous situation, mentally and physically. We don't know who you are, where you came from, nor what is waiting for you back home. The unresolved issues that forced you to psychologically escape your life could trigger more stress, perhaps another fugue episode. It's your call, but I'd prefer to hold off. This is my professional advice, not an attempt to keep you from your loved ones. Let's take a couple of days and see if your memory returns on its own."

Just the thought of walking blindly back into whatever horrors I left behind is enough to set me on edge, making it easy for me to accept the doctor's recommendation. "Okay. I understand. I'll wait."

With my reply, the doctor's demeanor changes. With her arms now relaxed, the worry in her face gone, she is obviously relieved, though I'm not sure why. Is she afraid of those I left behind, the police, maybe both? Her reaction leaves me hanging, doubtful her let's-wait-and-see approach will work.

"What about medication?" I ask, hoping for a magic pill to make this all go away. "Is there something you can give me to stop my brain from holding my memory hostage?"

"I hesitate to put you on antianxiety meds. As a psychiatrist, I'm an anomaly, more into cognitive behavioral therapy than big pharma. Those drugs have many awful side effects, some of which may be dangerous if contraindicated from your medical history, which of course, is inaccessible at the moment. Even then, it can take a while to find the right dosage and stabilize your system, too. Now, you certainly have anxiety issues. But we don't need to uncover the source of that anxiety for you to regain your memory. What will help is relaxing a bit, taking it easy."

A nervous laugh bursts from my mouth. "Take it easy? Really? I'm facing an identity crisis here. A big one."

Keep hiding.

I wince as the words echo in my mind once more.

"How can I take it easy when I can't stop my fears from ricocheting around my empty head?"

"Well, you have a point. So, let's fill up your head with focused, mindful observations, ones that will push aside those worrisome thoughts, and at the same time, may offer you clues to—well, not necessarily to your identity—but who you are as a person."

"Mindful observations? What do you mean?"

"It's part of a therapeutic approach I use with many of my PTSD patients. For you, I would start out by checking yourself out physically, maybe while you shower. What do you see or otherwise sense about your body? Any scars? Stretch marks? Are your muscles toned or flabby?"

The doctor picks up my left hand and examines it, then wiggles my ring finger. "What can you notice just from examining your hand, especially this little digit?"

I pull back my hand and stare at it. "No ring. I guess I'm not engaged or married. Maybe divorced?"

"Perhaps, but maybe you lost the ring, or took it off before heading off in your car."

Puzzled by the conjecture, I return my gaze to Dr. Malone. "What's your point then?"

"Simply, that it's not just the absence of the ring you should notice, but the physical clues that we might expect to see if you had worn a wedding band for more than a few months. A bit of an indent, maybe, if you had a ring sized to fit snugly enough to keep it from slipping off. Maybe a bit lighter shade of skin at the base of your finger, where a ring would have blocked the sun's rays."

"I see what you're saying. Pay attention to the little things, ones often overlooked." I re-examine my left hand. I see no sign I wore a ring, at least not for any extended period of time, but my nails are pretty, perfectly shaped and painted a neutral tint. Either I have a good manicurist, or I'm skilled at doing my own nails. Either way, the color suggests I'm not a flamboyant dresser. I flip my hand over and draw my right hand across my palm. My skin is soft and supple. No calluses. If I have a job, it probably doesn't involve manual labor.

"Focusing your attention is important, especially with my second suggestion, which is to keep your mind open to what you see, feel, hear, smell, and touch, and notice how you react. Try also to experience things using different points of view. These perceptions can offer clues to your life, bread crumbs, in a sense, leading you back to recognizing yourself. They may reflect your likes, dislikes, interests, even knowledge and education as they relate to what kind of job you may have left behind. Keep a journal of what you observe, your reactions, too. As you do, you should find yourself less connected to negative thoughts, and consequently, feel less stressed and anxious. Perhaps, enough to free your memory from lockdown mode."

It's that lockdown that has me worried, anxious about my condition and its causes, leaving me lingering with doubt about the doctor's approach. "Has this worked with your other patients, the one's with amnesia like mine?"

"To be honest, I've never worked with someone with psychogenic amnesia to this degree before, but yes, this has worked with patients with episodic memory loss linked to some traumatic event in their lives."

"So, you don't really know if this will work with me? This is all just a guess on your part?"

"An educated guess. But you're right, I can't guarantee this approach will work, but I believe it will. The key is to not judge what you see or otherwise sense, just accept it without emotion. This will be the biggest challenge for you, especially if something triggers an unpleasant memory that leaves you struggling with anxiety."

"You're not making this an attractive option. Isn't there any other way you can help me?"

"Hypnosis can be helpful, but that has its drawbacks, too, such as the tendency to induce false memories. Dream therapy can be effective but may take a while to produce results. After I leave here, I'll do some research, see what more I can find out about dissociate fugue and the best approaches for treatment. For now, just give these mindfulness techniques a try. Okay? Whenever you feel a bit of anxiety coming on, use your breathing exercises to shut it down. You're good at that, enough so you should be fine until we meet tomorrow."

I nod. That's all I'm capable of doing at this point. I'm overwhelmed with all the information Dr. Malone has given me.

"When you feel up to it, I suggest you get out of bed," she continues. "Take a long shower, get dressed, then stop by the nurses' station for materials to start that journal. As you move about, make your first observations, and record your impressions. Visit the PT room for a walk on a treadmill, if that seems like something you would do. The community room has a TV, DVDs, books, puzzles, and other diversions you might enjoy."

I nod, although I cannot imagine that anything will hold my interest enough to distract me from my predicament.

"If that goes well, you might use the computer there to search the Internet for regional newspapers or newscasts to see if anything or anyone seems familiar to you. Listening to music can trigger memories, as well. Again, journal if anything you see, read, or hear that stimulates your memory, even if it's just an inkling of emotion or recognition. Dreams, too."

Staring across the room at the door, I ponder what I might encounter beyond the confines of this place that would jog my memory enough to pull me out of my fugue. I can't think of a thing. I return my attention to Dr. Malone as she gives me a benevolent smile, the kind that reassures a fearful patient, like me, that everything is going to be all right.

She opens my file, pulls out a sheet of paper, and hands it to me. "At the same time, I need to make you aware of some things to watch out for—symptoms of PTSD that you should take as a warning to slow down, take a step back, get in touch with me."

I scan the list: depression, extreme mood swings, flashbacks, panic attacks, and then—"Paranoia? Hallucinations?" The last two symptoms leave me quaking.

"Those two are quite unlikely with fugue." She shakes her head. "So, don't give them much thought. But if you start thinking everyone is out to get you, or see or hear things that others don't, have the staff contact me. But really, all this can wait. We'll talk more tomorrow morning. I scheduled an appointment for you at eight. We'll work in the conference room. It'll be more comfortable there, and we'll have complete privacy."

She turns and pulls back the curtain, revealing another bed, one occupied by a still form.

"Privacy? You're concerned about privacy now, after talking all this time with another patient in the room, listening in on our conversation?"

"Stop," she says, holding up a hand and shaking her head. "Don't work yourself up. Your roommate is comatose. I'm told she's been here a few years. Brain injury from a skiing accident. She was only twenty-three when it happened. If she can hear us that would be a miraculous improvement in her condition."

As I stare at the unfortunate young woman, my heart sinks inside my chest, the tenseness in my body dissipates, leaving me feeling an odd mixture of grief, terror, and relief. If a nightmare hadn't jolted me awake, I'd be dead to the world, like her.

The doctor steps toward me and extends her hand. I grasp it. Despite her soft skin, her grip exudes strength, confidence.

"I'll stop by for you tomorrow morning." She moves toward the door. "For now, all I'm prescribing is rest."

"Thank you for your help." I force a weak smile.

I watch her leave, then lay back down, mentally exhausted. My thoughts are frenzied, dominated by the words the doctor used in explaining my condition. *Confusion. Wandering. Trauma.* Words that leave me with one question I can't answer—if my past is so stressful, traumatic enough to cause me to forget everything I am and the people most important in my life, am I better off not remembering any of it?

CHAPTER 4

Although I feel weak, I climb out of bed and make my way to the bathroom. I prop myself up at the sink. My spirit plummets at the sight of my face in the mirror, bruised, broken, and bandaged, and swollen. Did a car accident really do this damage? My arms quiver, as if the weight of the question is too much for me to handle.

Keep hiding.

My chest tightens, squeezing my lungs as the words bounce around my brain. Hide from who? Why?

My arms go limp. I slide to the floor and heave a deep breath. Then another. I recall Dr. Malone's slow, soothing count and follow along. Minutes later, with the words in my head finally silenced, I pull myself back up and stare into the mirror, determined to follow the doctor's prescription to study myself as best I can without emotion or judgment. Cringing at my unruly mess of blond hair, I know this task is not going to be easy.

I start by running my fingers through my hair and squirm at the greasy, awful mess. Still, I spy no dark roots, so perhaps, I'm a natural blond. I wince as my gaze travels past shapely eyebrows and the bruised skin around my right eye and settles on my nose, or rather the big white gauze pad taped across it. I resist the urge to rip it off, see what I look like under the bandage, and instead, stare at my fat lip. I flinch with pain as I smile at myself, a wide grin, revealing perfect teeth—straight and white. The product of great genes or dental work? The rest of my mouth feels like a fuzzy caterpillar crawled inside and died. I grab the toothbrush and toothpaste sitting atop a nearby shelf and scrub my mouth until the creature is gone.

At last, I stare into the mirror to assess myself, but all I see is wretchedness. Clearly, I'm someone who takes care of herself. But if that's true, how did I let this happen to me?

"I may not know who you are, or what is going on in your head," I say to the image in the mirror, "but at least I can make you look and feel less like someone who belongs in a loony bin."

Moments later, standing beneath the showerhead, I focus on the spray of hot water pouring over my head, down my back, over my limbs, my body. The welcoming heat of the water melts the tenseness in my muscles. My fingers massage away my worries as they work the shampoo through my hair. My hands glide thoughtfully across my body as I soap myself down. I discover firm muscles—arms, abs, muscular buttocks and legs. Am I a runner? Soccer player? Maybe a dancer?

After stepping out of the shower and toweling off, I take a minute to examine myself further, but discover no scars or stretch marks that might hint at past life experiences—injuries, health issues, weight loss. I pause to consider the absence of stretch marks, unsure whether it reflects the lack of children in my life or resilient skin post-pregnancy. A twinge of sorrow courses through me. What does that mean? Am I sad because I'm separated from my child? Unhappy that I don't have children, perhaps not by choice?

I don fresh clothes pulled from the bathroom shelf—a hospital gown, disposable underwear, bootie socks, and a robe—then blow-dry and brush my hair. I now feel more like a sane human being, even if I don't know who that might be.

As I swing open the bathroom door, a man's face pops into view. Startled, I stumble backward.

"Oh! I'm sorry," he says, wide-eyed, grasping for my hand. "Are you okay?"

At his touch, an unexpected tingle shoots up my arms. Every red blood cell in my body seems to rush to my face.

"No, uh, I'm fine." Mortified and confused by my reaction, I jerk my hand from his hold and flee to my bed, pulling the covers up to cover my thinly dressed self.

He moves to the side of my bed. "Good. Again, I'm sorry. I didn't mean to walk in on you."

"Apology accepted," I reply, as look him over. My heart flutters at the way his dark blue suit fits his tall, lean body, his broad, athletic shoulders. But it's more than his good looks that has me bothered. Something about him is vaguely familiar. "Should I know you?"

Our eyes meet. His soft, brown, searching. I look away, uncomfortable with his penetrating gaze.

"I'm Nick, Nick Costa." He seems a bit flustered. "I'm here to visit Emily, your roommate."

Something—his deep voice, perhaps his name—elicits a flicker of familiarity inside me, a confusing gut rush of attraction and angst. I stumble over my own words, rushing to introduce myself as Kay, then blather on about my amnesia. From the confused look on his face, I'm not making a good first impression.

I'm saved from my ramblings by the sound of a phone ringing, drawing Nick's attention. He pulls a sleek, black cell phone from his coat pocket and glances at the display. "Excuse me. I better take this," he says, then leaves the room.

As the door swings closed, I lay back on my bed and close my eyes, willing my mind to open, to let my memory out of its prison, to tell me if there is someone in my life who looks and sounds like Nick. Given the odd mix of emotions that bubbled up from my subconscious, I'm not sure I'm ready to remember.

Minutes later, Nick is standing at the foot of my bed, his arms outstretched at his sides, as if opening himself up to my will. "So, how about we start over? Hi, I'm Nick. I heard you just woke from a coma. I'm happy for you and wish you a speedy recovery."

Though he has a big grin on his face, his narrow eyes betray worry, not something I'd expect from a total stranger. I pause for a moment, still trying to figure out if the two of us have some connection that I can't remember. "Thank you for your good wishes. I'm Kay, at least that's what they tell me. Seems I have a full-blown case of amnesia."

"That's what I've been told. I'm sure it's just temporary," he replies with a gentle grin.

"I hope you're right." I nod toward the bed across the way. "I'm sorry about Emily. My doctor said she's been in a coma a few years, ever since a skiing accident. That must be hard for you. Is she your wife?" I ask, hoping my attempt to learn the nature of his relationship with my roommate—and, perhaps, me—isn't obvious.

I flush at my duplicity. Is this justified suspicion or the beginnings of paranoia?

Nick crosses in front of me to Emily's bedside. That's when I notice her half of the room.

Unlike my side—stark, colorless, devoid of any personal signature—Emily's space looks like some rainbow fairy descended upon it. The still, silent, and unseeing young woman is surrounded by rich visual stimuli with colors everywhere in her bedding, pillows, wall decorations, and flower vases. The only thing that seems out of place is a black wool coat lying across the back of a chair—Nick's, most likely.

"No, we're not married. If anything, she's more like my kid sister. Her brother, Dan, is my best friend. He's out of the country on a three-week assignment. I'm taking over his daily visits while he's gone. Dan and Emily have only each other now. Both parents are dead."

He picks up Emily's hand and caresses it, a heartwarming gesture that melts mine.

"Poor kid. She's been like this for three years. Suffered a brain embolism after a bad fall on a black diamond slope."

The grief I see in Nick's eyes tells me he really cares for the young woman. It fills me with sadness, too, not just for her, but for him.

He strolls over to the foot of my bed. "You probably don't remember, but I was here, reading to Emily, when you started coming out of your coma. I tried to talk to you, but you were rather groggy and confused."

I'm not sure how to respond. Could the familiarity I sense with Nick be something as simple as seeing and hearing him as I regained consciousness? "I'm sorry. Like you said, I was barely awake."

"That's okay. Anyway, as soon as you stirred, I hit the nurses' call button and let them know you were coming to. When the first nurse arrived, he hustled me out of the room. The staff went in and out for a few minutes. Then some doctor showed up."

I struggle to stifle a yawn.

"You're tired. I'll leave, so you can get some rest. I just came back to get my things." He retreats to the chair across the room, grabs his coat, then starts for the door.

"Please don't leave on my account. I'm not all that tired. Really. I'm here, all alone, without a memory to my name. Left to my own devices, I'll only dwell on my miserable condition." I don't wait for him to decide whether to stay or go. "How often do you visit?"

"I live close by and try to come in once a day, like Dan does when he's in town." Nick drapes his coat across the back of my bedside chair. "I read to Emily, talk to her, exercise her arms and legs. We hold out hope that her brain will heal. The doctors aren't so optimistic, but we keep trying."

The story is tragic, and at the same time, endearing. Is there a man like Nick in my life, someone compassionate, attentive, and selfless? *Not likely.* Otherwise, I wouldn't be here, alone without a single soul to vouch for my name or face.

With nothing to do but lie in bed and rest, as Dr. Malone insisted, and no personal history of my own to share, I convince Nick to sit and tell me his story.

I listen as he offers snippets of his life. Growing up in the Little Italy section of Baltimore with a handful of brothers and sisters and his parents—a cop and his wife, a high school lit teacher. Studying criminology at Old Dominion, a full ride paid for with a Navy ROTC scholarship. Graduating in 2001 with a four-year commitment to the Marines and plan to join the Baltimore PD after he'd fulfilled his service obligation. Deploying to the front lines of Afghanistan two months after 9/11 to hunt down Osama bin Laden and his band of Taliban terrorists.

As Nick speaks, there's something in his voice, his choice of words, even his stories, that seems so comfortable, so right. Suddenly, he falls quiet with a pensive look on his face.

"Do you remember 9/11, Kay? Anything of the terrorist attacks on the World Trade Center and the Pentagon? Most people who lived through that day can't forget it."

I hadn't expected the focus to turn on me, but I train my mind on the task anyway, hoping for a few memories to seep through the dam my subconscious has created. Surprisingly, and tragically, all I can summon are a few images from the media coverage. Planes flying into the Twin Towers. The collapse of the buildings. Billowing clouds of smoke. People running, screaming.

"Nothing specific." I shake my head with regret, disappointed at being unable to recall any personal memories of a day that should have been indelibly etched in my mind.

"That was a long time ago. Fifteen years. Perhaps you remember something more recent? How about last year's election? The presidential race was a heated one. The polls had the incumbent president, Jason Hayward, leading his challenger, Virginia Governor William Lockhart, only by a point or two in the popular vote. The electoral college map was up for grabs, too. Two weeks before the election, news broke of a purported pay-for-play scandal involving Hayward. The media ate it up. It was all over the Internet, too. William Lockhart won the election rather handily."

A flash of anger tears through me. I pause to reflect on the emotion and Nick's words but come up empty. "Sorry," I reply, shaking my head. "I don't remember."

"Really?" he asks, seemingly dismayed by my response. "It was a huge story, especially after the election, when the allegations proved false."

Despite my denial, there's something in Nick's story that triggers not just disgust, but a deep sense of distrust. Am I a Hayward voter outraged at the political shenanigans that may have cost my candidate reelection?

"Sorry. I just don't remember. Maybe I'm not into politics." My excuse is weak. The tightness in my jaw, the jitteriness in my limbs, tell me so.

"No need to apologize. I'm the one who is sorry. I didn't mean to rattle you. No more from me." He pretends to lock his lips and throw away the key.

"That's not necessary. Please, tell me more about yourself. You spent years in war zones. Were you ever injured in battle?"

Nick hesitates for a moment, as if uncertain he wants to go there.

"Please," I plead. "Your life is so much more interesting than mine. I promise to tell you all about myself when I finally have something to remember."

As Nick rolls up his left pant leg, I seem to know what's coming. I recoil as a long, red scar along the side of his calf comes into view.

"I got this souvenir in a gun battle with Iraqi insurgents in 2004." He places a hand on the left side of his abdomen. "I picked up a nice memento right here to match."

"What happened?" I ask, grateful Nick didn't pull up his shirt and flash me another horrific scar.

He pauses for a moment, rolls down his pant leg, then starts. "My unit was patrolling a rough area of Baghdad when we were pinned down by a rooftop sniper's nest. We took refuge inside an abandoned store. After tending to three wounded men, I took two others and made a run for the apartment building where the snipers were positioned. My unit provided cover, but Private Hardy was hit crossing the street. Corporal Jackson took one in the shoulder while we pulled Hardy to safety. I made it to the roof and took out one sniper before he knew what hit him. I took a couple bullets from the other thug, but somehow got off a kill shot as I went down. I spent the next three months recuperating stateside."

Something about his story kindles an elusive memory, something I can't quite put my finger on. Hoping the answer will come if don't press myself to remember, I return my attention to Nick.

"I guess what they say is true. War is hell." My face blushes with embarrassment. "Sorry. I guess I haven't lost my memory for pathetic clichés."

"No need to apologize." Nick turns toward me. "You're right. War really is hell. Unfortunately, sometimes it's just unavoidable. You have to stand up to bullies, whether you're on the playground or on the world stage. The only good part is the friends you make fighting side by side. You become as close as brothers, each willing to give his life for the other. I won't deny that it's hard when someone is killed or maimed." His gaze shifts to the floor.

A somber silence hangs in the air. When Nick looks up, he's regained his composure. "You cope by staying in 'Mission Mode,' focused on the job. Those who don't, end up with PTSD."

I flinch. The acronym reminds me of my own diagnosis, leading me to imagine myself wandering around a minefield, addled and unaware, bombs bursting around me, bullets whizzing past my head.

"I'm sorry," Nick says, his voice melancholy. "War isn't a pleasant topic. We can talk about something else."

"No, that's not it." I hesitate, trying to decide how much of my own story to reveal. The little I'd learned from Dr. Malone was discouraging. Still, Nick has poured out his story to me, painful stuff to be sure. He deserves at least a brief explanation from me.

"My psychiatrist thinks some severe psychological trauma is behind my memory loss, something awful enough to make me snap. She compared my condition to soldiers suffering from PTSD. It's not something I really want to talk about."

Dead air falls between us once again. Nick has carried almost all of our conversation, much of it rather difficult emotionally. The sadness in his face leaves me wrestling with guilt. I'm responsible. I was insensitive. I pressed him to talk about his military service, and now, I don't know what to say to change the mood or direction of our dialogue. The quiet seems to get louder with each passing moment.

Nick ends our conversational stalemate with a smile and a hopeful gleam in his eyes. "So, you really don't remember anything about yourself?"

Keep hiding.

The words rush at me once more.

I cross my arms as a twinge of nausea hits me. "No, nothing." It's not a lie, just not the whole truth. I remember Nick or someone who reminds me of him—a faint memory of someone from whom I should hide.

Nick's smile falls. "Well, I wouldn't worry too much about that. I've seen a few cases of dissociative fugue, as your doctor calls it. It doesn't last long."

I struggle for a new topic of conversation but come up with nothing. Uneasy with the direction our discussion has taken, I give in to my fatigue and yawn. "I'm sorry. I guess I really am tired. Maybe we could talk more next time you visit Emily." I rest my head on my pillow and pull my blanket to my shoulders.

A soft smile lights up Nick's face. "Sure. I'd like that. Since you're all alone, I'd like to offer you my phone number, you know, in case you need anything." He pulls a pen from his jacket and jots his information on a piece of paper lying on my bedside table.

"I'll leave you to rest now." He slips on his coat. "Promise me you'll call if you need anything, even if it's just to talk."

"I promise—and thanks. I enjoyed our chat." I offer him a sincere smile. "I really mean it."

Nick responds with his own broad grin. "Me, too, Kay." He flips the light switch as he opens the door. "Sweet dreams."

A second later, he's gone.

I close my eyes, but Nick's image lingers in my mind. Something about him has me conflicted: I am eager to be with him, and at the same time, disturbed by his presence.

My reaction to Nick must be a bit of PTSD paranoia, a reflection of a mind with nothing better to do than worry. Most likely, he simply reminds me of someone else in my life, someone I really should be wary of—once I remember him.

CHAPTER 5

I awake with a start, blanketed in darkness, my heart racing, my breath labored. It takes me a few moments to remember where I am before the dream that startled me awake flashes through my mind.

I'm standing in a long, dim hallway watching Nick walk away. His dogged gait, his unwavering silence reveal his intention—he is never coming back. "I'm sorry. Please, you must forgive me," I call out to him, but he doesn't stop, nor hazard a glance back. To him, it's clear—I no longer exist.

Uncertain what the nightmare means, but desperate to put it behind me, I flip on the overhead light, blink my eyes to adjust to the glare, then head to the bathroom. The bad dream fades quickly as I wipe a cool wet cloth across my face and neck.

As I exit the bathroom, I glance at the digital clock on the wall. 6:13 p.m. On my bedside table, I spot a food tray. Realizing I haven't eaten for days, I'm suddenly famished. I hop back into bed, pull my meal close and start to eat.

The baked chicken breast is cold, dry, and bland as cardboard. The broccoli is bitter, the salad wilted, its tomatoes overripe. I gobble up the dessert—raspberry gelatin—the only course that isn't somehow ruined. Needing to keep my body strong to help my mind recover, I resolve to suffer through the rest of the unpalatable meal and rely on the TV to distract my taste buds.

Scrolling through the channels, I settle on a 24-hour news channel. But listening to the grisly stories of suicide bombings in the Middle East, domestic shootings, and deadly car pile-ups is harder to swallow than my chicken.

"On an equally somber note, a spokesperson for President-elect William . . ."

My stomach lurches, my body tenses. *I can't watch anymore awful news.* I snatch up the remote and flip through a slew of celebrity gossip shows, classic sitcom reruns, and a variety of game shows, then settle on *Jeopardy.* I recognize the host, Alex Trebek, the game, and decide to play along.

"Let's try 'Henry the Eighth' for six hundred, please," says the tall gangly young man standing behind the middle podium with the name "Lenny" scrawled across its front. Alex reads the answer as it appears on the screen. "Alone in my prison strong, I wait my destiny. Woe worth this cruel hap that I should taste this misery!"

The rest of line pops into my head. *Toll on, thou passing bell. Ring out my doleful knell. Let thy sound my death tell. Death doth draw nigh. There is no remedy.*

"Anne Boleyn," I say, as the name comes to me. My face flushes with sadness as I recall the title—"Oh Death, Rock Me Asleep."

The current champion, a woman with a mass of curly blond hair buzzes in. "Kendra," Alex calls out.

"Who was Anne Boleyn?"

"Correct. Select the next clue."

"Wow," I say aloud, casting aside my momentary melancholy. "I must know my classic literature." That I would even have such a thought seems to prove the point.

I focus my attention on the show, hoping for more clues to my knowledge base. Over the next few minutes, I beat the contestants to the buzzer across the category and three others—"AP U.S. Government," "World Geography," "Pardon My French"—making it clear I'm at least well-read, if not well-educated. I bomb with "Baseball Hall of Fame." The last column of clues is a chance to redeem myself, though the name of the category is a bit unnerving.

"'Heaven and Hell' for $200, please," Kendra calls out, after retaking the lead in the game.

Alex reads the blue-and-white clue as it appears on screen. "The lyrics of this number one-selling hit by King's Gambit tells the tale of an emperor lamenting his life choices and the fate awaiting him after death. Listen."

Music erupts through the television's speakers, a catchy collection of staccato notes, led by a string section. I hum with the melody. Pulled into the beat, I suddenly find myself playing along, my left hand fingering the neck of some imaginary stringed instrument, while my right hand draws an invisible bow across my lap.

My heart leaps with excitement. "I must be a musician, but what do I play? Violin? Cello? Bass?" I mumble, frustrated with my inability to answer my own question. "Why can't I remember anything important, like my life?" I blurt out.

"Your memory will come back soon. It's simply takin' a rest, girl."

I flick the OFF button on the TV remote and turn toward the voice. In the doorway stands Jimmy, the nurse I met earlier in the day. The equipment tray he carries signals it's time for a vitals check.

"I hope you're right, but, like Anne Boleyn, the answer to another *Jeopardy* question, I feel like a prisoner held without just cause and beyond any hope of ever being set free."

"Well, I've hope enough for the both of us." Jimmy offers a friendly nod, then crosses over to Emily's bedside, where he trades out the IV bags. "As for what's causin' you to forget yourself, well, I'm sure the good Lord will reveal everythin' to you when you're good and ready. Just be patient while He works His will."

As I watch him go about his duties, I reflect on his thick Southern drawl. "I love your accent, Jimmy. It reminds me of some place. Where are you from?"

"A small town just west of Lynchburg in the Roanoke Valley—God's country here in Virginia. Big, beautiful mountains, clear blue streams. Perfect in any season. Green as far as the eye can see in the spring and summertime. A mix of red, yellow, and orange in the fall. A blanket of Divine white in the winter."

I close my eyes and easily picture the setting in my mind. "It does sound idyllic." Although I don't share Jimmy's accent and can't remember having been anywhere near his hometown, I sense we share some sort of kinship for the area.

"Did you sleep all afternoon?" Jimmy asks, after returning Emily's chart to its clear acrylic pocket on the wall. He pulls off his latex gloves, tosses them in the trash, then stretches on a new pair.

"Yes. I don't know why I was so tired. After all, I was in a coma for days, not running a marathon. The nap felt good, though. Or maybe I just needed to get some food in me. Either way, I am more rested."

"Probably the food, honey. But bein' unconscious ain't sleepin'. Nothin' restful about it. I've been around comatose folks for a while now and know what I'm talkin' about. None of them wakes up and hops out of bed ready to go gangbusters. I'm glad you got that nap in." He glances at my dinner tray. "Girl, I know the food here is not the best, but you're gonna need to do more than pick at your food to get your strength up."

I grimace at the half-eaten dinner but keep my review of the meal to myself. "I'll try to do better. I promise."

"I'll hold you to that." He pulls a digital thermometer from his pocket and slides a sterile plastic cover over the tip.

"Nick, that is, Emily's visitor, seemed nice enough. Have you met him?"

"Just once. Earlier today. If he's Emily's visitor, it's a surprise to me. I thought he was here for you."

Jimmy's comment dumbfounds me. "Why? He seems to know Emily well. At least, that's the impression I got as he spoke about her and her family."

"I checked on you an hour or so before he notified the staff that you were stirrin'. When I walked into the room, he was hoverin' over you, holdin' your hand, not Emily's." He thrusts the thermometer at me. "Put this under your tongue, please, and sit still while I check your other vitals."

I follow Jimmy's instructions and watch while he finishes my exam, but my mind wanders to his revelation.

My thoughts flash back to my first few confused moments of consciousness. Nick was there, leaning over me, holding my hand, as I came out of my coma. Could there be more behind Nick's attentiveness than what he's let on?

When the thermometer beeps, I pull it out of my mouth. "Well, if Nick's part of my past, he's doing a good job of hiding it."

Hide. My heart jumps at the word. Am I being justifiably suspicious of Nick?

"Don't go by what I say. I usually work a different floor, so I don't see who's comin' and goin' around here."

The nurse's words ease my mind, convince me I'm letting my mind play tricks on me. Perhaps Jimmy misinterpreted Nick's behavior, simply caught him checking on me after seeing me move or hearing me grunt. That makes more sense. Although I'd just met the man, he seems to be a stand-up guy. He's given me no reason to mistrust him.

Jimmy finishes jotting some notes on my chart. "Your vitals are all normal. Is there anything else I can do for you, hon? Maybe a little somethin' to help you get a good long rest tonight?"

After losing almost two days of my life to a self-inflicted coma, sleep is low on my list of priorities.

"No, thank you, Jimmy. I'll be fine. Anyway, Dr. Malone thinks my memory might come back faster if I stimulate it, observe my surroundings, journal my perceptions and impressions. She also encouraged me to use the computers in the Community Room to search the Internet for familiar people and places."

Jimmy nods. "Sounds like a good idea. You'll have the room all to yourself. Nobody goes in there after dinner. Is there anythin' else you need before I tend to my other patients?"

"I'll need some paper and a pen, if there's some handy."

"Sure. Follow me."

—

The public-use computer, a dinosaur with a big, white bulbous monitor, sits atop a gray counter in the corner of the Community Room, next to a small printer and corded telephone. As Jimmy reviews the instructions for using the equipment—speaking of browsers, websites, and social media that I might find useful—I find his tutorial unnecessary. Apparently, my subconscious sees no danger in letting me remember how to use modern technology.

After Jimmy leaves, I sit down in front of the computer and splay my fingers across the keyboard. My hands tremble. I pull them back and stare at the blank screen but can't control my growing fear about what lurks in my past.

I bolt from the chair, away from the computer, and stand with my eyes closed, metering my breathing. *Inhale . . . exhale . . . inhale . . . exhale.* After my jitters subside, I open my eyes and scan the room, determined to go a little slower, make some tame, meaningless observations, as Dr. Malone suggested, as a calming distraction.

I listen. The room is quiet, the only noise stems from the buzzing of activity by the staff down the hallway as they go about their business. Looking around, I notice the space, about three times the size of my small double room, is warm and inviting, decorated with soft yellow walls and a large brown sectional. I'm drawn to the sturdy oak shelving filled with books, worn paperbacks mostly, with a few hardcovers thrown in. Scanning the titles, nothing seems to interest me, though it's clear mysteries and romances are the favorites among the patients and staff.

Wandering about the room, I come to a standstill next to a small, square table and gaze at a jigsaw puzzle left halfway completed. I reach for a small, irregular-shaped fragment of the flowery meadow scene, examine it briefly, then turn my attention to the puzzle. I zero in on where the colorful piece belongs in less than a minute. Five more pieces quickly find their homes, revealing the image of a big, bright sunflower. I may have problems mentally reconstructing my identity, but otherwise, my brain seems to work fine.

I take a chair at the table and continue working on the jigsaw, trying to give my stressed-out mind a chance to relax. Even so, the puzzle of my identity continues to haunt my thoughts.

What will I see when I finish the hidden image of my past? A loving circle of family and friends that I'll run back to as fast as my legs can carry me, or something or someone so terrifying that I'll run away, wishing I'd never remembered?

CHAPTER 6

The only way to settle the question is to forge ahead. I take a couple of calming breaths and return to my seat in front of the computer. Staring at the browser, I recall Dr. Malone's suggestion that I look for familiar people and places in the newspapers and newscasts. That strategy seems a fruitless effort. Not if I want to track down my identity. A simpler, more direct approach is in order—search for "Kay Smith," as if that is my real name. At this point, I have no reason to doubt it is, but with a name like "Smith," I know it will be like scouring a rock quarry for a lost diamond. But success will open a world of online information for me—jobs, family, and friends, even my own social media pages—a better bet for stimulating my memory.

I dive into the task. A few keystrokes later, I've set up Gmail and Facebook accounts under an alias, "Mary Brown," then start my search for what I expect will be an avalanche of other Kay Smiths.

I'm not wrong. A few dozen are listed on the social media site. With no way to winnow the possibilities with demographic search filters, I set about scrolling through all the photos for an image I might recognize as mine, but the cache is quickly exhausted. There wasn't one photo that bore enough resemblance to me to suggest even a few shared genes. A LinkedIn search yields similar results, leaving me with two alternative explanations. One, I wasn't into social media in my past life, which is doubtful, given how easily I navigate these sites, or two, Kay Smith isn't my real name.

I decide to write down everything I know about myself, along with what I don't.

Description:
- ✓ *White female, mid-thirties(?), blond hair, green eyes. Weight? Height?*
- ✓ *Where am I from? Parents? Education? Job?*
- ✓ *Am I a wife? Mother? Do I have family? Friends?*

January 5: Car accident on country road during blizzard.
- ✓ *Specific time and location?*
- ✓ *What make and model of car was I driving? License plate? Registration?*
- ✓ *Has my car been pulled from the lake, my purse, wallet, ID, cell phone retrieved?*
- ✓ *Treated for minor injuries, hospitalized for psychogenic coma.*
- ✓ *What hospital? Who treated me? Was I ever conscious?*

January 6: Transferred to Summer Oaks
- ✓ *Who initiated this on my behalf? Who's paying my bills?*

January 7: Awoke from coma with psychogenic amnesia, diagnosis: dissociative fugue
- ✓ *What traumatic experience led to my fugue? What chronic stress did I experience prior to losing my memory?*

The facts are sketchy, but the glaring holes offer me hope. Some of the blanks in my history can be filled by the police report for my car accident, others from the hospital that treated me. And my file here at Summer Oaks is a good place to start.

I log off the computer, snatch up my writing materials, and hustle down the hall to the nurses' station. The young man sitting behind the tall, gray counter checks my patient wristband to confirm my identity as "Kay Smith," then pulls a manila folder from the stack of files in front of him. After agreeing to examine the file where I stand, I flip through the few sheets of paper in the thin folder, jot some notes on my writing pad, then return my file to the nurse and thank him.

Back in front of the computer, I pick up the phone and punch in the number for St. Christopher's Memorial Hospital, the facility on record for my medical care after the accident. I reach a "not in service" recording—twice. An online search for the correct contact number comes up a blank. The only hospital I can find with the name of the good saint is located an ocean away in London. I return to the nurses' station to recheck my notes but find no discrepancy. My transfer paperwork is apparently wrong, a big dead end in my quest for answers, leaving me to wonder how best to proceed.

I search for reports of car accidents in Virginia for January fifth, the date I was admitted to the hospital. A couple minutes into my search, a news item catches my attention:

Car Accident Leaves Woman Comatose, Identity in Question
Posted: Jan 5, 2017 11:15 PM EST (*Charlottesville Courier* e-edition)

Albemarle Co., VA – Charlottesville Police are investigating a blizzard-related car accident on Hwy. 15 that left an unidentified woman in a coma at Albemarle County Hospital. John Harris was driving south-bound around 5:15 p.m. the evening of January 5 when the car in front of him veered off the road, down an embankment, and into Lake Monticello. He stopped and rescued its driver before the car sank beneath the lake's surface. Mr. Harris took the lone occupant of the car, a woman, to Albemarle County Hospital for treatment. She was comatose upon arrival and remains hospitalized.

The victim, described as 32-37 years old, 5' 5", 110 pounds, with green eyes and short blond hair, was reportedly driving a silver Audi sedan. Tentatively identified as Erin Johnson, the woman's name has yet to be confirmed. Anyone with any information that could lead to a positive identification should contact Sergeant Robert Montgomery of the Charlottesville Police Department (434-828-9122).

Erin Johnson. I stare at the name and repeat it in my mind, then aloud. Like "Kay Smith," the simple moniker doesn't strike a chord with me. Still, the noticeable similarities between our two cases are too compelling to ignore.

Am I Erin Johnson?

I reread the physical description, the details of the woman's accident, and convince myself to follow the lead. After printing a copy of the article, I look up the contact information for Albemarle County Hospital and carefully dial the phone number. My call is picked up by an automated switchboard, forcing me to wait through a glut of useless extensions before instructing me to stay on the line for "all other calls." A few seconds later, a live operator is on the line. I explain my inquiry, then wait while she checks the inpatient status of Erin Johnson.

"I'm sorry. She is no longer a patient here," the operator says when she returns to the line. "For further information, you'll need to talk to Records. The office closed at five, so you'll have to call back tomorrow or leave a message."

My call is transferred before I can reply. I'm about to hang up when a woman's voice addresses me. "Patient Records. This is Anita. How may I help you?"

"Oh, uh, hello. I didn't expect anyone to answer. I was told the office was closed."

"Normally, it is," Anita replies. "I volunteered for the night shift this week to digitize old records into the system. It was getting lonely around here, so I answered your call. How may I help you?"

"My name is Kay Smith. That is, I think that's my name. I'm not quite sure." I ramble on about my situation, leaving out many of the specifics, then tell the clerk about the news article I'd read.

"Can you tell me Erin Johnson's status?"

"I'm sorry. That's confidential information. I need permission from the patient or her family before I can release any information."

"That doesn't make sense. The news article reported that Erin Johnson arrived unconscious with her identity unconfirmed. If that's the case, how does she or anyone else give permission to release information?"

"Again, I'm sorry. That's the law. HIPAA rules."

After a few more rounds of futile persuasion, I'm exasperated, ready to give up when another approach occurs to me.

"I've got an idea," I say, hoping a friendly, personal appeal will help soften the clerk's firm grip on the information I'm seeking. "If we keep this inquiry anonymous, if we use no names, can you help me? All you'd have to do is search the records for the evening of January fifth for my description: white, adult female; age probably mid-thirties; short blond hair; brought into the ER after a car accident."

Dead silence hangs in the air. I'm not sure if the clerk has disconnected our call or is considering my request.

"Listen, Ma'am, I don't really know if that's legal or not. I'm all alone here, so I can't ask my supervisor. Give me a minute to look over the file and see if there's anything I can tell you."

After thanking Anita for her compassion, I'm put on hold. A couple of minutes later, the clerk is back on the line.

"What I'm about to share with you is public information, so I'm not breaking any laws in answering your question." Anita pauses, as if her silence is a forewarning of what is to come. "Yes. There was a comatose woman matching your description, brought into the ER the evening of January fifth. Erin Johnson. She was admitted that night. I'm sorry to tell you she died the next day. She never woke up."

CHAPTER 7

'm stunned. I pinned my hopes on Erin Johnson and me being the same person. With no other leads to follow, I press on with my inquiry.

"Please, bear with me. I know it sounds crazy, but maybe the woman didn't die. The file could be wrong. It might just be a clerical error. Not on your part, of course," I hastily add. "Do your records note whether Erin Johnson had any unusual identifying marks?" A tattoo, scar, or other noticeable marking would prove the woman and I are two different people.

"That type of information wouldn't be in the woman's medical file, but it would be part of her autopsy report."

"An autopsy? For a car accident?"

"Unnatural deaths always require an autopsy. In this case, the police would have been called in, a report filed, and the body taken to the county morgue for examination and storage until it could be positively identified and claimed."

The mention of the police catches my attention. "Were police called to the hospital after this woman arrived at the ER? Is there some sort of accident report in her file?"

"Yes," Anita says, a few moments later. "Sergeant Montgomery left a preliminary copy for our files. It's only a page long. The Charlottesville

Police Department will have a more complete report on file. That's public information, too."

She reads me the report. A minute later I've recorded only two new pieces of information: the police report number and the D.C.-area phone number for John Harris, the Good Samaritan who pulled "Erin Johnson" from her car. Nothing else in the preliminary report adds to or deviates from the online news account I'd read of the woman's accident and her condition, nor reveals anything more about John Harris. Even so, I have enough information to move on, though I'm not sure where I'm headed.

Staring at my notes, I can only contemplate the long search that lies ahead for the truth of my life. I try to talk myself into making the call to the county morgue, but it seems a futile effort. What are the odds that the hospital mixed up the identities of two patients—one dead, one alive—or worse, transferred a living, breathing Erin Johnson to the morgue? Not likely. Those kinds of mistakes only happen in horror movies.

"Thank you, Anita. You've been very generous with your time and assistance."

"My pleasure. Good luck, Ma'am."

Good luck. I could use some of that. Suddenly, a different take on my troubles hits me. Could it be that I am fortunate indeed? That this is a chance to leave my wretched life behind and start over with a new identity and a clean slate?

Once again, I walk away from the computer. This time, I fetch the TV remote, click the ON button, and plop myself down on the couch. The local news might jog my memory, but the clock on the wall reads seven-forty, too late for the evening broadcast, too early for the late-night news. I surf the channels, looking for something, anything to pass the time. In my present mood, the sitcoms come off silly, the one-hour dramas too dark, the reality shows too pathetic. I settle on *Headline News* when it appears on screen, just as it goes to a commercial break. I pick up an old copy of *People* from the coffee table and begin reading an article about a young starlet. Halfway through, something mentioned on TV catches my attention.

"... State Emergency Management personnel from five East Coast states hit hard by the recent blizzard report that the storm claimed more than twenty lives," a young Black anchorwoman says. "The hardest hit was Virginia, where eleven fatalities include a family of five who died from hypothermia after being trapped in their snowbound car on a rural road in southern Virginia. Officials fear the totals could rise. More than a dozen people across five states remain missing ..."

My heart skips a beat. I rush back to the computer, where my fingers stumble over the keyboard in a search for photos of the missing storm victims. Ten minutes later, the faces of five women lost while driving in the snowstorm glare back at me from the computer screen. The names don't matter. I bear little resemblance to two Black women, two elderly Latinos, or a heavyset white woman.

Though disheartened, I realize I don't want to be haunted by my past, forever looking over my shoulder for whatever—or *whoever*—is lurking behind me. No matter how tempting it might seem to just start over, I can't leave my mystery unsolved. Though it's a long shot, a crazy idea, I grab the phone sitting next to the computer and place a call to the morgue.

CHAPTER 8

Leaning back in his overstuffed brown leather recliner, Felix Jager basked in the warmth of a hot, glowing fire after a dinner of baked salmon, steamed asparagus, and sautéed potatoes. In for the night, he wore his favorite loungewear—a worn, gray warm-up suit emblazoned with the name "Camp Peary," known more familiarly as "The Farm." Despite having been forced out of the clandestine intelligence service ten years ago, he kept the items in his closet because the fabric was warm and cozy, far from the feeling he held for the agency bosses, who hadn't the balls to appreciate his methods. Now, he worked occasionally with two of his former Defense Intelligence Agency colleagues, dedicated, talented people, who, like him, were dishonorably discharged for violating what all three considered absurdly strict rules for extracting intelligence from sources.

Felix sipped his coffee. A sigh of contentment escaped his lips. "What do you think, Roscoe?" he asked, gently stroking the sleek, black cat lying next to him. "Have the cops found that popsicle yet?"

The cat rubbed his head along Felix's thigh and purred.

He stroked his pet's soft, black fur. "You do, huh. Let's see if you're right." He set his cup on the coffee table, grabbed his tablet, then pulled up traffic-accident.com and searched the website for new reports of vehicle mishaps in the Albemarle County area. He found three, though none that alarmed him the least bit.

"Things look good, buddy." He smirked and checked his watch. "Time to check in."

He pulled his cell phone from his pocket and pressed "1" on its speed dial. His call was answered after the first ring.

"Hello, sir," Felix started, "I checked the news reports again. There hasn't been a single account of a car or accident victim being pulled out of the Rivanna River in the last three days. There's no evidence she made it out of her car, dead or alive. I think it's safe to conclude that the target has been neutralized."

"That's no longer good enough. I need proof of death. A photo. Without tipping off the cops. Now. I'm running out of time."

The doubt Felix heard in his boss's voice rattled him. Still, Felix knew better than to challenge his employer. The last time he lost his cool, the agency fired him, forcing him to ply his trade as an independent contractor. He loathed everything about contract work. He hated the insultingly low pay. He despised his clients, pissed-off fools, cowards all too eager to have someone else obliterate their spouse, business partner, or other target of their greed or rage. Worst of all, he hated not being in control. Clients couldn't be trusted to keep their mouths shut once the job was done. There was always a better-than-even chance they'd cave and rat him out when the heat was on. Working for his current employer, the work was steady, the money good, and he'd never had a problem with loose lips.

"You can trust me, sir. I did my due diligence," Felix said, hoping to quell his boss's uncertainty in the matter. "There were no witnesses. No one stopped to rescue the target. I neither saw nor found any evidence that emergency vehicles were called to the scene that night or the next morning."

Felix paused, waiting for some acknowledgment from the man. When there was none, he continued. "I'm betting it'll be a good long time before that ice queen melts and somebody finds her. April at the earliest, after the spring thaw. Otherwise, my guess is July when the dry season hits and the river's water level drops. Either way, I think we're in the clear for a while. When she's finally found, it'll appear as if her death was an accident, per your instructions, sir."

"That's all well and good, but I still need proof of death. Get that photo by tomorrow morning. No excuses."

"Yes, sir. Anything else you need from me?"

"No." The line went dead.

A photo of a dead body inside a car submerged in the waters of an icy river? "Fuck!"

CHAPTER 9

I pull up the phone number for the Albemarle County Morgue. An energetic-sounding clerk answers the phone identifying himself as "Danny." Five minutes after explaining my unusual situation, I learn the morgue has no doppelganger for me lying on a slab in cold storage, no female corpse with "Erin Johnson" written on her toe tag. Maybe this idea that Erin Johnson and I are one in the same person isn't so crazy after all.

"Would you like me to check NamUS? That's the Department of Justice's online database for missing and unidentified persons. I can run a check using your name and description."

I jump at the attendant's offer, adding "Kay Smith" to his search. When he returns to the phone a few minutes later, he has nothing to report. The database holds no record for a missing woman matching my description under either name. With both names in question, I ask him to try "Jane Doe," but that search, too, results in a dead end.

"I'm sorry I wasn't more help. We don't often have bodies comes through that lack some sort of identification, even if it's flimsy. The last Jane Doe was a few months ago, a tragic case, just awful. Turned out to be a local girl who'd gone missing. She was found in a shallow grave after a couple hunters stumbled across it. Some animals had disturbed her remains."

My heart starts to race.

"She'd been strangled . . ."

My lungs wheeze for air, suffocated by something deep inside me.

". . . I knew her from high school. Her name was Madeline . . ."

Maddy. The nickname peals through my head like a warning bell, drowning out the clerk's voice.

It's your fault.

Horror loops over and over in my mind like a bad movie. The room starts to spin. Like a movie, everything fades to black.

—

"Hello? Hello? Ma'am? Are you still there?"

The words are faint. I open my eyes and drag my head off the computer keyboard.

"Ma'am? Are you okay?" the morgue attendant's voice shouts from the phone handset, swinging by its cord over the side of the desk.

I reach for the receiver with a trembling hand and press it to my ear. "I'm sorry. I just, um, that is, someone interrupted our conversation." I stumble through the lie, too embarrassed to admit to my panic attack and fainting spell.

"I'm sorry. I have to go now," I say, rushing my words. "Thank you so much for your help." I hang up without giving the helpful clerk a chance to say good-bye.

I close my eyes and take a few deep breaths to settle myself, trying to get a grip on what just happened, but my panic attack defies any explanation without some memory to bring it to light. I want to believe there is a reasonable explanation for my intense, paralyzing reaction to the name "Maddy," something unrelated to the forgotten trauma that sent me running from my life. My churning gut tells me otherwise.

I take a few more breaths and refocus on Erin Johnson. It doesn't take long to see where our lives merge. Our physical characteristics are a close match. Our accident descriptions are too similar to be ignored. Even the absence of her body from the morgue lends credibility to the idea that we are one and the same person. And now there is one new name that complicates the picture—Maddy.

I rise from my chair and shuffle around the room, doing my best to avoid the computer, as if my refusal to set eyes on the machine, the only portal I have to my past, could cause all the suspicions I harbor about my forgotten life to disappear. It's irrational, I know, but I do it anyway. Instead, I pick through the books on the shelves and scan a few back covers. I read the first few pages of a mystery novel, but soon find myself rereading entire paragraphs because my mind is too distracted to draw meaning from the author's words.

I reshelve the book, meander over to the window, and stare into the dark night. The lights in the room reflect off the glass, causing me to gawk at a ghostlike image of myself staring back at me, as if my bruised and battered twin is outside, desperate for me to let her in. The fear I see in those eyes raises the question I'd asked myself earlier: Do I even want to remember my past?

When it comes down to it, I know I have no choice. My situation can't be resolved by a decision to keep my life before the accident buried. Just not possible. Even if I never regain my memory, my past will always be there, hovering in the shadows. If I don't actively work toward resolving my amnesia, it'll catch me unawares. *Yes,* I decide, *it is better to know.*

But now, I'm faced with a new question, one that leaves me shaking with fear. *Who is Maddy?*

CHAPTER 10

elix had no doubt the woman was dead, so to his thinking, a return trip to the scene of the crime for a death photo was a futile gesture. A risky endeavor for him, his employer, too, but he had no choice in the matter. Not following orders, angering the big guy, would make him a target, the prey of his replacement.

He glanced at his watch. With a midnight departure and a two-hour drive, he'd arrive at the scene around two. The rural road would likely be deserted at that hour, the risk of witnesses almost nonexistent.

With time on his hands, he set his cell phone on the end table, picked up the remote and turned on the TV. After scrolling through the menu of movie offerings, he settled in to watch "Misey," a film he'd never seen. The plot, about a famous writer injured in a car accident then rescued and held captive by a deranged fan, held Felix's interest until something in the back of his mind started to gnaw at him.

Did I miss something?

He replayed the job in his mind but saw nothing that would even hint at a slipup. The only possible witness had been in a car he passed, a Dodge Charger at least a half-mile behind him, struggling to stay on the snowy road. Since no emergency vehicles were called to the scene, it was clear the muscle car's driver saw nothing.

Felix went into the kitchen, refilled his coffee cup, and returned to his recliner, but his mind continued to nag at him. *Something went wrong.* He shut his eyes, oblivious to the story playing out on the TV, and summoned his memory of that night, mentally retracing his steps for anything that could lead him to question the certainty of the woman's death.

I didn't pass any emergency vehicles on the road into town. I pulled into a McDonald's drive-through for a coffee and burger, then parked and watched the road for the next half hour. The only vehicle that drove by was a snowplow. Not a single cop car or fire engine. No EMT truck or ambulance. I checked into that cruddy, little motel a block away and never heard a siren whiz by. I listened to my police scanner for hours that night, but never heard one bulletin about an accident anywhere near the river.

He opened his eyes and stared at the cat sitting at his feet. *I called all the urgent care centers and hospitals, but the only woman brought in was some dumb chick who drove her car into Lake Monticello. "Erin Johnson" or "Erica Jones." Some lame-ass name like that.*

Felix ran through the scene in his mind a second time but nothing he remembered changed his conclusion.

The cat meowed and sprang toward him. Felix's cup flew from his hand, splashing coffee across his shirt and pants. "Dammit, cat!" He jumped from the recliner and stripped down to his shorts. At that moment, he realized one small gap in his recollection. A hole in his surveillance that could sink him. He'd knocked over his coffee that night, splattering himself with liquid so hot he thought it would burn a hole in his pants.

"Fuck!" He paced the room, his step heavy. *I soaked up the mess, but I couldn't've been distracted for more than ten, fifteen seconds at the most.*

Felix replayed the incident in his head over and over, and finally backed into a scenario in which the car behind him stopped to rescue the woman. The timing of the coffee fiasco—no more than seven or eight minutes into his surveillance—might have caused him to miss the car if it sped by on the way to the nearest hospital. That the bitch failed to surface anywhere on his radar, dead or alive, didn't put his mind at ease.

Felix gaped at the TV screen, tossing other scenarios around in his head, when something he hadn't considered hit him.

What if the people in the car behind me did stop, rescued the woman, then took her home with them like that whack job in 'Misery'?

Felix considered the possibility for a moment, but decided that it wasn't likely, though over the next few minutes the question lingered in his mind. He couldn't shake the feeling that there were loose ends he needed to tie up.

He dashed to the garage, wrenched open the glove compartment of his truck, and yanked out a burner phone, one of three he kept charged for situations where total anonymity was required. Back inside the house, his first call was to Albemarle County Hospital, the medical facility nearest the crash site. It took one lie about looking for his missing wife and three transfers to reach someone who could address his concerns, a woman working the late shift in the Records Department.

"Yes, sir," said the clerk, who identified herself as Anita. "According to the records, a woman was brought in the night in question matching the description you gave me. The man who brought her in said her name was Erin Johnson, but I guess that was never confirmed. Is Erin Johnson your wife?"

Felix's heart started to race, beating faster and faster, while he considered the possibility that the woman he left for dead was still alive.

"Sir, did you hear my question?"

"Yes, ah, yes," Felix quickly recovered, then stumbled into another lie. "That's her. That's my wife." He moaned, trying his best to sound like an overwrought husband. "She was visiting her mother that day and left for home around five, even though I told her to stay put and wait out the blizzard. I haven't seen or heard from her since. Where's Erin now? What's her condition?"

"I'm so sorry, sir," the clerk said, with genuine sorrow in her voice. "My records show that the woman on record as Erin Johnson died the next day, January sixth."

Felix smirked without saying a word, thankful the clerk couldn't see his face over the phone.

"Sir? Are you still there?" From the distress in her voice, the clerk was clearly more upset about the woman's death than he was.

"I'm sorry. Yes. Yes, I'm still here," Felix said, feigning a whimper. "I . . .I'm just startled, shocked to find out my wife is, uh, dead."

"Sir, if this is your wife, her body should still be at the county morgue. Do you want the phone number and address?"

"Yes. Thank you. You're very kind." He let out another groan for good measure, then recorded the information while the clerk read it over the phone.

"I'm really sorry, sir. I know it's not the answer you were looking for, but that's what is recorded in your wife's file. Off the record, though—"

"Yes?" Felix interrupted, barely able to control his impatience.

"I think there's a chance that your wife is still alive."

CHAPTER 11

"**A**live? You think my wife may still be alive?" The joy Felix had felt a moment earlier drained from his body. He braced for bad news.

"I can't say for sure," the records clerk said, "but I took a call earlier this evening from another woman, one suffering from amnesia after being involved in a car accident the same night as your wife. She's going by the name Kay Smith until she figures out her real identity. I don't mean to give you false hope, but she does match your wife's description."

Felix barely held back a string of cuss words, then pulled himself together. "Oh, my god!" he exclaimed, with a more appropriate mix of surprise and elation. "That's great! What was that name again? Where is she?"

"Kay Smith. She was calling from a rehab facility, but she didn't mention its name or location. Anyway, I thought she had the wrong hospital and the wrong patient, so I told her to check the morgue for Erin Johnson, just like I suggested to you a moment ago."

"Thank you. Thank you very much. You've been very helpful." He disconnected the call with a swift flick of his finger, then slammed the phone onto the coffee table.

"Damn!"

The cat bolted across the room and took refuge underneath a rocking chair.

"If that motherfucking bitch made it out of her car alive," he screamed, "if she's this Kay Smith, I'll track her down and finish the job! If I have to, I'll put the fucking toe tag on her myself and drop her cold, dead body at the morgue."

After calling the Albemarle County Morgue, Felix found himself on hold, forced to listen to a sickening playlist of soft rock music. When the morgue attendant came back on the line five minutes later, Felix held his anger in check and continued his imitation of a frantic husband. The clerk promised to check into his inquiry, then put him on hold once again. Felix's patience wore thin as he paced the room, waiting for the attendant's return.

"I'm sorry, sir," the clerk said ten minutes later. "I've done everything you asked. I double-checked our computer and hard copy records, the logbook of funeral home transfers, the FBI unidentified person's database, and checked every cadaver in the place, but I can't find any woman named Erin Johnson. There's no Jane Doe matching the description you gave me either. Maybe the hospital got it wrong, and your wife didn't die. Perhaps Erin Johnson isn't your wife. Either way, she's not here."

Felix grumbled at the news, unsure what it meant.

"If I were you, I'd take this as a good sign and assume she's still alive. In fact, I had a similar call from a woman a few minutes ago. She had amnesia and was looking for information on the same woman. I guess she was hoping there was a mix-up of some sort, one that would confirm she was Erin Johnson. She could be your wife."

Felix took a deep breath to calm the anger boiling up inside him, then spoke. "Where was she calling from? Did you get her name?"

"I'm sorry, sir," the clerk replied. "She offered two names, Erin Johnson and Kay Smith. She didn't seem to know which one was correct. I have no idea where she was calling from."

Felix howled and hurled the phone across the room. It shattered against the wall, leaving plastic, glass, and metal scattered on the floor. After fetching another burner phone from the truck, he placed a follow-up call to the hospital's Records Department, and was put on hold yet again. He hung up, then used the phone to search online for the police report for Erin Johnson's car accident. When he found it a few minutes later, he knew he was in trouble.

Fuck! There was a witness!

CHAPTER 12

It took more than a few minutes of deep breaths, in and out, to leave me calm and clearheaded enough to realize that my imagination was getting the better of me on all fronts. Without any real memories to anchor my reality, gruesome suspicions about my past are likely to continue. Truth is, I have no reason to suspect that Maddy, whoever she is in my life, is in any danger, much less dead. I need to guard myself against such mental distractions in the future, or, at the very least, be better prepared so that I can control them, rather than the other way around.

I place a return call to the Albemarle Hospital Records Department to follow-up with Anita.

"So, you see, Anita," I say, after filling her in on what I learned from the morgue attendant. "There's no record of Erin Johnson at the morgue. Isn't it possible that there was a mix-up, and her death certificate was meant for someone else? Because I think I'm that Erin Johnson. Everything about us matches up, our physical descriptions, our car accidents, even the timing of it all."

The phone goes silent. I'm not sure the lapse in conversation reflects Anita's earnest consideration of my theory. Perhaps she's on another line, calling the psych ward to come and lock me away.

"I believe you. I do," she says finally, with a wariness to words. "At least, I believe that there might be more to what's going on here than a simple mix-up in patient records. I got a call from a man just after I talked with you. He asked a lot of the same questions you did."

A chill rushes through me. "Did you get his name?" I ask, rushing my words. "What did you tell him?"

"I don't remember his first name, but he was looking for his wife. He seemed frantic, desperate to find her. Said her name was Erin Johnson. He reeled off the same physical description you gave me. I told him exactly what I told you, that Erin Johnson died January sixth. I referred him to the county morgue to confirm her ID."

"Did you tell him anything else?"

"He was really upset, so I told him about you."

My teeth clench, my heart flutters as alarm surges inside me. I should be overjoyed at the news, relieved that a concerned husband is looking for me, but instead, I have grave doubts about anyone trying to find me, especially a husband. If what Dr. Malone says is true, that I'm running deaf, dumb, and blind from a traumatic reality, I must consider the possibility that the man looking for me does not have honorable intentions.

Instinctively, I touch my bandaged nose. *Am I a battered wife?*

"Maybe this man knows me." I pause to catch my breath. "How much did you tell him?" I brace for bad news.

"There wasn't much to tell. I gave him your name—Kay Smith. I repeated what you told me about your accident, your amnesia and all. He wanted to know where you were. I said you were in a rehab facility. That's all. You never gave me the name or location of the place."

I heave a sigh of relief. I'm safe. Unless he finds a way to track me down to Summer Oaks.

"After the call, I was curious, wondering if you two really were looking for each other, whether there really was a mix-up in the files. So, I poured over Erin Johnson's file to see if I could figure out what happened. I was hoping to give you two a happy ending. I found anything but that. I'll tell you what I know, and maybe we can figure this out together, but you can't breathe a word of this to anyone, or I risk getting fired. Do we have a deal?"

My pulse quickens as my already heightened sense of wariness escalates. Nonetheless, I jump at the clerk's offer. "Yes. Of course. You have my word and my deepest gratitude. So, what did you find?"

"For starters, the death certificate in her file doesn't look right to me. In the three years I've worked here, I've processed probably a thousand of these documents, including dozens signed by Erin Johnson's doctor, Dr. Arjun Patel, a neurologist on staff here. I searched his patient files, looking for other death certificates to be sure. I'm convinced the signature on Erin Johnson's paperwork is *not* Dr. Patel's. It's not even close. He's one of the few doctors whose signature is consistently legible."

"Are you saying it's a fake?" I ask, stunned by the news.

"That's what I wondered, so I checked Erin Johnson's treatment log. I didn't find anything that would suggest her life was in danger. She arrived unconscious with a broken nose, other minor facial injuries, and a possible concussion. The CT scan report Dr. Patel ordered showed no abnormalities. Same for the blood work. There's a diagnosis listed here, 'Coma – Psychogenic.' I've never seen that term before, but I'm guessing it's a coma with psychological causes."

Anita's words rock me. If there is any evidence to prove I *am* the missing Erin Johnson, this is it.

"I came out of my coma earlier today. My doctor says I'm suffering from global psychogenic amnesia." I explain the terms and diagnoses to Anita as best I can.

"So, let's think about this for a minute." I consider what we know, what we don't, and where to look next for answers. "Let's assume I'm not Erin Johnson," I continue, though everything I've learned so far seems to point in that direction. "If her death certificate is fake, where is she? Was she released to someone or transferred to another facility?"

"That's the other problem," Anita replies, clearly irritated. "Her paperwork shows her body was released to the county morgue. But as you discovered, it never arrived at the facility. It's possible her body was delivered to the wrong place, but given a suspicious death certificate, I'm inclined to think the transfer paperwork was doctored, too."

Nothing associated with Erin Johnson's case makes any sense. So much of her medical records appear to be outright fraudulent. At the same time, there's no concrete information to confirm my identity as Erin Johnson, only circumstantial evidence based on the similarities of our physical descriptions, our accident histories, and medical diagnoses.

"I really don't have anything to offer as proof," I say, exasperated by the lack of answers in what should be a simple matter. "But I'm convinced Erin Johnson and I are one in the same person. Maybe Kay Smith is my real name. Maybe it's Erin Johnson. Maybe it's neither. I just don't remember." I sigh. "If only you could give me some solid information."

"I wish I could help you, but all I can offer you is what's in my records."

From the heavy dose of sympathy in the clerk's voice, it appears Anita is starting to believe my crazy theory.

"Do the records show if anyone ever identified Erin Johnson as Kay Smith?"

"Give me a minute, and I'll see what I can find." Anita puts me on hold.

"I'm sorry," she says, when she returns. "According to the records, no one came forward to ID Erin Johnson. The name Kay Smith doesn't show up anywhere in the digital file or the hard copy."

I frown. I don't know if Erin Johnson is my real name, but I'm not about to bet my life on this generic name, like Kay Smith, one that anyone could have made up on the spur of the moment. I dread the prospect of another tedious Internet search trying to match my face to another commonplace name. The only way to avoid it, I realize, is to talk to whoever tagged me as Erin Johnson.

CHAPTER 13

"One last question, Anita, then I'll let you go. From the news story I read, I know that a man by the name of John Harris rescued me after my car went off the road. Is there a witness statement anywhere in the file, something that tells us how John Harris knew my name was Erin Johnson?"

After a short pause on Anita's end, she replies. "No. Nothing. Maybe he snatched your purse from the car and kept it. It's been known to happen. Not everyone is as good a Samaritan as they claim to be. You could just ask him. I gave you his phone number on our last call, didn't I?"

I scan my notes and quickly find the information. I repeat the number from the page.

"That's correct," she confirms.

I stare at the page. Neither the name nor the number mean anything to me, but maybe it should. Perhaps my rescuer wasn't just a passing motorist. Maybe we have a more personal connection than he let on. When I get John Harris on the line, I intend to ask him just how well he *does* know me.

"Thank you for all your help, Anita," I say, taking a much-needed breath to settle my nerves. "I'm not sure what all this means, probably just a series of unfortunate errors. Who knows? Maybe something else is going on, something fishy, as you suggested. Until I figure this mess out, please keep everything we've talked about quiet, don't tell anyone what we've learned. Don't correct any records, or, for that matter, tell anyone I exist. In fact, I think it's best we keep this whole conversation between ourselves. I need more time to remember, more time to figure out who this mystery man is, and whether he poses any threat. Can you do that for me?"

"Nothing gets past these lips, to anyone, until I hear from you. Promise," Anita says, her voice firm in relief as much as conviction. "Cross my heart and hope to die. And listen, honey, if there's anything else I can do to help, please let me know. I'm working the night shift through the end of the week if you need me. Say, why don't you give me your phone number? That way I can let you know if this guy calls back, or if I run across some helpful information."

I hesitate. "I'd rather not give you the number here. It would reveal my location. It puts you in a difficult position if this man, or anyone else I'm not sure about, comes asking."

Anita agrees and offers me her cell and home numbers, so I can check in with her. I jot the clerk's numbers on my notepad, then promise to keep her updated on my search for answers. After thanking her again, I say good-bye and hang up.

Staring at my notes, I shudder. *What is going on?* My medical file contains so many errors and omissions that I can't help but infer that there's more than just plain, old incompetence at play. But if the mistakes in my file aren't due to human error, they must be intentional. Someone tampered with my records. But who? And why?

My conversations with Anita provide answers to a few of my questions, but instead of bringing clarity to the picture of my life, they only raise more puzzling questions. I record them on my notepad:

The man who called Anita claiming to be Erin Johnson's husband: Is he legit?

If so, am I his wife, or is he looking for someone else?

If his story is a lie, why is he trying to find me?

I raise my left hand and stare at my fingers, reflecting on my relationship status. There is no ring and no indentation that suggests that there ever was one. I consider alternative explanations this man might have for tracking me down. One, the mysterious caller and I are married indeed, but I don't wear a ring for one reason or another. Perhaps, we are not well off financially, so we didn't exchange rings. Two, our marriage is common law, so no bands were ever exchanged. Three, I don't wear a ring because my husband and I are separated or divorced, ours was either a short marriage that didn't leave any telltale ring marks, or a long departed one whose evidence has faded away. Four, the mystery caller is my boyfriend or just a friend who claims to be my husband to get answers. Five, the guy really is looking for his wife, but I'm not her.

Two more disturbing explanations exist. One, there is an unknown link between that man and me, some hidden agenda. A relationship I can't explain just yet.

Keep hiding.

The words ring inside my head, underscoring the second disturbing scenario, the one that seems to best fit the puzzle. I *am* Erin Johnson. The man Anita talked to is my poor choice of a life partner, one so abusive I had no choice but to flee when he busted my nose and gave me a fat lip. I took off intending to start a new life with a new name, a new identity.

Maddy.

The name tears at my heart. Who is she? What are we to each other?

From the terror I feel at the least recollection of her name, she must be important to me. I consider another possible scenario—that I'm not running *from* an abusive man, but instead, I left home, took off in a terrible blizzard, because I was running *to* her—Maddy—to protect her from him.

Fear rises in my throat. I want to believe the existence of this man is a good sign, a hopeful harbinger that help is on the way. But I can't. Not with a little voice in my head whispering its ominous warning over and over.

Keep hiding.

Should that warning now include someone in my life named Maddy?

CHAPTER 14

Felix knew he'd hit a dead end at the morgue. To him, the irony of the situation was no laughing matter. The conflicting reports of this woman's death—whatever her name was—didn't make any sense. With a possible witness to his crime—some guy who pulled the living, breathing woman from her car—he quite possibly still had a job to finish.

He punched the number for Albemarle County Hospital into his phone and asked for the Records Department, only to have his call rerouted to voicemail. He tried again a couple of minutes later with the same result. Ten minutes after that, his call finally went through.

"This is Mr. Johnson," he shouted into the phone when the Records clerk answered. "I called the morgue about my wife. They don't have her body. They don't even have any record that she was ever there. What's going on? Where is my wife?"

He heard the anger in his voice and realized he had to tone it down. Yelling at the woman on the other end of the phone wouldn't get him very far. "I'm sorry. That was rude. I'm just upset. Can you please check the records again? Maybe Erin didn't die."

"I'm sorry, sir. I've already checked both the digital and hard copy records for Erin Johnson. They both report her death on January sixth."

"Are you absolutely sure there's no mistake? Maybe there was mix-up with patient records and my wife is still there. Maybe she was transferred or released. Do you have any paperwork on that in her file?"

"No, sir. There's no release, ah, that is, no transfer form," the clerk stuttered, as her voice squeaked. "I mean yes, there is, but it's a transfer release for the county morgue."

He peppered the clerk with more questions, hoping to rattle her into slipping up, show her hand if she was lying. "Maybe my wife is that woman you mentioned earlier—Kay Smith. The one who doesn't know her own name or who she is. I should talk with her. Where was she calling from? Can you give the phone number?" He focused his attention on the woman's voice.

The loud sigh Felix heard on the other end of the line spoke volumes. He said nothing in response, left the conversation hanging, dead air, waiting for the next telltale sign of lying.

"No, sir. I don't have her number. But I do have good news there, at least for Kay Smith, that is." Her words were rushed, almost breathless. "I was mistaken about her, uh, that is, she was. She called back to let me know that, well, someone from her family had arrived and confirmed her identity. She really is Kay Smith. She's *not* Erin Johnson. She's *not* your wife."

"You sure about that?" Felix said, his words heavy with accusation. It was the type of question, delivered as he did, that often broke the weak ones, left them confessing everything Felix needed to hear, and sometimes more.

"I . . . I really don't know what else to tell you."

She was lying to him. He was convinced. There were too many indicators—the change in her speech pattern from their earlier conversation, the rise and fall of her voice, rambling on, stuttering, as if making everything up on the fly. That she didn't crack in the end didn't tell him much. Grilling someone over the phone rarely produced that effect. In person, he utilized strong incentives for people to talk. He'd make that visit, get her to talk, if he couldn't get the information any other way.

"I'm not satisfied with where this conversation is going," Felix said. "I need to speak to your supervisor. Please transfer this call."

"I'm sorry, sir," she replied, her sigh signaling relief. "I'm the only one working Records tonight."

Fury raged inside him. He hurled the phone to the floor and stomped on it, repeating the assault over and over until the device lay scattered in jagged shards. Spotting Roscoe trembling under a nearby chair, he rose, strode across the room, and scooped up the frightened animal, then paced the floor of his living room, furiously stroking the thick, black fur on the animal's back.

That clerk is covering up something. I'm sure of it. Why? Did someone get to her, tell her to keep her mouth shut sometime after our first conversation? If so, who?

There was no time to waste. He had to make the trip to Charlottesville and get that proof of death, though now, Felix doubted he'd find a corpse to photograph, forcing him to hunt his prey one last time.

CHAPTER 15

eep hiding.

My heartbeat echoes in my ears, drowning out the voice in my head, but the uncertainty remains. Is the ominous warning—my voice, my words—a subconscious message from my imprisoned memory? Or is it a hallucination, yet another step into the depths of PTSD-induced paranoia?

Just because you are paranoid doesn't mean that people are not out to get you. I try to laugh off the old cliché, but I can't. Everything I see or otherwise sense is just too real.

I close my eyes. *Breathe in . . . breath out . . . in . . . out . . .*

A minute later, the only sound I hear is the slow whoosh of air as I inhale, then exhale. At last calm and relaxed, I open my eyes and thoughtfully ponder what I know. Someone *is* looking for me, a man my mind seemingly wants me to forget. If the dread now haunting me is any indication, he's someone I fear, perhaps intent on causing harm to me or someone I care about. Perhaps Maddy.

I have no choice now, I must press on, do what I can to remember my past, and continue my search for answers. I can't waste any more time in a state of frenzied worry. But the road of inquiry ahead is full of potholes—odd, glaring craters of missing and fraudulent information I'll fall into if I keep relying on secondhand sources for information. Instead, I need to go straight to the people involved to get at the truth of Erin Johnson's case.

I pull my copy of the news bulletin detailing her accident and scan the story for the name and cell number of the police officer handling the case. He's my best bet for answers and would know if my car has been recovered, and if so, what identifying information was found inside. As I punch Sergeant Montgomery's phone number into my cell, Dr. Malone's warning peals in my brain. Contacting the authorities is risky if I offer them the truth of my situation, which could bring my past life crashing down on me before I'm ready. I need an alias and a cover story, one that will get Sergeant Montgomery talking without exposing myself.

As I stare at the news story in front of me, an idea occurs to me. *A reporter.* I give the ruse a bit more thought and decide it's best to pose as a journalist from the local desk, a recent hire, working a human-interest angle on Erin Johnson and the tragedy that befell her, rather than someone from the crime beat. *Have I always been this duplicitous?* I shake off the unsettling thought and dial.

My call goes to Sergeant Montgomery's voicemail. I hang up without leaving a message or callback number and make a mental note to try again later.

The next best source is the Sergeant's accident report, but the website for the Charlottesville Police Department offers yet another obstacle—requests for motor vehicle accident reports are accepted only in person or by mail.

Online, I identify several alternate websites promising access to traffic accident reports, but my request is stymied by my lack of plastic money. Though advertised as "free," the sites require an upfront fee, chargeable on a credit or bank debit card, guaranteed refundable before the end of a short trial period. My accident report will have to wait until I can somehow pay for my "free" copy.

John Harris is next on my call list. One glance at his phone number and my chest grows tight. When I pick up the phone, my palms start to sweat.

What is it about this Good Samaritan that has me so nervous? Does the name ring some unconscious bell? Are we more than strangers who just happened to be in the same place at the same time? If so, why did he deny it and dump me at the hospital?

One possibility immediately comes to mind—we're having an affair. His odd behavior makes sense if one or both of us are married. I try to imagine alternate explanations for his actions but can't manage even one. My hand quivers as I replace the phone in its cradle. With my courage in retreat, I opt to look for a photo of John Harris on the Internet on the off chance that I'll recognize him and remember how he fits into my past.

I stare at the computer screen, unsure how to proceed. John Harris is as commonplace a name as Erin Johnson and Kay Smith. Woefully, I have very little to work with in narrowing my online search. No address or city, no physical description, no employer. Nothing but a phone number with a D.C. area code.

I type a question into the computer's browser: *How do I find a person from a phone number?* I scan the page of websites offering free reverse lookups and settle on one that promises to deliver not just a name and address, but also personal history, work history, social media links, even known relatives and associates.

I enter John Harris's phone number into the search line and await the results with eager anticipation. After a few clicks of my mouse, I locate a site that provides names and addresses without an upfront fee. My search comes up empty again. John Harris's number is not his. It belongs to 78-year-old woman living in Sitka, Alaska.

Why am I not surprised?

CHAPTER 16

I lean back in my chair to consider my options, but my thoughts are muddled. My neck aches, prompting me to stand and do a few head rolls to work out the kinks, when suddenly, two hands grab my shoulders from behind. A scream catches in my throat. I pull away and spin around, only to find myself in the arms of Nick Costa. The sheepish grin on his face shows he is surprised by my reaction.

"Sorry," he says, taking a step backward. "You looked like you needed a little neck rub."

"Well, maybe so, but you really shouldn't sneak up on people."

Uncomfortable with the intimate gesture, I pull my robe close and retie the belt. As I do, Jimmy's words echo inside my head: *I thought he was here for you.* Doubt floods my mind—qualms about me, about Nick—indicating that perhaps we have a history together, some connection I can't remember.

"What are you doing here, Nick?"

"I really enjoyed our visit this morning, so I decided to stop by and see if you wanted company this evening."

The response seems benign enough until I catch him peering over my shoulder at the computer monitor. Jarred by a pang of anxiety, I bolt to the keyboard and log out, then grab my notepad and clutch it to my chest. I'm not ready to share anything I've learned tonight. Not with Nick. Not with Dr. Malone. Not with anyone. Not until I can make sense of everything and present the crazy—no—paranoid thoughts running through my head with some sane evidence. Without it, my next stop might really be the nuthouse.

"Sorry," Nick says, with a note of disappointment in his voice. "I caught you at a bad time. I'll leave."

As he turns and starts toward the door, my mind flashes back to the dream that woke me earlier—Nick walking away while I plead for forgiveness. The twist of panic I felt in my dream returns. Is the dream a reflection of something from the past or, perhaps, a premonition of what is to come?

I won't know until I get to know Nick better. Not an unpleasant task, I must admit. He is, after all, very attractive with his dark, wavy hair, his warm brown eyes and strong square jaw.

"Nick, I'm sorry. Please stay."

He stops at the hallway and turns back. "You sure?" he asks with a gentle smile, one that starts to melt the lingering tension in my shoulders.

I return Nick's smile and nod. "Yes, I'm sure. I need a break anyways." I point toward the puzzle table. "We can visit while we work a jigsaw."

A moment later, we're sitting across from each other, examining the colorful pieces that lay before us.

"It's a flowery meadow." I pick a random puzzle piece off the table. Just as I did earlier, I examine its shape and colors, pour over the unfinished scene looking for its home, and in less than a minute, nestle the piece where it belongs, completing the image of a bright, white daisy.

I watch Nick out of the corner of my eye as he selects a puzzle piece and focuses on the half-finished scene. After a minute trying to force the piece into several different areas of the picture, he admits to being stumped.

"Guess I'm not good at puzzles," he says with a sheepish grin. "Want something to drink?"

"Yes. Thank you. Nothing with caffeine. I conked out after you left. Woke up hours later. Caffeine will only make it harder for me to fall asleep later tonight."

My gaze lingers on Nick as he rises from the table and walks to the refrigerator in the corner of the room. Pulling open the door, he peers inside. "What's your poison? Sprite, apple juice, or water."

"Water, please."

He grabs two bottles and lets the refrigerator door swing closed, then twists the caps off both bottles and tosses them in the recycling bin next to the refrigerator. Back at the puzzle table, he sets a bottle next to me.

"I'm sorry for monopolizing the conversation this morning. I'm not prone to talking about myself, at least not that excessively. Not very gentlemanly." He sips his water, then sits.

"No apology necessary. I was the one asking all the questions. I enjoyed listening to your stories." That's not the whole truth. I'm unsettled by them, too, shaken by a vague sense of déjà vu. As if I've heard his stories before, but from whom? Can't be Nick. He'd tell me if he knew me, wouldn't he?

I brush aside the nagging thought and continue. "Your life is like something out of a book or a movie—working-class boy works his way through college, then goes off to war and becomes a hero. I assume you left the service."

"You're trying to get me to talk again," Nick says with a shake of his head.

"Seriously, I'm really interested in hearing more." It's the truth, though part of that interest is learning if the next broadcast of Nick's life will seem like repeat episode, too. "I promise to tell you my life story—when I finally remember it." *If ever.*

Sitting across from me, I can't stop wondering if Nick is part of that forgotten life story. Part of me is drawn to him and wants the answer to be "yes." But, at the same time, the little voice in my head is terrified that it's true, that there some awful reason for him hiding not just his identity from me, but for him hiding me from, well, me.

"Okay," Nick responds. "I'll talk, but I'm holding you to your promise." While his grin is playful, the furrow in his brow shows worry.

Uncomfortable keeping his gaze, I pick up a jigsaw piece and stare at the puzzle. "So, you served in the Marine Corps?" I ask, without looking up.

"Yes. Two tours of duty. I'm a reservist now. Left active duty five years ago after Pop was shot during a raid on a gang drug lab. The docs had to replace his hip. He had a hard time of it. Ma, too. So, I resigned my commission early. I moved home and helped Ma nurse Pop back to health."

If what Nick says is the truth, it's remarkable. How many sons would drop everything and put their careers on hold to care for a sick or injured parent? Not many, I'm betting. "I'm sorry to hear that. How's your father doing? Has he recovered?"

"He's not a hundred percent, but he gets around well enough with a cane. I know he misses the force." Nick's eyes twinkle with amusement. He chuckles. A wide grin spreads across his face.

"What's so funny?" I ask, unsure how a parent's misfortune could draw even one laugh.

"It's just that Ma nagged Pop for years to retire. She was tired of worrying about his safety. Tired of his long hours and the difficulty leaving the job at the door when he came home at night. I was told that Ma was at it again, pleading for Pop to retire the evening before he was shot. The next day, she got her wish. Pop took a bullet and was off the force for good." Nick chuckles.

Clearly, I'm missing something funny. "Again, where is the humor?"

"The joke was on Ma. After a couple of months, my parents didn't need my help, so I got a job in D.C. Within two weeks, Ma was begging me to come back home. Having Pop around 24/7 was driving her nuts. She said she couldn't do anything or go anywhere without him underfoot. Things are better now. Pop volunteers in the neighborhood schools. In the summers, he umpires for the local Little League. Everyone's happy."

The anecdote must be true. My gut tells me it is. There was too much emotion, too much detail, too much intimacy in the storytelling to be a lie. And the account rings true—as if I'd heard it before. I hide my face to conceal the growing suspicion weighing me down—Nick is playing a game with me. But toward what end?

At the same time, I can't help feeling that Nick's intentions, whatever they may be, have a bright side to them. How else could he have told such a charming and moving tale, showing that with love and humor, close families can weather any difficulties that come their way.

I turn away from Nick, hiding the tears pooling in my eyes, woeful reminders that beyond the walls of Summer Oaks, I have no such family. If I did, I wouldn't have run from them when things turned bad. I would have run *to* them. My only choice is to keep my guard up.

—

Nick and I work in a comfortable silence for the next half hour, each of us focusing on a different area of the puzzle. At one point, Nick leans over to my side of the table to place a piece. I catch a whiff of his scent, a hint of both citrus and musk, a fragrance that hits me as comfortable, even intimate.

"That's an interesting cologne you're wearing."

He looks up with a curious look of surprise on his face. "Oh, that's my aftershave. Acqua di Parma. It's from the old country, you know, Italy. Pretty pricey. My mother gives a bottle to each of the men in my family every year for Christmas to remind herself of her grandfather and father, both of whom passed when she was young. Do you like it?"

"Yes. I do. Very much." Is this scent, and the welcome memory of it, a reminder for me of family members long gone? Or is this one more clue—proof even—that Nick and I share some past connection?

I steal a glance at Nick. Across from the table, he's staring at me with an odd, almost melancholy grin on his face. "You look so sad. Why?

"Nothing, really," he says, shaking his head. "It's just that the last woman to comment on my aftershave was my girlfriend. She loved it, too. We're, ah, not together anymore."

A sudden pang in my gut tells me not to ask any more questions, so I respond with a simple "sorry" and return my attention to the puzzle.

As the night wears on, there are moments when I spy Nick staring across the table at me with that furrow in his brow. He smiles and looks away, but I can't help wondering if he knows something I don't.

I stand and stretch, an effort to mask my deep-breathing exercises.

"If you don't mind me asking," Nick says, "did you see anything on the Internet that jogged your memory?"

I hesitate to answer. I want to trust Nick. I really do. But my continuing apprehensions about the man make that impossible.

"Sorry. No luck there. My doctor thinks it's just a matter of time, though."

Nick's eyelids droop, his smile sags. Clearly, he's disappointed by my lack of progress, perhaps as much as I am. I decide to go a bit further to gauge his reaction.

"I do have two good leads in tracking down my identity, however. One is the Charlottesville police officer heading up the investigation of my car accident. The other is the man who pulled me from my car and rushed me to the hospital."

"That's great. Sounds promising." The smile on Nick's face is hard to read, but the strain in his voice betrays his words true feelings. He's not happy.

CHAPTER 17

The tension I'd felt earlier in the evening returns. My shoulders ache, my head throbs. Obviously, this rollercoaster of psychological distress I'm riding is getting to me.

"I think I'll turn in. I'm more exhausted than I thought." I lean down, retrieve my notepad and pen from beneath my chair, then turn to Nick. "Thank you for coming by. I enjoyed our visit."

"Me, too." Nick rises from his chair. "I hope we can do it again soon. In the meantime, if there is anything you need, don't hesitate to call me."

The soft, genuine smile on Nick's face warms my heart.

"You still have my number, don't you?" he asks.

"It's on my bedside table. Thank you for the offer. I'll let you know if I think of anything."

"I'll walk you to your room," he says, pulling on his coat. In one swift move, Nick slips my arm through his, rests his other hand on mine, then escorts me down the hallway. The feel of his hand on mine, gentle yet strong, lends an air of familiarity to the gesture. Rather than unnerve me, I feel safe, even at the end of a day that has left my nerves frazzled.

When we arrive at my door, he turns to me. "Can I bring you anything? Books, maybe some magazines?"

I pause to think, then glance down at my robe. That's when an idea hits me. "Actually, I'd like to get out of these bedclothes," I remark, tugging at the collar of my robe.

"Really?" Nick says, with surprised grin on his face. "And you want me to help you?"

I blush at my verbal blunder. "No. That's not what I meant." The words rush out of my mouth, but I know it isn't the whole truth. My gut and my mind tell me to keep my distance from Nick, but my heart and body want him close.

I take a deep breath and start again. "I'd like something else to wear around here. I don't need anything fancy, nothing designer, just something more presentable than the standard-issue hospital gown and robe." I smile, hoping what I'm about to ask won't come across as being too forward with a man I've known less than a day.

Nick wrinkles his nose, gives me a once over, then smiles. "Not a particularly fashionable look for you, but I think you'd look good in anything."

Emboldened by Nick's flirtatious compliment, I continue. "Well, actually, one of the nurses took pity on me today and offered to buy me a couple of outfits and undergarments, but I don't want to burden her. I hate to ask this, Nick, but would you get me a debit card with a hundred dollars preloaded on it? I'll give to my nurse, so she won't be burdened when I accept her help."

It was all a lie, of course. I never spoke with any nurse about buying me clothing. That deception rolls off my tongue so easily is a little disconcerting.

"You want something like a Visa gift card?" Nick asks.

"Yes, that would work. It could easily buy me a few changes of clothing at a discount store and leave a few dollars for other needs that may arise. I promise to pay you back as soon as I can."

I gaze at Nick to gauge his response and find myself mesmerized by the twinkle in his eyes.

"Sure. No problem." He draws out his wallet and pulls out some bills. "If you'd rather, I can give you cash now, or I can pick up what you need myself."

"No. That's okay," I blurt out. I take a calming breath and start again with another easy little fib. "That is, I don't want money lying around. I'm sure the people around here are honest, but you never know."

The truth is that cash won't work. Without some sort of plastic money, online access to my accident report and John Harris's background information will remain out of reach. I hate lying to Nick. Despite my lingering suspicions, he seems a generous, caring man, one who doesn't deserve deception after offering help. After paying for the free trials, I'll access my accident report and John Harris' background information, then, to make good on my words, ask one of the female nurses to run my shopping errand.

"It can wait until your next visit," I continue. "Anyways, I'd prefer a woman buy what I need. I hope you understand."

"Again, no problem." After putting away his wallet, Nick says goodbye and turns to leave, but stops abruptly. "Say, I have an idea. There's this great French deli nearby that has the best breakfast sandwiches around. Why don't I bring us a couple of my favorite? Toasted baguette with ham, Gruyere cheese, Mornay sauce, and a fried egg. It's called—"

"Croque Madame. I'd love one," I blurt out, startling myself, more so from the French accent that exited my mouth than the name of the sandwich itself. As for Nick, he looks more amused than surprised. He joins in as I chuckle. "I guess my taste buds have a better memory than my brain. Seems my tongue speaks French, too."

"That's great. A clue to who you are. I guess our being together is helping. It's drawing out instinctive memories."

The high-pitched buzz fills the air between us. Nick pulls his cell phone from his jacket pocket, looks at it, then tucks it back inside his coat. "I have to go. So, we have a date, right? Or should I say, rendezvous?" He laughs. "Seven-thirty tomorrow morning? I'll bring your debit card with me."

I nod. "Thank you. Sounds wonderful. My mouth is watering already." That last comment isn't a lie. It's the truth, prompted by the memory of tonight's dinner that I couldn't bring myself to finish.

Nick starts to leave, then pauses, and turns my way. "Listen. I can't begin to imagine the emotions you're experiencing, the fear, the anxiety associated with your amnesia, or the knowledge that some awful tragedy caused it." His words come soft and slow. "But I think you're stronger than you give yourself credit for. I know it. I can see it in your eyes."

My eyes meet his. The worry I felt earlier is gone, replaced by confidence.

"You're going to come out of this fine. I know it, even if you don't. You, well, you just need to believe in yourself. I know I do."

An almost overwhelming urge comes over me, but somehow, I resist the desire to grab the man and kiss him. Instead, I lean in and hug him. He hugs back with a squeeze far too intimate for two people who have just met. Still, my heart leaps at his warm embrace until a confusing sensation develops between us, like a bipolar magnet— attraction and repulsion.

Nick's cheek brushes against mine. I feel his breath on my face. I yearn for a kiss, his lips on mine. But I can't. Without any inkling about the nature of our relationship, I don't want to propel us in the wrong direction. At the same time, I'm not ready to trust Nick—nor myself.

"I better go," Nick says, gently pushing me away before I can do it myself.

Both disappointed and relieved, I open my eyes and turn away for a brief moment. I can't let him see the conflicting emotions in my face or ask questions I'm not prepared to answer.

As I watch him leave, the dream I woke to earlier flashes in my mind—Nick walking away from me, the desperation I felt knowing

I would never see him again. When the doors slide open, he turns toward me, offers a friendly wave and a gentle grin, then disappears into the elevator.

My instincts are telling me that Nick is more than just a close friend of my comatose roommate, if that's even true. There's something between us. My attraction to him is obvious, at least to me. That I don't seem to hold the same appeal for Nick suggests that our relationship, if there is indeed one, isn't a romantic one.

Even so, why would Nick feel the need to keep whatever relationship there is between us a secret? Is all this just his way of playing with me, a tease to see if I will remember him, recall what we are to each other? It's a theory that doesn't make sense unless Nick is a psych case himself. Otherwise, what does he have to gain from continuing such a deception, hiding himself from me?

Keep hiding.

I can't escape the echo of these words.

Is Nick hiding *me* from someone else?

CHAPTER 18

After deciding to head to Charlottesville, Felix took ten minutes to learn online what he needed to know about the Records clerk: the make and model of her car; the names, ages, and genders of her kids; her age, physical characteristics, and other important personal data. It took another hour to don a disguise, print out a fake hospital ID, and, finally, switch out his truck's license plate for a dummy one. Then, with the back tires spinning and squealing, he hit the road headed back to the edge of the Rivanna River where he'd left the woman inside her car to meet her icy, watery demise.

By the time Felix arrived at the scene, the night sky was hidden behind a thick cover of clouds and falling snow, leaving the area blanketed in darkness and his heart racing in dread of what he'd soon see.

Carrying the flashlight from his glove compartment, Felix exited the truck and headed to the back of the vehicle. He lifted the cover to his truck bed, fetched the long-handled spade he kept there as a tool of his trade, and slogged through the soft, knee-deep blanket of snow down to the riverbank. After a couple of cautious steps onto the ice, he cleared a wide swath of snow, then trained his flashlight's bright beam downward. A few moments later, he spotted the reflective glare of a red taillight through the thick opaque ice. He couldn't see much else. The sight wasn't enough to prove the woman was inside, frozen to death, if not drowned.

He centered his spade over the rear window, thrust the blade into the ice and started chipping away. Fifteen minutes later, sweating from a mixture of exertion and anxiety, Felix knelt on the ice and peered through the two-foot hole he'd made. His blood pressure shot up at the sight before him. The car's rear window was shattered, its driver's seat empty.

The woman was gone.

Ten minutes later, Felix parked on the street alongside Albemarle County Hospital, away from the bright lights and video surveillance cameras monitoring the area. Now calm, cool and collected, he reached into his pocket, removed his cell phone, and placed the call that would hopefully yield the information he needed to finish the job.

—

Anita nearly jumped out of her desk chair when her cell phone rang. She pulled the buzzing device from her pocket and looked at the screen but didn't recognize the incoming number. She stared at the time displayed on her phone—*11:13*—and trembled, afraid of who was on the other end of the line. Late-night calls always meant bad news. She shut out the buzzing long enough to say a silent prayer that no one was dead, then steeled herself for the worst and answered the call.

"Hello?" The simple word eked past her quivering lips.

"Hello, Mrs. Hodges?"

Anita's heart skipped a beat. The voice on the other end of the call, deep and throaty with a "just the facts" tone, flashed her back nine years to the midnight call from a Florida State Trooper with the news that her husband was dead, killed when his rig jackknifed into a bridge piling on I-95. She tried to speak, but she couldn't summon enough breath to squeak out more than a "yes."

"This is Officer Anderson of the Charlottesville Police Department. I'm sorry to be calling so late, Mrs. Hodges, but we have your sixteen-year-old daughter, Vanessa, down here at Ivy Creek Park. My partner and I caught her in the back seat of a car with a boy. I don't suppose I need to tell you what they were doing. Suffice it to say that if you can get down here right away and take your daughter into custody, I won't arrest her for indecent exposure."

"Indecent exposure?" After a sigh of relief nobody was dead, Anita realized there had to be a mistake. "I don't understand, officer. I talked with my daughter earlier tonight. She had homework to do, then was going to bed early. If you put the young lady in question on the phone, I'm sure . . ."

"Listen, it's freezing out here. I'm trying to do everyone a favor here by not taking these two to the station and booking them."

Anita gave the only reply she could. "Thank you, sir. I'm on my way."

—

Felix stood next to the glass door used by hospital staff to enter the facility. Dressed in a blue parka over pale green scrubs, he fumbled through his pockets to give the impression he was looking for an employee security card. A few seconds later, he spotted the clerk, bundled up in a heavy black coat and red scarf, moving at a fast clip down the hallway toward the door. Despite wearing a black wig and mustache, he turned away to hide his face from her. When he heard the door open, he brushed up against the woman, then ducked inside the door before it swung closed.

He loitered in the hallway, watched the clerk's red Chrysler PT Cruiser speed out of the parking lot, then entered the stairwell and made his way down to the basement floor, where he'd learned the Records Department was located. Standing in front of the office door, he pulled a small, black device from his pocket and held it to the door's key reader. The telltale click of the lock release confirmed his radio frequency ID thief had successfully stolen the clerk's personal office access code from her employee access badge when he brushed up against her.

Once inside, Felix scanned the room. Alongside the outer wall stood three cubicles, each with a flat-screen monitor, a keyboard, and a heap of file folders piled on the desktop. The rest of the office was packed with rows of gray metal shelving filled with more folders. He went straight to the stacks and searched for the hard copy of Erin Johnson's medical records but couldn't find it.

He left the shelving area, surveyed the three cubicles, and spotted two framed photos of Anita's teenaged children on the desk nearest the door. He sat down in the clerk's chair and jiggled the mouse, causing the screen to pop up with a blank password box. He pulled a flash drive out of his coat pocket and plugged it into the monitor's USB port. A few seconds later, the blinking red light on the device turned green, confirming the clerk's password had been overridden. He typed Erin Johnson's name and admittance date into the patient records database and smirked with satisfaction when her file appeared onscreen.

Felix scanned the first few pages of the record, looking for any piece of information to explain what the hell was going on with the missing woman. He breezed past her physical description, the notes about the uncertainty surrounding her name, the preliminary police report, then went straight to the digitized copy of her medical certificate of death. He took careful note of the name of the attending physician, Dr. Arjun Patel, then skimmed the supporting medical record to better understand how the woman died but found it confusing. The official cause of death was a brain aneurysm, but not one test or treatment record offered any support that the woman's injuries included even a minor concussion.

He shuffled through the dozens of folders stacked atop the clerk's desk, found the hard copy of the woman's file, and tore through it, looking for anything that hadn't been included in the woman's digitized record. When he fell short again, he laid out the pages on the desk and examined each one carefully. It took him a minute to realize what was off-kilter. The sloppy signature of the attending physician on the death certificate didn't match the doctor's orderly signatures in the rest of the file. Not even close.

Felix threw the file folder across the room, then slammed his fist on the clerk's desk. The death certificate was a fake. Erin Johnson didn't die, at least not at Albemarle County Hospital. He wasn't sure if what he'd discovered was a case of basic incompetence by some stupid clerk who didn't know her job or didn't care, or whether it reflected someone playing a game of hide-and-seek with the woman he'd left for dead.

He knew there was only one way to find out.

—

Five minutes into the trip across town, Anita Hodges finally thawed out enough to thoughtfully consider what she'd been told by the police officer.

Her daughter had never caused any problems before. She hadn't even had her first date. Vanessa spent most of her waking moments either studying, practicing her flute, or working on projects for one of her many after-school clubs. *At least, that's what she tells me.*

Anita had always trusted her children implicitly, but now she wondered if her daughter could be keeping secrets from her.

"Good God Almighty," she prayed aloud. "If I'm one of those clueless parents whose kids sneak out of their bedrooms and run wild at all hours of the night, please help me. Please, help my baby."

Still, Anita couldn't believe she'd be so blind. There must be some error.

She pulled into a McDonald's parking lot and called her home number. Five rings later, she was greeted by the yawning voice of her daughter. Anita sighed, relieved to know that someone else's teen was being detained by the police. She apologized to her daughter, told her to go back to sleep, then hung up.

With the stress of the moment behind her, Anita felt the chill of the cold winter's night blow through her. She pulled into the late-night drive-through for a cup of coffee, then parked again in the lot. The first sip of the dark, rich brew flowing over her lips and down her throat, warmed her, allowing her to forgive the police officer for making such a huge error. She picked up her phone, pulled up the number for the last call received, and pressed the green phone button to dial the number. When the call didn't go through, she looked up the number for the Charlottesville Police Department and asked the switchboard operator for Officer Anderson.

"Hello. This is Lieutenant Anderson," a woman's voice came over the phone.

"I'm sorry. I'm looking for another Officer Anderson . . . a man. He called me about ten minutes ago. Said he caught my daughter and a boy making out in the back seat of a car at Ivy Creek Park."

"I'm sorry, Ma'am. I'm the only Anderson on staff with the department. Perhaps you got the name wrong. Would you like me to transfer you to the Patrol Bureau? They should be able to confirm the name of the officer detaining your daughter."

Anita apologized for the confusion and thanked the lieutenant for her assistance. The sergeant who eventually took her call couldn't shed any light on the late-night mix-up involving her daughter.

"I can assure you that none of our units have detained any lovers tonight at Ivy Creek Park, or any park for that matter," the cop said. "It's colder than the devil outside. No one in their right mind is horny enough to have sex in a parked car in this weather. I hate to tell you this, but it sounds as if some smart-alecky kid played a joke on you."

This made no sense to her. She knew all her daughter's friends, good kids, sweet and respectful. *They wouldn't pull such a cruel trick on me.*

She resolved to get to the truth behind the prank during a frank talk with her daughter in the morning. She took another sip of coffee, then pulled the car out of the parking lot and started back toward the hospital.

—

Felix stood in the shadow of the stacks holding Erin Johnson's file—with its contents restored—and waited for the clerk's return.

Click.

He recognized the sound. Someone with a key card was at the door. He checked his watch and frowned. He didn't expect the clerk back from the false emergency he'd concocted for at least another twenty minutes.

Play it cool, man. Whoever it is, play it cool. He listened carefully to the swish of the door opening, the soft clatter of shoes on the low-pile carpet, the squeak of an office chair, the clickity-clack of a keyboard, and waited for some clue to the person's identity to determine his next move.

In the next moment, he recognized a woman's voice.

"Hello, Dr. Patel. Sorry to have missed you. This is Anita Hodges. I'm calling from the Records Department for Albemarle County Hospital.

I have some questions regarding a patient file. Please call me back at 434-828-5684. Thank you."

When the clacking of the keyboard resumed, Felix stepped out of the shadows and toward the clerk. "Hello. How are you?" Felix didn't care a whit about the woman but needed a friendly opening to keep her off-guard enough to get some easy answers.

She jerked around in her chair, clearly startled. "How did you get in here? This office and its files are restricted. I locked the door before I left."

"No one was here, so I got a janitor to let me in," he lied.

"Who unlocked the door for you? Was it Pat?" The clerk's voice held a note of irritation. She stood up, clenched her fists, and rested them on her hips.

"Yes. I think it was Pat. Nice guy."

She was clearly angry. Felix saw it in her piercing gaze and the downward curve of her thin, red lips. *Play it cool, man,* he reminded himself. *Don't set her off.*

"Pat is a woman. Whoever let you in this office is in big trouble. So are you. Who are you anyway? Let me see your badge."

"I'm Tom Morgan," he said, referring to the name he'd printed on his fake ID card. "I'm new here, a nurse in the cardiac unit, and this is my first night on the job." The words rolled off his tongue as smoothly as if they were the truth. "Don't you just hate the night shift, uh, pardon me, may I have your name?" he asked, hoping to deflect the conversation and get the woman off his back.

"I'm Anita, and don't try to change the subject. You're in my office, where you're not supposed to be. Somebody should have at least told you that."

Felix followed her gaze to the folder in his hands.

"I'll take that, please." The clerk extended her hand. "Before you can see anything in these files, you'll have to show your ID and clearance orders. No exceptions."

Felix held back the folder. Once she eyed the name on the file, his cover would be blown, but then it would be time for answers. He waited until she started toward him, then reached inside his coat and pulled out a small sleek pistol.

"This is all the authorization you need, Ms. Hodges." Felix aimed the weapon at her heart. "This gun may be tiny, but it's very lethal. Now I suggest you cooperate, or the next call your family gets from the police won't be a false alarm."

CHAPTER 19

I awake from a fitful night's sleep with tears streaming down my face, struggling to forget the nightmare I'd just lived through, but I can't get the horrifying sights, sounds, and feelings out of my mind.

I'm riding in a pickup truck, the driver a dark, malevolent figure. Fear rages through me as I try to speak to him. He parks in a wooded area. In the next moment, I'm observing him from a distance, frozen in place, watching as he pulls a woman out of the truck. Except for the long blond hair trailing down her back, she looks a lot like me. I stand by in horror, unable to move or speak, helpless to intervene as the cloaked figure clutches the woman's throat and squeezes the life out of her. I sob as the woman slumps to the ground, watch as the masked figure digs her grave and buries her, watch until, at last, the demon stands over me and speaks, "You can't hide from me."

Curled up in my bed, bawling as in my dream, I try to chase the vision out of my mind but fail. I struggle to convince myself it's just a product of my overactive imagination, a one-act horror film written and directed by my subconscious based on the morgue clerk's mournful recollection of a murdered classmate. But while I lie in bed, shaking almost uncontrollably, I'm not so sure the night terror is a pure work of fiction. If what Dr. Malone said was true, my subconscious is trying to tell me something. But what? Having just witnessed a murder in my dream, I'm not sure I want to listen.

Afraid to expose myself to more nightmares, I resolve to stay awake and find something to occupy my mind. I flip on the bed lamp, then glance at the clock on the wall. 5:45. Too early to do much of anything, I switch on the TV, keeping the volume low so as not to disturb the patients in the rooms adjacent to mine. Surfing through the channels, I find an odd mix of programming available and settle on an old game show rerun, hoping that the combination of comedy and trivia will boost my spirits and benignly occupy my mind. But I fight to stay awake. It's a losing battle. I slip in and out of consciousness, reliving the horror of the dream each time I doze off.

I give up the effort when my head and shoulders start to ache. I pull myself out of bed and take refuge in the shower, vigorously scrubbing my scalp with shampoo, as if doing so will wash away the terrors that plague my mind. After a while, the hot, powerful spray of water proves a therapeutic success. I feel cleansed of the ache in my head, the soreness in my shoulders, and the horrors in my mind. All are now distant memories.

After toweling off, I put on the fresh nightgown and robe left on my chair last night by some staff member. As I pull on the yellow, one-size-fits-all knee-high stocking slippers, I realize one of the day's priorities must be arranging for one of my female nurses to do some shopping with the debit card Nick promised me. With a mysterious stalker on my trail, I need some street clothes, something to wear if I need to flee Summer Oaks at a moment's notice to avoid facing my traumatic past before I'm ready.

I hear a knock on the door.

"Good morning, Kay," says a voice from the doorway. I look up to see a young Asian-American nurse holding a brown paper grocery bag. "I'm Jenny. Someone dropped this off for you last night."

Unsure what's inside, or who it might be from, I accept the bag with a bit of trepidation. Cautiously, I open the package and peer inside. *Clothes.* I spy a piece of paper and dig it out.

Hey, girl. Summer Oaks can be a bit cold and drafty during the winter. Since you're up and moving around, I thought you'd like some warm threads to wear. My roomie, Natalie, is about your size. She pulled a few items from her closet for you and added a new pack of panties she had on hand. Fruit of the Loom, nothing fancy. The tennis shoes are size seven. I hope they fit. I'm off tomorrow. Take care. See you soon.—Jimmy.

"How thoughtful," I say, oddly unnerved. "Jimmy brought me some clothes to wear." And serendipitous. At least I hope that's what it is. Or did Jimmy eavesdrop on my conversation with Nick last night?

"He's such a sweetie. Always thinking of others," Jenny says, with a knowing nod. "Well, I need to get back to the nurses' station. Let me know if you need anything."

Once she leaves, I close the door, then set about trying on clothes. As it turns out, the only items that fit are the undergarments and shoes. The long-sleeved shirts and sweaters hang on me, the blue jeans a bit short. Looking at myself in the mirror, I can only cringe at my reflection. Comfortable, just not my style.

I'm not really surprised by my reaction. Everything I've sensed about myself thus far suggests I'm highly educated, classically trained possibly, in music, language, and cuisine. It makes sense that my fashion tastes would reflect such an upbringing. At the same time, I'm grateful for the clothes, so I don't seem to be too much of a snob. *That's a relief*, I think and smile at my reflection.

When I approach Jenny at the nurses' station, she takes one look at me and stifles a laugh. "You need longer arms and shorter legs, or better-fitting clothes. Maybe I could ask around, see if some other nurses may be more your size."

"Thank you." I offer a grateful smile. "But that's not necessary. If you're willing, I have another way to get some clothes that fit and other things I need. My roommate's friend, Nick, is bringing me a prepaid debit card this morning." I pause, hoping that the request I'm about to make isn't too big of an imposition. "Would you be willing to pick up a few things for me at a store?"

"Of course. I'd be happy to." She hands me a pen and sheet of paper. "Just tell me what you need. There's a Walmart just down the road. I can stop there after my shift ends at three. If you're not in a hurry, I can bring everything in tomorrow morning. Otherwise, I can swing back at five-thirty tonight. My husband has a basketball game not far from here at six."

Given the choice, I opt for the latter. The sooner I have some decent street clothes, the sooner I'll be ready to run for my life. If I have to.

CHAPTER 20

Jenny and I discuss my likely clothing size, my wardrobe and other personal needs, and together we come up with a list of items she'll buy for me that afternoon. As I start back to my room, I hear my name. I spin around and spot Nick walking toward me carrying a small white sack and a beverage tray with four cups nestled atop it. Bundled up in a long winter coat and hat, the sight of him makes my heart ache and my gut twist. What is it about Nick that has me battling such conflicting emotions?

As Nick nears, I catch a welcome whiff of the savory breakfast sandwiches he'd promised to bring. My worries take a back seat as my salivary glands shift into overdrive. "Smells wonderful."

I reach out to relieve Nick of the drink tray, but he nudges me away. I lead the way to the Community Room and a corner table by a window, far enough away from the media area, so that if anyone comes in to watch TV, they won't be able to hear our conversation.

Nick unburdens himself of the bag and drink tray, then sets the table with our food, drinks, plasticware, and napkins. He pulls out a chair. "After you, Madame," he says with a bow. "A feast fit for the Queen of France and her humble servant. Croque Madame, orange juice, and coffee."

"Thank you. This all looks scrumptious, *délicieux*," I say, laughing off Nick's antics. "But you need to work on your accent." I offer the correct pronunciations, drawing giggles from both of us.

Nick removes his overcoat and lays it across the back of his chair. Underneath, he is dressed much the same as the previous day—dark suit, white dress shirt, and a blue tie. He takes the seat across from me, and we begin to eat.

After the first bite, I can't keep my delight to myself. "Wow. This is amazing, and just as I remember it. I just wish my palatal memory came with a bit more context, like where I was and who was with me when I last enjoyed it."

Nick, happily chewing, nods in agreement. We eat in silence until I hear a muffled laugh. When I look up, Nick appears to be stifling a laugh.

"What's so funny? Do I have food all over my face?" I grab my napkin and swipe it across my mouth and cheeks.

"No. I was just enjoying watching you eat. You surprised me, attacking your food like a ravenous lion. I've never seen you . . ." The mirth in his expression disappears. ". . . I mean, I didn't expect that."

I feel the blood drain from my face. *I've never seen you . . .* Is Nick's slip of the tongue, his change in his demeanor an aborted confession, proof, finally, that he is hiding a past relationship between us? I don't see how it can be otherwise.

Although I've lost my appetite, I take another bite to give me a moment to consider my response. My instinct tells me to let Nick think his gaffe went unnoticed.

"You'd eat like a lion, too," I say with a full mouth, "if you hadn't had a decent meal in days."

"No excuses needed," he says, with a grin.

"So, is there anything new with you? Perhaps a recovered memory or two?"

A sip of coffee buys me some time before I answer. It's a simple question, innocent enough if coming from most people, but now that I'm convinced Nick is being evasive, perhaps up to no good, I'm not inclined to tell him anything, much less my disturbing dreams and recollections.

"No, no progress, unfortunately."

"Something wrong?" he asks a few moments later, staring at the half-eaten meal sitting in front of me.

"Guess my appetite was bigger than my stomach," I reply with a weak smile.

The wariness in Nick's eyes tells me he doesn't buy my excuse. I jump in to divert the attention from me and back on Nick, hoping he'll reveal something, anything that will help me understand who he is to me.

"I know you're tired of talking about yourself, Nick, but you haven't told me about your job. Yesterday you mentioned that you wanted to be a police detective after you left the Marines. Did that work out?"

Nick shakes his head in reply as he wipes his mouth with a napkin. "I went in a different direction. I'm a security specialist."

"A security specialist? What does that mean?"

"Basically, I'm a bodyguard." He picks up his juice bottle and takes a big swig.

The muscles in my jaw, neck, and shoulders stiffen. "Oh. For whom?" My mind runs wild with a host of nefarious possibilities. With his ruggedly swarthy good looks and a name like Costa, could Nick—perhaps, me, too—be connected to the Mafia?

Nick looks down, then dabs at his mouth with his napkin again. This time it seems like a ploy, a delay tactic to give him time to consider his answer.

"CEOs and other bigwigs, mostly." He pauses, takes another bite of his sandwich, then grins at me before starting to chew.

His answer, short and to the point, is vague, shifty even. I need to know more, a lot more. My life could depend on it.

"Why do CEOs need bodyguards?" I clutch my coffee cup with both hands as it sits atop the table, an effort to squash the nerves inside me threatening to erupt. "And who would want to kill them anyway?"

"You'd be surprised," he replies, wadding up his sandwich wrapper.

"So, surprise me." I feign a friendly smile to hide my desperation.

"My current assignment receives threats every day," he says, while gathering the trash from the table and stuffing it in the paper bag. "Some people don't like how he does business. Then there's kidnapping. Anyone with money or power is a target there. There are plain old nutcases, of course, with no motives based on reality. The press can be a problem, too—intrusive, even a bit hostile at times. There's a host of other reasons, too. My team works together well, though, so the worst-case scenario is just that, something that never comes to pass."

"So, who do you work for? Do you travel everywhere your boss goes?" I ask, hoping Nick's s answer will trigger a memory that will clue me into our past activities.

"I'm bound by confidentiality agreements, so I can't reveal any details of my employment. But yes, there is a good deal of travel involved. In fact, the worst threats come during business trips abroad, often goodwill trips whose purpose is to build economic opportunities for people in the countries my employer visits. Unfortunately, there are extremists and malcontents who don't see it that way; not everyone is welcoming. My team is always on guard for terrorists, criminals, and other crazed lunatics."

Silence hangs in the air as his words sink in. "Do you carry a gun at all times, or just when you're on duty?"

Nick stands and pulls open the right side of his suit coat, revealing the butt of a large, black gun tucked inside a thick, leather shoulder holster. "SIG Sauer .357 Magnum."

Even though I'd asked the question, the sight of the firearm startles me. My heart races, its beat echoing inside my head. As I squeeze shut my eyes and turn away, an image flashes in my mind.

A dark truck . . . a big one . . . driving alongside me, matching my car's speed . . . the truck's passenger-side window sliding down . . . a face in the shadows . . . a gun aimed at my head . . .

Suddenly, I feel myself falling, gasping for air as a scream dies in my throat.

CHAPTER 21

"**K**ay, what's wrong?" Nick's voice breaks through the pounding inside my head.

I feel his hands grip my arm. I open my eyes and find myself sprawled on the floor with Nick kneeling beside me.

"Talk to me. What just happened?"

The terror on his face mirrors what I feel inside. I take a deep breath and let it out. That dark face—*that gun*—lingers in my thoughts. I'm in no shape to consider its implications. "Give me a minute," I say, my voice trembling.

Nick, his hands cold, yet strong, hold me while I breathe. *Inhale . . . exhale . . .*

As I try to collect myself, a young woman shuffles into the room with an old man in a robe and slippers by her side. "Do you need some help?" she asks, after looking our way. "Should I get a nurse?"

"Thank you, no. She's fine," Nick replies. I nod in agreement.

The woman smiles kindly in reply, parks the old man on the couch, then picks up a nearby remote. "There you go, Dad. I've turned on your favorite morning show. Stay here and watch. I'll be right back."

Once she's gone, I quickly regain my composure and turn my attention to Nick. "I'm sorry. The sight of your gun set me off."

"Did you remember something?" His voice reflects a mix of fear and excitement. "Did someone pull a gun on you?"

I balk at revealing the truth. "I . . . I don't know." The sight of Nick's gun triggered a memory, and that riles me. In my dream—or memory—I can't see the face of the man pointing a gun at me. Is it Nick? *Oh, my god, is it Nick?*

I try to calm myself with slow, deep breaths, but the effort barely keeps my panic at bay. Kneeling next to me, Nick's face is contorted with concern. I don't want to believe the gun I saw in my mind is Nick's, that at some point he tried to kill me—or still intends to. If he wanted me dead, he had the perfect opportunity to do it before I woke from my coma. Moreover, he keeps urging me to try and remember my past. Is my fugue-filled brain hiding something he's desperate to uncover?

It's clear Nick is not going to reveal himself anytime soon, a potentially dangerous situation for me if his intentions are not altogether innocent. I need to keep pushing without giving him any reason to turn my suspicions back on me.

Ready to dig a little deeper into Nick's story, I grasp his hand and let him help me back to my seat. I clutch my cup and take a couple sips of my coffee, focusing on the warm liquid as it flows down my throat. "Thanks. I'm feeling better."

The note of skepticism I see in Nick's eyes tells me he's not buying it. "Seriously, I'm fine. Sit. Let's finish our coffees."

After Nick takes his chair, I move to another line of questioning, taking it slow this time. "I thought you wanted to be a cop, like your father. How did you end up in the private security business?"

"You are relentless. Why are you so curious about me?"

"Honestly, I don't know," I reply, trying my best to project innocent curiosity, though it's my own distrust of Nick driving my interest now. "Perhaps hearing about other people's lives will jog a memory of my own," I reply. "Maybe I just need a distraction. It's better than talking about subjects I don't even know I cared about, such as music, books . . ."

Across the room, the old man has pumped up the volume on the TV. I recognize the deep male voice booming from the speakers, drawing my attention to the screen and causing my teeth to grind. ". . . or politics."

"Politics? Kay, do you recognize the guy on TV? Do you know who he is?" Nick seems startled, even slightly excited.

I stare at man on the screen. Tall and broad-shouldered, with thick brown hair, a straight, aristocratic nose, and a strong, square jaw, he exudes confidence, success, control. A flood of odd emotions rushes at me as I listen to him speak: anger, grief, regret, futility.

"He's the president-elect, isn't he?" At least that's what the caption denotes at the bottom of the screen. That I can't member a man who elicits such negative emotions from me is curious. Is this normal for amnesia sufferers?

"Yes, you're right. That's Governor William Lockhart, president-elect of the United States. Remember? I told you yesterday that he defeated President Hayward in the general election."

I cringe at the name and the way it rolled off Nick's tongue. I take a deep breath to brush aside my emotions and consider my odd response, as Dr. Malone suggested, and what it might reveal about me.

One explanation is easy to come by. My reaction simply reflects voter disappointment because my candidate, Hayward, lost the election. Perhaps my reaction reflects a belief that Lockhart's campaign cheated to win, planting false pay-for-play accusations that unfairly drove some voters to reject Hayward.

At that moment, the old man's daughter enters the room. "Let's go, Dad. It's time for your physical therapy." She helps him up, and together they shuffle out the room, leaving the TV on.

"It seems you haven't forgotten everything. That's huge. That's great!"

I don't see the point. Nick seems overly enthused that I remember even the tiniest fact.

"If you say so."

"It's a start. Every memory can lead to another. Is there anything else you remember about William Lockhart? Anything at all?"

There he goes again, pushing. The needle on my internal trust meter plummets to the danger zone. Where is Nick going with this?

Keep hiding.

The two little words are back, hounding me from somewhere deep inside. From whom? Why? I cast my gaze at the TV, and as I do, an idea flashes in my mind, a possible scenario that makes perfect sense.

"What's going on here, Nick? Who are you, and why are you pressing me to remember this guy? Was I involved in this election scandal? Do I know something about the pay-for-play hoax? Are you a reporter trying to dig up dirt?"

CHAPTER 22

Nick is clearly stunned, but from the odd smile on his face, he seems more bemused than alarmed, not what I'd expect if my accusations hit the mark.

"What? Where'd you get a crazy idea like that?" he asks with a snicker.

I feel my face flush. "Don't laugh," I snarl. "I have my reasons." Despite Nick's reaction, I'm not ready to walk back my allegations, especially since he didn't outright deny them. "Even as I came out of my coma, I sensed there was some connection between us. You've been so attentive, bringing me food, promising me money, hanging on my every word waiting for me to remember something."

My words are rushed, breathless almost, as if I must finish my thoughts quickly or lose my chance to speak up. "Every time we're together, you're grilling me, like a reporter working a big story. Now, you're pushing me to remember the man who benefited from a political hit job. Well, this election scandal is not just a big story, it's huge. Blowing the lid off what happened may not change the outcome of the election, but it could ruin careers, and make you a media darling . . ."

Inside my chest, my heart is pounding, waiting for Nick's response.

"Take it easy," he finally says. "You have it all wrong. I'm not a reporter chasing you for a story."

His words ring hollow.

"I am who I said I am. An ex-Marine who now works as a body-guard. Emily really is like a kid sister to me. Her brother, Dan, and I are best friends. We served together in Iraq, and now, work for the same security firm. You want to ask him?" He pulls out his phone. "Go ahead. Give Dan a call."

I want to believe Nick. I do, but everything I sense about the man says we have a prior relationship. If Nick is not a reporter, he's looking to get something else from me. I need to press harder to determine how much of what he says is truth.

"So, if I talked to the nurses on this floor, asked how often you came to see Emily, ask if they'd seen you putting her through her exercises, they'd back you up, too?"

From the silence hanging between us, it's obvious I caught Nick in a lie.

"No. Not lately, at least. The first year, yes. One of us was here every day, but it became too much of an emotional burden, especially for Dan. Emily's condition never changed. The second year, with the demands of our jobs, we had to pull back. But Dan hasn't given up on Emily. He visits when he can. We both do. Dan also pays a couple of nurses on staff here to exercise Emily a few times a week after hours. They can vouch for the arrangement with Dan, but I'm not sure which staff to approach."

Nick's explanation seems earnest, reasonable even, but it doesn't explain one thing. "So, what are you doing hanging out with me?"

He shakes his head, obviously frustrated by my continuing doubts. "I was here visiting Emily when you started to emerge from your coma. I was so excited. It gave me renewed hope for Emily. And once you were wide awake and we started talking, well, . . . I like you. Okay, maybe I have been a little clingy, a tad too accommodating, but you seemed like you could use a friend. Now, let's move on. I promise I won't bring up politics ever again."

If Nick is trying to be funny, it's not working, especially since I don't believe he's being completely honest. Maybe there's some to truth to what he says, but there's been too many little tells on Nick's part for me to cast aside my suspicions. For now, it seems, all I can do is play along, stay alert and keep my guard up until I have some answers I can trust.

"Sorry, Nick," I reply, offering my best sheepish grin. "I don't know where that came from. Must be some of that paranoia Dr. Malone told me to watch for, you know, from my PTSD."

"No worries. We're good. Don't give it another thought." He rises from his chair, collects our trash and my uneaten food, then strolls over to a nearby garbage can and tosses everything. Back at the table, he pulls a small, plastic card from his wallet and hands it to me.

"Judging from the clothes you're wearing, borrowed, if I'm not mistaken, you could really use this debit card. I put three hundred on it. The D.C. area is an expensive place to shop. Even the clothes at Walmart can have designer prices."

I waiver for a moment, but accept the card from him, nonetheless. "Thank you. That's very generous. More than generous. I promise to pay it all back, every penny. When I can."

I mean it, although I have no idea when or even if I'll be able to keep the vow. I hadn't considered yet whether money, or rather, the lack of it is an issue in my situation. If I drive an Audi sedan, as stated in the news article and on my accident report, I couldn't be too poor.

"That's not necessary," Nick says, shaking his head. "Please consider it a gift. Pay it forward when you meet someone who could use a little hand up."

"Thank you. I will." I tuck the card into the back pocket of my jeans.

"I took the liberty of bringing you something else." Nick reaches into his right coat pocket then sets a cell phone and a charger on the table in front of me.

"The phone is charged and ready to go. You can reach me by pressing one on your speed dial. Call or text if you want to talk or need anything. Any time. Day or night. You won't bother me."

I hesitate, unsure if there is more behind the gift than a quick, easy way to stay in touch. *Can he keep tabs on me with this device?* "The debit card was too generous of a gift to begin with—" My voice trails off as I push the phone across the table.

"It isn't costing me a dime if that's what you're worried about. It's a prepaid phone I used abroad last summer. It still has unused funds. Take it. It ensures your anonymity when making calls. No one can track you to Summer Oaks with this."

The hair on the back of my neck stands up. "What do you mean by that?" The question blurts from my mouth.

"I'm just looking out for you," he says, taking a step back.

"I'm sorry. That was rude. I know you have my best interests at heart." At least, I hope he does.

"That's true. Really, it is." Nick cups my hand in his, his touch, once again, sending a confusing mix of emotions through me. I pull away and take a sip of coffee to hide my retreat.

"In fact, I brought you this old phone because I was worried about you. Yesterday afternoon, you told me your doctor advised you against contacting the police for help until you could recall the tragedy that triggered your amnesia. Then last night, you revealed different intentions. You were ready to ignore that advice and call the police sergeant who handled your accident investigation. I was concerned that if you used the house phone, the cops could track you down. They can't do that with a throwaway phone, no one can."

I guess I should be grateful that Nick is on the ball, doing a better job of keeping me safe than I am. But I can't help wondering if there is more behind Nick's offer of an untraceable phone than concern for my well-being. Does he have some ulterior motive for keeping me under the police radar? Should I be wary of the police, too? For that matter, who is the "anyone else" that Nick thinks might be looking for me?

CHAPTER 23

Worried I've already exposed myself with the calls I made last night, I pick the phone and its charger off the table and offer a smile. "Thank you for looking out for me."

Nick's relaxed smile returns. "Whatever you need, just call or text. Any time of the day or night. I'm here for you."

After Nick leaves, I hustle to my room to retrieve my notes and pen. Back in front of the public-use computer, I'm ready to access the "free" website services that could yield information on my accident and rescuer. With any luck, I'll soon have a name for myself and a virtual past to go with it.

A moment after I pull up the Internet browser, someone calls my name. I spin around in my chair and see Dr. Malone standing in the doorway, holding a notepad and a thin, manila file folder.

"I stopped by your room to pick you up for our eight o'clock appointment, but you weren't there. A nurse said I could find you're here." Her voice trails off as she scans the room with a look of confusion on her face. "She said you had a visitor," she continues, walking toward me. "Who? Did someone you know come forward? The staff should have notified me."

"No, nobody from my past, I'm afraid." Given the doctor's diagnosis of PTSD-induced amnesia, I *should* be afraid to have my past show up here.

"My roommate's friend stopped by with breakfast," I continue, rising from my chair and snatching up my materials. "I'm sorry you had to come looking for me. Our appointment slipped my mind. I had a rough night. Didn't get much sleep. I had a bad dream."

"Believe it or not, that is a good sign," she replies, her voice confident, strong. "As I noted yesterday, nightmares can reveal a lot about what is troubling us. In your case, it could provide the clues we need to better diagnose the circumstances that led to your fugue state. Why don't we adjourn to the conference room, so you can tell me about your dream?"

With a gentle hand on my back, the doctor escorts me down the hallway. But with each step, I grow more anxious. My throat narrows. My gut churns. I don't want to relive my dream, but more than that, I don't want to face what I suspect is the truth behind my nightmare—that the trauma I'm fleeing involves a ghoulish murder.

Behind the closed doors of the conference room, I take a seat on the sofa, then summon the strength to speak. "Doctor, what if we forget my nightmare and try something else? You mentioned hypnosis yesterday. That just might work—you know, break that dam holding my memory at bay."

Sitting across from me, Dr. Malone starts to speak, her cadence slow, her tone soothing. "Kay, I know nightmares can be confusing and frightening. Horrible things happen in them. But not everything is as it appears in a dream, especially the ones that frighten us. For example, it's not uncommon for death to be part of a dream, but that doesn't mean someone has died. Nor is it a premonition of an impending death. Did someone die in your dream, Kay?"

Feeling like a naughty child caught in the act and forced to own up to her bad deeds, I divert my gaze and nod in response.

"Was it someone close to you?"

"Yes, uh, no. I'm not sure." My words come out in a whisper. "I saw a woman. I'm not sure who. She looked a lot like me." My eyes begin to water. A tear escapes my right eye and dribbles down my cheek.

The doctor's hand appears in front of my face with a tissue. I take it and wipe the wetness from my face.

"Yet here you are. Alive and well. You're perfectly safe here at Summer Oaks. I can assure you of that. But more importantly, you must not take dreams literally. In fact, death in a dream usually reflects an ending of something in your life, most often a relationship."

With my tears dried, I look up at the doctor.

"When you are the victim of a violent death at the hands of another during a dream, it could simply mean that you feel like you're dying inside that relationship, usually from some unmet needs, such as self-fulfillment, happiness, or security." She leans across and pats my hand. "Trust me. Discussing your nightmare could provide clues that will help us understand why your unconscious self has hijacked your memory. Now, why don't we talk this out?"

The doctor's gentle voice calms my fears as much as her words, so I agree. A few minutes later, I've spilled the details of my nighttime ordeal.

"There's a lot of revealing symbolism in this dream, Kay. Given my diagnosis that you are suffering from dissociative fugue brought on by some severe psychological trauma, it's my professional opinion that you are running from a relationship with someone close to you, a husband or boyfriend perhaps, and he is the murderous figure in your nightmare. The radiologist's report included in your medical file gave you the all-clear, no sign of broken bones recently or in the past, so most likely, we're talking about a relationship involving psychological rather than physical abuse."

I'm not sure what to say, so I simply nod.

"Communication is likely a big part of the problem in this relationship. In your dream, you try to speak, but the figure glares at you, effectively silencing you. Then he chokes you to death. It's not uncommon in psychologically abusive relationships for the victim to be deathly afraid to speak up out of fear her words will be met with more abuse."

I'm not convinced the psychiatrist has the right interpretation. She must have seen the doubt in my eyes because she continues pressing her point.

"I'm not dismissing the possibility that, prior to your fugue state, you feared for your life. That is a legitimate interpretation of your nightmare. Psychological abusers can, and often do, escalate to physical violence. It's something we can explore in our therapy sessions."

She speaks with such ease and an air of authority that her theory seems almost undeniable. Running from an abusive husband—could it be that simple? I have no other explanation to offer.

"Your interpretation makes sense, doctor." A quiver in my voice betrays my emotional state. I take a deep breath to calm my worries, then continue. "But I'm still not sure how understanding this nightmare will help me recover my memory."

"The one overriding theme of your nightmare is a sense of helplessness, a lack of personal control you feel in your life. That's typical for victims of abuse, both physical and psychological. I think I can help you there. If we use our sessions to work on developing in you a greater sense of self-efficacy and self-confidence, I'm sure we can bring you out of this fugue and, at the same time, prepare you to successfully cope with any personal threats that you may encounter back home, should you choose to return home. Of course, your situation is quite unique because of the amnesia."

"Why is that?"

"Helping victims of abuse overcome their fears and stand up to their abusers usually involves an honest, open discussion of past threats and safe, effective strategies to defuse and otherwise cope with such threats. Until your memory returns, we can't fully explore your situation. You'll need to give me another day to research a suitable approach for accomplishing our therapeutic goals."

"If you think it will help." We spend a few minutes discussing my observations and the conclusions I've drawn about myself. I hold back, offering only the most benign perceptions about who I am as a person: natural blond; no kids; physically fit, perhaps, a runner; educated and cultured, as suggested by my *Jeopardy* performance, musical proclivities, and my penchant for French language and haute cuisine. I say nothing of my political leanings except to note my displeasure at Hayward not winning reelection. I leave it at that, making the excuse that I slept most of yesterday, leaving little time to make observations.

What I leave out are the suspicions plaguing my mind, about me, the man searching for me, Nick, and someone named Maddy. Dr. Malone seems convinced that my nightmare reflects nothing more than my involvement in an abusive relationship, but I'm not so sure.

"That's a good start, Kay. You seem to have the hang of mindfulness," the doctor says, rising from her chair. "Let's meet tomorrow, same time. Eight o'clock. I should have some answers by then. In the meantime, keep up with your mindful observations. Your breathing exercises, too." With that, she leaves.

Suddenly left by myself, panic returns and all the mindfulness in the world doesn't answer the one question that counts—how do I defend myself from a potentially violent man I can't recognize?

CHAPTER 24

ack in front of the Community Room computer, I pull up a commercial public records website, authorize a payment of $3.95 from my debit card, and print a copy of my accident report. A quick scan of the document confirms what I'd learned from both Anita and the initial news story I'd read but goes into much more detail. I turn my focus to John Harris's statement:

I was driving alone, going west on Highway 15, just outside of Charlottesville, on my way to help a friend caught in the storm. The car ahead of me swerved off the right side of the road. I pulled over to help. The car, a silver Audi, had broken through the ice of a lake and was sinking fast. I grabbed the tire wrench from my trunk, bashed in the car's rear window, then crawled inside, and pulled the woman behind the wheel to safety. There were no other passengers inside the car. She didn't seem too terribly hurt, just dazed. I put her in my car and set my GPS for the nearest hospital. I tried to keep her talking in case she had a concussion, but mostly she mumbled. I did get her name—Erin Johnson. She was unconscious by the time I pulled up to the ER. Hospital personnel took over from there.

The statement is signed and dated: "John Harris, 01/05/2016, 6:14 p.m." Where the witness's driver's license should have been recorded is a notation: "Unavailable." The officer's report continued:

> Mr. Harris reportedly lost his wallet at the scene of the accident. He asked to use the restroom before being escorting to his car in the parking lot to retrieve his car's license and registration information. He didn't return after 10 minutes. This officer searched the restroom, then the parking lot. John Harris was gone.

The hair on the back of my neck stands straight up as a tingle runs down my spine. From Sergeant Montgomery's account, I can only draw one disturbing conclusion—the lone witness to my accident snuck away before the police could confirm *his* identity. This doesn't exactly make me feel warm and fuzzy about my Good Samaritan, if he even was that.

As I read further, I discover a Virginia State Police APB with a physical description of the missing John Harris and his car:

> Male, Caucasian, approx. 6' 2", 180 lbs., 35-40 years old, wavy black hair, brown eyes. Last seen 6:15 p.m. wearing blue hospital scrubs marked, "Property of Albemarle County Hospital." Observed on hospital security video entering a black or dark blue Dodge Charger, exiting the ER parking lot, and driving north on Jefferson Drive. License plate not visible on video footage.

The only other notation in the report reads: "Accident under investigation." If I were a little child waking up to no presents under the tree on Christmas Day, I couldn't be more disappointed. I had counted on a follow-up at the scene of my crash to provide some definitive evidence of my identity. Instead, I have nothing. If this is the extent of the

Sergeant's work since that night, then my car is still at the bottom of Lake Monticello, along with my purse, driver's license, car registration, and any other documents that might help identify me by name and address. For now, I remain Kay Smith or Erin Johnson. I really don't know which name is mine—if either.

All in all, Sergeant Montgomery's report raises a lot of questions. I have no choice but to try once more to contact the officer and hope that he'll be able to give me some solid answers. The biggest questions surround John Harris. The witness's retelling of the accident seems plausible enough, but his flight from the hospital calls his whole statement into question. John Harris, if that's his real name, may well have been my brave knight that cold, snowy evening, but running off shows how tarnished and dark his armor is. Perhaps, as Dr. Malone suggested, this man is the abusive partner I'm running from.

After plugging the name into the computer, I'm inundated with images, too many to scroll through. I make a quick assumption about John Harris and add "Virginia" to the search parameters. I scroll through the dozens of faces the search produces, hoping to recognize John Harris. Not one of the young brown-haired, brown-eyed faces does it for me. Perhaps, one of them is my hero. I just don't know.

I pour over the APB once more and focus on what it tells me about John Harris. That's when it hits me—John Harris's description matches Nick's. I read the words aloud this time, as if bearing witness to what I suspect is true. I shudder from the questions echoing inside my head. Is Nick the elusive John Harris? Did he rescue me, unconscious, from certain death after my car accident? Was it even an accident at all?

Curious how much of Nick's story is true, I punch in his name into the browser and hope for answers. A good hour later, my plea has fallen on deaf ears. Among the hundreds of men with the same name online, including those with varied spellings for "Nicholas," not one post or image belongs to my Nick. He doesn't show up on any database, government or otherwise. Either he has some way of keeping his face and information off the web, or more likely, Nick is not who he claims to be.

CHAPTER 25

Throwing caution—and good sense—to the wind, I punch Sergeant Montgomery's phone number into the cell phone Nick gave me and press SEND. Even if Nick bugged the phone somehow, I won't be asking any questions about him, not directly by name, at least, and then only about a car accident we haven't even discussed. That'll either confuse Nick, or if he's John Harris, make him consider coming clean.

"Montgomery here," a deep, male voice answers after three rings.

I hesitate for a moment, startled that I finally have the officer on the line. I scan the room to confirm I'm alone, then speak. "Hello, Sergeant. My name is Mary Brown. Thank you so much for taking my call."

I rise from my chair, grab my notebook and pen, then head toward the corner window to ensure that I can speak freely if someone enters the room. "I know you're a busy man, so I'll get right to the point. I'm a reporter with the *Charlotte Courier* working on a human-interest piece, a story following up on a single-car accident involving a woman, tentatively identified as Erin Johnson, the night of January fifth. The woman was transported to Albemarle County Hospital, where you took a vehicle accident report from a witness by the name of John Harris. I have some questions about the accident,

Mr. Harris, and any follow-up investigation conducted by you and your department."

"I'll do the best I can." The Sergeant's tone is friendly and relaxed. "What do you want to know?"

I stifle a sigh of relief, pleased that Sergeant Montgomery doesn't suspect I'm anyone other than who I claim to be. I need to watch myself, neither reveal my ruse nor come across as pushy. If I don't, the sergeant might terminate our call before I can get answers I need.

"First off, can you tell me what happened to Erin Johnson? Were you able to talk with her about the accident or confirm her name?" I know the truth, or what I believe to be the truth, but want to know if the police do, too.

"Unfortunately, no. She was comatose upon arrival. I followed up with a call to the hospital the next morning, but the victim was still unconscious. I called again the next day but was transferred to Records. The clerk there told me Erin Johnson died January sixth."

From the Sergeant's answer, it's clear the police are unaware of the mix-up or outright fraud associated with the woman's death. I follow up with another question.

"To your knowledge, Sergeant, has anyone come forward to positively identify Erin Johnson?"

"Not that I know of, but the case would've been referred to the VSP, the Virginia State Police. You should check with them."

"Yes, sir, I will." With the preliminary role-playing questions asked, I hope my next inquiry will reveal something I don't already know.

"Next, have you completed your accident investigation, including the recovery of Ms. Johnson's car?" My heart jumps into high gear in anticipation of his answer.

"I don't usually give out that information, but in this case I will because the Charlottesville PD will need some help from the public to close this case. The answer to your question is 'no.'"

The sergeant's answer, the anger I hear in his voice, confuses me. "Was there a problem that impeded your follow-up investigation?"

"Yes, a big one. And this is where we'll need help from the public. We don't know where the woman's car went off the road. The witness was mistaken with regard to that important piece of information. Based on what he told me, I was convinced the victim's vehicle went off the road near a bridge spanning Lake Monticello, approximately seventeen miles southeast of Charlottesville. When the blizzard subsided, my crew went to the scene but came up empty. Our department searched other possible water entry points along the reported route, but still found no submerged car."

His words rattle me, leaving me speechless.

"Please ask your readers to contact me if they have any information that might help us locate the woman's vehicle," Sergeant Montgomery continues. "It's our best chance to positively ID her, find out what really happened that night, and notify her next of kin."

"Of course, Sergeant. I'll make sure your request is prominent in the story," I say, playing my part as cool as I can. I take a deep breath and continue. "You have me a bit confused, Sergeant. Do you think the witness just got it wrong, or did he lie?"

"I can't say. That would be speculation."

The way things are going, my bet is John Harris lied. But why? I need to find out as much as I can from Sergeant Montgomery about my so-called hero.

"Your accident report notes that the man who rescued Erin Johnson, a Mr. John Harris, gave you a statement and then took off. Can you tell me more about him? How did he act? Do you think his sneaking out of the hospital was an attempt to avoid further questioning?"

"The witness was agitated, jumpy, but that's nothing unusual in these cases. He'd been through a rough situation. Why did he flee? Again, I could only speculate."

From the strain in his voice, I can tell the Sergeant is feeling agitated himself, understandable, given that John Harris gave him the proverbial slip.

"Sergeant, during your many years on the force, you probably developed some sixth sense to tell you when someone is lying, either in part or entirely. Given your interaction with John Harris, his unexpected and unexplained flight from the hospital, and the lack of results from your follow-up investigation, how much of John Harris's signed statement do you believe?"

"Off the record?"

"Of course. You have my word."

"Very little."

I pause for a moment to consider how to proceed. So far, the sergeant hasn't said anything that blows my case wide open. If what we discussed to this point is all I get from him, I'll be at another dead end. With nothing to lose, I put the big question out there.

"So, what do you think really happened that night?"

"I could speculate, but I won't. Department policy prohibits us from making such statements, especially with open cases."

I can't let it go. I need to hear Sergeant Montgomery's theory about what went down the night I disappeared from my own life. His observations and deductions might be way off base, but I have to think a man with enough years in law enforcement and public safety to become a police sergeant would come closer to the truth than I ever will.

"Off the record, then. Just to give me an idea of what to do next, where to look for answers." I brace myself, unsure if I'm ready for his take on the mysterious John Harris.

There is a hesitation on the other end of the phone. I hold my breath and wait for him to speak.

"All right, but strictly off the record." It's a firm command, not a request or a suggestion.

Inside my head, I'm jumping and screaming for joy, but outwardly I maintain my cool. "Yes, sir, you have my word."

"I considered four possible explanations of what happened that night," the sergeant begins. "First, John Harris saw Erin Johnson's accident and rescued her out of the goodness of his heart but ran when he had the chance because he's running from the cops for one reason or another. That explanation came up short when he lied about the whereabouts of the woman's car wreck."

"I agree. That doesn't make much sense."

"Second, I considered the possibility that the two were in a relationship and had a big fight. She took off, and he followed, hoping to make up. He forced her off the road accidentally, or she lost control of the car herself. He saved her because he loved her. He took off because he wasn't prepared to confess all, but again, his lies about their names and the crash location defy logic."

The sergeant's reasoning, again, is sound.

"I also considered that maybe John Harris was angry enough following their fight to force Ms. Johnson off the road. When he saw her car sinking into the water, he panicked and saved her, either out of regret or his perverse sense of love. In this case, his flight from the hospital made sense. If there was damage to Harris's car from driving the woman off the road, he may have feared I'd detain him. If not, maybe he just didn't want to face the consequences of his actions when his lover came to and accused him of attempted murder. But again, what reason would he have for lying about their names?"

"I can't think of one," I reply, worrying about Sergeant Montgomery's fourth scenario, the one he's willing to hang his hat on in explaining my Good Samaritan's contradictory statements and behavior.

"In my mind, there's only one story that makes sense of Harris's suspicious behavior. The name is an alias, something the witness has used before or just made up on the spot. Why? He's a criminal.

Maybe he has a police record, perhaps some outstanding warrants. I think he knows Erin Johnson, too. She's his Bonnie, he's her Clyde. They're a couple on a crime spree, possibly already wanted by the police and on the run."

The sergeant's theory leaves me speechless. I hadn't considered that I might be a criminal running from my crimes. The notion doesn't sit well with me.

"As for the accident, my guess is he did see his girl's car go in the water and lied about the location to throw off our follow-up investigation. Why? Because he couldn't risk us recovering the vehicle. There's something incriminating inside it. Guns, drugs, stolen property, money, maybe all of the above. Perhaps the car was stolen. Career criminals swipe vehicles all the time to transport their loot, sometimes even murder victims."

Up to that moment, I'd considered murder in my past a worst-case scenario.

It's your fault.

My head starts to throb. What is my unconscious mind trying to tell me? That I'm involved in some murder? Nick, too? Perhaps that of someone named Maddy? Is that what my nightmare has been trying to tell me all along? Something inside me tells me I'm not a killer, though I'm not so sure about Nick.

"Sergeant," I say, trying to shake off the frightful jitters threatening to erupt from inside me. "Do you think this couple could really be murderers?" I hold my breath awaiting his answer.

"Probably not."

I exhale with relief.

"More than likely, Bonnie and Clyde are con artists. Scammers often work in pairs, and they dress well to impress their marks."

"They were well-dressed?"

"Yes, at least our Bonnie was. The ER removed the woman's clothes and bagged them. I examined them for identifying marks, but only found some expensive labels. Her pantsuit was Chanel, her fashion boots Dolce and Gabbana."

Somehow that sounds like my style.

"No jewelry, though. No rings. No earrings, unusual, given her ears were pierced. My bet is Harris removed her jewelry before arriving at the hospital. Likely very expensive baubles, distinctive, probably stolen or otherwise illegally obtained."

Reflexively, I touch my ears. I make a mental note to check out my ears after the call.

"What about John Harris? Was he wearing expensive clothing, too?"

"I don't know. Hospital staff said he came in soaking wet wearing a dark suit, white shirt, and blue tie. By the time I'd met him, he'd changed into a pair of hospital scrubs. His clothes were in a plastic bag that disappeared with him when he drove off, but I'd bet those duds were designer, too."

Sergeant Montgomery's theory softens my fears about my possible involvement in a Bonnie and Clyde couple. Scheming people out of their life savings, jewelry, too, is reprehensible, but it doesn't leave behind dead bodies that need dumping, or the strangled corpses of pretty, young women buried in off-road, unmarked graves. At the same time, pegging me as part of a pair of con artists would explain why I seem to be such a talented liar.

"I think Clyde really did rescue Bonnie from a sinking car," the officer continues. "He brought her to the hospital because he thought she was badly hurt, and he cared too much to let her die. At the same time, he couldn't stick around because he'd get IDed and end up in the clink, so he gave me the slip the first chance he got. That's my best guess. If that scenario doesn't do it for you, you're welcome to speculate on your own."

"No, Sergeant, your theory sounds very plausible."

I really can't find any hole in his reasoning. If John Harris and I didn't have a relationship prior to my accident, he wouldn't have cause to give a false statement about our names and the location of my submerged car, nor would he have had any reason to escape further questioning by the police. I press on with my inquiry.

"Your report says an APB was issued for John Harris and his car, a black or dark blue Dodge Charger. Any luck finding him or the vehicle?"

"None. Both vanished into thin air. He never came back to check on his girl. I didn't really expect him to. He may have called the hospital looking for information, but there's no way to verify that one way or the other."

I pause to recall my last conversation with Anita and her revelation that a man had called claiming to be the husband of Erin Johnson. That call was likely a ruse. According to last night's news, seven women went missing in the aftermath of the blizzard, and none of them went by the name Erin Johnson. The only explanation is that Anita's caller was John Harris, Sergeant Montgomery's "Clyde." If John Harris pursued the same leads I did, it stands to reason he made a follow-up call with the Records clerk. I jotted a reminder on my notepad to check in with Anita.

"Do you have any more questions for me, Ms. Brown?" The sergeant's voice booms across the phone line, interrupting my train of thought.

"I'm sorry. Yes. One moment while I check my notes." I linger with my thoughts to consider my next question.

"Sergeant, may I bother you for a few more details."

"Sure. Your article may uncover some new leads from the reading public, so go ahead."

For a brief moment, I'm wrenched by a pang of guilt, remorse over continuing my deception of a man being nothing less than honest with me. Still, I press on undeterred.

"Are you aware, Sergeant, of any unsolved crimes in the area that could be linked to this couple or a dark blue or black Dodge Charger? Not just scams, but thefts, burglaries, maybe even assaults?" My heart races inside my chest. I don't want any of his conjecture to be true, but it's something I must face if his Bonnie and Clyde scenario reflects the truth about my past.

"I checked our open cases for the Charger, as well as cases involving a man and a woman matching the description of the couple. I didn't find anything, but that doesn't mean those two are innocent. It happens all the time. People who get scammed are often unaware they've been taken. And those who do know may be too embarrassed to report the crime to the police. Eyewitnesses to crimes are rare, especially with burglaries and some violent offenses, like kidnapping and premeditated murder. Unfortunately, cases go cold pretty darn fast when there's not much evidence to go on."

Good news or bad? I'm not sure. "Do you think John Harris is still in the area?"

"If he's working a lucrative scam, he may still be in the vicinity. If that's the case, he's ditched the Charger and is driving something that blends in more with the rest of the vehicles on the road. But with his partner-in-crime dying under suspicious circumstances, my bet is that he's long gone by now. Probably working an angle to recruit his next accomplice."

Keep hiding.

The little voice in my head says to bet against the Sergeant on this point. I have no doubt that John Harris knows I'm still alive. If I could figure it out, so could he. If I'm right, he's not long gone, and he's eager to find me. Still, the sergeant's theory doesn't explain everything. If I am to assume that John Harris is the man looking for me, then who's behind my clandestine transfer to Summer Oaks and why?

I scan my notes and realize I've covered every question I have for the sergeant except for one I'm terrified to ask. "One last question, related to another story. Do you have open cases involving a woman or child named 'Maddy.' I hold my breath awaiting the sergeant's response.

"Name doesn't ring a bell. Sorry."

"Thank you," I say, heaving a sigh. It's clear he is almost as much in the dark as I am. With so much at stake here—my sanity for one—I'm not sure if his lack of information is good or bad. With nothing else to ask, I thank the officer for his help and wish him well with his investigation.

"Good luck to you, too. And again, if someone comes forward with a tip about this case, let me know. We don't have the time or manpower to cover these cases like you reporters. I would really appreciate anything you can give me to help close this file."

I agree to let him know what I find, but it's another lie. No way am I going to tell him the truth of what I learn. At least, not until I figure out who I am and whether I'm running from the law myself. There's a lot more work ahead of me before that happens, starting with tracking down the elusive John Harris—even if that means going after Nick.

CHAPTER 26

felix sat in his truck as the rays of the rising sun lit the sky chewing on a sausage biscuit and grumbling about the lack of progress he'd made in hunting down his prey during a long, sleepless night. He'd failed in wresting any helpful information from the hospital records clerk, even less from the neurologist who treated Erin Johnson. His efforts to gather information on John Harris proved the witness was no more than a phantom, a faceless, nameless man who told one lie after another to cover up what he knew about the woman and her car wreck.

An all-night wild goose chase and what do I have to show for it? Confirmation I screwed up. That bitch is alive. Somebody somewhere knows where I can find her.

A dozen phone calls and an hour later, Felix identified the ambulance service that had whisked comatose Erin Johnson away from Albemarle County Hospital, a small operation just outside of Culpeper, Virginia. The phone receptionist, an older woman by the sound of her voice, confirmed the January sixth pick up of a patient from Albemarle County Hospital and her subsequent delivery to Kenney Hospital in Roanoke, Virginia.

A quick Google search later, Felix was convinced the facility was a ruse, another red herring designed to hide the woman. He put the truck in gear and headed to Culpeper to give his inquiry a more personal touch.

—

It was close to ten o'clock by the time Felix drove past the faded red-and-blue sign for Harmon's Ambulance and Medical Transport Service two miles outside the small town's limits on a remote section of State Route 3. The cinder-block building suffered from a serious case of neglect. White splotches of paint showed beneath a thick coat of dirt and grime. Plywood sheets covered two of its four front windows. The lone garage door was open, revealing an empty bay. Two vehicles were parked off to the side of the building. Even so, the place was far from a hotbed of human activity, not a person in sight.

Felix parked around back, then quickly entered the building through an unlocked door that led into a short hallway. The front office was a few steps away. On his right was an open door to a vacant restroom. On his left, another door was closed. From the loud giggles, grunts, and high-pitched squeals escaping the room, it was obvious he'd found two possible sources of information.

After Felix kicked open the door, he almost burst out laughing. It wasn't the startled looks of embarrassment on the couple's faces that amused him. It wasn't the black studded- leather they wore and the other gear in the room. It was the amateur way the blubbery twosome had every piece configured, how they were using them. In his mind, these jokers had no business playing bondage games if they couldn't be bothered to learn how to use the equipment properly.

But Felix's mission was no laughing matter. He couldn't do his job properly with the two dressed as they were. After forcing them to strip down, he bound their naked bodies and mouths with duct tape and left them where he'd found them. He locked all the exterior doors, then searched the office and everything in it for the one little piece of information he needed. He found the paperwork showing the pick-up and delivery of Erin Johnson to the phantom facility that was Kenney Hospital, but nothing else.

Felix turned to the two hapless lovers locked in the storeroom for answers. Thirty minutes later, the man and woman were dead. They'd succumbed to his interrogation methods all too quickly without giving up any useful information.

When he heard the rumble of a powerful engine pulling into the garage bay, he smiled. The man with the answers had just arrived.

—

Fifty minutes into his interrogation of the company's lone ambulance driver, Felix was filled with an odd mix of anger, frustration, and admiration for the lean, well-muscled, young Hispanic man lying bound on the table before him. Running out of time and patience, Felix couldn't wait any longer for the information he needed. He had to step up his game to convince the ambulance driver to reveal where he'd delivered that bitch.

With his favorite pearl-handled hunting knife at the young man's throat, Felix saw something in his eyes that he hadn't in the others—combative defiance. He hadn't come across such resistance in years, not since his days at the agency working over terrorists, stupid, low-level operatives brainwashed into thinking that some unseen, all-powerful god would grant each of them a glorious afterlife for giving up their mortal souls in battle against their enemies. Those misguided jihadists had been no match for him. His power had always been far greater than their god. He'd broken them all, squashed their spirits, left their bodies behind bloody, bruised, burned, sliced, and diced. So, it would be with the subject lying before him now. His deity, no matter whom he prayed to, couldn't save him any more than the terrorists' god could.

"Why are you protecting the woman?" Felix asked, his voice calm and measured. He knew restraint in such situations was necessary. Any overt show of agitation or frustration would only serve to embolden his subject, make it harder to extract the information he needed.

"You must know that you'll die a horrible death if you don't tell me where you delivered that comatose woman the afternoon of January sixth."

Felix circled the table, examining his work, its results, and realized physical torture wouldn't work on the ambulance driver. He needed to find another incentive for his subject to surrender the information. Rummaging through the young man's discarded clothes, he found a wallet and rifled through its contents: a driver's license, an ID card for the U.S. Marine Corps Reserves, a Visa card, a McDonald's scratch-off ticket good for a Big Mac, and $26 in cash. He pocketed the money and the coupon, tossed the wallet aside, then found a cell phone in the back pocket of the man's pants. After bringing it to life, he went straight to the archived photos. Within seconds, he had what he needed.

"All right, young man, you've proven yourself a worthy opponent. The Marine Corps would be proud of you, but enough is enough." He strolled around the table, watching the man's defiant glare follow him with each step.

"All right, Sergeant Enrique Sanchez, you and I both know you'll never make it out of this room alive. You knew it all along. That's why you've been so stubborn. Up to now, the question was a simple one. Would you be willing to go through all that pain and suffering to protect the woman I'm looking for? Apparently, yes. Does *this* change your answer?"

Felix held the cell phone over the man's face, close enough so that the former Marine couldn't avoid the screenshot of a young, beautiful, brown-skinned brunette cradling a tiny, pink-blanketed infant in her arms. He pulled back the cell phone without saying another word and stared into the young family man's eyes. The guts and determination he'd seen earlier was gone, replaced by terror, the look of a broken man ready to spill his guts.

CHAPTER 27

I stare out the back window of the Community Room. My mood matches the bleak, overcast sky in front of me. The sergeant was my best hope for answers to my identity and background, a chance for a ray of light in the blackness of my forgotten past. But I'm still in the dark. Between my witness's likely lies and Sergeant Montgomery's speculations, there's not one single fact I can rely on. I have only my gut to trust—and it's not feeling too good right now. It's hard to stay focused with my body gripped with tension, my shoulders weighed down with worry.

One thing is clear. If Sergeant Montgomery's theory is true, and John Harris is an alias and I'm his partner in crime, continuing to search for him online will be an exercise in futility. A call to Anita to check on any further contact from John Harris must be my next move. With all the confusion and outright lies swirling around in my mind, I first need to clear my head.

"You're doing great, Mrs. Pascucci. You're really getting the hang of this walker."

I turn and spot a large bald man escorting a petite dark-haired woman around the room. "One more lap down the hallway and we'll be done with your physical therapy for the day."

Physical therapy. Exercise. That's what I need to declutter my thoughts. My muscles could use a good workout, too, a physical release from all the tension and inactivity.

Back in my room, I dig through Jimmy's bag of clothes, change into a baggy pair of gray cotton sweatpants and a light-blue T-shirt, then head for the PT room.

—

The yellow-walled physical therapy room is occupied by two people, a burly male therapist supervising a rotund gray-haired man leisurely strolling atop one of three treadmills in the far corner of the room. A large, flat-screen TV hangs from the ceiling nearby. A variety of massage tables, weight machines, and other exercise equipment are scattered around the room.

"May I use the treadmill?" I ask the therapist. "I need a good long walk."

He gives me the once-over and nods. "Knock yourself out."

I hop on the nearest machine, set it on a low speed and take my first steps, then increase my speed regularly until I'm running comfortably at a brisk pace. Running feels natural. The therapist, glancing my way, gives me a thumbs-up.

After five minutes of vigorous exercise, my endorphins kick in. I feel strong, confident, ready to handle anything that crosses my path. For the first time since waking from my coma, I experience a measure of peace. My serenity is short-lived, interrupted by a loud *harrumph*.

"How much longer?" the old man grouses.

"Seven minutes down, thirteen to go," the therapist replies, his voice betraying his own boredom. "Want me to turn on the TV? That'll help you pass the time."

"All right, but I don't want to listen to any of those daytime female gab fests. I hate game shows and old sitcoms, too. Find me some news. Real news. Not a bunch of talking heads debating what they think is news or making it up to draw viewers."

The TV comes to life and the screen jumps from one channel to another until it settles on a news station featuring a pretty anchorwoman with a square face and a long mane of wavy, auburn hair. Most of what I've seen or read in the news the past day has been rather morose, so I decide to ignore the TV altogether.

Instead, I focus my eyes on the treadmill's read-out and mentally count along with the timer. *Four minutes . . . and one second . . . two seconds . . . three . . .*

"Louder," the old man shouts. "I can't hear."

The TV's audio level goes from barely discernible to a dull roar in a matter of seconds, making it hard to shut out the words blaring from the speakers.

The big stories surround William Lockhart and his growing list of cabinet choices. Next to me, the old man rants on about each nomination, drowning out the reporter. He sums up his displeasure with the president-elect a few minutes later. "The country's headed for hell in a handbasket with this guy in charge. Always thought he was a crook. That phony corruption scandal against Hayward proves it. Lockhart couldn't chance losing, so he had an October surprise ready to go. President Hayward got screwed, the American people, too. I don't trust this guy any farther than I can throw him."

I don't trust him either. The thought doesn't startle me, but it does spark a recall of the heated discussion I had with Nick earlier—well, fiery on my part at least. Nick had been so cool, so calm in denying he was a reporter out for a big story. Was that all a show, an act to throw me off, to get me to somehow remember and admit my role in political dirty tricks?

The old man rattles on, drowning out my ability to think. When he finally shuts up, I look up from my treadmill to the TV screen showing William Lockhart standing at a podium flanked by two American flags with a throng of reporters hanging on his every word.

Dr. Malone's advice pops into my head. *Be mindful. Observe. Don't judge.* She was convinced that managing my stress was the key to my recovery, the return of my memories. With a big breath in and out, I'm ready to return my attention to the TV.

"Governor Lockhart, on behalf of the entire press pool, I'd like to express our condolences . . ."

From out of nowhere, two words strike me like a lightning bolt. *She's dead.*

I can't control myself. Anger rises in my throat. My blood feels ready to boil. My legs go weak and wobble beneath me. I reach for the handrail to steady myself, but my grip goes limp. I fall, hitting the treadmill's emergency stop button as I go down. Lying in a heap on the pad, I struggle to catch my breath. Suddenly, I feel a hand on my shoulder.

"Are you okay?"

I recognize the therapist's voice over the blaring TV and nod my head in response. I draw in a deep breath, then roll myself to a sitting position. "Yes. I'm okay. I just tripped over my own feet."

"Well, just to be on the safe side, I'd better check you out. Does anything hurt? Your ankle or your knee? Did you bump your head?" He reaches toward me, but I wave him off.

"No. Please. I'm fine." I blush with embarrassment. "I must have looked like a complete klutz. The only part of me that hurts is my pride." The statement is not wholly true. My pride is not the only part of my psyche that is wounded.

"No worries, I didn't see what happened. Don't rush to get up. Just sit there. I'll get you some water."

The room goes silent for a moment until the old man growls another complaint. "Why'd you mute the TV? I wanna hear the rest of this asshole's lies."

The therapist returns a few seconds later and hands me a paper cup. I take a sip of the cold drink and hear a loud *harrumph*.

"I'm done," the old man barks. "My twenty minutes are up. Get me off this damn contraption and back to my room."

With a note of annoyance in his grin, the therapist turns toward his patient. "I'll be right there." Turning back to me, he asks, "Will you be all right by yourself?"

I nod, thank him for his concern, and quietly sip my water as I watch the old man shuffle out of the room with the therapist by his side.

Finally, alone with my thoughts, I sit and focus on those two little words that set me off—*she's dead*. My heart sinks with despair. Who died? Do I bear some responsibility for her death? I must. Why else would my locked-down memory haunt me with a singular charge—*it's your fault*. Is this woman and her fate at the heart of my fugue? Is my mind struggling with itself to reveal our shared secrets?

I hazard a glance at the TV screen, at the now-silent image of the president-elect, and wonder if I was close to the truth when I accused Nick of being a reporter chasing me for a story on election tampering. Every time I see or hear William Lockhart, my emotions go into overdrive—anxiety, anger, distrust, all directed at that man. Is there a connection between him, me . . . and some dead woman?

Am I a campaign operative, perhaps, the one responsible for spreading the false pay-for-play narrative that cheated President Hayward out of his rightful reelection? Did the woman have damning evidence and threaten to go public?

The scenario seems weak, far-fetched even, especially as a motive for murder. The stakes are just not high enough. Spreading vicious lies about a political opponent is reprehensible and immoral, but not illegal. There must be more to what's going on here.

John Harris is still the key to all this, especially if he and Nick are one in the same man. It doesn't matter either way right now. Without my memory to rely on, my only recourse in my search for answers is to depend on people with whom John Harris has come into contact. Right now, the only person I know who might be able to help is Anita.

I pull myself up and scurry back to my room. I rush to my bedside table, tear through my notes, and place the call to the clerk's personal cell phone number.

"Hello." The male voice on the other end of the line is deep, gruff.

"Hi." Confused, I glance at the phone number on my notepad. "I'm looking for Anita, but maybe I misdialed."

"No. You got it right. This is Mrs. Hodges's phone." The response is cold, unfriendly.

"May I speak with her, please?"

"It depends. Who's calling?"

I don't know what to say. If someone is screening Anita's calls, something is wrong.

"Uh, I'm just a friend. If she's not available, I'll catch up with her later."

"A friend? I guess you haven't heard . . ."

"Heard what?" My heart sinks inside my chest, my breathing becomes labored, as an overwhelming sense of dread takes hold of me.

The man's voice softens. "I'm sorry that you have to find out this way."

"Find out what?" Fear seems ready to burst through my chest.

"Anita Hodges is dead."

CHAPTER 28

"**A**nita . . . dead?"

"Yes, Ma'am. You're speaking with Detective Sam Warren of the Charlottesville Police Department. It appears Mrs. Hodges was murdered last night."

Murdered. The phone tumbles from my hand. I mouth the unspeakable word to myself, shaking with a mixture of disbelief and horror.

"Hello? Hello?" The detective's faint voice calls out to me from my cell phone.

I fumble to pick up the device, then struggle to speak. "I, uh, I'm sorry. I dropped my phone." My voice shakes with genuine sorrow.

"I know this must be a shock, but maybe you can help me catch her killer." Against all odds, the detective's just-the-facts-ma'am voice calms me down. "Please tell me your name and how you know Mrs. Hodges."

I stammer for a moment, trying to figure out what to say. I don't know whether to tell the truth or fabricate another story.

Keep hiding.

I can't ignore the voice in my head. I choose to lie. "My name is Mary Brown. I'm a friend of Anita. What happened?"

"Mrs. Hodges was found this morning at her place of work, the Records Office at Albemarle County Hospital. It appears she was killed last night between 11:38 p.m. and 2:00 a.m. Where were you last night at that time?"

I couldn't be more shocked by the news if the detective reached through the phone and Tasered me.

"I was asleep," I answer truthfully after recovering my wits. "Do you know who did it, or why she was killed?" I have my own theory.

"I'm not at liberty to comment at this time, but maybe you could help. How well acquainted were you and Mrs. Hodges?"

I want to help. I really do. But I'm not ready to spill my guts and reveal myself.

"Did you know Mrs. Hodges well enough for her to tell you if she had any enemies, perhaps someone stalking her or bothering her in any way?"

"She never mentioned anyone like that."

"Mrs. Hodges was a widow. Do you know if she was seeing anyone? Maybe a tall Caucasian with dark hair and a mustache?"

A lump seems to form in my throat. The description vaguely describes John Harris, Nick, too, if either man disguised himself with a fake mustache.

"No. Why?"

"We have a person of interest caught on the hospital's security video."

I need to see that surveillance tape. "If you send me a copy of the video or a clear photo from it, I might be able to identify him," I say, hoping for an affirmative reply.

"I'm sorry, that's not possible, Ms. Brown, at least, not at this time. If you give me your email address and phone number, I'll send you the video if and when it's cleared for release."

"Yes. Thank you," I reply, following up with Mary Brown's Gmail address and the number for the burner phone Nick gave me. It's a risky move, but it's a chance I must take. I need that video. It represents the first solid lead on my stalker, an opportunity to get a look at him before he catches up with me—if he isn't closing in already.

"By any chance did you know a doctor on staff at Albemarle County Hospital?" the detective continues. "A neurologist by the name of Patel?"

My lungs constrict with fear at the name and the detective's use of past tense regarding my doctor. "No. W-why?"

"I was just wondering if they knew each other. He was found dead this morning after failing to report for work. I can't say anything more."

My knees go weak. The tight-lipped detective doesn't have to reveal my neurologist's cause of death. Murder. It has to be, and by the same hand that took Anita's life—the man looking for me—my husband, assuming the man Anita talked to was telling the truth, which seems increasingly doubtful.

"How good a friend did you say you were with Mrs. Hodges?" the detective continues with a note of suspicion in his voice. I gasp for air, afraid that I have slipped up, given the detective reason to doubt my answers. I take a calming breath and find strength in the truth.

"We were no more than casual acquaintances. I, uh, I didn't know her all that well."

"Too bad. I hoped you might be able to help me find a connection between the two victims, if there is any."

With his last statement, the detective confirms the doctor's murder.

"Wish I could help you there." I really do, but I can't risk exposing myself.

"Listen," the detective continues, "if you think of anything, no matter how small or insignificant you think it might be, please call me."

"I'll help any way I can." I copy down the detective's name, phone number, and email address, then end the call.

I lay on my bed, breathing in and out, trying to get a hold of myself, but I can't stay still. I crawl out of bed and start pacing the floor, trying to make sense of the fact that someone is willing to kill to find me. *What have I done to be on someone's hitlist?*

One possibility is that Sergeant Montgomery's theory is true, that I'm half of a crooked couple, a pair of high-class con artists, who dress in designer clothes, dine on the finest cuisine, and speak French like a member of the aristocracy—the *haute bourgeoisie*—to bilk the gullible rich out of their wealth with our lies and manipulations. Did we kill in the heat of the moment when faced with an angry victim determined to put us in prison? Perhaps we never leave witnesses behind to ID us and our crimes. The whole thing doesn't really make much sense, though. Where in this scenario is my PTSD and the last straw, the trauma that triggered my flight from myself and my memories?

I'm left hoping that Dr. Malone's theory is more on target, though that is also what frightens me the most. I am an abused wife, a woman dominated by an abusive man with a simmering propensity for violence. With my high-class tastes, my fluent French, he might be cultured, perhaps a rich and powerful man. Maybe even connected to William Lockhart, which would explain my antipathy for the president-elect. It makes sense and would explain why I'd rather run than speak up even if I witnessed a violent crime, a murder even.

It's your fault. The haunting refrain fits this gruesome scenario.

My body starts to tremble as I imagine it in my mind. My husband and I, driving around in the dark in his big black truck, stopping to help young pretty women, isolated, perhaps stranded by the side of the road next to a broken-down car, maybe caught in a rainstorm while out for a run. Each one naïve, unaware that the presence of another woman in a vehicle does not make accepting a ride from a strange man safe. We drive to a lonely patch of woods, somewhere no one can see what is about to happen. Steps away, I'm forced to watch a gruesome one-act show—my husband, his brawny hands at the woman's throat, squeezing as she struggles, until at last, her body goes limp and slumps to the ground, the gleeful look in my husband's eye as he buries his victim. My role is unspoken, coerced. I cover for this monster, his vile deeds, serving as his alibi should suspicions ever fall on him, complicit myself, keeping me from going to the police and confessing all.

It's your fault.

The words taunt me now. Are they trying to tell that I have more to account for than my imagination has offered? Am I a reluctant partner to murder, perhaps, someone named Maddy, or is my imagination running away with me?

I move about the room trying to lay out the possible players in what has become a very deadly game of hide-and-seek—the man lurking in the truck's shadows, the mysterious John Harris, Nick. I close my eyes hoping for a blinding light to illuminate the answer to what is now the most critical question—how many men are involved in this horrific drama? Three? Two? One man playing all three roles? A multiple personality of sorts, or just an incredibly talented actor?

Two makes more sense than three. If my flashback reflects reality, one man chased me down in his truck, driving me into some unknown body of water, while another man, driving a Dodge Charger, rescued me and delivered me to the emergency room. Are John Harris and Nick the same man? They share similar physical traits, but so do thousands of other men in the area.

One thing is clear—Nick is holding back from me, lying even. That he does so smoothly, deflecting my suspicions as deftly as he does, only heightens my sense that he is up to no good. But still, that doesn't prove John Harris and Nick are one and the same. It just means I can't trust either man.

It's your fault.

My heart falls, my spirits drop. Whatever unknown failures I may have been guilty of in the past, I know what I have done now. Two people are dead, murdered by someone looking for me. And that is, indeed, my fault.

CHAPTER 29

rust no one.

My subconscious is right. That must be my approach.

Anita was killed by someone trying to learn my whereabouts. She didn't divulge that information. She couldn't. I never told her where I was. But the death of my neurologist has me worried. Despite the forged documents, it's possible he knew how I ended up at a rehab facility, even if he was clueless about where I was taken.

I pace the room, trying to identify my options, and decide my next move. One possibility is going to the police and telling them what I know, what I don't know, and let them take it from there. On the one hand, giving a detailed account of my conversations with Anita could be the key to finding her murderer and my stalker. The police would be here asking all sorts of questions I can't answer, and probably a lot more I shouldn't with my own criminal past a real possibility.

I have no doubt Detective Warren would be circumspect about my story. I wouldn't blame him if he thought I was faking my amnesia. If I were in his position, chances are I'd think that, too. He'd put his men to work corroborating my account, of course. With access to all sorts of government resources, the police would likely uncover my identity well before I recovered my memory. Even if the police didn't have enough evidence to hold me as either a material witness or a suspected criminal, I doubt I'd be free to leave the area or move on with my life.

Either way, I'd be exposed. Reporters and cameramen would camp outside my door. My face would be plastered on TV, newspapers, the Internet, every possible news outlet, all connecting me to two brutal murders and, if my nightmares have any basis in fact, likely more. Every minute of publicity would be a gift to my stalker, the information he needs to track my movements and plan my demise.

I could request police protection, or at the very least, anonymity until the killer is caught, but that's a risky move, too. Even if the police and district attorney agreed to such an arrangement, someone somewhere would leak my name, face, and whereabouts to the media for one reason or another.

The flip side, of course, is to simply wait a few days to see where the investigation goes, who the police suspect, and what progress they make. It's possible my theory about the killings is way off base, that someone else, perhaps two separate people, killed Anita and Dr. Patel. If not, and the police don't uncover any viable leads, I can call in my statement. Even then, I won't have to stick around for the cops to come after me.

I don't know what to do. My mind is racing light years faster than my feet. I stop in my tracks, grab the footboard of Emily's bed to steady myself, then close my eyes and draw in two deep breaths. *Inhale . . . exhale . . .inhale . . . exhale . . .*

When I finally open my eyes, I gaze upon the still form of my roommate. Suddenly, I know what to do. I refuse to be like Emily, held hostage in place and time, mind and body, waiting for a chance to reclaim her life. Not when I have a choice in the matter. There's only one option going forward—I need to get away from Summer Oaks and leave without anyone knowing where I'm going. Once I'm away, I'll be able to take a more active approach to jump-starting my memory. Most importantly, it'll put distance between me and the dark past that seems to be coming for me.

There is one sticking point. I have no place to go, no way to get around, and less than three hundred dollars on a prepaid debit card to support myself. I can't ask for help from any of the staff or leave behind any hint of my intentions. That would only put more innocents in harm's way.

There's just one person I can consider asking for help. Nick.

CHAPTER 30

ime is not on my side. Neither is fear nor anxiety. Nick has shown me nothing but compassion and has proved willing to go out of his way to help me. Even his touch echoes safety and security. That he hasn't been completely open and honest with me doesn't mean he's dangerous. With no other options, I shove aside my apprehensions about our possible criminal past together and place the call. Nick picks up on the first ring.

"What's up?" His tone is terse, worried.

"I hate to ask, but I need another favor." I hear the quiver in my voice, feel the fear rising in my throat.

"Whatever it is, you can count on me," Nick replies, his voice softened.

I take a deep breath and slowly release it. "I need to leave Summer Oaks. I was hoping you could pick me up, maybe let me stay at your place for a few days until I decide where to go next."

"Leave? Why?" His voice deepens with concern but, curiously, lacks any indication of surprise.

"I think someone from my past, someone dangerous, might be close to finding me here." Now that I've said it aloud to someone other than myself, it seems less like a nightmare, or some crazy figment of my imagination, and more like reality. I can't explain my predicament to Nick, not without tipping him off about my suspicions about him. And at this point, keeping secrets from Nick is my best defense. I have to hope that he hasn't seen through my deceptions, that he will trust me enough to accept my plea for help without asking a lot of questions.

"Who? Have you remembered something or someone from your past?" Nick asks, with a note of guarded hopefulness in his voice.

"I don't want to go into details over the phone. Can you just come and pick me up? I'll explain later." Suddenly, my body starts to tremble as fear rises inside me. Asking Nick to whisk me away was the wrong move, and I am tempted to withdraw my request.

"Of course. I'm at home. I can be there in fifteen minutes, ten minutes if I catch green lights all the way."

Too late. He's made the choice for me, so I go with that.

"It's pretty damn cold outside," Nick continues. "Twenty-nine and dropping. I'll bring you a coat and hat. The coat will be too big, but it'll do until we can stop somewhere and buy you something that fits."

"All right, but don't come inside. You can't be seen bringing me outerwear. I don't want anyone to know I'm leaving. I need to slip out a door and be long gone before anyone notices I'm missing. It's safer for me, you, and the staff here, too."

"Sounds like a plan," he says.

I'm thankful to have only a short wait. I won't need more than a minute to get out of the building. I don't have anything to pack or take with me other than my notepad and cell phone, the only items I don't dare leave behind for my stalker to find, or anyone else for that matter. Too much information in the wrong hands is dangerous, not just for me but for everyone I've encountered since awaking at Summer Oaks.

"Where should I meet you?" I ask.

"Take the back stairs, then look for a rear door. That will be the employees' entrance. It will be unmanned. I'll meet you there."

It's obvious covert operations are nothing new to Nick. That he's already familiar with Summer Oaks' layout, especially the exits, is not surprising whether he's a bodyguard, as Nick asserts, or a con man. Reconnaissance is part of either job description, allowing him to make a getaway at a moment's notice with anyone being the wiser.

"What kind of car should I look for?"

He doesn't answer right away. "A black sports coupe."

At first, I don't understand Nick's hesitancy, not until I put two and two together. "What make and model?"

"A Dodge Charger."

CHAPTER 31

Felix broke from his routine and sped into the Summer Oaks parking lot without the usual reconnaissance drive-by. He settled for a quick spin around the back of the building to locate the exits. Four doors: front lobby, emergency exits right and left, employee and delivery entrances at the rear. He pulled into an open spot directly by the side door giving him the quickest, least-guarded exit to his car if he needed to make a hasty retreat.

Not that he expected that to happen. This wasn't his first extraction, and it wouldn't be his last, if that's what the situation called for. Finding that bitch struggling to remember her own name would make the job easy enough to come back in the dead of night and abduct her without anyone being the wiser. If she saw him, recognized him for who he was—*that* would be a problem.

—

I was wrong to trust Nick more than my instincts. His familiarity, his attentiveness, his actions, even the attraction we seem to have for each other—it all confirms my suspicion that we have a prior relationship, that he is John Harris. Still, his motives for deceiving me remain elusive.

If anything, Nick's ruse quells my fear that he is out to kill me, at least for the time being. He could have smothered me with a pillow any time before I emerged from my coma. Still, I can't trust him.

Fool me once, shame on you. Fool me twice, shame on me. I'm not about to let that happen.

I rush to the Community Room, find the computer free and search online for a local taxi service. I pick the first one on the list and make the call on the house phone.

"How soon can you get a cab to Summer Oaks Rehab Center?" I ask the dispatcher when she answers my call.

"Do you have an address?"

"No. It's in the metro DC area."

"One moment, please."

My nerves are on edge, waiting for what seems an eternity.

"I can have a driver there in approximately twelve minutes."

That isn't fast enough. With Nick already on his way, I'll have to find some way to delay him.

"Great. Have the driver come around to the back door. I'll meet him there."

I give the dispatcher a fake name and cell number to complete the reservation, a ruse to prevent Nick from somehow tracking me.

—

Felix nodded and smiled at the uniformed guard standing by the lobby door. Tall and gangly with a face full of acne, his opponent was easy to assess. *Kindergarten cop. Not even a billy club to defend himself.* If Felix ran into a problem, the man-boy wouldn't know what hit him.

He approached the woman seated behind the reception desk. "I'm here to visit a patient. Alicia Simmons. Where can I find her?"

"Let me check."

He already knew. He'd called from the parking lot a couple of minutes earlier, asking the operator to connect him to the patient in room 213. When a woman answered the phone, he jumped at an old trick, pretending to be a radio show calling with a chance to win prizes. The woman fell for the ploy, answered a few easy questions, including her name, the only information he really needed. It gave him cover he needed to enter the building and pass himself off as a visitor. Once past security, he'd search the building's top three floors reserved for inpatient rooms. With any luck, he'd spot Kay Smith quickly, without alerting her or anyone who might be guarding her.

"Alicia Simmons is on the second floor, room 213," the receptionist said. "You're welcome to go up after you sign the registry. Include your name, the name of the patient you're visiting, and room number. I'll also need to see some ID."

Felix pulled out a pen from an interior coat pocket and signed using his usual nondescript alias, "Jack Martin." He returned his pen to his pocket, pulled out his wallet and flashed the fake driver's license that went with the name and disguise. Seconds later, he was inside the elevator and headed for the second floor, where he would start his search and work his way up. With patient rooms limited to three floors, Felix was confident he'd soon have the answer to one question—was Kay Smith the woman he needed to find and kill?

—

I hustle back to my room. As the door closes behind me, my cell phone buzzes. *Nick.* I let it ring a few times before answering, biding my time for some inspiration, but my mind is a blank. Afraid Nick will come for me if I don't answer, I press the CALL button.

"Nick. Hi." I do my best to hide the apprehension rising in my throat.

"Good. You're okay. I was beginning to worry."

His words are rushed, almost breathless, as if he's sprinted the distance between his place and Summer Oaks. "Anyway, I'm here. Parked by the back door. Are you ready?"

His words give off an air of cool confidence, as if my desperate escape is part of his own plan. Is that what he has been pushing for, a chance to get me away from the security of Summer Oaks and isolate me for his nefarious purposes?

I fall into another quick lie as I pace the room. "No. My nurse just left. Dr. Malone is on her way to see me. I can't go anywhere now, not without raising alarm."

"I'll wait. Call me when you're ready to go."

Waiting isn't enough. I need Nick to leave and stay away long enough for my taxi to arrive and make my get away. I stop in front of the window and spot a woman huddled against the cold, crossing the parking lot.

"I have a better idea," I reply. "Instead of wasting time sitting in the parking lot, why don't you buy me that better-fitting coat you promised me? The nurse who agreed to do my shopping mentioned a Walmart near here, just a couple of miles away."

"I don't know. You sounded so desperate earlier. I'd feel better staying close."

"I'm sorry," I say, feigning a sigh. "I was having another of my panic attacks, maybe even a bit of paranoia. I'm better now. I don't think I'm in immediate danger. Really. I'll call after I finish up with Dr. Malone. Then I'll slip out the back, and we'll be on our way. I promise to explain everything once we're settled at your place." I stifle the truth. *No way am I going anywhere with you.*

Nick protests again.

"Please. A snug-fitting woman's coat will do a better job keeping me warm than something that hangs on me," I say, doing my best to sound more lighthearted than our last phone call. "A size six, I think, maybe an eight. You be the judge. I could use a scarf to help hide my bruised face and a pair of gloves, too."

After Nick grumbles a "yes" and hangs up, I post myself in front of the window and wait for Nick's Charger to pull around the side of the building. I flash a smile and wave when he passes by, hoping that if he looks up, he'll see there is nothing pressing to worry about.

Except there is everything to worry about, at least for me.

CHAPTER 32

At best, my cab is still ten minutes away. A sweaty mess from my workout, I hustle into the bathroom and pull off my shoes, shirt, and sweatpants, then clean up with a bit of soap and water. As I comb my hair, I stare into the mirror at the bandage taped across my nose. I'm hesitant to remove the gauze, fearful that doing so might set back my healing or leave me disfigured, but I know it has to go. If my escape is less than perfect, Nick could easily spot the big white bandage on my face from a block away or in a crowd.

I hold my breath, peel back the tape, and pull the gauze from my nose. After washing off the adhesive left behind, I examine my bruised and swollen nose from every angle. For the most part, it's long and slender, culminating in a slightly upturned point. I heave a sigh of relief, pleased that my injury isn't as disfiguring as I'd feared. Still, I can't imagine that I look much like myself.

I exit the bathroom, pull on my too-short jeans, don a blue sweatshirt from my bag of borrowed clothes, and slip on my sneakers. Ready to make my escape, I drop my cell phone on the floor, stomp on it twice, then toss it in the trash. After snatching up my notepad, I cross the room to the door and peek out. With no one in the immediate vicinity, I step out of the room.

The only person in sight is a tall man at the far end of the hall. Wearing a long, black coat and black cap with his back to me, he glances at each door as he passes by. For some reason, the figure gives me the creeps, so I scurry for the stairwell at the opposite end of the hallway. As I grab the door handle, I steal a glance back down the hall. The man in the black coat stands next to my open door staring inside the room. He turns his head in my direction. In that moment, I recognize the cloaked figure— the ghoul in my nightmare, the monster who tried to kill me. And he recognizes me.

I pull open the door and barrel down the stairs to the first floor so fast, I'm not sure my feet ever touch the steps. Moving as fast as my racing heart, I head for the rear of the building, hoping my taxi is early.

It takes only a second's glance out the plate glass door to dash my hopes. Behind me, the sound of a door opening startles me. I spin around and see a young, thin man with shoulder-length blond hair dressed in gray coveralls emerge from a room just steps away. With the door opened wide, he pushes out a cleaning cart, sets the lock on the knob, then strolls away, leaving the door to swing shut.

I squeeze my body inside the room just before the door clicks closed.

—

Felix bounded down the stairs two by two until he reached the first floor. He pulled his gun—a 9mm semiautomatic with a built-in silencer— from his shoulder holster, then peeked through a crack in the door and listened. The place was quiet. No commotion, no shouts, no alarms. Poking his head out the door, Felix looked both ways but saw no one.

He returned the pistol to its holster, then emerged into the hallway and dashed toward the rear of the building. He held the door as he stepped outside and searched for any sight or sound of the woman. The only movement he saw was a tall man, bundled up in a thick winter coat, creeping across the icy parking lot toward a car parked under an overhead light.

She must still be in the building.

Back inside, Felix strode down the hallway, checking locked doors, inspecting the spaces behind those left unsecured. He passed only one person in the hallway, a young janitor pushing a cleaning cart. Dressed in gray coveralls and heavy leather work boots, the blond man sniffled and coughed as he shuffled by.

—

I fumble around in the dark room for the light switch and flip it on. I check the door to ensure it's locked, then turn around and examine the janitorial supply closet. Small, with little room to move around, the shelves on either side of me are neatly arranged with a variety of cleaning solutions, spray bottles, paper towels, garbage bags, and brushes. Lined up along the back wall are brooms, buckets, mops, and an empty cart. Gray coveralls of varying lengths hang nearby. On the floor, next to a large rolling bucket, is a sign "Caution: Wet Floor" with a picture of a stick figure slipping and falling.

With my heart still racing, I pull in a deep breath through my nose. The strong smell of ammonia assaults my airways. A coughing fit ensues that threatens to give away my hiding place.

Suddenly, the doorknob rattles. Is that him? Did he hear me cough? If this guy could hear the frantic thumping of my heart, it would be all over.

Time seems to stand still waiting for something to happen. Is he gone? Is my path clear to the rear exit? What should I do if my taxi is not there?

There is only one way to find out. Get out of here, now. I must act quickly and do so armed, ready to defend myself as part of my escape. I take a second survey of the room and quickly spot my weapon of choice.

—

After inspecting the ladies' room, Felix glanced down the hallway, but the only person in sight was the janitor. As he watched the figure receding toward the rear of the building, something seemed off with the man. It wasn't that his blond hair seemed a bit long on the back of his neck. It wasn't just that his gray coveralls seemed to hang on his frame and puddle around his ankles.

No boots this time. Sneakers!

Felix burst into a sprint.

—

The footsteps grow louder, quicker. *It's him! Oh, my god, it's him!* I hoist the bucket from the cart, count to three, then turn around and chuck two gallons of ammonia down the hallway with perfect timing. My would-be killer tries to put on the brakes, but slips and falls, then slides across the floor on his back, legs and arms flailing for a hold. I snatch another improvised weapon, a spray bottle of bleach, then thrust the cart out of my way and race for the back door.

At the glass entryway, I strain, looking for my cab. Nothing. A quick glance back into the hallway proves my plan worked. Coughing and struggling to stand, it's clear I've blinded the monster with the potent cleaner, at least temporarily. Although still struggling, the man reaches inside his coat. I bolt through the door without another look back, determined to make my escape any way I can.

In the next moment, I'm grabbed from behind. The spray bottle slips from my hand. Now defenseless, my screams are smothered by a gloved hand, my arms pinned by a thick, strong arm. Fear teems from every pore in my body. My attacker drags me backward. I strain to pull away, but he holds me fast. There is no air between us. Through his jacket, I can feel the muscles in his thick arms, his broad chest, and his lean torso.

I dig the heels of my tennis shoes into the snow-covered ground but find no purchase. I fight against my attacker's hold, kicking and thrashing. The effort is useless. He's too strong, too overpowering. Within seconds, he has us both concealed behind a thick row of snow-capped bushes. Tears blur my vision, and I squeeze my eyes shut as I'm forced to the ground, pinned by a pair of strong, sinewy legs.

I can't give up. I won't. I continue to struggle.

"Stop. Stop it, Kay." I hear the urgent whisper through my muffled cries for help. "I'm here to help you, not hurt you."

I recognize Nick's voice but hear no truth in his words. In no position to throw him off, I give up the fight and open my eyes. His gaze meets mine. He looks as terrified as I feel. His eyes, his brow, his frown, show real worry, although I can't be certain if he is scared for me or himself.

"I know you're afraid of me," he continues in a hushed tone. "But you shouldn't be. I haven't killed anyone outside of combat, and I don't plan to start with you. Please, you must believe me."

Nick's voice is urgent, pleading. I want to believe him but can't.

"I'll tell you everything once we're safely away from here. For now, all you need to know is that I'm a member of the Secret Service. I'm here to protect you. You're Angela Lockhart, soon to be FLOTUS, the First Lady of the United States."

CHAPTER 33

Angela Lockhart? *That can't be.* Not a battered woman? Not a wife covering for her murderous husband, or a Bonnie scheming with her partner-in-crime, Clyde?

In one quick move, Nick hoists me up, then hurries me to his car parked a few feet away. After hustling me into the passenger seat, he slams the door shut, then darts around the front of the car and jumps behind the wheel.

"Put on your seat belt," Nick shouts, as he puts the car in gear and punches the accelerator. The car lurches forward.

Before I can move, the side window behind me shatters. Nick jerks the steering wheel to the left, spinning the car around. The rear window shatters.

In a flash, Nick is on top of me. "Get down and stay down!" Just as quickly, he's off. The growl of the Charger's powerful engine fills the air. I feel the tires spin, the car pitch forward and accelerate.

With the wind knocked out of me, my screams go silent. In between gasps for air, I feel the swoosh of the bullets whizzing overhead, but all I can hear is the frantic drumming of my heart. I sneak a peek toward Nick just as the rearview mirror explodes. Glass and plastic rain down on me. I throw my hands over my head and press my arms against my ears to shut out the horror of the blasts. My body rolls with a sharp right turn of the car as Nick accelerates again, the Charger's engine roaring like thunder.

Soon, the only thing I hear is the pounding of my heart, an eerily calming sound, each *thumpa-thumpa* offering proof I'm still alive.

A few thousand heartbeats later, when the car slows to a stop, Nick's muffled voice breaks through my defenses. "Are you okay, Ma'am? Are you hurt?"

I didn't expect to hear panic in his voice, but it's there, offering a glimmer of hope that Nick's story is on the up-and-up. I want to believe the man is a decorated war hero, a Secret Service Agent, someone who could be overwhelmed with fear when facing death. But I just can't. No self-respecting Secret Service agent would have left my side in a hospital ER, especially if I really was the comatose wife of the president-elect. Nor would he have left me unprotected at Summer Oaks, even for a minute. *If he is Secret Service, why is he the only agent protecting me?* That Nick had saved me from another murderous attack moments ago does nothing to bolster his claim. His life was in danger, too.

Amidst the confusion and uncertainties swirling around in my head, I squeak out a response. "I'm okay. Can I get up now? This position is extremely uncomfortable, and it's making me sick to my stomach." It's the truth, although I suspect the whole getting-shot-at thing is more to blame for my nausea than my posture.

"Yes, Ma'am. You can sit up. We're safe for now."

Nick sounds confident, but I'm not so sure. Nevertheless, I pull myself up and survey our location. The filthy, peeling paint on the long cinder-block walls, the boarded-up windows, the piles of garbage and refuse on the pavement suggest we are parked behind an abandoned strip mall. Glancing around the car, I realize the damage is not as bad as I'd expected. The dashboard has taken a half dozen shots. The back window is shattered. Shards of glass

are strewn across the floorboard. The rearview mirror, hanging by
a thin thread, is the main fatality. It isn't until I look at Nick that I
realize there was more damaged in the attack than the car and my
sense of security.

- 170 -

CHAPTER 34

"**Y**ou're bleeding!" I shout at the sight of a thick, red line of blood seeping down the right side of Nick's face. "We've got to get you to a doctor." The urgency in my voice startles me, forcing me to admit to myself that, perhaps, sometime in the past, I cared for Nick. Still, I know I must keep my distance, keep my emotions in check and put my own safety before Nick's.

I search the car, frantic for a tissue or small garment to stem the bleeding but find nothing. I start to rip the sleeve from my coveralls when Nick stops me.

"Hold on, Ma'am." He pulls my hands away from my shirt. "You need every stitch of clothing you have on to keep from freezing to death. Besides, I haven't been shot. It's just a little cut, probably from flying glass. Nothing I can't take care of myself."

After reaching into the back seat, Nick produces a large navy pea coat. "Here. Put this on."

Freezing, I quickly unbuckle my seatbelt, grab the coat, and pull it on.

"It's too big, but it'll keep you warm until I can make that trip to Walmart. I never made it there. I saw a black truck in the parking lot and stopped to investigate. It looked like the one that ran you off the road."

Anger wells up inside me, boiling hot, ready to erupt like a geyser. "I knew it! You *are* John Harris. You lied about my car crash. Lied about who I am, who you are, then abandoned me at the hospital. Who are you really? What the hell is going on? Who is trying to kill me?" I shake my head. "Please. My gut tells me I'm not Angela Lockhart. I can't be." I don't want to contemplate that the soon-to-be most powerful man in the world might be behind my trauma-induced amnesia. The implications are just too huge. "Just tell me the truth."

With a sigh, he reaches into his jacket pocket, pulls out a brown leather case and hands it to me. I flip it open to see a gold badge with a five-point star inlaid with a crest and the words, "U.S. Secret Service." A raised banner across the bottom edge reads "Special Agent." Opposite the badge, tucked behind a clear plastic pocket, is an ID badge with Nick's name and photograph.

"I'm Special Agent Nick Costa, Secret Service, Counter Assault Team, Presidential Protective Division," he says. "And you *are* Angela Lockhart." He takes the badge from me, tucks it back inside his coat, then takes my hands in his. His touch is warm, gentle, familiar, radiating a tactile sense of trust I never felt before.

I pull back as the frightening reality of my situation hits me. Even if I am Angela Lockhart, I could still be a battered woman. Still be a Bonnie to a Clyde. A criminal. Except, my Clyde might be moving into the White House soon. My visceral reactions to seeing and hearing William on TV suggest an unhealthy, if not downright dangerous relationship. Is Nick protecting me from my husband? Or is he protecting my husband from me and whatever it is *I* know?

"I'm sorry for deceiving you these last two days, Ma'am. Really, I am," he says with a sigh. "I misled you and everyone, but it was necessary. I made up aliases to protect us and those around you from a professional killer. Even your psychiatrist was in the dark about your identity and mine. In fact, the doc and I have never met in person. We communicated only by phone or text. The only thing I told her was that someone ran you off the road. I held back that little detail from the police, too, and lied about the make of your car and where to find it."

His explanation sounds plausible, but still comes up short. "But why not tell me the truth?"

"That was Dr. Malone's recommendation," he says, while inspecting his scalp with what is left of the rearview mirror. "She thought it was dangerous to just blurt out everything. We talked about options, but it all came down to giving you time and space to trust your instincts and let your memory recover on its own. As it turned out, we didn't have that luxury. We barely escaped with our lives a few minutes ago. I don't know who is behind it all. Nor why. We'll just have to figure it out together."

Before I can ask more questions, Nick reaches for the door handle next to him. "Listen, now is not the time to go into all this. We've got to get to a safer place, but not in this car. There's a busy Walmart across the street. I should be able to find something there we can borrow."

"Let me clean that cut first. You're bleeding all over yourself. You'll attract attention." I scan the interior of Nick's car again. "Do you have anything in here that I can use as a bandage?"

"I have a first-aid kit."

After Nick retrieves the kit from his trunk, I open the large black satchel and gawk at its contents—much more than the usual kit of Band-Aids and antibiotic cream.

"You've got a stethoscope, drugs, syringes, a sewing kit, and surgical tools in here."

"Every agent is trained and equipped to give lifesaving medical aid in the field."

"Hopefully, you won't need any of that. Lean your head down so I can see what I'm dealing with here."

Nick's wound turns out to be a small abrasion, although from the looks of it, I'm not convinced flying glass is the culprit.

"You're lucky. Looks like a bullet just nicked you."

Nick looks up and flashes a crooked smile. "Is that supposed to be a joke, Ma'am?"

"What? No. No pun intended. Just the facts. Be quiet while I finish." I push Nick's head back down, wipe the cut clean, then place a piece of gauze on the wound and tape it down. I comb his hair with my fingers to hide the bandage. "There. Barely noticeable."

Nick thanks me, then exits the car and takes off running. The minutes seem to drag on as I sit shivering from the frigid air pouring in through the shattered rear window, staring at the bullet holes in the dashboard, and grappling with one confused thought after another.

Is this really happening to me? Is a hitman truly out to kill me?

My mind replays the frantic scene until another thought occurs to me. He was chasing me but didn't start shooting until Nick appeared. Was he trying to kill Nick, not me?

The hum of an engine invades my thoughts. I turn around and spot Nick behind the wheel of a car. He pulls alongside me in a beat-up silver hatchback, then jumps out of the vehicle, opens my door, and escorts me to the car. Our gazes meet as he pulls open the passenger-side door. The fear I see in Nick's eyes sets my heart racing.

Despite the biting cold, I can't hold back any longer. "Nick, talk to me." My voice quivers. "If I'm really Angela Lockhart, what are we doing here? Does my husband know what's going on? What about the Secret Service? Why aren't there more agents protecting me?"

"I haven't said one word to anyone, not a soul, where you are or what happened to you, Ma'am, for one simple reason—I don't know who we can trust."

The little voice inside my head knows. *No one.*

CHAPTER 35

Moments after the Charger peeled out of the parking lot, Felix jumped into his truck and did the same, but his pursuit was short-lived. The puddle of ammonia he'd slipped into had seeped into his clothes, covered his skin and face. The fumes stung his lungs and blinded his eyes. Desperate for relief, he pulled over to the side of the road, jumped out, and thrust his face and hands into a snowbank. He flung off his coat and shirt and, despite shivering from the freezing temperatures, rubbed snow across his torso. When the effects of the ammonia subsided, he grabbed his clothes and tossed them in the bed of his truck, then took his seat behind the wheel and jacked up the heater to full blast.

Fuck! There was no getting around it. He'd seen her with his own two eyes. And she'd seen him. How much did she remember of him, of his maneuvers to run her car off the road and kill her? How much did she remember about her life? Who was the driver of the Charger? These were all questions his boss would ask, questions he wouldn't be able to answer if he picked up the phone and delivered the bad news now.

In Felix's mind, there was no advantage to making that call, not until he could offer something in the way of answers that wouldn't put a target on his own back.

—

After a quick shower at a commercial truck stop, Felix returned to Summer Oaks wearing a second disguise from the duffel bag of clothing, hats, and hairpieces he kept in his truck. As before, he smiled at the guard and signed at the front desk with another false ID.

"I'm here to visit Kay Smith," he told the receptionist.

While the receptionist accessed her computer records, he added his new alias to the sign-in sheet.

"Kay Smith is in room 418."

As Felix completed his check-in, he scanned the list on the off-chance Kay had other visitors that morning. There were none, though it appeared someone paid an early morning visit to her roommate, Emily Campbell. The name next to the patient's was Nick Costa.

After a quick elevator ride, Felix stood surveying the room assigned to Kay Smith. There was nothing remarkable or alarming about it, but the sight of the woman sleeping in the bed across the room was an unwelcome complication.

"Hello? Hello?" he said.

The woman offered no response.

"You won't get any greeting from Emily. She's in a coma. Going on three years now, poor girl. Can I help you?"

Felix spun around, surprised to see a petite Asian-American nurse standing in the doorway. He cast his eyes on her name tag.

"Yes. Thank you, Jenny, isn't it?" Felix said, offering his most courteous persona. In his line of work, good manners rarely got him what he needed. Still, not every situation required him to beat the living crap out of someone to extract the information he sought. "I'm looking for Kay."

The young nurse's face lit up with a smile. "A visitor for Kay? That's great. Are you family or friend? Either way, I should warn you. She has amnesia and might not remember you."

"Yes. I'd heard she has problems with her memory."

That tidbit of information wasn't enough to satisfy his need to know. He also didn't want to tip his hand. To cover his tracks, he needed an out, a way to disclaim any familial connection between him and "Kay." He was ready with a story.

"Actually, I'm not sure if Kay is the woman I'm looking for," Felix continued. "I'm just checking out a lead on my missing stepsister, Greta. She disappeared a month ago. The family has been frantic with worry. If I can just get a glimpse of her, I'll be able to tell if she's Greta. If she isn't, there's no sense meeting her."

"It's worth a try. But it may take more than a glimpse to recognize your sister, if that's who she is. Kay has a large bandage covering her nose. She injured it in a car accident."

"A car accident? Is she okay?" Felix asked, giving his best impression of a worried brother.

"Not to worry. Kay's fine. Other than amnesia, she only has a few bumps and bruises."

"Good. Well then, I guess I'll have to meet Kay after all. If we're lucky, she'll recognize me and set the matter to rest."

"It would be wonderful seeing Kay reunited with her family. Let's see if we can find her. Maybe she's in the Community Room. She spends a lot of time in there on the computer."

Felix knew they wouldn't find the woman there, but he had to keep up the ruse long enough to return to her room and search for clues that might lead him to her current whereabouts.

When they arrived at the Community Room, Felix watched as the nurse scanned the room.

"She's not here," the nurse noted.

"Where else could she be?" Felix didn't have to feign the impatience in his voice.

"I don't know, sir. I'll check her chart. Maybe she's in a session with Dr. Malone or having a test done."

"A session? With a doctor?"

"Yes. Kay's psychiatrist. She's treating her amnesia. I may be a few minutes. Why don't you wait in her room in case she returns before I do?"

As he walked down the hallway, Felix tamped down the fury threatening to erupt inside him. He had enough on his plate just tracking down the bitch. Getting his hands on her file and the psychiatrist's notes would take time he didn't have. He'd have to bring in some help to do that job.

Once inside Kay's room, he shut the door and quickly set to work, searching for anything left behind that could offer him answers. A slip of paper lying on Kay's nightstand immediately caught his eye. Nick Costa's phone number.

Jackpot! If that Charger belonged to Costa, a quick hack into his phone should lead him straight to her.

Felix tucked the note in his coat pocket and continued his search. When he spotted a cell phone in the trash can, he nearly burst out laughing. His mirth died when he picked it up and noted its condition. Somebody didn't want anyone to access this phone. Hoping the data on the SIM card would still be accessible, he tucked the device into his coat pocket.

Having failed to find any other clues, Felix stepped across the room, pulled Kay Smith's medical chart from its plastic wall pocket, and gave it a once over, but found nothing of use, except some corroboration of Kay's medical condition further linking her to Erin Johnson. He'd just tucked the chart back into its holder when the nurse reappeared.

"I'm sorry, sir, but I can't seem to find Kay. I really don't know where she is."

Felix didn't either, but he knew where she *wasn't*. Summer Oaks. "Has Kay had any other visitors?"

"No. But she seems to have struck up a friendship with one of Emily's visitors. He was here earlier today. Kay shared breakfast with him in the Community Room."

Nick Costa.

Convinced there was nothing left to discover, Felix feigned a pressing appointment and promised to return later. He left certain he had the answers that would satisfy his boss until he could finish the job he started.

CHAPTER 36

The car Nick stole to better facilitate our getaway stinks of beer and cigarettes. The front passenger seat is covered in thick purple faux fur. The windshield is pockmarked with chips, the vinyl dashboard cracked from sun damage, and the passenger side mirror missing. The carpet is worn through to the rubber over much of the floor mats, and what is left over is stained by a rainbow of colorful substances. I can't help but wonder if the old junker is reliable enough to keep us moving away from danger.

"Seriously, Nick? Is this car safe?"

"Sorry. It was unlocked and a model I knew I could hot-wire quickly. It started up without any problem and got me here, so I think we're good for now. We need to get moving quickly. Before we take off, I need to strip my car of anything that might identify me as the owner. I'll just be a few minutes."

Once we're back on the road, I stare out the window, but I don't really see anything. My mind is too preoccupied with trying to find some sane reason for someone wanting me dead. My thoughts linger on William, raising questions I can't answer. Why am I married to a man I seem to detest, fear, or both? What's behind the intense distrust I feel for him?

As part of my Secret Service detail, Nick must have some answers. As I glance at him, wondering what he knows, I'm reminded of the one thing he was most eager for me to remember—the election. "Tell me the truth, Nick. I can handle it. Is my husband behind all this? Did he direct someone on his staff to kill me? Do I have evidence that he cheated to win the election, and he doesn't trust me to keep my mouth shut?"

I have no idea why I trust Nick with my theory—after all, he could be working for my husband. Why else would he so intentionally keep bringing up the election? The worry on his face doesn't reveal his role one way or the other.

"I don't know Ma'am, but I don't think so. I only touched on the election hoping to stir your memory enough to—"

"But it's the only explanation that makes sense to me," I jump back in, determined to extract some answers. "I ran away in the midst of a dangerous blizzard because I couldn't handle what I'd discovered—evidence proving William was responsible for the lies painting Hayward as a crooked politician."

Even as the words leave my mouth, I still don't believe them myself. That my husband may be a deceitful, duplicitous bastard explains my instinctive distrust of the man, but not the primal fear I'm experiencing in my nightmares, my panicked flight from my life, nor the murderous brute willing to kill to find me and finish the job he started.

Maddy.

The name sends a shiver down my spine. Whoever she is, the woman must somehow be involved in this all-too-real horror story, but I'm not sure I'm ready to know just yet. I can barely process what little Nick's already revealed. My frustration bubbles up as tears threaten to erupt.

"Come on, Nick. You must have some idea about what's happening here. What sent me driving off into a raging snowstorm all by myself without even one Secret Service agent to protect me? My car went off the road somewhere in rural Virginia, so where was I even headed?"

"I have few answers, but we really need to get out of here first, Ma'am," Nick says, shaking his head. "We can't afford to be spotted so close to the parking lot where I stole it. And we also need to put some distance between us and the thug who's after you. We'll find an out-of-the-way place to check-in and get this hot car off the road. We need to avoid the freeways and main roads, though. There are cameras everywhere recording vehicles, their licenses plates, and routes. Once we're settled somewhere, I'll tell you what little I know, then we'll put our heads together and try to figure out what's going on."

I fear I already know. The target on my back speaks volumes, so does that little voice in my head. My husband, the president-elect, is involved in some criminal behavior, an act or acts that threaten his power, his move into the White House, enough for him to resort to murder—mine—to protect himself. Somewhere in the deep recesses of my mind, I've buried the proof.

I hazard a peek at Nick wondering if I'm right about William, and if so, whether I should be more distrustful of the man who so conveniently rescued me—twice—when I was most in need of help. "Tell me, Nick, do you work for me, personally, or for the president-elect?"

He glances my way and speaks in a just-the-facts tone of voice. "I work for the Secret Service, Ma'am. I serve at the pleasure my superiors and their boss, the president, whomever that may be at the time. But you are my charge. My job is to keep you safe. From everyone. No matter who or what threatens you or why."

His answer doesn't go far enough for me to give him a pass. I need to know more. "So, in my case, how did you pull all of this off by yourself?"

Nick returns his gaze to the road ahead, then goes on to explain the elaborate measures he'd taken to protect my would-be killer from learning he'd botched the job. The false names, the lies Nick told the police about my crash, his flight from the hospital when it appeared his cover would be blown, were just the start. He hadn't abandoned me either but had been near my bedside almost 24/7 using different disguises with fake IDs to gain access to me and my chart. When I was physically out of danger and my coma diagnosed as psychogenic, Nick expedited my transfer to a facility where he could keep me safe under another alias until I regained consciousness.

"A Marine buddy of mine who drives for a small ambulance outfit just outside Culpeper agreed to transport you to Summer Oaks with no questions asked. I picked the place because it's close to both home and work. Plus, Emily really is the sister of a good friend, Dan. I served with him Iraq, too. He took a corporate security job after his sister's accident. He needed a bigger salary to cover her care at Summer Oaks."

I listen in awe as Nick details his efforts to obscure my trail, from the moment he fished me out of a freezing river until I arrived at Summer Oaks. It's clear now that he's not taking orders from anyone, including William.

"The easiest ruse was lying to Sergeant Montgomery about the make and model of your car and its location; the hardest, doctoring your hospital records, both the digital and hard copy."

When Nick finishes, I offer my thanks, but rather than be happy to have been saved by someone so clever, I'm distressed about it. "I guess I should thank you for all the trouble I've caused you," I say, my voice quivering. "Running away wasn't a smart move. I realize that now. It put not just you and me in jeopardy, but others, too."

I draw a deep breath to calm myself, exhale, then continue. "I know you were just doing your job, Nick. Your bag of tricks saved me, but two innocent bystanders are dead because of your deceptions—a hospital records clerk and the neurologist whose signature you forged on my fake death certificate."

I stare at my trembling hands and summarize what little I know about the man looking for me and my suspicions about his role in the two murders. I turn away from Nick to hide the tears rolling down my cheek. "He killed two people trying to finish the job he started, Nick."

"I'm so sorry. Really, I am." Nick's tone reflects regret, but no hint of surprise.

Gritting my teeth in anger, I turn toward him and punch his shoulder. "You already knew, didn't you?"

Nick deflects his gaze from the road and glances my way. The remorse in his eyes confirms my suspicion.

"Yes, Ma'am. I knew. I loaded your cell phone with spyware to track your Internet usage and listen in on your calls. I heard about the murders from Detective Warren the same time you did. I won't apologize for my deception. It's my job. You were keeping secrets from me. I couldn't protect you like that."

Nick's revelation leaves me speechless, though in hindsight, I shouldn't be surprised.

"Please believe me, Ma'am. Nobody regrets what happened to those people more than I do. If I could have done anything to stop this killer, I would've done it. I had no idea those two were in danger." The sorrow I hear in his voice seems sincere, but it doesn't change the facts.

"How far will this madman go, Nick?" My heart starts to race as a sense of panic rises inside me. "Hiding me is a bad idea. The worst. It puts people at risk of dying in my wake." The gruesome reality grips my throat, making it hard to breathe.

"You're right, Ma'am." Nick glances in the rearview mirror, then returns his attention to the road. "It *is* dangerous for anyone who encounters you. The best way to minimize the risk to everyone is precisely by lying low. There will come a time when you'll need to come out of hiding—after your memory returns." He turns his gaze on me. "That's our best weapon in this fight. The only one we can wield that will lock up those responsible for these murders and the attempts on your life."

I sigh. "All right. We'll do it your way, for now at least." Nick's point is a good one, but it isn't enough to convince me. I turn away and watch as the world goes by my window. Every day that passes increases the likelihood of more innocent deaths—perhaps, even Nick's.

I return my gaze to Nick, my heart filled with pain. I couldn't live with the weight of more deaths on my soul—especially his. I'm left with one sobering resolution. If I ever suspect I've put any more lives in danger, I need to be prepared to come out of hiding and face down the fiends behind these murders alone.

Drained from the intensity of the last few minutes, Nick and I agree to settle in somewhere safe before continuing our discussion. For the next few minutes, I lie back, bask in the warmth of the heat pouring out the vents, and listen as the radio replaces conversation, filling the car with the soft, melodic notes from an NPR broadcast of a piece I recognize as it moves toward the finale, Brahm's *Violin Concerto in D*.

After the music ends, the program announcer follows up. "That beautiful recording was by the Boston Philharmonic with guest violinist, Katica Feher. Stay with us past the upcoming station break for a real treat, my favorite aria, and likely yours, too, "O mio babbino caro" from Puccini's comic opera, *Gianni Schicchi*. But now, it's time for an NPR news update," the radio announcer says. "Here's Latisha Owens with the latest."

Across from me, Nick reaches for the radio dial.

"No, please. I love "O mio babbino caro." It's a beautiful aria."

"I just thought, well, the news—" he stutters.

Too late I understand his concern.

"Our next story tugs at our nation's heartstrings. A tragedy surrounding our new First Family, the murder of Amelia Bulloch, the sister of soon-to-be First Lady—"

CHAPTER 37

*A*my.

My chest seizes, my throat tightens as the name peals like a warning bell inside my head. I glare at Nick. He looks as horrified as I feel. Once again, he reaches for the radio button.

"Stop, Nick," I growl, as the horror inside me erupts into fury. "I can't trust *you* to tell me the truth, so I need to hear it from someone who has no reason to lie."

We struggle over the radio controls, casting a garbled mix of static, music, and voices, over the car speakers. Finally, Nick gives up. I scramble to recover the NPR station until the car swerves hard to the right, pulling me away from the radio as I lurch left. I push off Nick and bolt upright, alarmed. Nick has turned into the parking lot of grungy convenience store.

"Nick, slow down," I scream, but he doesn't listen. The car accelerates past the store and careens around the rear of the building. My body pitches forward against the seat belt as Nick slams on the brakes.

"I'm sorry I didn't say anything before," he says, almost breathless.

I turn to face him, ready to unleash the fury inside me threatening to erupt.

"I wasn't sure you could handle it."

His face betrays the panic in his voice. I try to speak, but the words catch in my throat.

"Your frantic flight from the hotel, the attempt on your life, your memory loss—it all happened after FBI agents informed you and your husband that your sister had been murdered. Please, Ma'am, you have to believe me. I kept this awful secret from you out of fear that telling you would bury your memory even deeper. And we need your memory back. I'm certain it's the key to uncovering why someone is out to kill you."

My mind is racing, struggling with horror, trying desperately to remember my sister. *Amy.* Tears pool in my eyes as it dawns on me that her nickname is all that I can recall. How is it I forgot everything about her, what she looked like, how she talked, our life together—her murder?

But I must remember. Nick has made that clear. He seems to think I have the answers that will explain who wants me dead and why.

"Do I know something about my sister's murder that threatens her killer?" I blurt out. "Is that why someone is gunning for me?"

"Yes, that is, I think so. I have no evidence, no solid suspects yet. That's why I've been hiding you."

Keep hiding. My subconscious was right. I needed to keep hiding. I still have to. I'm not safe yet, and now, Nick isn't either.

I shake my head in utter dismay. "This is all a lot to take in. It's all too horrible to even think about. Perhaps that's why my mind has barricaded my memories, left me with nothing but her nickname— Amy—to remember." I sigh, saddened by my inability to recall the one person in my life I should remember the most.

"I believe that you withheld my sister's murder from me to protect me, but the cat is out of the bag now. You can't safeguard me anymore by keeping me in the dark, not with Amy's killer targeting me. Tell me about her, what happened, how she died. Maybe it will spark my memory enough to break this dam in my mind."

"You're right, Ma'am," Nick says, hanging his head low. "I've done a poor job protecting you. I failed Amy, too—"

I throw my hands up. "That's not what I meant at all! Whoever is after me ran me off the road and left me to drown. If it weren't for you, I'd be an ice cube by now." I don't know what to make of Nick's lament about Amy. "And how did you fail Amy? Were you supposed to protect her, too?"

Nick sighs, then looks up and stares out the windshield, then starts. "Your sister served as your personal executive secretary until October twenty-third, when she decided to head home to Richmond after a campaign stop in Raleigh." His voice is steady, his words deliberate, spoken like a cop delivering testimony at a trial. "She insisted on driving herself and going alone. Amy—" Nick chokes on my sister's name.

Tears well up in my eyes, blurring my vision, but not so much that I can't see the pain in Nick's face. As part of my security detail, he must have spent a lot of time around Amy, too. Still, I hadn't expected him to be so aggrieved. I flip open the glove box and spot a small box of tissues. I grab one and hand it to Nick, then take another and wipe my eyes.

A moment later, Nick starts again. "I was part of the Secret Service detail that found her rental car at an I-95 rest area in Virginia, a few miles north of the North Carolina border. There were no signs of an attack or struggle. Nothing to suggest she was sick or hurt. No ransom demand was ever made, so she hadn't been kidnapped."

Nick shrugs his shoulders and shakes his head. "There was no evidence of robbery. Her rental car was unlocked with her purse inside. Her cash, credit cards, and cell phone were all there. Her luggage, briefcase, and laptop were in the back seat. She even left the keys in the ignition. The only thing missing was, well, Amy. She was just . . . gone."

Nick turns away, but not before I see a deep sorrow in his eyes, one that betrays a hurt that goes far deeper than I would expect from a Special Agent grieving for someone he protected, even peripherally.

"You . . . were you in love with Amy?" My words come in a strained whisper, almost inaudible, even to me.

He nods in reply and loses the fight to hold back his tears. "The first moment I met her, I knew she was the one for me. Sweet, smart, kind. I used two weeks of vacation time to look for her, but every lead I followed went nowhere."

Seeing Nick in so much agony is more than I can bear. I unlatch my seat belt and launch myself at him, throw my arms around his chest, and hug him with all the strength I can muster. Nick reciprocates, holding me as tightly as I do him. We sit together without saying a word while the windows fog up. In the quiet moments that follow, my heart aches for him, for Amy.

Nick finally pulls away appearing cooler and more controlled, then begins again. "Amy's body was found five days ago near a trailhead in Pocahontas State Park, that's about eighty miles from the I-95 rest area where her rental car was found. The Chesterfield County morgue identified her using dental records. The FBI took over the case immediately. Two agents showed up at D.C. hotel three days ago to inform you of Amy's death. You were sitting for a *People* magazine interview when they arrived, so your husband took the meeting. He told you the news later, after you finished the interview."

I shudder as the memory of my nightmare flashes in front of me. "How did she die?"

"I don't know, yet. The Bureau is keeping a tight lid on the autopsy results, but I'm working on getting a copy."

It's your fault.

The words eat me up inside. I turn away from Nick to hide my distress over the cryptic message and its meaning. Am I somehow culpable in my own sister's murder?

Maddy. That my mind chose now to thrust this name forward can't be good. I can think of only one possible reason for the psychic communiques. I can't ignore them anymore.

CHAPTER 38

"Is there a hitman after me because I know something about my sister's murder, and maybe the death of another woman, someone named Maddy."

Nick's eyes grow wide, his jaw drops. "You remember Maddy?"

"No, but I talked with the morgue attendant last night inquiring about Erin Johnson. When I followed up asking about Jane Does, he recalled a murder victim brought into the morgue a couple of months ago. When she was finally identified as local woman, he mentioned her name, 'Madeline.' The name 'Maddy' immediately popped into my brain. It set off another panic attack, so I figured there must be some connection to me. If I'm Angela Lockhart, then Amelia Bulloch is my sister. But who is Maddy, and where does she fit in all this?"

Nick pauses, casts his eyes down, as a note of sadness crosses his face. "Maddy O'Brien was a campaign intern. She worked for your husband's organization until mid-June when she was transferred to your staff." He returns his gaze to me. "She was a sweet girl—smart and a hard worker. She disappeared last July driving home from a campaign stop to spend the holiday weekend with her family. She never arrived. Her body was found in a shallow grave in October."

He pulls out his phone, swipes his fingers across the screen, then turns the phone toward me. I wince as my insides twist with heartache.

I'm looking at the photo of a young woman, pretty with long blond hair. I recognize her, more than I care to.

My hand seems to have a mind of its own as it gravitates to my neck. "Was she strangled to death?" I gaze into Nick's eyes, hoping they will tell me I'm wrong.

"Yes, that's what the coroner's report concluded. The body was badly decomposed, but the hyoid bone in her neck had been crushed, so that was listed as the cause of death. How did you know?"

I hedge on my answer, unwilling to confess my nightmare until I know what it means. "I'm not sure. It just came to me. More of a vague hint than a memory of any kind."

"That's a good start," Nick says, his eyes reflecting a glimmer of hope. "Let's keep going and see what else jumps out at you. And to answer your original question, I do think Maddy and Amy's murders and the attempt on your life are linked. I just don't know how."

Suddenly, a thin, dark shadow materializes in the foggy window behind Nick. It knocks on the window, startling the both of us. Nick pulls his gun, then turns and swipes at the window with the tissue in his hand.

Outside, a thin gray-haired Black man waves his hands at us. "You can't park here," he shouts. "Move on. Now. I have delivery trucks coming."

Nick flashes the man a thumbs up, then flips on the defrost, and turns to me. "Listen, I know this has been hard. For me, too. But we need to leave, and I'm not comfortable driving around in the open. There's a business district not far from here, not the best, but there are a few low-rent motels in the area may offer a safe place to hide. Once we're out of sight, I'll tell you everything I know. We'll sit and talk and figure this out together. I promise."

I nod, too weary to argue. For now, that promise is good enough for me.

—

Ten minutes later, Nick and I are parked in the lot of a motel, a small seedy establishment. The "ey" on the flashing red sign of Morey's Motel is burned out, casting a mottled purple hue to the cinder-block building's peeling blue paint. The office windows are covered with grime. The place gives me the creeps.

"Seriously, Nick, what are we doing here?" I cringe.

"I know it's not what you're accustomed to, Ma'am, but we're stuck with places like this right now. Cheap motels don't require ID if you pay cash. And that's how we'll have to live for the time being. Using my credit and bank debit cards would expose us and our location."

"Wait! Use the debit card you gave me. I have it in my jeans pocket." I unbutton my coat and pull at the zipper of my janitor coveralls. "Just give me second to dig it out."

"No, thank you, Ma'am. I got this. Ma always told me it was dangerous to walk around without any money in my pocket, so you keep that card until we're low on cash." He tips his head toward the motel office. "I'm sure this place is not as bad as it looks. Just let me check it out. Keep the doors locked and your head down."

A few minutes after Nick enters the office, our car is parked in front of room 10, the last one on the far end, and Nick is inside, doing a quick security check. After he returns, he escorts me through the door.

"I'll be right back," he says, standing in the doorway. "I'm going to park the car around back, get it out of sight."

After the door closes behind me, I turn and survey the white-painted cinder-block room and its furniture, mismatched pieces best described as Goodwill rejects. A blue vinyl sofa, its thin cushions patched with duct tape, sits beneath a bank of filthy windows. Scarred nightstands flank a queen-size bed covered with faded linens. A small, tube TV sits atop a worn laminated desk next to a sad little coffeemaker holding a stained carafe. Against the back wall stands a small sink atop a dark-stained base cabinet. A door, presumably to the toilet and bath, is off to the right. I walk over to the bed and test the mattress. A bit lumpy, saggy, too. The room's only saving grace is the smell of disinfectant permeating the air.

"Are you certain this place is safe?" I ask, after Nick walks through the door.

"As long as you stay out of sight, we should be fine, Ma'am." He locks the door behind him. "The room itself may be sketchy, but the place is built like a fortress. The door is an inch-and-a-half of solid metal with a dead bolt, swing guard, and a chain lock. It would take a wrecking ball to break through these cinder-block walls. The windows are double-paned with blackout drapes. If we aren't loud and keep the car around back, nobody should even know this room is occupied. We have the last two rooms on the end to ensure our privacy."

"No!" I jump up from the bed, run to Nick's side, and clutch his arm. "We don't need two rooms. Stay here with me. I'll take the sofa." I couldn't have acted more like a little girl frightened of the monsters under her bed, but I don't care.

"I promise nothing will happen to you under my watch, Ma'am." He pries my fingers from his arm and holds me at arms-length. "Don't worry. I'm staying here with you. The extra room is a buffer between us and the room two doors away. If we see or hear anyone outside our room or next door, where no one should have any business, we'll know to be ready for trouble."

He nods toward the couch. "As for this poor excuse for a couch, I have dibs on that, Ma'am. Not that I expect to grab many zs. I'll be sleeping with one eye open."

I slump to the couch relieved Nick isn't going anywhere. He pulls off his coat and lays it across the arm of the couch, then walks over to the desk, picks up a packet of coffee, and examines it.

"I don't know about you, Ma'am, but I could use a cup of joe. How about you? I can't promise it'll be good. The grind is something packaged for the motel trade."

"That would be nice. Thank you." Nick and I have a lot to discuss, and a little caffeine, even cloaked in a bad cup of coffee, is welcome.

A couple minutes later, Nick hands me a Styrofoam cup.

Thank you," I say, with a smile.

"Cream, one sugar, right?"

"I guess so." I take a sip. The warm brew feels good going down.

Nick takes a couple of slurps of coffee, then sets his cup atop the desk. At his direction, I sit on the bed, while he pulls the desk chair over and sits next to me.

"Now I know you have lots of questions, Ma'am, and I'd like to tell you I have all the answers, but I don't. I can only tell you what I do know. The rest we'll have to figure out together unless we can find a way to break that logjam of memories in your mind. I caution you, though. What I'm about to tell you is not pretty."

"I understand." The words squeak from my mouth, reflecting the fear percolating inside me.

Facing the cold hard truth of my past by myself, I'm not sure I can hold it together alone. Nick seems to be off-limits now, clear from the physical and emotional distance he's put between us after resuming our real-life roles. So, I cling to the only thing providing me comfort. I grasp the simmering container of coffee with both hands and draw consolation from the heat radiating from my fingertips to my wrists. Warmth spreads through my insides with each sip of the sweet, creamy brew. I know the aftereffect will be temporary. What I'm experiencing now is the eye of a raging storm. The worst is yet to come. I heard it in Nick's voice just now, saw it in his eyes.

"Are you ready, Ma'am?"

I nod, clutching my coffee cup, holding on to one hope—that there is enough coffee in the pot to get me through the chilling horrors coming my way.

CHAPTER 39

Nick reaches for my hands. His soft touch calms me. I draw in a big breath and let it out slowly. "Okay, I'm ready. Tell me everything you know."

"Let's start with some personal background. There are some people in your life you should be eager to remember. Maybe talking about them will get your memories flowing."

He reassures me that everything he'd told me about himself, his past and his family, is true, except for his job working private security. That little lie was necessary cover, another effort to not force reality upon me before I was ready.

Nick follows his story with mine, reiterating what I already know and adding details I don't. I am Angela Bulloch Lockhart, the thirty-four-year-old daughter of U.S. Senator and Mrs. Beau Bulloch.

Once again, Nick shows me a photograph, a couple, probably mid-fifties, she blond and beautiful, he balding, but handsome. As I gaze at the image, I struggle with a mixture of emotions: for my mother, a sense of longing, sadness; for my father, submissiveness and fear.

"They were killed ten years ago when their private jet went down off the coast of Virginia."

"My parents are dead?"

"Sorry. I only thought to start there because they were in your life the longest. More memories. Hopefully, some happy ones."

I focus on the photo, searching for hint of joy, but don't. "Let's move on."

"Yes, Ma'am. You and William Lockhart married in 2008 when he was a rising star in the party, and together, you are the parents of two sweet little girls, Olivia, age six, and Sophia, age three." Nick taps the screen, then hands the phone to me. Two little sunny-haired girls, dressed in pink frocks and sitting behind a pink doll cake, smile back at me.

My heart leaps inside my chest. "My daughters?"

"Yes, Ma'am. That photo was taken last June. Olivia is on the right. Sophia is the birthday girl. Aren't they beautiful?" His voice is sincere and carries a note of affection.

I focus all my energy on the photo, hoping that by sheer force of will I'll remember the two most important people in my life. Bits and pieces from that night fall into place.

I see Sophia's face, smeared cheek-to-cheek with pink icing. I taste her sweet, strawberry-frosting kiss. I feel her hug, the warmth of her tiny body wrapped around mine. I bask in the comforting scent of her baby shampoo as her soft hair grazes my face. My heart leaps with happiness hearing her little-girl squeals of delight as they rise above the laughter of the other partygoers.

"Yes. They are lovely!" I spring from the bed. "And I remember them, Nick. I remember that party, too!"

For the first time since waking from my coma, I feel joy. With a sudden burst of energy, I jump up, throw my arms around Nick and squeeze.

"That's wonderful," he says, hugging me back. When we finally pull apart, I can't contain myself. I blather on, moving excitedly around the room, detailing every image, every sound I remember from that evening, which in the end is very little but just enough to offer one thing I desperately need—hope. Hope that I might soon remember all that was good about myself, my family, and my life.

When my burst of energy finally fizzles out and my memories fade, I retake my seat on the bed and reach for Nick's phone. I flip through more photos of the girls with cake and presents, smiling at each one, until I come across one with two women who look identical—hair color, complexion, facial structure, eye color—except for differing lengths of hair. *Amy and I were twins.* My heart sinks inside me as my gut twists with despair. At a loss for words, I utter a feeble comment. "Amy looks good with long hair."

"Long hair?" Nick asks.

I flip the phone around, displaying the photo. "Isn't this me on the right with short hair."

"No, that's Amy."

Puzzled, I stand and move to face the mirror on the wall, then glance back at the photo staring back at me from Nick's phone. "But that means I had long hair when this picture was taken. When did I cut it?"

"Not too long after that photo. It was mid-July. The campaign laid over at your family beach house to prep for the nominating convention. Much of the East Coast was suffering through a heat wave. It wasn't supposed to get any better. Amy remarked how much she liked her short hair, how it helped with the scorching heat and high humidity, so you asked the stylist for the same cut."

Nick pauses for a moment. When I turn, I spy a glint of tears in his eyes. My heart fills with regret for not considering how Amy's death might have affected Nick. With the two of them working so closely with me, interacting as needed, I could see how they could grow so close enough to have fallen in love. I return to my seat on the bed, and lay a comforting hand on Nick's arm, igniting a spark of temptation inside me.

I pull my hand away and return my gaze to the photo, trying my best to summon a memory of my only sister. But I can't. The emptiness I feel in my heart is as big as the black hole in my mind.

"Amy's haircut looks good, huh? Kind of sassy," Nick remarks.

I hold back the tears welling up in my eyes and respond in kind. "Yes. I like it. I really do."

"Well, your husband didn't. He was livid," Nick continues. The grief in his voice is gone, though now, he seems a bit agitated. "I was there when he blew his top with you. It wasn't the image he wanted you to project, he said. The cut and style wouldn't test well with older women and male voters. So, for the rest of the campaign, and even after the election, he insisted you wear a wig everywhere you went, one identical to the style you wore throughout the primaries. Amy told me you removed the wig off only after you were in for the night, but to spite your husband, you kept your real hair short."

Anger rises in my throat. I want to scream, but I hold it in. "Does he also pick out my clothes and makeup? Does he decide what toothpaste I'm allowed to use based on marketing promises to keep my smile bright enough for his voters?"

Suddenly, it all makes sense. Dr. Malone was right. She pegged my problem. I'm a weak-willed woman, the wife of a psychological abuser. No wonder every memory of William is filled with anger and distrust.

"I wouldn't know, Ma'am," Nick replies, shaking his head. "I do know you hated that wig. I heard you grumbling about it often enough. But as it turns out, that wig helped keep you safe. You had it on the night of the blizzard. As I was pulling you out of your car, I noticed your hairline was cockeyed. Once I had you safe and warm in my car, I removed your wig, hair pins and all. I stashed it under my seat before heading to the hospital. With your own natural hair, short as it was, and the injuries to your face, I thought it would be tough for anyone to think you looked like Angela Lockhart, not that anyone was aware you were missing just then. Either way, I didn't want anyone to recognize you, not just yet. I guess it worked. No one was the wiser for it."

I can't keep my sarcasm in check. "Then I guess we should thank my controlling husband and that damn wig for saving my life."

CHAPTER 40

A marriage based on fear and loathing is no marriage. I need to know more about my relationship with William to better consider our roles in what is clearly an extremely perilous situation now for both Nick and me.

"As a member of my Secret Service detail, you probably saw everything that went on in private. So, tell me, from what you've seen, do you think there's any love between me and my husband?"

Nick shakes his head and looks away, obviously uncomfortable with my question. "Ma'am, we're not privy to everything that goes on behind closed doors. Nor is it my place to interpret what I may or may not have seen or heard."

I frown at Nick's response. "You're being evasive again when you promised to be open with me. Further, it's your job to be observant and to assess people's intentions from their behavior, so I ask you again, from what you've observed of my husband and I, do we love each other?"

Nick takes a moment, as if to consider his answer, then turns and speaks. "No, Ma'am, not from my perspective. I'm sorry. I guess protecting you, at least from distressing news, is a tough habit to break. I'll be more conscious of my obligation from here on out." He pats my hand, draws a sigh, then continues.

"I know that you and your husband slept in separate bedrooms. As a couple, you never showed affection when I was around, except in public, and even then, it seemed one-sided, your husband giving you a peck on the cheek, more like a photo op. When you two were alone, the only talk I ever overheard was about the kids and his work, sometimes your schedule in support of his career. I saw no physical intimacy behind the scenes—no hand-holding, no hugs, no knowing smiles."

Nick's description portrays a rather lackluster marriage, but nothing that would cause me to loathe William, nor distrust him as I do.

"In private, your husband was often harsh, critical, overbearing. It was hard to watch sometimes. You never fought back. It seemed like you hated being a political wife, despised it. You never said so, but I could hear it in your voice and see it in your eyes. Again, that was only in private. Otherwise, you always looked the part of a happy politician's wife whenever the occasion warranted it."

I shake my head in disgust. "So, my marriage was a sham. Neither of us loved the other. This explains a lot."

"What?" He seems confused.

"The hostility I feel for William. My instincts tell me not to trust him."

"Don't take this personally, Ma'am, but nothing I saw surprised me. I've seen a lot of rocky marriages in this business. Distance between couples is par for the course. It doesn't necessarily mean there's a lack of personal integrity. Politics can exact a big toll on marriages. There are lots of pressures on both sides, especially at the highest levels of government. Love doesn't always keep these people together, even though they may have started out that way. Power does. Divorce doesn't play well in elections either."

I take a moment to consider Nick's words, his impression of William and me, our marriage. As I do, a few shadows emerge in my mind—vague recollections of interviews, some with William, most not. Campaign stops, luncheons, visits to schools and hospitals—everything expected of a devoted politician's wife during an election. There is only one element of Nick's revelation that doesn't quite fit.

"Yes, a lot of what you say is familiar, but I'm not getting an angry vibe about campaigning, like I hated being in the spotlight saying nice things about William. It's more, well, like I was going through the motions, dazed, weighed down by a mix of sadness, grief—" I stop as two more words form in my mind—*remorse and guilt.*

My heart sinks into my chest. I struggle for air just for a moment, then heave a deep breath and start to count.

"What is it?" Nick's voice reaches out. "Did you remember something?"

My breathing eases quickly, but the guilt I feel is still there. I look away. I don't want Nick to see my face when I lie.

CHAPTER 41

"Talk to me, Ma'am." Nick's voice is frantic. "Tell me what's going on."

"Nothing. I'm not sure. Guess I just had a bout of sorrow." Inwardly, I grimace at my deception. Continuing to hold back from Nick, deceiving him at every turn, especially now that he has promised to be truthful with me, is tearing me up inside. There's a part of me that wants to expose myself, everything I'm seeing, sensing, remembering. But another part of me knows I can't. I shouldn't. The part that remembers that dream—Nick walking away from me as I plead for forgiveness. Forgiveness for what? Did I let William bully me into doing something indefensibly vile?

He takes a seat next to me and wraps his arms around my shoulders, a gesture that allows me to relax and release some of the tension wracking my body.

"What you're feeling, Ma'am, is perfectly natural. Anyone would feel the same even with their memory intact. To be honest, I think you're drawing from recent memories. Those last two weeks of the election, after the news of Maddy's death and Amy's disappearance, you were despondent, withdrawn. But in public, you were perfect—happy, upbeat. I don't know how you pulled it off, though Amy once told me you two did some acting in college. Anyway, you were better, if just a little bit, after the election. Without the stress of the campaign, you were more relaxed. Probably from spending more time with Olivia and Sophia. You seem to draw strength from being with them."

Nick's last words strike me as true, causing me to smile inwardly, and at the same time, leaving me sad. I must rely on what little memory I have of them to push me through this perilous situation, far enough, at least, to allow me to see them again before submitting to whatever justice awaits me.

Nick rises from the bed and fetches me a glass of water. I guzzle it down, taking comfort in the cool liquid as it runs down my throat. I know we need to take this slower, shy away from discussions that will trigger my dark emotions.

"I really don't want to talk about William or my girls right now. It's too painful. Tell me about Amy, instead," I ask, hoping it will help both of us focus on Amy's life, rather than her death. "That is, if you're up to it, Nick."

He nods, takes my empty glass, and sets it on the desk, then sits in the chair across from me. "It'll be tough, but we need to do this. Maybe sharing some stories, or perhaps, a few more photos, will help you remember her and your life together."

Nick pulls out his phone once again, flicks through the screen, then shows me a photo of the two of them, together. "I don't have much in the way of photos. Our jobs were both quite demanding, not just because of your campaign schedule, but because you were determined to make sure the girls received all the time, love, and attention they needed from either you or Amy. That left little private time for us to really get to know one another, much less take a selfie together."

My heart breaks from yet another regret. I monopolized my sister's time, keeping her from fulfilling her own dreams.

"We managed to share a quick lunch or dinner once a week or so. When I was off duty, I sometimes helped Amy babysit your girls." His smile returns as he relates an endearing story involving a particularly funny game of hide-and-seek with Olivia and Sophia in a Philadelphia hotel suite. Nick follows up with other recollections, mostly fleeting moments he and Amy shared when their schedules allowed.

"A lot of these stories are awfully familiar, like I've heard them before."

"She probably told you about them. You two seemed very close," Nick says, nodding. "She texted me this one the day before you disappeared."

Nick hands me his phone revealing a photo of Amy and me, what must be a rare, candid shot of us making silly faces. How could I forget my own sister?

Keep hiding.

I shudder from a chill that seems to seep through to my bones. Did Amy's murder send me running from my past? Or did the guilt I feel for her death wipe my memory of her?

I shove the phone at Nick, pick up my coffee and sip it, finding comfort in its warmth. "Seems like my campaign activities were hard on your budding romance. I'm sorry."

"Nothing to be sorry about, Ma'am. We had jobs to do. Neither of us would ever give less than a hundred percent to our work. For Amy, it was closer to a thousand percent. She worked hard, too hard sometimes, but I understood why. She was totally devoted to you, your husband, and the campaign. Amy believed you both belonged in the White House, that you were good for the country. I respected her for that."

My sister believed in my husband. Was she naïve? Or am I wrong in the contempt I feel for William?

A weak smile appears on Nick's face. "I knew the craziness wouldn't last forever. She knew it, too, and was ready to walk away from it all. She wanted a more normal life, one with a family of her own. I was going to give that to her when things settled down after the election. I had my grandmother's ring ready to put on her finger."

My eyes start to water. I reach for the tissues just as a tear runs down my cheek, but Nick beats me to the box. With his smile wilted, he pulls out a couple tissues, hands me one, and keeps one for himself.

"Now, I wish I hadn't waited." He leans over, places his elbows on his knees and rests his head in his hands. "I should've proposed when I had the chance. If I had, maybe Amy wouldn't have turned me away that last night when I offered to drive her home."

I can't look at Nick. His anguish is more than I can bear. My gaze falls upon his cell phone, resting on the bed. I pick it up and flip through the photos, hoping th_____ will distract me, if not jar loose the recollection of my _____ otos seem familiar, but nothing sparks my mem_____ t of a petite, white-haired woman stand_____ each. A flush of happiness overta_____ "Where was it taken, and ____

He wipes hi_____ you and Amy. She was y_____ describe her, though 'a_____ part of the vast estate you a_____ It's located on a small private _____ band's campaign laid over for two_____ for a much-needed rest and family t_____ husband Ed to join your family for the h_____ them still work for you as resident caretakers_____ at's in Lynchburg. Your family estate."

"Mimi." The name tumbles easily from my lips. I s___ at the photo, willing myself to remember what I can about my life with the woman, but all I come away with is a warm feeling of love. "Well, my brain doesn't remember much, but my heart does."

"It should. Mimi was more a mother to you and Amy than your own flesh-and-blood mother. You both loved her as such. Amy told me so. Mimi adores you both, too. Seeing the three of you together, well, the affection was obvious. I confess to being sweet on the old gal myself. We got to know each other pretty well that weekend."

"Really? What did you two talk about?" I ask, eager to know if Mimi had said anything that could help me remember my past.

"Mostly about your family, what it was like for you and Amy growing up. She said your parents were rarely home. Your father was the senior U.S. Senator from Virginia. Like you, your mother was a politician's wife. She had her charitable and social responsibilities in town but spent most of her time in D.C. Mimi and Ed were the only other stable adults in your life. Apparently, the rest of the staff, your in-home tutors included, never lasted long. From Mimi's stories, it seemed that you and Amy were poor little rich girls. She did her best to give the two of you the loving home you deserved."

Nick's summary is depressing but goes a long way in explaining the negative emotions I suffered looking at my parents' photo. I return my focus to Nick's screen, flipping through his photos until I spot one of Amy and Nick in a backyard setting, surrounded by a throng of people, most of whom share a keen resemblance to Nick.

"This is the last photo of Amy and me together. That's my family. We were all at my parents' house for a party. My brother, Frankie, was home on leave from Afghanistan."

The sadness in Nick's voice tears at my heart. I lean in and examine the photo. "Amy must have shared her own party pictures with me. The people in this photo look familiar."

"That was October fifteenth. The last day Amy and I had any real time together before she disappeared." Nick's eyes grow wet. He wipes away a stray tear and looks into my eyes. "As I said before, I think Amy's murder, Maddy's, and the attempts on your life are related."

"Why do you think that?" I ask, taking his hands in mine, an effort to comfort the man, as much as to brace myself for whatever awful revelation he's about to share.

"Because on the evening of October twenty-third, two agents with the Virginia State Police showed up at the Raleigh hotel where your husband's campaign was staying. They broke the news that shattered the staff—Maddy's body had been found and identified. That same night, Amy went missing."

CHAPTER 42

The memory of my nightmare flashes through my mind, bringing with it the horror, the desperation and hopeless paralysis I felt at watching the slow torturous death of a woman at the hands of a dark phantom.

It's your fault.

In a fog of uncertainty, I rise from the bed, cross to the mirror, and stare at myself. I want to come clean to Nick. But it scares me that I can't trust myself enough to remember what sent me running from my life.

"I think I know who is behind all this."

"You do?"

Without looking at him, I can sense Nick tense up. "Yes. The answer is here," I say, pointing to my head. "Somewhere in the back of my mind, buried deep where I can't get to it. I know who wants me dead."

I close my eyes and push myself to remember, but the memories stay hidden. When the warmth of two hands falls on my shoulders, I open my eyes and see Nick standing behind me. For a second, I am terrified, but then our gazes meet in the mirror. His eyes reflect hope. I'm sure he sees futility in mine.

"I'm sorry. I wish I could remember everything, but I can't." I slip away from Nick and retrieve my coffee. The warmth is gone, both from my shoulders and my cup.

"Don't worry, Ma'am. I'm hoping that by reviewing the facts of Amy's case, we might jog your memory enough to figure out who is responsible for her murder, perhaps Maddy's, and the attempts on your life."

Though Nick's words exude confidence, his voice projects doubt, sadness.

"Absent any solid evidence or a confession," Nick continues, "I think that's the only way we're going to be able to get at the truth. It seems the key memories we need are from January fifth, the day you took off, the day our truck-driving hitman first tried to kill you."

He glances at the cup in my hands. "Your coffee's probably cold. Want me to freshen it up?"

I nod, hand him my cup, and return to my seat on the bed.

A moment later, Nick hands me my steaming cup. "Maybe I could start by telling you what I know about that day."

"It's worth a try." I take a sip of coffee, hoping the hot brew will chase away the dread-induced shivers coursing through my body.

After taking a calming breath, Nick starts. "Well, to set the scene, the day you drove off, you, your family, and some key staffers were staying at the Fairmont Hotel. You had come to town earlier that week to get Olivia settled in her new school. She's in kindergarten."

In my mind, I see her. My little girl. Dressed in a white blouse, plaid skirt, navy knee socks, and tennis shoes. I smile at the memory. "Yes. She's at a private school, isn't she?"

"Westminster Academy," Nick replies, nodding. "Good job. Let's keep going and see what else jumps out at you."

"The floor is all yours."

"Anyway, that afternoon, around two o'clock, I got a call from an FBI buddy of mine. He knew about Amy and me, that I was nuts about her. He tracked me down, found out I was on duty that day, and broke the awful news to me. Said two agents were on their way over to the

Fairmont to inform you and your husband. He thought I deserved better than to be a fly on the wall when I learned of Amy's fate."

I close my eyes and follow Nick's words, hoping for a glimmer of memory to shine through.

"As I mentioned before, you were in the middle of an interview when the agents arrived, so your husband met with them alone in your penthouse suite. When you finished with the magazine reporter, I escorted you upstairs. I don't know what happened behind those closed doors—"

Nick's words jar loose a memory, sending my heart racing. "Wait, Nick. I can see myself. I'm standing in the middle of the living room. William's there, pleading with me."

"My presidency is on the line. The future of our country is at stake."

Inside my chest, my heart is thumping hard and fast, ready to burst. I struggle to speak, but the words catch in my throat.

"If you turn your back on me now, we'll all go to jail."

Sorrow and regret wash over me. I still can't answer.

"If for no other reason, do it for the girls. They need their mother."

Oh, god, what have I done?

CHAPTER 43

I bolt from the bed, stumble to the bathroom, and lock myself inside. Feeling dizzy, I flip down the toilet lid, then sit and lean over with my head hung low. *Breathe. Breathe.* The ringing in my ears fades to a dull roar, allowing Nick's frantic pounding and strained voice to reach me through the door.

"Ma'am, are you alright? Angela? Please speak to me."

I pause to catch my breath, then squeak out a reply. "I'm okay. Just, ah, just give me a minute."

"Are you sure?" Nick's voice softens, though the strain is still there. "We don't have to do this."

Yes, we do. I need to hear the whole story, at least what Nick can tell me, and make it through without cracking up. Time is not on our side. A vicious killer is out there somewhere, stalking my every move, and leaving behind a trail of bodies. He won't stop until he finishes the job he started—and neither will I.

I rise from the toilet and prop myself up, trembling, in front of the bathroom mirror, then stare into the pair of eyes looking back at me and the pain behind them. At that moment, I realize there's only one path forward if I'm to escape the terror I feel. I need to keep my eyes open, be ready to acknowledge the tough, unpleasant facts Nick needs to tell me. The truth will save me. From myself. And from whoever wants me dead.

I flip on the bathtub faucet and splash my face with cold water. After toweling off, I open the door. Nick greets me with a nervous smile and a glass of water.

"Thought you could use some cool water. Hot coffee, all that caffeine, well, it probably didn't help."

I drink the clear liquid in two greedy gulps.

"Thanks. It wasn't the coffee." I brush past Nick to the sink and refill my glass. "Your words did the job. I saw bits and pieces of my past, nothing specific that will help us, but distasteful snippets all the same. My memory is trying to emerge. It is. I need to relax when it presents itself, control my reactions, just as Dr. Malone taught me."

Nick rests his hand on my shoulder and leans in. Our gazes connect. "We don't have to rush this."

"You know that's not true, Nick. Any further delay could cost more innocent lives." I perch on the edge of the bed, then motion for Nick to take his seat. "Let's keep going. Now, what happened after I entered the hotel suite?"

Nick returns to his chair and begins again. "I don't know. I waited in the hallway for you. It didn't take long. You stormed out of the suite after only five minutes. You were fuming with anger."

My mind flashes back to the scene behind the door. I cringe.

"What's wrong. Do you remember something?"

"Just an emotional memory," I lie. "You're right. I was mad. I don't remember why."

What role did I play that fills me with such anger and self-reproach that I'm afraid to be totally honest with Nick?

Keep hiding. The words peal the truth in my head. Now, more than ever before, that seems to include hiding from myself. Still, I know I must press on. Hiding is not working, keeping neither me nor Nick safe.

After a few deep breaths, I'm ready for Nick to continue. "So, what happened next?"

He stands and starts to pace. "Yes, well, your behavior was startling. I expected you'd be upset, maybe crying. Instead, you stomped right past me before I had a chance to talk to you. I followed you downstairs, where you met up with Lauren, one of your assistants. I didn't hear the conversation. When she walked away, I approached you. You were incensed, said you wanted to be left alone. No security detail. Especially me."

My words had hurt him. I can see it in his eyes.

"Lauren returned seconds later, so I backed off. Another agent distracted me for a minute. When I turned around, you were gone. I asked Lauren what was going on. She didn't know, just that you asked to borrow her car, so she gave you her valet ticket. The agents in the hallway told me that you jumped in the elevator, giving orders that no one was to follow."

It seems too easy. "So, one word from me, and the Secret Service shirks its responsibility to go everywhere I do?"

Nick stops in front of me. "You have the right to refuse protection. But I knew you were hurting and probably not thinking clearly, so I took off after you. Does any of this spark a memory?"

I close my eyes, take a sip of water, and will the clear liquid to wash away the shame imprisoning my memories. But it doesn't. Some of what Nick says does feel familiar, but nothing stimulates a recollection, visual or otherwise. But there, in the shadows of my mind, I can still feel them. Lingering emotions—guilt, anger—bottling up my memory, keeping it from breaking free.

"I'm sorry, Nick." I open my eyes and shake my head. "I'm still blocked. You'll have to fill in the blanks until I can do it myself."

Nick straddles the chair by the bed and nods. "Well, that was three days ago, the day of the big blizzard. It was already snowing heavily. Traffic was slow. I thought maybe you were on your way home to Richmond. After confirming the make, model, and color of Lauren's car, I took off after you. When I finally spotted what I thought was her bright blue Jeep Cherokee, it was pulling off I -95 just south of Fredericksburg. Traffic was bumper to bumper and crawling, so by the time I pulled off the freeway the Jeep was nowhere in sight. I was low on fuel, so I pulled into the only gas station at exit. I was standing by the pump when I called you. That's when I heard your ringtone. I found your cell phone in a nearby trash can."

I pick up Nick's phone from the bed. The touch of the smooth plastic case elicits a vague memory. Instinctively, I fling the device away from me. Nick catches it. "I think I threw it away."

"Yes. That's what I thought, too. You hated cell phones. You once told me you felt chained to them, like a slave, compelled to answer every call and text." He tucks his phone in his coat pocket. "My instincts kicked in. I assumed you tossed it to get everyone off your back. Even your security detail. You wanted to be left alone. You were running away from everyone, going somewhere other than your home in Richmond."

"Why would I do that? Where would I go?" I don't have the answers, and from the puzzled look on Nick's face, he hasn't a clue either.

"That's part of what you need to remember. I wanted to give you space while still watching over you. I removed your phone's battery and followed, hoping to keep interference from the agency or your husband's staff to a minimum. The gas station attendant couldn't tell me which way you drove off, so I had him show me the last few minutes of the surveillance video. It showed the Jeep headed west. I gave him fifty bucks for the disk and his silence, then left. Soon thereafter, I saw a car ahead which I assumed was yours.

"My Charger wasn't built for driving in snow, but I did my best to catch up. A black pickup passed me going too fast for the weather. I was less than a quarter mile away when I first saw the truck driver make a move on you. I watched in horror while he ran you off the road."

I close my eyes, inhale deeply, and let it out. Flashes come in bits and spurts. "I'm driving on a quiet country road . . . snow is falling hard and fast . . . the sun is almost set . . . a bright light bounces off my rearview mirror." My chest tightens. "I can't see. His headlights . . ." The words catch in my throat.

"You don't have to do this, Ma'am."

"Yes . . . I do." I breathe—*in and out, in and out*—keeping my eyes closed to retain the memory. "The only way to unleash my memories is to relive the worst of them."

I feel Nick's hand on mine. The memory continues.

"The truck's tinted passenger side window begins to roll down. The dark figure of a man comes into view . . . in the dim light, I see his face—and a gun. He's pointing it at me . . . laughing like the Devil." I gasp for air. "I'm sorry. That's all I can remember." I open my eyes and look at Nick. "I guess you saw what happened, though."

He leans over and grasps my hands. "I'm so sorry. I should have—" He looks away, shaking his head. "I had no cause to suspect he was a threat."

I pull my hands from his and place them on his shoulders. "Nick, it's okay. We've both made mistakes. But that's all in the past."

Nick's phone buzzes inside his coat. "Excuse me, I should take this."

He walks into the bathroom and shuts the door. When he returns a few minutes later, he crosses to the bed, sits down, and hands me his phone, revealing a photo, a headshot of a pale man with a bald head, a protruding forehead, dark eyes, and a wide flat nose.

My blood runs cold.

CHAPTER 44

*f*elix wasted no time tearing out of the Summer Oaks parking lot. Desperate for information, he pulled into a McDonald's a block away and parked his truck around back in a corner spot. He snatched his phone from his coat pocket and pulled up the spyware app. After digging out the slip of paper in his pocket, he punched Nick Costa's phone number into the device and pressed SEND. The call went directly to an automated voicemail message without the live connection he needed to hack the mystery man's phone.

Fuck! I can't catch a break!

He pulled a tool kit from his center console, dug out the cell phone he'd collected from the trash and popped open its backside. He smiled.

With the phone's undamaged SIM card installed in a burner, Felix brought up the call log. He recognized only one number among those received or dialed within the last five days. *Nick Costa.* The other two he tracked to the Charlottesville Police and the records clerk he'd dispatched earlier that night. The calls added nothing to what he knew, but the dearth of other numbers, especially any linked to federal law enforcement, suggested he could still contain the situation.

Still, Costa's identity eluded Felix. If he were a betting man, he'd put money down that the man was the original owner of the burner phone. It could be brand new, or it could be one he used for one purpose or another. If his assumption was correct, Felix had one last trick to get at the man's hidden data on the card, a forensic analysis program he kept handy for just such purposes.

Minutes later, the SIM card revealed another D.C. area number in the phone's call log. He punched the number into his own burner phone and pressed SEND.

"Good afternoon, you've reached the White House Office of the Secret Service. How may I direct your call?"

Although alarmed by the receptionist's greeting and dying to rattle off a few choice words of anger, Felix held back. He needed to go further to confirm what he suspected.

"Nick Costa, please."

Placed on hold, the operator returned a minute later. "I'm sorry, Special Agent Costa is on personal leave from the agency. If you tell me the nature of your business, I can direct—"

Felix punched the OFF button and screamed in frustration. When he finally calmed down, he thought through the implications.

If that brain-addled bitch is on the run with a Secret Service agent, chances he's revealed that she's Angela Lockhart. The more important question remained. *Does she remember anything at all, especially what she did?*

CHAPTER 45

"That's him!" I gasp. "That's the guy who tried to kill me." Nick grimaces, looks at the photo, then tucks his phone in his coat pocket.

"How did you track him down? Who is he?" I clutch Nick's hand, hoping to draw strength from him. His skin, as cold as mine, betrays the fear he holds inside.

"Remember that black truck I mentioned earlier, the one I saw in the Summer Oaks parking lot?"

I nod. "You thought it looked like the truck that ran me off the road."

"I stopped when I saw it. I recorded the license plate, VIN, make and model of the truck, then sent it off to a buddy of mine in the FBI. The plate was stolen, but the VIN matched up to this guy. His name is Felix Jager, ex-DIA, Defense Intelligence Agency. He was stationed in Afghanistan in the early years of the war, Iraq later. Had a rep for working over terrorists and jihadists a little too well. Waterboarding was the least of his tricks. When the Abu Ghraib torture scandal became a hot button, Jager was ordered to scale back his methods. He blew his stack with command and was promptly discharged."

I meet Nick's gaze. The dread I see in his eyes tells me we're in deep trouble. I steel myself for the worst. "Go on. Tell me the rest." My words come out strong and firm.

"Jager is no amateur. He turned to contract work after getting tossed from the DIA, doing dirty jobs—torture, kidnapping, murder-for-hire, and such—for anyone willing to pay his fees. It's rumored some of his work is government-connected, not just foreign players, but the U.S., as well."

"So, you're telling me a government-contracted hitman is out to kill me?" Not that I am surprised. With my nerves on edge, I bolt from the bed and start pacing the room.

"William must be behind this. Inauguration is only a couple weeks away. He must already have connections with the country's federal intelligence agencies and their operatives on both sides of the law. If he thinks I know something about these murders that threatens his claim to the Oval Office, I don't doubt that he'd use the resources at his disposal to silence me."

"Ma'am, there's no basis for accusing your husband of anything." Despite his steadfast words, the worry on Nick's face tells me he has at least considered the possibility.

"From what I've been told," he continues, "Jager is not that exclusive. He could be connected to any number of people outside the government, your husband's campaign, for instance. In fact, it seems most likely that the attempts on your life are connected to Maddy and Amy's murders. Both worked for the campaign well before your husband was elected and given access to federal agencies. Still, Amy disappeared the night the campaign was told of Maddy's murder, and you were attacked hours after learning of Amy's murder. In my mind, the campaign is still the most logical link."

I pause to consider Nick's reasoning, and somehow, I know he's right. "So, you think Amy knew something about Maddy's death, too?"

"Yes."

I pace the room once more, now, too jumpy to stand still. "And you think someone connected to the campaign killed her to silence her?"

He nods. "Or contracted the hit on Amy."

I stop in front of the mirror and stare at my image.

It's your fault.

I turn away from the mirror, afraid I'll see the truth of the frightful cryptic message in my own eyes. I climb onto the bed, thrust myself up against the headboard, then grab a pillow and clutch it to my chest. "And now, this someone has set Felix Jager after me, believing I know something about Amy's murder or Maddy's or both?"

"That's the most coherent theory."

"But what is it I know?" I scream, slamming my fists into the pillow. "I can barely remember anything good about my life, let alone anything sinister, like two murders!"

Nick stands, walks over to me, and sits on the bed. He takes my hand in his. This time, I don't pull away. I need his touch to ground me, tell me I'm not the awful person I fear I am.

"I don't know the answer to that either, Ma'am. But whoever wants you dead must believe you have incriminating evidence."

"So, what the hell is it, and where am I hiding it?" I ask, throwing my hands in the air. "All I have are nightmares or vague figments of my memory-starved imagination. That kind of evidence doesn't hold up in court."

"I guess it's possible you hid something somewhere, maybe compromising pictures or papers. If you had the evidence on you when you drove away, that could be why Felix ran you off the road into that river. He wanted both you and whatever dirt you had on his client to disappear. Perhaps, it's simply that you are the evidence."

"I'm a witness? I suppose it's as good a guess as any." I shrug, hiding the truth once more. It's not a guess, not on my part anyway. Nick's inference is a gut punch, right on the money. My emerging memories seem to confirm that. My dreams, too. If that little voice in my head is also on the mark, I'm to blame, at least in some part, for this waking nightmare. Until I know more, remember more, I can't reveal my fears about my role to Nick.

"Yes. But I prefer to think of them as suppositions based on known facts." He rises from the bed, approaches the window, then peeks out. He turns around without a hint of alarm on his face, easing my own worries. Felix the bogeyman is not lurking outside our door. At least not yet.

From atop the sofa's armrest, Nick continues. "One fact involves the timing of Amy's abduction and the attempt on your life. Both acts are so closely timed, that whoever is behind all this must have felt that finding Maddy's body, and later Amy's, posed a risk of exposure so significant that he had to act quickly to silence you both."

I jump at the chance to connect the dots. "The guilty party must have been in the room when the FBI broke the news of Maddy's murder. And he must have been with me when I learned Amy had been murdered." After all, I think to myself, I wouldn't have put a hit out on myself. William is still my prime suspect otherwise.

"I don't think we can go that far, Ma'am. When it comes to a story like this, the news travels fast, especially with reporters dogging the candidates at every turn. If I may be frank, Ma'am, a dead cold body is a serious threat to any public career, so anyone in Washington who has—or had—political aspirations could be behind Maddy's murder. We could be way off here, too. People kill for a host of nefarious reasons. Regardless of why Maddy was murdered, though, I still believe Amy's death and the attempts on your life are part of the killer's cover up."

I can't see the flaw in Nick's analysis. Still, I'm not so sure he's right to dismiss my theory this easily. I'm convinced William and his campaign are caught up in the middle of this deadly intrigue. If I am, so is he. "This could still be about the fraud perpetrated on President Hayward, couldn't it? Are people dying over political dirty tricks?"

"The timing doesn't work," Nick says. "Maddy was murdered in July, long before the fake pay-for-play story made the headlines. There must be some other reason Maddy was targeted."

It's your fault.

I wince as the words pierce my heart, reminding me that I may be hiding deadly motives of my own.

CHAPTER 46

across from me, Nick looks as worn as I feel. Lying on the bed, I realize I'm exhausted. But now is not the time to sit back and rest. We have to press on, both mentally and physically. I drag myself from the bed and walk the room once more and offer my thoughts on our next move.

I recap. "We have good reason to assume that Maddy's and Amy's murders are connected to each other and to the attempts on my life. If we assume Amy knew something about Maddy's murder, then we need to focus on who had reason to kill Maddy. If Maddy wasn't part of the plan to ruin Hayward's chances for reelection, we need another motive for someone to want a young campaign intern dead."

I catch Nick's gaze. The wariness I see in his eyes hints at something he'd rather not mention.

"What is it, Nick?"

He shakes his head and shrugs. "Nothing, really, Ma'am. Just some rumors."

I march over to the sofa and glare at him. "Rumors?" It takes me less than a second to understand what he's insinuating. "My husband was cheating. With whom?" I ball my fists. "Not that I care." Did I ever have real feelings for William, love him with all my heart, soul, and body? I dig deep but the only answer I find is "no." And yet, my clenched hands suggest otherwise.

I look at Nick, waiting for a response, but all I sense from him is an uneasy reluctance to speak.

"Come on. Spill the beans, Nick. Our marriage was a sham. This woman, whoever William was messing around with, could be the key to all this horror."

Nick finally relents. "It was just a rumor. No names were ever mentioned, at least that I heard. But every campaign is rife with gossip about who's sleeping with whom."

This discussion is getting old, but I can't let it drop. There must be some reason beyond William being an arrogant control freak to explain why I don't trust him. A reason that could explain why two women are dead, and I'm next on the list.

"I hope you're not trying to protect me from the truth, Nick. I can handle it. William wouldn't be the first politician to have a wandering eye. If my memory of history is correct, adultery among the political class is almost a job requirement." The anger growing inside me suggests that I'm on the right track. "I have an idea of what might have happened. Just hear me out."

"I'm all ears," Nick replies.

I drop down on the couch next to Nick. "Maddy disappeared the same day she left the campaign. Let's go on the assumption that William was having an affair, probably with someone on his staff. Maybe Maddy discovered what was going on, perhaps walked in on them *in flagrante delicto*. A young, disillusioned intern might be upset enough to go to the media. Or maybe William was shacking up with Maddy herself, and at some point, he considered her a threat to the campaign. Either way, Maddy disappears, until her body is discovered months later. My gut instincts are with me on this. Maddy was killed to cover up William's affair, either with her or some other woman."

From the exasperation I see on Nick's face, he's clearly not buying my theory. "I hear you, Ma'am. I'm not trying to spare you any bad news, and I don't mean to dismiss your instincts." He pauses for a moment, then continues. "But we need to avoid jumping to conclusions that could cloud or otherwise alter your memories when they finally emerge. False memories will not help us nail Jager and whoever hired him."

He draws in a big breath and sighs. "But let me address your theory, Ma'am, and why I'm skeptical."

"Be my guest," I say, crossing my arms.

"It goes back to motive. I'm just not sure that a fling is reason enough to kill. Again, campaigns are hotbeds of gossip about one affair or the other among staff. Candidates, especially, can draw lots of speculation. There was scuttlebutt about your husband, that he had a wandering eye for pretty blonds. But there was even a whisper or two about you and member of your staff."

"Me? An affair? With whom?" I ask, shocked by the revelation.

"As a member of your protective detail, I can assure you there was nothing behind the gossip. All I am saying is that such rumors come with the territory. They don't mean anything and even if they do, they can easily be dispelled."

Nick's explanation leaves me hanging, struggling with the idea that the disgust and distrust I feel for my husband is over nothing other than old-fashioned marital infidelity. Am I a jealous person? Somehow this doesn't ring true to me. And besides, it seems I am not without blame. It's obvious that my heart no longer belongs to my husband. I would have gladly fallen into Nick's arms on any number of occasions over the last couple of days—even today, after learning our true identities.

How long have I felt this way about Nick? Did Amy know? Perhaps, William?

The questions startle me, leaving me fearful of what the answers might reveal about me and the vague sense of guilt weighing me down.

"The only person immune to the rumor mill was Andrew Novak, your husband's chief of staff. No one would dare risk that man's wrath by telling secrets or spreading tales about him. I wish I could give you a more concrete answer, but I can't."

My jaw clenches at the name and Nick's impression of the man. I try to visualize his face, but my memory comes up short. Before I can ask Nick to pull up a photo, his phone chimes, causing him to leap up from his seat on the sofa.

"Listen, Ma'am. I have an appointment with that FBI buddy of mine, the same one who gave me the head's up about . . ." He looks away without finishing his thought. "Anyway, I'm supposed to meet him at a cafe a couple of miles away in ten minutes."

My heart leaps inside my chest. "You're meeting with the FBI? Why?"

"He's going to fill me in on recent developments in the investigation of your sister's murder and report on some leads I asked him to check out."

The jitteriness I see in Nick tells me he's nervous about this meeting. Hoping I can help, I bolt from the sofa and grab my coat. "Then why are we wasting time here? Let's go."

Nick jumps ahead of me and blocks the exit. "No, Ma'am. I'm sorry. No one deserves to sit in on this meeting more than you, but that can't happen. You need to stay put. If you show your face anywhere around town, you risk exposing yourself to Jager. At the same time, I can't be sure my buddy will keep our secret either. Asking him to fill me in on Amy's murder investigation is a small indulgence, but expecting him to keep our confidences and conceal your whereabouts is too big of a favor. Let me take this meeting alone. Hopefully, what I learn will help you remember what happened the day you learned about Amy's death."

Nick's suggestion rattles me. "What about Felix Jager? He could be nearby. What if he sees you leaving? I'll be good as dead."

"Don't worry, Ma'am. Now that I have you safely stashed here, I'm going to text my buddy and change our meeting to the parking lot across the street. The grocery store there is busy, enough so that nobody should notice two men sitting in a car, and easy enough for me to keep an eye on this place. I doubt Jager is close by, not yet. We put a good bit of distance between him and us when we left Summer Oaks."

Nick pulls out his cell phone and punches the keypad. "Now, if you'll excuse me." He walks into the bathroom and shuts the door. A minute later, he emerges.

"Everything is set, Ma'am. I'll be right across the street." He crosses the room, reaches into his overnight bag, and produces a cell phone. "This is another burner phone. I use it in emergencies." He turns it on, punches the screen, then hands it to me. "If you hear or see any-thing suspicious, or if anyone knocks on the door, lock yourself in the bathroom, press ONE and hit SEND. On the first ring, I'll come flying back. I promise."

He puts his hand on my shoulder and gives it a firm squeeze. The strength of his grip reminds me that I'm in good hands, no matter how far away they are, whether across the room or across the street.

"How long do you think you'll be?"

"It depends on how much information my buddy has for me. I'll have some questions, too. Maybe twenty-five, thirty minutes tops."

"I don't want to sit here twiddling my thumbs while you're gone. Let me use your laptop, see if I can find something to nudge my memory along."

"It's not safe to use the motel's Wi-Fi. I'll set up a private hot spot with your cell phone."

All too quickly, Nick's laptop is connected to the Internet, and he is bundled up in his coat, ready to head out.

"Do you really have to go? Why don't you meet with this FBI agent in the empty room next door? You paid for it. You have a key to the room, don't you?"

He draws the drapes back and peeks out. "I don't want him to be privy to everything I'm doing, where I am and such. The fewer people who know, the less likely there will be leaks, and the safer we'll be."

The confidence I see in Nick's face eases my worries.

"I'll be back soon. I promise. Now, I really must go. I need to get into that parking lot before he shows up. I don't want him spotting me coming from this motel. Lock the door behind me." And with that he leaves.

I follow Nick's instructions, then peek through the window and watch him jog across the street. He loiters along the edge of the busy store lot for a minute. When a blue sedan pulls up next to him, he hops inside. The car, parked with the driver's side facing the road, offers Nick an easy line of sight to Morey's Motel.

I linger at the window, surveying the area. The afternoon sky, overcast and snowy, is darkening rapidly. Out on the street, a flurry of cars and trucks speed past the motel and its defective neon sign. The low rumble of the traffic permeates the windows. Glancing across the motel parking lot, I spot a lone car, a dirt-caked white compact sitting outside the rental office. There's not a person in sight.

Satisfied that no one is lurking nearby, I sit down behind Nick's computer. A flash of nerves hits me as I prepare to type in my name: Angela Lockhart.

CHAPTER 47

pull up several brief biographies online confirming all sorts of public details about my life. Age. Family history. Education: home-schooled through high school, Communications degree from Wilton College, a small, private women's school in Virginia. My marriage to William nine years ago and my dutiful role in his political life. The birth of our daughters, Olivia, six years ago, and Sophia, two years later. Lingering over the few photos of me, William, and the girls, I'm filled with bittersweet emotions, tears, and smiles.

I scroll through the dozens of photos of me, portraits showing me in a variety of poses, some alone, the rest with William staged at campaign events, our private home in Richmond, the Governor's Mansion. Although my clothing differs from photo to photo, my face appears frozen in character from one shot to the next, the same green eyes seemingly twinkling with pride, the same bright smile gleaming with happiness. No hint that life, at those moments in time, was anything but picture-perfect. At least, not until ten days before the election. In the waning days of the campaign, I see a different me, a more subdued character, one struggling to show the world a happy face. Clearly, worry over Amy's disappearance was weighing heavily on my mind back then.

I abandon my unsuccessful attempts to jump-start my memory, and, instead, decide to focus on the event at the heart of this maddening mess—Maddy's murder. Who wanted her dead and why?

Online, I find little information about the young woman's murder, only one article detailing the basic facts of her disappearance and the discovery and identification of her badly decomposed corpse. The piece includes a short bio covering her family, hometown, high school, and college activities. My interest is piqued in the second to last paragraph detailing Maddy's internship with the campaign, including a comment from me:

I'm sure I speak for everyone on the campaign when I say we are deeply saddened by Maddy's death. Everyone loved her. Whoever did this horrible deed robbed the world of an amazing young woman. She was smart, hardworking, likeable, a real team player. Most of all, she was honest. There was nothing fake about her. That's something rare in politics.

The words, my own, seem to substantiate my theory about Maddy's murder, that she left the campaign in disgust over William's philandering. At the same time, the sentiment nauseates me. Though the puzzle of my life is far from complete, these words and my emerging memories reveal one clear picture—I'm not among the authentic few in politics. I'm as phony as William and the rest of them, harboring a vile, guilty secret like the worst of those in the game.

At that moment, I feel strangely free, empowered even, as if a great weight has lifted from my shoulders. With renewed vigor, I press on, confident that I'm close to the answers buried deep inside me. I just need to keep digging to uncover the truth.

I pull up Maddy's Facebook page, hoping to see what was going on in her life around the time she disappeared. The computer screen fills with memorial posts, pictures, and videos, all extolling her virtues.

Scrolling down the page, I find Maddy's posts for the two months preceding her disappearance on July 2. Almost exclusively focused on

William's campaign, the young intern sung his praises and encouraged people to get out and vote. She posted pictures of packed campaign rallies and videos she captured with her cell phone of William working the crowds. There was one video, a selfie from mid-May with the two of them in the shot. The taped conversation was rather innocuous, but the way he looks at her, the way she looks at him, the closeness of their bodies, strikes me cold.

They're more than casual acquaintances.

At the end of the video, William moves on, leaving Maddy behind to make a final comment. "Listen, ladies, there are lots of great reasons to vote for William Lockhart for president. But if that's not enough, vote for him because he's smoking hot, and I mean sizzling! Let's get real, ladies. Who would you rather see as our president for the next four years, fat balding Hayward?" She pauses and points to William moving through the crowd. "Or that gorgeous hunk of a man?"

If the statement wasn't so disgusting, I'd be snickering along with the joke. But this is no laughing matter. Maddy is dead.

It's your fault.

I cringe at the words which, now, take on new significance, revealing a hideous, though well-worn motive for murder.

CHAPTER 48

*I*s Maddy's death on me? Did all this happen because of William's infidelity after all? Was I jealous enough to do something about it? As a bullied wife, would I dare take such action on my own? I don't want to believe it. I can't. My brain is having a hard enough time even coming to grips with being William's wife, so why would I lift a finger against any woman willing to satisfy his needs? I should be thanking those bimbos for letting me off the hook.

I chase away the ugly thoughts with a glance at the clock and gasp at the time. Nick has been gone more than fifty minutes. With my heart racing with worry, I dash to the window and peek through the drapes. The blue sedan is gone, and Nick is nowhere in sight. When I turn my gaze toward the motel office, I see it. A large black pickup with dark-tinted windows pulling into the parking lot and headed my way. Trembling, my heart seems to drop to my stomach.

I race across the room to reach the cell phone atop the desk, but trip over the chair. As I scramble to my feet, I hear the lock jiggle.

I grab the cell phone, hit "1" and "SEND," then scan the room for a weapon, something I can use to defend myself. Within seconds, I'm standing behind the door armed with a lamp. Gripping the long metal stem with every ounce of my strength, I raise it above my head, focus my aim, and hope to hell I land a knock-out blow on the intruder.

Fear seizes me as the door jerks open a crack, straining the door chain and swing latch along with my heart.

"Hey, I'm back, Ma'am. Unlock the door and let me in."

"Nick!" I try to scream, but his name catches in my throat. Gasping for air, I throw the lamp on the floor, shove the door closed, then release the locks. When Nick pushes open the door, I pull him inside.

"Felix! He's out there. Didn't you see his truck?" I shout, as I slam the door shut and lock it.

The alarm on Nick's face tells me he hasn't. He tosses a large manila envelope on the bed, then darts to the far side of the window. "I don't see him," he says, peering out the window from behind the drapes. "There's a pickup parked three doors down that looks a lot like Jager's, but it's the wrong make and model. A lot older, too." He drops the curtain and turns to me. "A short Latino man stepped out of the truck just as I passed by."

He eyes the lamp on the floor, walks over, and picks it up. "You thought I was Jager, huh?" He offers a sly grin. "Planned on putting my lights out with this?"

"Very funny." I sneer. "I had to defend myself, didn't I?" I wrench the makeshift weapon from his hands and return it the nightstand then, with a heavy sigh, collapse on the bed.

"Listen, Ma'am. I'm sorry about the joke. Not my best."

I sit up, cross my arms, and give him a sheepish grin. "You're for-given, but you were late. Thirty minutes tops. Remember? That's what you said. You were gone almost an hour. When I saw that truck, what was I supposed to do? You weren't anywhere in sight. What were you doing in the motel office anyway?"

Nick reaches into his pocket and holds up small silver object. "My FBI buddy gave me a flash drive with Amy's file on it. I'm kind of old-fashioned. I like paper, so I can make notes in the margins, highlight details I think are significant. The motel manager let me print out a copy and charged me a buck a page. Forty-seven bucks. Highway robbery!"

He returns the flash drive to his pocket, pulls off his coat and lays it on the couch. "I haven't been through the whole file yet. It'll take some time to sort through all the forensics and interviews, but my buddy gave me the highlights. Unfortunately, he didn't tell me anything that would break open the case, at least from our perspective."

"Can I see the file? Maybe something will jump out at me, spark my memory."

Nick eyes the envelope on the bed. "Are you sure you want to know what's in Amy's FBI file?"

"It's not that I want to know, Nick. I *have to* know." I don't offer what I'm really hoping to find—information that somehow proves I couldn't be involved in any of this, not in Maddy's murder, much less my own sister's. "You said so yourself. The attempts on my life must be related to Amy's death. Why else would someone sic a hit man on me?" I pick up the envelope and wave it in the air. "Talk. Tell me everything, or I'll read it for myself."

"Yes, Ma'am."

Nick takes the packet from me, then stares at it. That's when I realize . . . How could I be so insensitive? This is just as hard for him. Probably more so. He loves Amy and wanted to spend the rest of his life with her.

"Nick, I'm sorry." I rush to his side. "We don't—"

"No," he interrupts, turning his gaze on me. "You're right. We need do this, and we'll get through it together." He draws a big breath and lets it out. "First, there's no doubt the body is Amy's. Dental records confirmed her identity." Nick pauses for a moment. "Some of this may be hard to hear, Ma'am."

"I'm ready if you are."

With his head hung low, Nick continues. "The autopsy showed the hyoid bone and thyroid cornu in Amy's neck were crushed, evidence that she was strangled. Her body was too decomposed to determine if she was . . . ah, well . . . assaulted."

A tear appears on Nick's cheek. My eyes begin to water. I jump to my feet, fetch the tissue box from the far side of the room, and extract tissues for both of us. Sitting on the bed, dabbing at my tears, I hazard a glance at Nick. He's doing the same. The sight of him struggling with his grief sends me longing for him again. I want to wrap my arms around him, take away his sorrow. I want him to do the same for me.

Nick touches my hand.

Afraid of my feelings, what I might do, I pull back, jump up and walk away. "I need something to drink."

At the sink, I guzzle a tall glass of water. As the cool liquid streams down my throat, I somehow expect it to extinguish the intense emotions I have for Nick. But I know that won't happen. The feelings I have are beyond my conscious control, just like my memories.

In the next moment, I see Nick, reflected in the mirror, standing behind me.

"I apologize for losing it," Nick says, his voice melancholy. "Just the facts, Ma'am, going forward."

I reply with a nod. But the exchange does little to change one truth, a glaring one for me, at least. Nick still has a hold on me, forcing me to keep my distance, both physically and emotionally.

Nick excuses himself to the bathroom. I settle into my corner awaiting his return, planting myself against the bed's headboard, my legs fully extended, a pillow across my lap—as many physical barriers between Nick and me as I can manage. Emotionally, I can only hope that a cold, hard review of the facts surrounding Amy's murder will put the freeze on the fire burning inside me for the man.

My thoughts are quickly overwhelmed by a lurid possibility I hadn't yet considered. Jealousy may, indeed, be at play here. My feelings for Nick could have blown my dissatisfaction with my own marriage out of proportion. Maybe I was jealous enough of Maddy to have her killed, or of Amy because Nick loved her, not me. Perhaps, Felix was chasing me, because I reneged on paying him the blood money he earned. My body goes limp, as if surrendering to the wild theory that casts me as the jealous, cold-blooded killer of my romantic rivals.

After Nick returns, he picks up where we left off, helping me to deflect these wild, irrational fears from my mind.

"There's one big discrepancy between Amy's case and Maddy's, Ma'am. The Medical Examiner found blunt force trauma to the back of Amy's head. Not enough to kill, but enough to knock her out, at least temporarily. If Amy was choked to death, it likely happened while she was unconscious."

Did I do that? I draw my arms tightly across my chest, an attempt to control my trembling hands. "She probably didn't suffer. I guess we should be grateful for that."

The trite consolation draws a feeble smile from Nick, but the comment seems too weak to offer any peace of mind. Even so, I find an odd sense of comfort in Nick's revelation. Amy never battled for her life. It was likely she never knew death was at hand. *Making it easier for me to lay my hands on her, perhaps?*

Nick says nothing as he turns away from me. "Yes. Let's hope that was the case."

Suddenly, he jumps up. "There's more in her file, but I haven't had a chance to look it over." He paces the floor, then stops in front of the desk. "So, did you make any progress while I was gone? Did you see anything on the Internet that sparked a memory?"

I pause to consider my words. I'm not ready to spill everything I know—or suspect. Both Nick and Dr. Malone cautioned me about jumping to conclusions that could create false memories. At the same time, I realize, I need to not let my emotions and imagination get the better of me. At this moment, the only thing I'm fairly certain of is that William and Maddy's affair set these murders in motion.

CHAPTER 49

"**S**orry, Nick. I wish I could report that surfing the Internet led to some miraculous recovery of my memory, but it didn't. That block in my brain didn't move an inch." Not a lie, technically, at least. "But I am confident of one thing."

"What's that?"

"William has his fingerprints all over this mess."

After moving to the desk and replaying Maddy's Facebook video for Nick, I offer my conclusion about William's affair. But even as he listens, I can see doubt in his eyes.

"I'm sorry, Ma'am, I don't see what you're seeing."

"Come on, Nick. The Secret Service knows what goes on behind closed doors, don't they?" I steel myself for the question I have to ask. "Admit it. William was carrying on with Maddy. She travelled with him and his people before she joined my staff."

Nick's stoic expression doesn't give anything away. "We really can't see through doors, Ma'am. I wasn't on your husband's detail, but yes, there were rumors. I mentioned as much earlier. Word was he was spending private time with some female staff member."

"So, it could have been Maddy." My emotions are mixed at Nick's news. Happy to be finally getting somewhere, disappointed at where we're headed.

"I can't say for sure. After Amy disappeared, I chased every possible lead trying to find her, even looking into Maddy's death. I came up short linking her romantically to anyone, including your husband."

"If there were any truth to the rumor, and Maddy was threatening to tell all, wouldn't that give William a motive for murder?" *And me? But I don't say that out loud.*

Nick shrugs his shoulders. "Maybe. Maybe not. The tabloids are full of stories like that in the run-up to a presidential election. Most are attributed to 'unnamed sources' within the campaign. 'He said, she said' stories don't get much traction in the media, not without solid evidence. Politicians seem to wangle their way past their indiscretions with lies, bribes, and spin, but not murder. Yes, affairs can end political careers, but it usually takes a love child to do that. That's what ruined John Edwards presidential aspirations."

A love child? Nick's words jolt a memory. *I'm in a bathroom, alone with Maddy. She's retching into the toilet. A pregnancy test sits nearby, atop the bathroom vanity, its pink plus sign broadcasts the truth.*

"Maddy was pregnant." The words burst out of my mouth. Without stopping to catch my breath, I close my eyes and focus.

I'm standing beside Maddy, patting her back, doing what I can to comfort her. "How far along are you?"

"Seven, eight weeks maybe."

"Who's the father? Is it someone on the campaign?"

She turns to me, grimacing from the nausea. "I can't tell you."

"Yes, you can. I'll keep your confidence. I'll do anything to help you."

"No. I can't tell you. I can't tell anyone. People will talk. It will hurt the campaign."

I open my eyes and sigh, shaken by the memory, but not debilitated, not panicked. A victory, offering hope I'm on the mend to recovering my memories.

I share my flashback with Nick. "Maddy *was* involved with someone working the campaign. But an affair with a staffer is not newsworthy. A leak wouldn't ruin a candidate. The father must be on the ticket. Since William's running mate is a woman, it must be him. Maddy interned with William's travelling staff, too."

The hairs stand up on the back of my neck as the full impact of my memory hits—a love child is a motive for murder, incriminating William—and me, too.

Standing next to me, Nick scrolls through the screen on his phone. "Working back, that would mean Maddy got pregnant sometime in early May. Four or five weeks before she transferred to your campaign. This could be the smoking gun we need to nail those responsible for her murder, perhaps even Amy's." He starts tapping away on his phone.

"I don't remember a positive pregnancy test in Maddy's autopsy report. Maybe the ME didn't check. Her face and hands were mutilated before she was buried, probably to make it harder to ID her. Some animals dug her up, leaving little tissue behind. I've contacted a source in the FBI to check anyway. Hopefully, they'll be able to test for pregnancy from whatever tissue they retained for evidence."

I crawl back onto the bed, horrified by these new revelations. The image of Maddy's body, assaulted by ravenous carnivores, echoes in my mind. I'd like nothing more than to shut off my brain, to sleep, chasing the horror away. But something about Maddy's story doesn't sit right with me. I swing my legs over the side of the bed and sit up.

"All along, we've operated on the assumption that these two murders, Maddy's and Amy's, are linked. The evidence, though circumstantial, is based on their work relationship and the timing of their disappearances in relation to key events. We suspect that Maddy was killed to cover up her pregnancy by William. But here's the thing I don't get . . ."

Nick looks as puzzled as I feel. "What is that?"

"Maddy confessed her secret to me. So, why was Amy killed?"

CHAPTER 50

From the expression on Nick's face, the proverbial light just flashed on in his head.

"You must have told Amy. We had lunch that last day Maddy was with the campaign. She was pretty upset but refused to tell me why. She also never seemed curious about why Maddy disappeared, just sad. That night we all learned of Maddy's murder, I could tell Amy was angry. I'm wondering if she put two-and-two together—Maddy's pregnancy and her death—and considered telling the police what she knew. In which case, Amy was a threat and had to be silenced. That leaves one very important question. Who else knew about Maddy's affair with William and her pregnancy? And who knew that you told Amy?"

It's your fault.

A pang of guilt wrenches my stomach. "I don't remember what I did with Maddy's secret." The words blurt from my mouth, a rush to my own defense, though hopefully Nick doesn't sense that's my intention. "I can't remember if I told anyone, let alone who." I turn away from him, hiding the remorse building up inside me.

"I don't know your husband well enough to answer this question, but if he *was* the father of Maddy's baby, would he kill to keep that little secret buried?"

It's your fault.

I spin around. "How would I know? I barely remember the man!" My hands fly to my cheeks. "I'm sorry, Nick. I didn't mean to snap at you."

"That's all right," he says, kneeling beside me, taking my trembling hands in his. "This must be tough, raising such awful suspicions about your husband. But listen, there's still a possibility he didn't know about Maddy's pregnancy, that he didn't order her murder or Amy's."

I push Nick away, stand up and start pacing the floor. "Don't patronize me. I know William is involved. My gut, my heart, my emerging memories, they all tell me he's involved." And, somehow, some way, I am, too.

Nick says nothing, just pulls out his cell phone. A few taps of the screen later, he hands it to me.

"What about him, Andrew Novak, your husband's chief of staff?"

An odd mixture of rage and shame sweeps over me as I stare at the image of an older man with thinning gray hair, a long, narrow face and nose, and thin lips. The longer I hold my gaze, the angrier and more ashamed I become. I squeeze my eyes shut, hoping to quell the intense emotions welling up inside me. That's when I see him. In my mind. Standing over me. His weasel-like face twisted with concern.

"If you don't do this, William will lose the election, and all the hard work and sacrifice everyone put into this campaign—your sister's, especially—will be for nothing. If you won't do it for William, do it for her. Do it for your country. Do it for the girls. They need their mother."

"What is it, Ma'am?" Nick's distressed voice breaks the spell. "Another memory?"

"Yes. An emotional one." My stomach churns at what it proves—that both William and his chief of staff pressured me into doing something I didn't want to do, something so desperate that refusing their demand would cost William the presidency. Are they trying to silence me now that I've done their bidding?

Disgust rises inside me, for William, Andrew, and myself. "He looks familiar." My words emerge with a growl. I thrust the phone at Nick. "He reminds me of a rodent, a rat."

"Yes, I guess he does." Nick snickers, tucking the phone back in his coat pocket. "My exposure to the man is limited. But what I've seen and heard is consistent with the rumor mill. Novak is ruthless. He'll do anything to protect your husband, his conduit for wielding power himself."

Nick is setting Andrew up for the fall guy, but I'm not ready to buy it. At least, not all of it. The only memories I have of William and his chief of staff involve both of them pressuring me.

Nick's phone beeps. He checks the incoming message.

"My guy at the FBI left a voicemail for the medical examiner. He'll get back to me about Maddy's pregnancy." He tucks his phone into his coat pocket. "In the meantime, we'll just have to keep going. Your recollection of that last morning with Maddy suggests your memory is ready to emerge. If we stick to the facts, try to keep our emotions under control, you might soon remember everything."

Nick is right. With my fear in check, I'd easily recalled a memory that revealed a possible motive behind the murders and the attempts on my life. I now feel less like I'm drowning in my own grief and fear, and more like I'm treading water. Even if, in the end, I can't save myself.

My head starts to throb as exhaustion finally catches up with me. I stretch myself out on the bed and tell Nick I need to rest.

"No problem. Meanwhile, I'll study Amy's file." He flips the light switch. "I'll try to not make any noise. You have a nice nap."

I shut my eyes and will myself to sleep, but rest eludes me. Nick's words echo inside my head. *You must have told Amy.* I wrestle with the same feelings I experienced in my nightmare. Despair. Helplessness. Guilt. My thoughts wander to Nick, how he described me when I stormed out of the hotel suite after learning Amy was dead—enraged.

My mind conjures a new theory. I revealed Maddy's secret to Amy, then let it slip to the wrong person. I failed to report my suspicions to the authorities when Amy went missing. I put my husband and his career over the life of my own sister and a young intern. It's a harsh judgment, but it is easier to swallow than the alternative. If I was careless, perhaps blinded by my aspirations for my husband's political career, I can tell myself that I had nothing to do with either death, that, consciously, I did nothing wrong. The truth rests on one thing—recovering my memory. Unless I can find some way to uncover the facts before Felix hunts me down, there's a good chance the truth will be buried with me—and Nick, too.

CHAPTER 51

"**Y**ou better be fucking with me, Jager!" The words blasted from Felix's cell phone though he held the device at arm's length. He'd learned early in his job to deliver bad news to his boss using his phone's speaker or risk damaging his hearing.

"No, sir. I'm not. She's alive." Felix rubbed his brow with his free hand. He could feel a headache coming on.

"How the fuck did that happen? Where is she now? I want to know everything. Don't leave out any detail!"

Felix didn't. Ten minutes later, without interruption, he'd finished the report he'd dreaded since he found the woman's icebound car empty. He fudged on how the two escaped his grasp at Summer Oaks. There was nothing to be gained from sharing that embarrassing detail and too much to lose—what little confidence remained with his boss after their conversation.

"So, let me get this straight, Jager. You screwed this up not once, not twice, but *three* times. First, by falling for a ruse concocted by this rogue Secret Service agent. He fooled you into thinking that bitch was dead, lost beneath the frozen river where you left her to die, when she was, in fact, alive but comatose at a nearby hospital. He put one over you again while you were resting on your laurels, had her transferred to a rehab facility, then obscured her trail. She woke from her coma yesterday with a complete case of amnesia, no fucking idea who she was. Even with this Secret Service agent hanging around, she was still clueless. When you finally had her in your sights, you let them both slip through your fingers. They're gone. Vanished. Sounds like three strikes to me. What do you think, dumbass?"

The way his boss summed up the situation irked him. After all, he wasn't the one who created the mess in the first place. His boss did. It was always him. Felix was just the hired help, there to clean up after a man more cold-blooded than himself.

"The game's not over yet, sir."

"This is not a game, you moron! I stand to lose everything if you fuck this up. I lose, you lose."

Felix knew what those words meant, at least as they pertained to him. He'd no longer be the hunter. He'd be the hunted.

"The situation is not as bleak as it seems, sir. I have reliable information on the car they're now driving, a hot silver Honda Accord with D.C. plates. It was stolen from a Walmart parking lot in Alexandria. I found Costa's Charger across the street behind a vacant strip mall. I have a source inside the DOT monitoring traffic cameras. It's just a matter of time until they're spotted."

"Damn it, man. We don't have time. The Secret Service is breathing down my neck. When that bitch drove away, I held them off, told the agency head that she needed time alone to grieve. She was going to stay with some friend in Richmond; who, she didn't say. The next day, when you told me she was dead, I set my plan in motion. I told the Director of the Secret Service that she was missing and hadn't checked in since leaving the hotel. There are now dozens of agents quietly searching the route to Richmond for the Jeep she borrowed. I can't keep stalling. They want to go public, see if someone knows something. Once that happens, the shit will hit the fan. Someone from that rehab facility could recognize her and blow the whistle.

Those two will come out of hiding. We'll have lost our chance to silence her for good."

"I don't think Summer Oaks' staff is such a big problem, sir. In fact, they might help us in the end."

"I don't need guesses at this point. I need certainties."

"Hear me out."

"You're batting oh-for-three, Jager," The man growled. "This better be a home run, or I'm benching you."

"Look at the situation, sir. This agent, Costa, has been by her side the whole time but apparently never revealed her identity to anyone, not even her. I'm certain of that. Her file, the staff at the rehab center, they all referred to her as 'Kay Smith.' With the two of them on the run and in hiding, we can further assume she doesn't remember who she's running from or why. They don't know who they can trust, either. Otherwise, Costa would've called in the Secret Service, the FBI, or some agency that could protect her better than he could alone."

That his boss hadn't interrupted him was a good sign. He was listening. Felix still had a chance to finish the job he started.

"Now, once I track them down, I work my magic, get the info you need to be sure this mess is contained. Then I stage their deaths as a murder-suicide. The White House spins Costa as a bad guy, an agent gone haywire, obsessed with the woman he was supposed to protect, keeping her hidden for his own nefarious purposes."

The line on the other was silent. "That sounds too farfetched to be taken seriously."

That was not what Felix wanted to hear, but he was ready for such a response. He'd spent a good deal of thought planning this scenario. He had to. His own life was on the line if he couldn't get his boss to give him another chance.

"Actually, sir, it's not. I checked this guy out. He took personal leave the day the FBI came to the hotel with news of Amelia Bulloch's murder. The two had more than just a professional relationship, they were an item. My sources tell me Costa was set to pop the question, but she went missing before he could follow through. After his sweetheart disappeared, Costa took two weeks off to look for her. He came up empty, of course, and returned to work on Angela Lockhart's security detail. Here's the clincher. The same day the FBI released the news of Bulloch's death, our girl runs off, he goes after her, they both end up MIA. The obvious conclusion—poor grief-stricken Costa has lost his mind, believes Angela Lockhart is his dead sweetie, and abducts her."

"Too many assumptions here, Jager. I don't do assumptions. I deal in facts. But you've left me with no other option. Against my better judgment, I'm giving you this one last chance. Do whatever you have to do to find them. Grill them on what they know and who they've told, then eliminate them both, once and for all. You better hope that contains the fucked-up disaster you created. You don't want me sending in someone to clean up after you."

Felix held back his anger. It was not in his nature to take shit from anyone, even his superiors. His termination from the DIA proved that. He wanted to chuck this whole mess entirely, pack his bags for his tropical island, and leave his boss high and dry to clean up the chaos with another stooge, but there was no way his boss would let him live if a new man had to finish the job. Even with a new identity, he'd be looking over his shoulder every day, waiting for his date with death.

"Yes, sir. I will get the job done."

"How? What's your plan? Do you have some idea where these assholes are holed up? What their next moves might be?"

Thankfully, he did. The questions his boss peppered him with meant the man still had a measure of trust in his abilities. With the reassurances he was prepared to provide, he'd be safe. There would be no bullet bought with his name on it today.

"Yes, sir. They know that time is not on their side, that I'm coming for them, that I found them once and will again. Their only way of staying alive is to come out in the open with her story. But that can't happen while that bitch's memory is still on the fritz. Costa is driving this thing. If I were him, I'd take her someplace that could jolt her back to reality with all her memories intact. Someplace safe, where she could meet up with someone she knows, who knows her well."

"And that would be . . ." The anger in his boss's voice had waned a bit, but not his impatience. "Come on, man, spill it!"

"From my research, there's only one place that makes sense, sir—Bulloch Hall. Her childhood home is full of memories, photos, and such. Her old nanny still lives there with her husband, too. You may remember them."

"That's right. Those two old coots," his boss replied with a snicker.

The phone went silent. Silence was a good sign. It meant the man was thinking, considering the usefulness of the information he just offered.

"You may have something here, Jager. Guess you're not as dumb as I thought you were."

Jager cringed at the man's words. He'd had enough of this asshole. Once this job was over and done, he was gone, out of the business for good.

His boss continued. "As tight as she is with the old woman, I'm sure those geezers would do anything to help her."

"That's my thinking, too, sir. It's a long shot, a dangerous one for her and Costa, but they don't have many options other than staying put and hoping her memory magically returns."

"Looks like they need a compelling reason to take their chances sooner rather than later. Knowing her as I do," his boss said, with his usual air of confidence, "I have the perfect fire-starter to smoke her out."

CHAPTER 52

My growling stomach nudges me awake. I check the time on the nightstand: 6:35 p.m. A couple hours of sleep. Not enough to overcome my fatigue, but my headache is gone.

"Nick?" I call out, as I sit up. He is nowhere in sight. Before I can raise the alarm, I hear the toilet flush. Relieved, I drag myself out of bed, step in front of the mirror, and frown. My bruises are an ugly sight against my pale skin, and my clothes are a wrinkled, frumpy mess. When Nick emerges from the restroom, my stomach rumbles loudly again.

"Hungry?"

"Yes. I haven't eaten since breakfast. Do you think it's safe enough for us to leave this place and get some food, maybe do some shopping? I'm wearing my only set of clothes. If I don't get something new to wear tonight, by tomorrow morning I won't need your protection. My clothes will be so foul, no one would dare come near me."

Poking fun at myself feels good and draws a chuckle from Nick. It's nice to see that again after the distressing conversation we'd waded through earlier.

"All right. But we'll have to be careful, Ma'am. We'll grab a bite to eat at a drive-through, then find a crowded Walmart. People there don't look at faces. Sorry we can't shop at a more upscale store more befitting your taste, Ma'am. Store security will peg you as a potential shoplifter the second you walk through the door looking like that."

Nick's politeness is grating on my nerves. "If that's the case, you should stop calling me Ma'am, Mrs. Lockhart, or referring to me as the First Lady. It feels awkward. If Amy were still alive, we'd likely be family by now and on a first-name basis."

My words cause Nick to flush.

"I'm sorry. That came off wrong. I didn't mean to scold you."

"No. You're right, Ma'am, uh, sorry, I mean, Angela. It is dangerous. 'Angela' is out, 'Kay Smith,' too, now that Jager is aware of that alias. He may be onto me, too. So, what would you prefer I call you?"

We take a minute to consider a slew of new names. I settle on an easy one to remember, Mary Brown, the name I used for cover when talking with the police. Nick takes on the same surname, so we can pose as a married couple.

"All right," Nick says, extending his hand. "Hello, Mary Brown. Allow me to introduce myself. I'm Nick Brown, your husband. It's nice to meet you."

I giggle at the serious expression on Nick's face. "Pleased to meet you, Mr. Brown." Taking his hand in mine, I feel a tingle of excitement, drawing me back to the memory of our first meeting after I woke from my coma, when our hands touched, making my blood run hot. Once again, doubts about my own marital fidelity resurface, questioning the appropriateness of my hidden feelings for the man. Was I jealous of Amy and her relationship with Nick?

Afraid Nick will see the anguish in my face, I pull away and excuse myself to the bathroom. I flush the toilet to hide my ruse, then splash my face with water from the tub faucet. When I've regained my composure, I emerge from the bathroom to find Nick standing by the door wearing his coat and holding out mine.

"All right, Mr. Brown, let's get out of here before my clothes are able to walk out the door all by themselves."

—

Thirty minutes later, after we'd satisfied our hunger with chicken sandwiches, fries, and bottled water, Nick and I walk into a crowded Walmart. He'd picked the Rockville, Maryland, superstore to minimize the risk we might run into someone from the D.C. area who might personally recognize either of us.

Hoping to avoid stares of my bruised face, I stroll the aisle with my head down, looking up only to peruse the racks and shelves. With Nick's help, I select two pairs of jeans, four shirts, a sweater, a warm winter jacket, a hat and pair of gloves, and a small duffel bag to carry it all. I protest at what I consider excess, especially in light of our limited funds, but Nick insists he has more than enough cash to carry us over until our dire situation can be resolved.

Ever the gentleman, Nick hangs back as I push the shopping cart through the ladies' lingerie department. Walking among the lacy bras, skimpy panties, and pretty nightgowns, my lustful feelings for Nick bubble up again. Flushed with shame, I grab a six-pack of panties, a set of flannel pajamas, and a practical bra, then rush to the changing room before Nick can see the embarrassment in my face. Inside the dressing room, the blue-checked pajamas covering me from neck to ankle make me feel anything but sexy, squashing my libido like a cold shower. Mission accomplished.

With my clothing needs complete, Nick and I make a pass through the Health and Beauty aisles.

"Let's go with dark brown," Nick says, handing me a box of hair dye. "We need you to look as little like you as possible."

I nod, take the box from Nick, and toss it in the cart. After selecting his-and-her toiletries and basic cosmetics for me, we swing by the men's clothing department, then finish up in the jewelry department, where Nick and I select his and her rings that could pass for wedding bands. Something about the simple gold ring on my finger doesn't feel right. And it reminds me that my own rings are missing.

"By the way, Nick," I whisper into his ear. "What did you do with my rings?"

Nick is taken aback, a look of surprise on his face. "You remember your engagement and wedding rings?"

"No. But I'm a rich woman, married to a powerful man. I'm sure he'd never let me sit for an interview with a major magazine, such as *People*, without wearing my rings. They're big gaudy things, aren't they? Bet my necklaces and earrings are, too."

Nick glances around, then whispers back. "You're right about the rings. Ostentatious is a better descriptor, I think, than gaudy, but they are especially distinctive. A dead giveaway to your identity. I slipped them off your finger before I pulled up to the ER. Took your earrings and necklace, too. Everything is tucked away in my safe deposit box."

"You don't miss anything, do you?"

"With my job, I can't afford to." Nick offers a slim smile, but underneath, I know he's deadly serious.

On our way to the check-out area, Nick snatches a bag of Starbucks coffee from an endcap display and tosses it into the cart. Five minutes later, with our purchases paid for and our bags in tow, Nick and I slog through the slushy parking lot to the car. With my new navy parka on and Nick by my side, I feel warm and secure for the first time since waking from my coma. I just hope it will last.

CHAPTER 53

The car is quiet as we drive back to the motel. I stare out the window, watching a light dusting of snow pass through the beams of the streetlights, giving my mind a rest from the stresses of trying to remember.

Nick's voice breaks the silence, startling me. "You're doing it again."

"What?" I turn to look at him.

"Fiddling with your ring."

When I look down at my hands, I discover he's right, then self-consciously jerk my hands apart. My new ring is cockeyed halfway up to my first knuckle. I yank it back in place, then look at Nick. "I, uh, I wasn't aware . . ."

He flashes a gentle smile. "No reason you should be. Most people aren't conscious of their nervous habits. I noticed it a while back. You started tugging on your rings a week or so before the election."

A nervous habit. Directed by my subconscious. I don't need a psychiatrist to interpret my behavior. My sister's disappearance had caused me to struggle further with my marriage to William. A guilty conscious at play?

—

The rest of the evening passes without another distressing incident or heart-wrenching thought. With my hair dyed and wrapped in a towel, I crawl into bed to watch TV. Nick, parked on the couch, flips through the limited cable channels for something benign to entertain us. Bypassing crime shows, newscasts, family dramas, and reality shows leaves few options. He finally settles on *Field of Dreams,* promising me it will be an uplifting movie about an Iowa farmer inspired to build a baseball field in the middle of his corn crop by a mysterious voice in his head.

About ten minutes into the film, I recognize the plot and the characters. "Good pick on the movie. It's non-threatening enough for me to remember it, although I can't recall when I saw it, or who may have watched it with me."

Nick offers a sheepish grin. "It was last summer with Amy and me. We were babysitting the girls while you were at a campaign event. After we put them to bed, we scrolled through the movies. Amy had never seen "Field of Dreams"—one of my favorites—so she wanted to watch it. You walked in a few minutes later and joined us. You both seemed to enjoy the film."

The specifics of that evening elude me, but I know he's right. Still, I find it hard to concentrate on the story. Every little sound outside— beeping horns, slamming doors, yelling voices—has me on edge. Nick, on the other hand, seems perfectly calm. I spot him peeking out the window several times, but he never once appears alarmed. I settle in to enjoy the film, hoping something about it will jog my memory of that night with my sister.

During the movie's last scene, when Kevin Costner's character finally realizes the beckoning voice in his head had been his long-dead father all along, I wonder if it's truly possible for our loved ones to communicate with us from beyond the grave, to guide us in seeking truth and redemption. I am a realist. I know that much, but nonetheless, in my mind, I give it a shot.

Amy, if you can hear me, please help me. Help me remember. Help Nick and me bring those responsible for your death to justice before it's too late.

When the film credits finally roll, I yawn and glimpse the time on the clock: 10:58. "I'm beat, ready to call it a night. You can stay up, though. The light won't bother me."

I stare at the door. "Do you really think we're safe here?"

Nick rises from the couch, walks over to the door, and checks the lock. "Yes. We should be fine," he says, peering out the window. "Jager would have to be psychic to know where we're hiding. Even if he found the Charger and knows what we're driving now, he can't know what direction we headed, or how many miles we put on the odometer. Moments after I arrived at that hospital, I disabled my own phone. I've been using a burner phone, too, so no one could track you through me."

Nick's voice, strong and resolute, leaves me confident of his safety assessment. "Good. Hopefully, that will allow both of us get some much-needed sleep."

Minutes later, I'm washed up and tucked into bed. I glance at Nick. Stretched out on the couch, using his laptop for a light source, he appears engrossed in the thick wad of paper on the keyboard—Amy's FBI case file, presumably. Clearly, he isn't planning on turning in any time soon. I'm sure the military hero and security specialist in the man will keep him up most of the night, looking for danger and formulating a plan to bring us safely out of this perilous mess.

"Good-night, Nick." I smile. "Please, try to get some sleep. If we're to figure this all out before Felix has another chance to kill us, we'll both need our rest."

He turns his face toward me and flashes a gentle grin. "I will. Promise."

I flip off the bedside lamp. In the dark, the light from Nick's laptop illuminates his face. Silently watching him, I take the time to consider everything that happened to me since I'd fled my life. Through it all, I've never been alone. Nick was always there, at the ready, doing his best to keep my spirits up, my fears and tears at bay, my body nourished and safe. He's a good man, unlike my own husband, whom I neither like, love, nor trust.

"For the record, Nick, I think you would have made a great brother-in-law," I say, turning away to hide the sorrow in my face.

"Thank you. That means a lot to me." I hear a note of sadness in his voice. "And for the record, I would've adored having you as my sister-in-law. Now get some rest. Sweet dreams."

I drift off to sleep without another thought.

CHAPTER 54

Aloud noise startles me awake. I train my ears and listen, but the only sound I hear is a low gurgle by the window. On the nightstand, the clock glows the time: 1:31. Across the room, Nick lies against the back of the couch, the light from his laptop still illuminating his face. His eyes closed, his mouth agape. The computer screen hasn't yet gone to sleep, but Nick has, and he's snoring.

I crawl out of bed, tiptoe over to the window and peek out, but see nothing that would account for the racket that woke me. At that moment, Nick lets out a roaring *snork*. He rolls onto his side, causing his laptop and papers to tumble to the floor. Relieved to have discovered a benign source for my sleep disturbance, I pick up Nick's computer and tuck the papers underneath. A quick glance at the open computer screen shows what Nick had been so engrossed in earlier—Amy's Missing Person's Report. My desperate need for information gets the better of me. I sit on the edge of the bed, perch the computer on my lap, and read.

The Virginia State Police document, filed by me on October twenty-third, contains the basics about my sister: name, age, physical characteristics. The last two people to see Amy before she left the hotel, the doorman and the night manager, provide other descriptive details:

Clothing: turquoise blouse, black slacks, black heels, camel-colored trench coat, gold necklace and earrings, watch

Rental car: gold 2015 Toyota Camry - North Carolina license plate PNJ-7891

Luggage: a black leather handbag; a soft-sided, burgundy computer case; matching suitcase

The file includes a summary of the events surrounding my sister's disappearance:

On October 23, 2016, at 9:10 p.m., Amelia Bulloch and four other members of the Lockhart campaign (Angela Lockhart and her husband, Governor William Lockhart; Lockhart Chief of Staff Andrew Novak; Press Secretary Valerie Gibson) met with two FBI Special Agents from the Richmond office, Carl Nimms and Herman Montoya, in the Lockharts' penthouse suite at the Hilton Raleigh Midtown.

With those few words, the scene appears in my mind.

I'm staring at two dark-suited men standing in front of me. They flash badges at our group. Their somber faces tell me they have bad news. The taller of the two, a stout, balding Black man, confirms my fear. Maddy's remains have been found and identified, her death classified as a homicide. No suspects. Suddenly chilled, I cross my arms then scan the room. People are talking, but I can't hear a word over the echo of my heart pulsing furiously inside my head.

It's your fault. My memory of the scene, and the pain that accompanies those three little words, deepens. A tear rolls down my cheek. I know more will come. When I stand to fetch a tissue, Nick's laptop and papers tumble off the bed. I set the computer back on the bed, gather up the papers, and carry the stack with me, feeling my way through the darkness toward the desk, where I'd last seen the tissue box.

I stumble into the wall with a loud thud. That Nick slept through the noisy impact rattles me briefly, but I let it go. He had promised me we were safe hidden away in this seedy motel, and I believe him. I trust him with my life.

I find the tissues without further mishap and let my tears fall behind the closed door of the bathroom. While I sit on the toilet, dabbing at my wet eyes and wiping my runny nose, my gaze is drawn to the stack of papers on my lap—the hard copy of Amy's FBI case file. The top page is covered with dozens of notations on various aspects of Amy's case, some of which are decipherable, others not so much.

Reading on, I learn that the authorities had pieced together Amy's itinerary on the drive home from the litter inside her car (including a McDonald's receipt for coffee), GPS coordinates from the cell phone towers she passed along the way, and her cell phone records. There's one piece of information Nick considered critically important, judging by the three hastily scrawled asterisks next to it. At 1:19 a.m. on the night that Amy disappeared, she took a seven-second call from an unregistered, prepaid cell phone with a 703-area code. The authorities determined that the call came in when Amy was two miles south of the I-95 rest area where her rental car was later found.

The questions Nick recorded on the page mirrors my own: *Who called Amy so late? Why did she stop at the rest area? Did she meet someone there? If so, who and why?*

My hands tremble while my mind grapples with a fuzzy vision. I close my eyes, relax, and let it come into focus.

I'm a passenger seated inside the darkened cab of a pickup truck, illuminated only by the lights of its digital dashboard. Though the vents are pouring out heat, I'm chilled to the bone. My body is stiff, my muscles sore from trying to hold myself together. Struggling emotionally, in the grip of overwhelming sadness, everything is silent. I feel so alone.

A deep male voice bursts from the truck's speakers. The words, initially garbled, slowly sharpen, until at last, my heart seems cut to pieces.

"Earlier this evening the Virginia State Police released the name of a young woman whose remains were found last week by a Boy Scout troop hiking through a wooded area an hour west of Charlottesville. Ruled as a homicide, the victim was identified earlier today as twenty-two-year-old Madeline O'Brien . . ."

My chest tightens as the cab fills with smoke and the stench of tobacco saturates the air. I hold my breath as a cough threatens to erupt, then turn toward the source of smoke. The glow at the end of a thick cigar casts the driver's face in shadows. When he returns his focus to the road, the dashboard lights illuminate his face. It's Felix Jager.

I stare at the man sitting beside me, watching as the smoke swirls around his thick bald head. Even in profile, his expression is a blank. There's no emotion there. Nothing in his expression to suggest he is moved one way or the other by news of a young woman's death. Then, for no apparent reason, he turns toward me, and with a leer in his eyes, he offers a tight, thin smile. The sight is unnerving. My chest constricts, my body trembles. I gasp for air.

The vision quickly fades from my mind. After my breathing eases, I try to come to grips with what I've seen, what I've heard, but I can't. I tear through Nick's notes looking for some clue to explain my memory, but the timeline I find for the night of Amy's disappearance offers nothing. I'd reportedly gone to bed at 11:00 p.m., a full half hour before Amy left. The implications confound me. Unless I'd lied to the police, my latest vision isn't a personal memory from the night my sister went missing.

I train my thoughts and search for a rational explanation of what I'd experienced. Is it possible I snuck out of the hotel and followed Amy, that it was me on the phone with her, convincing her to pull over?

If so, why? Did she have more than suspicions about Maddy's death, perhaps some evidence, that implicated William—or me?

I consider the logistics of the scenario and realize I couldn't have pulled that off by myself, not without an accomplice helping me evade my Secret Service detail, someone with a car or who had the skills to steal one. Or did I borrow a vehicle, like the day I took off in my assistant's Jeep?

Suddenly, a more sinister thought intrudes on me, one that explains my disturbing vision the night Amy disappeared. I hitched a ride with Felix, a last-ditch attempt to catch up with my sister and stop her, one way or the other, from going to the authorities with her incriminating evidence. Once again, I can't see myself hurting my own sister, not intentionally, at least. I run through the explanations to explain my vision, at least one I can live with. Nothing comes close to making any sense until I consider one seemingly impossible possibility. That the person inside the truck with Felix was not me, but Amy.

CHAPTER 55

*I*t's a crazy idea. I know that. Still, I can't get the notion out of my head, that somehow, I'd seen and heard a memory from the last night of Amy's life. I try to shrug the fantasy off on the movie Nick and I watched earlier. Admittedly, *Field of Dreams* has me wondering if the dead can guide us from beyond the grave, but the fact that I hedged my bets with an entreaty to Amy doesn't make it true.

What I just experienced begs questions I can't answer. Is my vision proof that I lied to the police and was not tucked into my bed the night of my sister's disappearance? Or is it a product of wishful thinking and an overactive imagination, a PTSD-induced hallucination? Possibly, a real, bona fide message from the beyond—Amy answering my appeal for help in solving her murder?

I sit there, holed up in the bathroom with my thoughts, and decide my imagination is once again getting the better of me. Even so, I can't deny that my heart yearns for a spiritual explanation. I want the vision to be real. I want to believe my sister is near me, watching over me. I want to believe that life is more than just what we live here on Earth, that our love for one another never dies, even when the memory of our deep bond is dim. I want to believe that nothing, not even death, can keep my sister and me apart.

Amy, if you are there, please help me. I want to remember what happened to you, how I hurt you. I want to do whatever I can to make things right for you, for Maddy. Help me. Please.

—

To my amazement, I sleep through the rest of the night without tossing, turning, or otherwise terrorized by my own subconscious. The room is pitch dark when I awake, so I can't see Nick, but I can hear him nearby, softly snoring. I'm glad. Even the bravest knight must rest to be fit for the next day's battle.

I let him be, then fumble my way through the darkness, finding the shopping bags and the bathroom door without walking into another wall. After a long, hot shower, I emerge from the steamy bathroom, clean and dressed in a blue-checked flannel blouse, jeans, and a pair of brown leather, fur-lined boots. Nick is awake and pouring coffee. Standing in front of me with a bad case of bedhead, wearing a thick shadow of beard and his wrinkled, day-old set of clothes, I can't help thinking that he looks adorable. Tired of battling my attraction to the man, I let the thought slide.

"Good morning. Sleep well?" Nick hands me a steaming cup of coffee.

The pleasing aroma that rises from my mug is welcome. I take a cautious sip of the dark liquid and enjoy the rich flavor and consider my answer.

"Surprisingly, yes. You fell asleep working. Your computer and papers slipped off your lap and the noise woke me up. When I picked them up off the floor, the computer screen lit up. I hope you don't mind, but I looked over Amy's Missing Persons' Report and your notes."

What I don't admit is my vision of riding in a truck the night of Amy's disappearance with Felix at the wheel, my fantasy that Amy is attempting to communicate with me, and my worry that she isn't, that it was me that me and Felix who met up with Amy in that parking lot the night she went missing.

"No problem," Nick replies, retrieving his small, black overnight bag from the top of the dresser. "If you're done with the bathroom, I need to get in there. I'll just be a couple minutes, then we can discuss the report. Afterward, we've got to hit the road. We both overslept. It's almost nine o'clock."

While Nick is in the bathroom, I blow-dry my hair, then apply a light coat of mascara, then dab concealer on my bruises, blush on my cheeks, and gloss on my lips. Looking at my reflection in the mirror, I don't recognize myself from the pictures I saw on Nick's phone or online. Though my bruises are hardly noticeable, my nose is still swollen. But dying my hair dark has made all the difference. Felix Jager will never recognize me. Neither will anyone else.

A couple minutes later, Nick and I are seated at the desk discussing Amy's FBI report and Nick's notes. The big questions surround the mysterious phone call just past 1:00 a.m., minutes before Amy pulled into the rest area parking lot on I-95. Who was on the other end of that call, and why couldn't the FBI trace the device? The lone security video, focused on the vending machine area outside the restroom, never caught Amy's image, confirming that she never used the women's bathroom, nor bought a drink or snack. So, what was she doing at there?

"Do you think Amy stopped at the rest area and met up with whoever called her?" I ask, worried that caller was me.

"That would be my guess, but whoever was on the other end of the line had to be someone she trusted. I can't see her parking at a deserted rest stop to meet a stranger or someone she didn't know well." His words pierce my soul like a dagger in my chest.

The confusion I see in Nick's face melts into grief. "I don't know if I'll ever be able to forgive myself for not driving home with Amy. I wanted to. We argued about it, but she wouldn't let me come along. I don't know why she shut me out. I know she was hurting over the news of Maddy's death."

I can't let Nick take the blame.

"You didn't kill Amy. We both suspect Jager did on orders from someone connected to the campaign. In my book, William and his chief of staff are our best suspects."

"Whoever is behind this, I believe we're getting closer to some answers thanks to your emerging memory."

I flush with guilt. What would Nick do if he knew how much I've held back? My mind knows. It saw him walking away, out of my life. But would he abandon me before we can nail a cold-blooded murderer and the person who set him after me? My heart sinks considering another reason for Nick to forsake me—he finally figures out that I am the one who must be held to account for Maddy and Amy's murders.

"Listen, Ma'am, uh, Mary—I need to get used to that name for the time being. We need to get moving. First thing is to dump this car. I thought we'd go to Dan's place and borrow his SUV while he's out of the country on assignment. We can leave this junker in his garage. Again, we'll need to avoid the main roads and traffic cameras, so it will take a while. With the usual traffic, about an hour and a half. We'll talk about next steps during the ride."

CHAPTER 56

By the time we leave Morey's Motel behind us it's 9:25. Outside, the morning is cold and foggy, a gloomy day if ever there was one. I feel the same way. Everything I've learned in the last twenty-four hours has done little to clear the clouds from my mind, warm my heart, or lift my spirits. I don't see much hope on the horizon. When and if I do recover my memory, at best I'll find myself married to an unfaithful husband who likely played a pivotal role in the death of a young woman, her unborn baby, and my sister. The same man who, I'm certain, wouldn't shed an honest tear if I were out of his life for good. At worst, I'll learn I played an active role in the these murders due to mindless jealousy or a misplaced sense of duty to my husband's aspirations.

When we pull up to a stoplight, the sun peeks out from behind a low curtain of clouds, illuminating the tiny passenger in the back seat of the gray sedan in the lane to my right. The little sunny-headed girl waves her tiny fingers at me and flashes me a grin. I return the gesture and smile. No more than four or five years old, she reminds me that there are two bright spots in my life—my daughters. I close my eyes and picture Olivia and Sophia in my mind, imagine holding them in my arms, breathing in their sweet little-girl scents. I see myself clinging to them, fiercely, using every ounce of my strength to keep the three of us from ever being separated again. From the sadness plaguing my soul, that option may already be closed.

When the car makes a turn and pulls to a stop, I open my eyes. We're parked in front of a convenience store. Nick's going inside, he says, to buy breakfast. He returns with two cups of coffee and breakfast sandwiches.

Back on the road and finished with our food, Nick opens a discussion about our next move. We agree that everything hinges on recovering my memory. Paramount are any recollections of the closed-door meeting with William, when he told me my sister was dead. Our conversation goes downhill when Nick suggests we pay Mimi a visit.

"Mimi is more than a household servant. She raised and loved you and Amy when your own parents couldn't be bothered. She knows you better than anyone else on this planet. She loves you like a daughter. You love her like a mother. She could be the catalyst that jump-starts your memory."

"No. No way, Nick," I reply, trying my best to appear cool and in control. Inside, I'm quaking in terror at the idea. "Felix Jager will kill anyone to find me. We know that. He's already killed two people in his effort to track me down. The man is no dummy. Now that he knows I'm not alone, he'll stake out anyone and everyone who might help me regain my full memory. Mimi has got to be at the top of his list. Outside of William and my daughters, she's the only family I have left."

I grimace at the thought of Mimi becoming Felix's next victim. "Showing up at Bulloch Hall would be a fool's errand. Mimi, you, me, we'd all be sitting targets for Felix Jager. I won't risk her life or yours on the slim chance that I'd get my memory back."

"You're right." Nick nods. "It is too dangerous. We'll have to find another way to get the answers we need."

Neither of us utters a word during the rest of the drive. The break from the constant discussion of our plight is a welcome relief. I pass my time staring out the window, looking at the trees, the houses, the occasional gas station, or neighborhood store.

After we pass an elementary school with dozens of kids laughing and playing games on the playground, I hear a sniffle. The sorrow I saw on Nick's face tears at my heart.

"Amy wanted a houseful of kids," he says, his voice a bit shaky. "I told her the bigger the better. She never said why a large family was that important. I think it was growing up so isolated, homeschooled with no close friends your age. But now that . . . well, Amy would've made a great mom. I could see it when she was around your girls. She couldn't have loved your daughters more if they were her own. Olivia and Sophia adored their Aunt Amy, too."

The pain on Nick's face fills my heart with regret. Somehow, I feel Amy close by, sense this is what she's feeling, too. "I'm so sorry, Nick." I am. Amy's death will leave a hole in all our hearts.

"Enough of this pity party." Nick sighs and turns to me. "Let's listen to some music. Something upbeat. Amy enjoyed a variety of music genres. Soft rock was among her favorites, especially if the band had orchestra backup. I guess that shouldn't be too surprising. You two were brought up playing piano and strings. If that's okay with you, I'll see what I can find."

"Sounds good."

Nick scans the stations and settles on FM 102.3. The songs become familiar quickly, allowing me to silently sing along. When the next song pours out of the speakers, a baroque rock piece opening with violins, violas, cellos, my musical acumen bubbles up from deep inside me. *Four/four time. A-Flat major.* I hum along, fingering the staccato notes with my left hand—quarters, half notes—C, D-flat, B-flat—drawing each note with an invisible bow. The song is familiar, yet I can't put a title or lyrics to the tune. Before the words can kick in, the song is interrupted by a traffic update.

Though the song is over, the tune is stuck in my head. The notes, playing over and over, taunt me to remember the lyrics, the title. The earworm disappears when I hear Amy's name echo from the car's speakers.

"—of Amelia Bulloch. The medical examiner's office released her remains yesterday for transport to the Bulloch family's estate in Lynchburg, Virginia. Ms. Bulloch and her sister, Angela Lockhart, wife of President-elect William Lockhart, were raised there in a stately mansion by their parents, the former U.S. Senator from Virginia, James Madison Bulloch, and his wife, Adelaide, both of whom were killed in the crash of their private jet into the Atlantic Ocean more than ten years ago.

"Unconfirmed reports from the president-elect's staff have him traveling to the Bulloch estate in the next few days to formally lay to rest the remains of his sister-in-law in the family mausoleum. We've been told Mrs. Lockhart, the last surviving member of her family, is taking the death of her sister particularly hard. President-elect Lockhart is hopeful his wife will find the strength to come out of isolation and attend the interment."

"Did you hear that, Nick?" The words burst from my mouth. "William is going to inter my sister without me, and he's trying to convince everyone I'm a basket case, holed up somewhere overcome with grief. I can't let that happen. We've got to solve this mess before they inter Amy and make a mockery of her death." I keep mum on what bothers me most, that I need to unburden myself, tell Amy, her remains, at least, that I'm sorry and beg her forgiveness.

"Hold on there, just a moment," Nick interjects. "Don't you think this is a bit too convenient, maybe happening just a little too fast?"

"What? You think this is some kind of setup?"

"It's possible. You've given Felix the proverbial slip more than once now, surviving not one, but two attempts on your life. Whoever this guy is working for, whether it's your husband, Novak, or someone else pulling the strings, he wants you dead yesterday. This may be a trap to draw you out, reveal yourself enough for Jager to finish the job he screwed up."

I sink into my seat, frowning. For the first time, I consider that I may never be safe.

"I don't like this any better than you do, and Amy . . ." He pauses for moment, then continues, his voice cracking with obvious sorrow. "Well, she deserves a hell of lot better than to be used as bait by a vicious killer."

I reach out, touch his arm, and offer a compassionate caress. "I agree."

"Once we get these cars traded out," Nick says, now with an unwavering note of purpose in his voice. "We'll work on a plan. We'll be there for Amy. I promise." With Nick's vow, silence falls between us once again.

After several miles, Nick says, "It won't be long now. We're a few blocks away. Before we pull into Dan's driveway, we need to surveil the area a bit, make sure that Jager, or one of his goons, isn't lying in wait for us somewhere nearby."

He instructs me to watch everyone on my side of the street, people strolling along the sidewalk, waiting for the bus, sitting in windows, in cars or vans. As I do, I'm drawn to what I see. The old section of town where Nick's friend grew up is filled with tree-lined streets, tall, narrow brick homes, and the occasional business. The few people on the sidewalks appear happy, friendly. It's an inviting picture of a slower, quieter, more quaint way of life—a life I never had and never will.

Five minutes later, neither Nick nor I have spotted anyone suspicious, so he navigates the car to an alleyway, then pulls to a stop in front of a red-brick, one-car garage.

"I'll just be a minute. I need to get inside and fetch Dan's car keys. We're blocking the alley by parking here. Stay with the car and move it if someone needs to get by. Just circle the block and park here again."

I can feel the blood draining from my face.

"Don't worry. You'll be safe," Nick says with a smile, as he lays a reassuring hand on my knee, then withdraws quickly, clearly embarrassed by the familiarity this suggests. "I'm sorry, Ma'am."

I wave off his apology as I feel my face flush.

Nick clears his throat. "If you feel threatened at all, honk the horn, and I'll come running."

I nod. Without another word, he buttons up his coat, then hops out of the car. A minute later, he waves at me with a key, then disappears inside the garage.

While I wait for Nick to return, I focus my attention on the radio, scanning the channels for some soothing music. I pause the scanner when a breaking news story catches my attention.

"—triple murder out of Culpeper, VA. As reported earlier, the bodies of three people, two men and one woman, were found late last night locked inside a building housing a small ambulance service—"

Culpeper. Ambulance Service. I brace for more bad news.

"The victims have been identified as Harmon Fischer, 53, the company owner; his office assistant, Marilyn Dennis, 42; and, an ambulance driver, Enrique Sanchez, 31, a former Marine who'd been with the company less than three months.

"The Culpeper County Sheriff's Department won't release details of the scene. A source close to the investigation revealed that all three victims were naked and appeared to show evidence of torture. Preliminary examinations of the bodies suggest the victims were killed yesterday sometime between 10:00 a.m. and 1:00 p.m. The bizarre nature of the murders prompted the Sheriff's Department to bring in the VSP—"

The frantic heartbeat drumming inside my ears drowns out the reporter's words. Gasping, I struggle to draw in air. Three more people have died in my wake. My mind becomes muddled. Close to panic, I know I must focus on my breathing. *Inhale . . . exhale . . . inhale . . . exhale.*

When the drumbeat fades from my ears, I open my eyes. At that moment, everything is clear. I know what I must do to end the madness.

Without another thought, I slide behind the steering wheel, shift the car into gear, and drive off to face down my past and the demons that come with it. Alone.

CHAPTER 57

I had only a germ of a plan in mind when I took off. Nick had said, time and again, that remembering what happened to me just before I fled my life is the key to figuring out who is behind these murders and the attempts on my life and why. But nothing I've seen, heard, or have done in the last two days has shaken loose those traumatic memories. I can't see any other way to end all the killing than to confront William. If our marriage is anywhere like what I suspect, I'm betting my bully of a husband will reveal his true colors once I accuse him of murder. If he implicates me as a coconspirator or accessory, at least I'll finally know, and no one else has to die in my stead.

It's a dangerous move. For my plan to work, I will have to rely on the familiar surroundings of my childhood home to jar my memory. In my mind, however, the risks to my personal safety—and the safety of others at the estate—are outweighed by the certainty that the body count will continue to rise in my wake if I don't come out of hiding.

I have no clue what roads to take to Lynchburg, so I pull over into a crowded mall lot and begin downloading a free GPS navigation app onto my cell phone. Quickly, I realize it's a careless move. Nick loaded my first phone with spy software. It's likely he did the same with this one. I fumble to dislodge the phone's battery from its slot, tuck both parts inside my coat pocket, then set about searching the car for a road map of Virginia.

By a rare stroke of luck, I discover a portable GPS in the glove compartment. When I punch the ON button the screen comes to life with a request for the address of my destination. I balk. I have no memory of an address or a nearby landmark to guide me to Bulloch Hall. Without a cell phone and an Internet connection, my hometown will have to suffice for now.

With a flick of a button, I choose a route that takes me on a series of rural highways, a better bet for staying under the radar and the cameras perched along the Interstate. My promised arrival in my hometown is late afternoon, just after four o'clock. The timing means I'll have enough winter daylight to get my bearings and map out a stealth approach to Bulloch Hall.

The drive is slow and uneventful. I distract myself from my trip's purpose by listening to a classical music station, following along with the familiar pieces.

When I finally approach Lynchburg from the northeast via Highway 29, the sun is hanging low in the western sky. The hilly, heavily wooded terrain looks familiar, but not enough to jolt my mind into remembering the route home. An exit sign for Madison Heights solves my problem. Without hesitation or question, I pull off the highway, turn left at the stop sign at the bottom of the ramp, and drive a quarter mile, then take another left onto a narrow tree-lined lane.

The country road winds me through a forest of pines and hardwoods. When I spot a snow-topped, whitewashed wooden fence running along the right side of the road, my heart starts racing and my hands start shaking.

Bulloch Hall.

I press down the accelerator. The wheels spin for a moment before the car lurches forward.

"What am I doing?" I shout to myself, slamming on the brakes, spinning the car ninety degrees on the snowy road.

It doesn't take too much thought to answer my own question. I'm letting my emotions call the shots once again. Eager as I am to race down the road, run into the house, and scream for answers, it's the wrong move. Just driving past the gated entrance will expose me, jeopardize me and my goal. I'd be detained by William's security detail, *his* bodyguards, not mine. Nick hadn't been sure who he could trust in the White House. He even seemed circumspect about his own Secret Service colleagues. He'd been right so far, and I'm still alive to prove it. I can't second-guess his instincts now. Or mine.

Staring ahead at the thick forest, I decide to scope out the situation via a different tack—making my way to Bulloch Hall on foot, using the trees to hide my approach. I return to the main road and hang a left. The snowy pavement ends a quarter mile farther down the road at the river, next to a small, rickety house that looks ready to collapse. With no sign of recent activity, I park the car around back, bundle up, and follow the river north on foot.

—

The freezing temperatures, deep snow, and waning sunset slow me down. Twenty minutes into arduous trek, when my face is numb with cold and my leg muscles sore from the strain of wading through the thick, thigh-high snow, I finally spot a building on my family's property.

I recognize the small, white-pillared building and its colorful stained-glass windows—the Bulloch family mausoleum.

I duck low, scurry from tree to tree, then nestle myself next to a thick row of evergreen bushes a few yards from the structure. I peek through a thin gap in the thick foliage. Overhead, the trees' heavy canopy blocks what's left of the waning sunlight, making it difficult to gauge the freshness of the tire tracks in front of the mausoleum's wide oak door. Their existence proves one thing, though—my sister's body has arrived. William and his entourage can't be far behind.

I close my eyes. *Amy, if you're here by my side, please help me. Help me remember. Keep me safe.*

This feels right, although I have no idea whether Amy would want me safe and sound or lying dead in the snow with a bullet in my head. I shake off the gruesome thought, open my eyes and survey the area. A black SUV parked near the garage is the only sign of activity, otherwise the property is bereft of people. What's going on? This place should be crawling with Secret Service.

The rear of the main house, a white-columned, three-story monster, rises before me shielded by a long hedgerow, the backdrop to my mother's formal gardens. At the corner of the house shines a lone light. Someone is in the kitchen, otherwise, the estate seems deserted.

Staying low and using the tree trunks to hide my approach, I make my way to the back side of the carriage house, then slink around the far corner for a better look around the grounds. The snow on the driveway is packed down, clear evidence of recent traffic, but there are no vehicles of any kind in sight. If William's Secret Service detail is here, they're doing a pretty good job of hiding their presence.

I focus my attention on the house, looking for any sign of activity. Suddenly, a shadow passes by the lit kitchen window. With darkness falling all around, I decide to investigate further while the house and grounds appear unguarded. I scamper across the open expanse and duck beneath the glowing window. After taking a few moments to muster up my courage, I raise my head just high enough to peek into the window, only to come face-to-face with a dark pair of eyes staring back at me.

CHAPTER 58

I instantly recognize the face that belongs to those eyes, but from Mimi's shocked look, I can't be sure if she recognized me or thought me a prowler. I drop to the ground, uncertain of my next move. Inside my chest, my heart is beating a fast retreat, while my legs seem frozen in place. Then I hear a soft voice.

"Miss Angela, is that you?"

I glance around the corner of the house to see Mimi standing on the kitchen step with the outdoor light above shining upon her. Pale-skinned with close-cropped graying hair and dressed in a dark skirt and sweater, she appears shorter and frailer than I remember her. I scramble from my hiding place and rush over to meet her.

"Shhh. Not so loud. Please, Mimi, I don't want anyone to know I'm here. Can you turn off the floodlight, please?"

Mimi's hand disappears inside the house, and quickly, the light goes dark. The next moment, I'm wrapped in her arms, a hug so fierce I think she'll never let go. Not that I want her to.

"Good Lord, Miss Angela, you're freezin' cold," she whispers. "Get in here where it's warm, and I'll get you a hot cup of coffee. What are you doin' here all by yourself? From what I hear on the TV, you're supposed to be somewhere else workin' through your grief."

Mimi's words, her accent, pull me back to Summer Oaks and Jimmy's familiar Southern drawl. The recollection offers me a twinge of conviction, that all along, home was where I needed to be to recover my memory. That Nick presented the idea earlier didn't make me wrong for rejecting it, I realize now. I just needed to do it my way.

"Is that a bruise 'cross your nose?" Her voice rises in alarm. "Are you hurt?"

"Please, Mimi, hold your voice down." I whisper back. "I'm fine. I had a little fender-bender. The rest is a long story, but I can't go into it now. Are you alone? Is my husband and his security detail here yet? It's important that no one know I'm here."

"There's just me back here," she murmurs. "There's a coupla of Mr. William's security staff up front in the library, one at the gatehouse. There might be a few more around here somewhere. I don't keep track of their comin's and goin's."

Mimi draws me inside, shuts the door, then grips my hands. "Miss Amy came home about an hour ago. She's in the mausoleum inside a fine, mahogany casket." Her eyes start to water. She strains to speak. "I . . . I'm so sorry for your loss, Miss Angela. My heart is broken. I feel like I've lost my own daughter." The grief in the old woman's eyes and the desperation in her voice are sincere. I feel it in my heart.

After a lingering embrace, I brush the snow from my coat and jeans onto the floor mat. A good bit of the wintry stuff has already melted through my pants, leaving my legs cold and wet.

"I heard a news report on the radio that William was on his way to inter my sister. Was that report wrong?" I ask, with a note of disbelief in my voice.

"No, Ma'am. He's coming, but no one's told me when to expect him. Could be tomorrow, maybe the next day."

My bet is tomorrow. If this is all a trap, neither William nor his rat-faced chief of staff could count on the news of Amy's interment reaching my ears so quickly. Even so, I would expect them to dispatch Felix here as soon as possible, so as to lie in wait for me, grabbing me before I could show myself.

"So, where is the rest of William's security detail? There should be at least a dozen more here."

Shaking her head, frowning, Mimi is clearly not happy with the situation. "I had three big, black SUVs full of them here most of the afternoon, makin' a mess while I tried to get the house ready for guests. They were lookin' all over the place, inside and out, for who-knows-what reason. Like anyone would be lyin' low way out here in this freezin' weather waiting to take a crack at your husband. He's not even president, yet.

"Anyway, a coupla of them came back here about an hour ago, askin' about supper. I told them I didn't have anythin' in the kitchen to feed a crowd. When I suggested they go to Della Mae's in town for her happy-hour drink prices and thick steaks, they were more than eager to leave. They've been gone about thirty minutes. From those stories I keep readin' about Secret Service Agents partyin' like college boys, I expect they'll be gone a good long while. Now let's get you inside and warm you up."

I step away from the door and allow Mimi to help me off with my coat.

"Ed will be back soon," she says, hanging my coat on a hook by the door. "I sent him out a few minutes ago with a grocery list. I've got a pot of leftover stew on the stove. I'm taking a coupla bowls to the agents in the library when it's good and hot. There's enough for you if you care to join Ed and me for supper."

The savory aroma wafting through the kitchen is enticing. I consider Mimi's offer for a moment. The temptation passes after I pull off my gloves, wiggle my cold, stiff fingers, and realize my mind has become just as numb as my hands.

"I can't stay, not while there are Secret Service agents in the house." I flinch at the thought of Felix nearby, lying in wait for me, like a hunter stalking his prey. "Anyway, Mimi," I continue, "I just need to thaw a bit before heading back out. Do you have coffee? It doesn't have to be fresh, just hot."

"Coming right up."

I survey the kitchen while Mimi sets to work. The restaurant-grade kitchen is as I remember it. The high-end stainless-steel counters and appliances, the gleaming, white-tiled walls, blue-tiled floors, all give the room a cold, impersonal look. But with Mimi at the counter and the aroma of her cooking pulling at my memories, the kitchen warms my heart.

"It feels good to be home, Mimi. How is Ed these days? Aren't either of you looking to retire soon?" A memory of her husband, a small, thin man with a balding head and a wide toothy smile, pops into my head.

After pulling a pair of mugs out of the cupboard, Mimi sets them next to the coffeepot, then turns to face me. "He loves workin' here, tinkerin' with the cars, fixin' things around the house that need fixin', keepin' up the grounds. I love it, too. It's our home, even if it doesn't belong to us," she says, with a wistful look on her face.

The joy vanishes from her eyes in an instant, replaced with tears. "I'm happy to be of service to you and Mr. William whenever you need me, Miss Angela, but this time, I just wish it weren't on account of Miss Amy ..."

Averting her gaze, Mimi shuffles over to the Sub-Zero refrigerator and pulls open the door. She stands with her back to me, her shoulders sagging, staring into the fridge's interior, saying nothing. I'm at a loss as to how to comfort her. The few words spoken between us about Amy have only worsened her heartache.

I cross the kitchen, grab a towel from the counter, then pull up a seat at the small, white Formica table in the center of the room. After pulling off my woolen hat, I shake out my hair, then set to towel-drying my jeans.

"You still like your coffee with cream and one sugar, Miss Angela?" Mimi asks, still staring into the refrigerator.

"Yes. Thank you," I reply, happy to be resting my cold-weary muscles, though I know the respite will be brief. I can't stay in the house overnight with the Secret Service guarding it. My plan now must be making my way back to the car, finding a motel to spend the night, and getting back before daybreak to lie in wait for William's arrival.

"I hope someday you, Mr. Lockhart, and those sweet daughters of yours will move back here to Bulloch Hall," Mimi says, without looking my way. "I sure would love havin' your two pretty, little girls runnin' around. This place needs youngsters again."

I still haven't recalled much about my past, but I'm wary of raising my children in the shadow of what was clearly an unhappy home for my sister and me. Still, I don't want to dash Mimi's hopes. In the face of my sister's death, she needs something to look forward to as much as anyone.

"Well, we're obligated for the next four years to a nice house in the D.C. area," I say, in a lighthearted tone, though inside, I'm cringing. "Our lease could stretch to eight. In the meantime, I think it would be nice for the girls to visit the house where I grew up."

"That would be wonderful." When Mimi turns around, the smile on her face disappears. "What happened to your hair, Miss Angela? You always had the prettiest long blond hair all your life."

"I needed to change my appearance, Mimi. Like I said, I'm hiding. No one can know that I'm here. That's all I can say. It's better you don't know why."

A gruesome picture forms in my mind. *Felix and Mimi. His hands around her throat, squeezing. The fragile, old woman struggling for breath.*

"On second thought, I think I'd better leave. I'll take a rain check on the coffee." I quickly don my hat and gloves, then hustle over to my coat and pull it off the hook. "Pretend you never saw me. Hopefully, by tomorrow morning, I'll be able to explain everything. Just tell me one thing before I leave. What's this all about, Mimi? Why the rush to inter Amy without me by her side? Do you know?"

Standing alone, in the middle of the kitchen, Mimi offers a sad shrug. "The only thing I was told was to make the house ready for Mr. William's visit. Maybe he's tryin' to do right by Miss Amy. She shouldn't be lyin' out there, all alone, without a few prayers said over her soul by a minister of God."

"I agree. And again, it's critically important that no one knows I'm here. Nobody, especially William. Promise me you won't tell a soul, not even Ed."

"I promise. I've kept more secrets around this place in the last thirty-some years than you can shake a stick at."

Mimi insists on filling a travel thermos with coffee. I make a quick trip to the bathroom off the back hallway as she does. When I return, she hands me the container. After exchanging brief hugs and good-byes, I open the outside door and scan the area. There isn't a body in sight. When my gaze falls on the mausoleum, I turn back to Mimi.

"I'd like to visit Amy before I leave. Is the mausoleum locked?"

"Yes. Ed gave his set of keys to the head agent, a Mr. Riggs. I have a spare in the back. Let me get it."

When Mimi returns with the key, she's bundled up in a long, black woolen coat with a matching hat. "I'll let you in. That old lock can be as cranky as my Ed sometimes. Take whatever time you need. I'll come back out and lock up after you leave. I brought you a flashlight, too. It'll be awful dark in there unless you light some candles."

After surveying the grounds one more time, we set out for the mausoleum. When we reach the building, Mimi unlocks the door, pushes it open, and turns toward me.

"Miss Angela," she says, with a quiver in her voice, "I need to caution you. Don't go peekin' at Miss Amy. I did it earlier. I wish I hadn't. Now, every time I think about her, I see only what's left—nothin' but bones."

We exchange desperate, grief-fueled hugs. All too quickly, I pull back and wipe the tears from my face.

"You got your cell phone, Miss Angela? I'll keep an eye out and call you if I see anyone comin'."

I'm tempted by the idea but know that plugging the battery into my cell phone is a risky move for both me and Nick. "That won't be necessary, Mimi. I'll just stay a couple minutes. Anyway, you said it yourself, those Secret Service agents are unlikely to return any time soon. As for Ed, well, if he comes home and sees me, can I expect him to keep my secret, too?"

"You can count on him, Miss Angela. He's a man of few words. He could go days without openin' his mouth to talk if I didn't force him to speak to me once in a while. If you need anythin', call my cell phone."

"I will." Though I won't. Even if I could remember Mimi's number, I wouldn't call and risk someone overhearing our conversation, a situation that could cost both of us our lives.

—

Moments later, I'm alone inside the small, stone building with my flashlight's beam reflecting off the mahogany casket that cradles my sister. My chest tightens at the sight. I struggle to breathe, but the bitter cold air only makes it more difficult.

With a few tentative steps, I reach the coffin and switch off my flashlight, hoping the darkness might ease my pain. It doesn't. The blackness only serves to remind me that my sister's eyes will never again see the light of day. I tuck the flashlight in my coat pocket and set the coffee thermos on the floor, then lay my hands atop the casket, lower my head, and whisper.

"Amy, if you can somehow hear me, please know that I am sorry for everything that's happened. I'm determined to stop this insanity. I'll do my best to see that you and Maddy get the justice you deserve and the chance to rest in peace, even if that means taking my share of the blame and accepting the consequences. All I ask is that you watch over me until everything is resolved."

I wait, hoping for some sign that my sister has accepted my apology and my pledge—a flicker of spiritual light, an angelic word or two—but sense nothing that would suggest my plea has been heard.

"Good-bye, Amy. I know in my heart that I love you. I always will."

As I pick up my flashlight, the stained-glass windows on either side of the mausoleum door light up like a Christmas tree. In a panic to douse my beam, the flashlight tumbles from my hands, hits the floor, and goes dark.

Outside, I hear a car door slam, then another. The voices I hear grow louder with each beat of my racing heart. Desperate to hide but with few options, I scramble to conceal myself in the only place I can imagine where no one will look.

CHAPTER 59

I ignore the horror of lying in a closed casket with the rigid bones of my sister pressed into my flesh and focus on the murmur of two male voices in the room. I can't make out what they are saying. Sound apparently doesn't carry well across the wood and fabric of Amy's coffin. At the same time, the casket's soundproofing works to my advantage. I doubt either man can hear the loud, frantic thumping of my heart.

I hold my breath waiting for the casket lid to open. Time seems to stand still, forcing me to gasp for air so loudly I fear the noise will give me away. But the lid never cracks, not even an inch. Relieved, I sink into the soft, silky fabric cushioning me and hug myself for warmth. The chill deep in my bones refuses to go away. Lying next to Amy's skeletal remains, how could it? The air suddenly feels thick, heavy, suffocating . . .

I thrust open the lid of Amy's casket wheezing for air and find myself in total darkness—and alone. The crack of a bone pierces the silence as I scramble of out the coffin. When I drop to the floor, my right foot lands on something hard. I realize too late what it is. The coffee thermos rolls out from under my foot. The rest of me goes with it.

I end up lying face up on the cold, stone floor with a dull ache in the back of my head and a chill running through my bones. I feel the back of my head and discover lump the size of a small egg on my skull. A wave of dizziness rushes my head as I try to sit up, and then, everything goes black.

—

When I finally regain consciousness, I push myself to a sitting position. I don't know how long I was out, but it must have been a while. My dizziness is gone, but my nose and lips are numb, my legs feel like cold, dead weight. The rest of me will lose all feeling, too, if I don't find a way to insulate myself from the freezing air. I can't go back to the house knowing William's security detail is likely back on the job. I crawl across the floor, inch by inch, in search of my flashlight. The effort drags on. The only thing I find is the cold, hardwood of the mausoleum door.

I want to bolt upright, fling open the door, and flee, but I don't have the energy. As I push myself back against the door to sit and rest, my hand lands on a familiar cylinder. A moment later, the aroma of the rich, dark brew from the coffee thermos greets me. After a few greedy sips of the hot liquid, I start to feel warmth return to my body. Soon, I feel my energy returning, my brain kicking in.

My courage renewed, I decide to venture back to the car and find a motel with a nice, warm bed for some much-needed sleep, rest I'll need to keep my wits about me when I get the chance to confront William, hopefully in the morning.

I fumble around for the door handle. I find it and pull. The door doesn't budge. My blind search for a bolt or latch release, even a key, comes up empty.

I consider breaking a window and climbing out, but quickly abandon the idea as too risky. The smallest hint of trespassers on the property will cause William's security detail to postpone his trip to

Bulloch Hall or cancel it altogether. I can't chance any delay in putting this horrid nightmare to rest.

At the same time, I'm certain Felix is closing in on me. He's a proven expert in finding and killing people. I have no doubt that if he saw the smashed window, broken from the inside, he'd figure out that I'm nearby, risking my neck to see my sister one last time. Mimi and Ed would be as good as dead. It wouldn't matter to Felix if they didn't know anything about my whereabouts or my plans. Like my poor unfortunate ambulance driver, he'd torture Mimi and Ed, keep them alive long enough extract information he needed to finish the job he started.

Still, I'm underdressed and unprepared to withstand prolonged freezing temperatures, making the prospect of spending a long, cold night inside the mausoleum a deadly one. I decide to throw caution to the wind by reactivating my phone. If calling Mimi triggers Nick's spy program and he finds me, then I'll just have to convince him my plan is the quickest way to end the bloodshed and bring those responsible for so many murders to justice.

I reach inside my coat pocket, pull out my cell phone and its battery, and struggle to connect the two in the dark. When the battery finally snaps into place, I find the ON button and wait for the screen to flash to life. It remains black. Repeated attempts prove futile. Whether the device is broken or the battery dead, it doesn't matter. Either way, I'm trapped, stuck inside a frigid tomb until someone unlocks the door in the morning. If luck is on my side. I'm not ready to bet my life on it.

The biggest challenge ahead of me is to stay warm. Already my hands and legs are growing numb again. I pull myself off the floor and start pacing room, flapping my arms as I go to generate some body heat. The effort proves difficult in the dark. I keep bumping into the casket and walls. The few jumping jacks I manage generate some warmth, but leave my head dizzy and my throat and lungs stinging from breathing the freezing air.

When I lean on the casket to steady myself, my fingers find the soft, pillowed fabric of the lining. At that moment, I realize my only hope of survival is sharing one last night with my sister by my side. Tucked inside, with the casket lid slightly ajar, I'll be protected from the ice-cold air inside the mausoleum. The padding will provide a measure of insulation. My warm breath and body heat will keep the air around me warm, too.

After bumbling around in the dark, I touch upon a thin candelabra to jam between the casket and its lid to ensure a supply of fresh air. Within minutes, I'm nestled alongside Amy's bones, praying I live through the night, so the morning's ceremony doesn't become an interment service for two.

CHAPTER 60

Soon, the feeling in my legs starts to return, the air I inhale no longer stings my insides. Even my face is beginning to thaw out. Freezing to death is no longer my biggest concern. My greatest fear now is staying awake, vigilant against the possibility that Felix Jager is lurking nearby, intent on finding and finishing me off. The little bit of coffee I consumed won't keep me alert for long. I have to keep my mind occupied if I'm to avoid falling asleep on my watch.

I don't have a game plan for what I will say and do when I come face-to-face with William in the morning, so I try to imagine the confrontation in my head but find it difficult. Extracting the truth from William requires me to have at least some inkling of what happened the afternoon I fled. Without any memory of that day to gauge whether he is being honest or deceitful, my efforts to confront him will be doomed, and likely, me, too.

To stay awake, I turn my thoughts to the people I'd met the last few days: Dr. Malone, Jimmy, and a half dozen other medical staff from Summer Oaks. The only person who can keep my mind fully occupied is Nick, but my thoughts drift to those lingering memories of the man, his strong, sinewy arms around me. Overcome with shame for wanting him so, I chase Nick from my thoughts.

Left without anything better to do, my mind wanders to Amy. If there really is an afterlife, what she is thinking and feeling? As I do, the musical earworm that stumped me earlier recaptures my attention. Lying still, next to Amy, allows the sharp, staccato notes to come into focus. The melody follows. The lyrics strike me like a bolt of lightning, shaking me to my core.

When Death comes for me, I won't be kissed,
'Cause my name was scratched from St. Peter's list.
Turned away for infamy and blame,
For a life lived for power and fame.

"Facing the Grim Reaper" by King's Gambit. The music, the words, the message. It's finally clear what my subconscious has been trying to tell me, what I've already come to suspect. I'd been on top of the world, allowed myself to be a tool to gain position and power for William. Maybe I'm to blame for everything, for not appreciating what I had, and killing out of jealousy for what I didn't. Now, facing death, my prospects for a peaceful heavenly rest, if that is really possible, grow dim.

—

I must have dozed off, because I awake to the sound of someone fiddling with the door lock. Peeking out from the casket, I notice it's still dark out, not a ray of sunlight visible through the stained-glass windows. A visitor to the mausoleum in the middle of a freezing cold night, the difficulty the person has unlocking the door, means one thing. Someone without a key is trying to pick the lock. I don't wait to find out who. I reach for the candlestick and pull it inside.

—

Felix heard the telltale click of the lock. He pushed open the heavy wooden door and smiled as his night-vision goggles picked up a movement, the fleeting flash of a green thermal image. *Hiding in the casket with her dead sister? Either that bitch grew a pair of steel balls, or she's gone crazy.*

Felix knew she would be here. The dumb bitch had left such an easy trail to follow through the woods and around the property. With only one pair of footprints in the snow, he was certain she was alone. But where was Costa?

He stepped up to the casket, lifted the lid a couple inches, and peeked inside at the green glowing face masked with terror.

"If you make a sound," he whispered, "I'll kill you right here, right now."

He pushed the lid fully open, pulled his gun from his pocket, and pressed the muzzle of its silencer to her forehead.

"I have some questions for you. You answer quietly and correctly, you may live. You lie, hold back on me, or scream, you die. Got it?"

The green face nodded in agreement.

"Do you remember who you are?"

"Angela . . . Angela Lockhart." The name came in a strained whisper. "My husband is the president-elect."

"Are you sure?"

—

I don't know what to make of the question, so I just answer it. "Yes. I'm sure." Inside my chest, my heart is sinking into my stomach.

"What else do you remember?"

It's clear now the dark face hovering over me—Felix, I'm quite certain—is testing me, trying to determine how much of my memory is intact. What he doesn't realize, though, is that while I may remember little of my past, I know so much more than he might expect. He likely knows too much for me to lie outright. I will have to consider my answers carefully, pepper the truth with misinformation to avoid spilling everything and putting more lives at risk. Maybe then, Nick, Mimi, and Ed will have a chance at staying alive. Me, too.

"I woke from a coma two days ago with amnesia. I couldn't remember much at all, not my name, the car accident I was in, nothing about my life."

"Yet, you do know your name, now? How? Who told you?"

He's after Nick!

"No one. Nobody told me," I stutter through a combination of fear and desperation, grasping for some small lie to hide the truth from Felix. "I only remembered it this afternoon. I was in a motel room, watching the news, when the anchor spoke my name and my photo flashed on the screen. That's how I remembered my name. Unfortunately, I still can't recall anything about my life before the accident. Maybe you can help me. What am I missing?" I don't expect Felix to oblige me but hope the question will bolster my claim of total amnesia.

"You're lying. You're on the run, hiding, and someone is helping you. Nick Costa. I saw the two of you yesterday peeling out of the Summer Oaks' parking lot in his Charger."

"Nick Costa? That name sounds familiar. Who is he?" I reply, trying to buy time to think up a lie that will throw Felix off Nick's scent.

"Don't play dumb, bitch. I know Costa was behind the wheel."

I can't give in so easily.

"He's not mixed up in whatever is going on here. He knows less than I do."

"Are you willing to die to protect him?"

"Please. He's no threat to you."

I feel the muzzle of Felix's gun press harder into my forehead. He's losing what little patience he has. It's time to talk.

"Okay. Okay. You're right. His name is Nick. He visits my comatose roommate every day. We got to know each other, became friends. He invited me to go out for lunch. I was on my way downstairs to meet up with him when I saw you in the hallway. I recognized your face but couldn't put a name to it. I ran because I was scared. How do I know you? Why are you after me?"

Felix says nothing, neither acknowledges nor refutes my assumption, so I continue my tale, providing details to support my lies.

"Anyway, he was waiting for me at the back door. When you started shooting at us, it spooked him. He turned out to be quite a coward. Not a friend at all. First chance he got, he dumped me in a parking lot with some money and told me to get lost. I didn't know what to do, where to go. I took a room in a cheap hotel nearby to calm down and figure out my next move."

I hold my breath waiting for Felix's response.

"That's bullshit. He's Secret Service and you know it. It's also clear you remember something about your life, otherwise you wouldn't be here, at Bulloch Hall, hiding inside your sister's casket."

"My sister. Yes. Her name was Amelia," I reply, careful not to use her nickname. Any familiarity would betray I remember more than I'm telling. "I don't really remember her. The news story I saw on TV said she is going to be interred here at Bulloch Hall. I wanted to see her one last time, pay my respects. I thought a quick visit would jar my memory loose, too, but my plan failed. I still don't remember, and I've been locked inside this place all night. I climbed in here only to stay warm."

With silence hanging in the air, I fear Felix's interrogation may be over. Despite his earlier reassurances, I doubt he plans to let me walk out of here alive. To have any fighting chance to live, I need to do it standing on my own two feet.

"It's really uncomfortable lying here. Can you help me out?" I make a move to sit up.

Felix reaches in and pushes me down. "Not so fast. We're not done here." He raises his voice. "If no one is helping you, how did you get here?"

"I stole a car left idling at a Walmart." The truth will work the rest of the way. "The car's GPS directed me to Lynchburg. When I got close, I recognized the area. I parked the car behind a shack a mile and walked through the woods. I spotted the mausoleum and came straight here."

"What did I tell you would happen if you lied?" Before I can answer, the casket lid slams shut. Stunned by Felix's action, my scream catches in my throat. Before I can raise an arm to free myself, I hear a sound, a click of metal on metal. I push on the casket's lid. It doesn't move. I struggle to open the casket again and again, but it doesn't budge.

Terror grips me. I pound the lid with my fists and scream. "Please. Let me out." I continue my efforts until I'm hoarse and can't utter another plea.

Felix has won at last. I survived his first two attempts on my life. His third attempt will leave me dead and buried, anonymously locked inside a coffin that will be entombed within hours, sealed forever.

I can't see any way out. Resigned to my fate, I lie back and breathe deeply, in and out, yearning for sleep to overtake me before death can.

CHAPTER 61

drift in and out of consciousness until a bright, white glow appears before my eyes, one more intense than the sun. Curiously, it neither blinds me, nor impels me to flinch, squint, or wince in pain. Is this the light that the dead see at the close of their lives? Or is it as they are dying?

Absent is the sense of peace I've heard so much about. The welcoming arms of loved ones dearly departed are nowhere in sight. No mother, no father. No Amy. My heart is weighed down with regret. It's too late to redeem myself. If I'm not dead yet, I want to be.

"Amy, if you are near and can hear me, please help me," I whisper. "Please. Help me remember what I did wrong to deserve this fate."

Let it go.

The voice. It's back. I've had enough. Whether it's my subconscious speaking, a hallucination from another part of my brain, or Amy's ghost, it's time for the two of us to have a heart-to-heart talk.

"Let what go? How? I don't understand."

The guilt. Let it go.

My chest weighs heavy with remorse, a burden I'm not sure I can cast off so easily. "I don't know if I can do that. My mind may not remember what I did, but you do. You told me so over and over again these last few days, reminded me that I am at fault for everything that has happened. Now, it seems, it's too late to make things right."

Let go the guilt. Trust the truth to set you free.

The words sting me. I know the voice, no matter where it originates, is right. The answers I seek are inside me, hidden somewhere in the darkness of my mind. The dreams, visions, and fears that haunted me since waking from my coma have done nothing to restore my memories, only pushed them farther away. Now, with death upon me, I know it really *is* time to let go and accept whatever horrors have kept me from the truth. I have nothing to lose in trusting the little voice inside me—this one last time.

I close my eyes, draw in a deep breath and release it, along with the blame I heaped upon myself, the shame for whatever role I'd played that led me to this ignominious end. Suddenly, I'm overcome by a sense of peace, then, just as quickly, seized by an epiphany, bursting the dam in my mind, flooding my consciousness with the truth of my past. The odd dreams, the guilty thoughts, the intense emotions I'd experienced since waking from my coma—all of it—finally makes sense. The voice, it was my memory all along, trying to force its way back into my conscious self.

My relief vanishes in a flash, forcing me to struggle with a truth so horrid, twisted and heart-wrenching that I want to believe it's a hallucination generated from my oxygen-deprived brain. But I know that isn't so. Nothing I could imagine is worse than the truth of my past.

I know now why the King's Gambit song stuck in my mind. My name *was* scratched from St. Peter's list for a very good reason.

With my memory restored, blackness returns to my world. There is no white light. No spiritual vision. No inner consciousness drawing me back from the precipice of an eternal abyss. It's just me in the darkness. I hear myself breathing, my heart thumping. The air is stale and stuffy. I can smell it, feel it. I'm alive, but for how long?

I can't believe this is the end. I can't accept that after finally being released from the prison of my own mind, after knowing the truth and making peace with myself, that it will all end here, before I can exact justice for my sister, Maddy, Anita, and the others murdered in my stead. But I see no path to my survival.

I close my eyes and wait for death.

CHAPTER 62

A flicker of light penetrates my eyelids. A cold gust of air engulfs my bare face. Prepared to see death, I open my eyes, but the face I see this time doesn't belong to my dead sister. It belongs to William. Backlit by the light of two wall candles, an aura appears around his head, a halo he doesn't deserve.

"You killed my sister!" I scream, surprising myself with the force of my words.

William sputters, obviously shocked at my outburst, though I don't know why. Is he surprised to find me in the coffin alive, or taken aback by my accusation?

"I told you before, it was an accident," he says, his voice urgent. "You *must* believe me. Please, Amy!"

I moan in response to his words. They confirm my worst fears, my understanding of the song's message. Saint Peter won't call my name, at least not yet. I'm Amelia—Amy—and I'm alive. The bones lying beside me in the casket belong to Angela.

"I don't know if I can believe you, William," I reply, as I scramble out of the casket.

"I never meant to hurt Angela. I swear it." The tears in his eyes, the catch in his voice, the trembling of his hands—it all seems so genuine, just as it had when he made the same confession five days ago. At the time, I believed my brother-in-law, thinking him incapable of faking such emotional distress. Now, I know better. The man is an adept liar, a manipulator. The story he told me wasn't the truth, not the whole truth, at least. With my memory now intact, I *know* I can't trust him.

"Really, William, so much has happened in the week since you first confessed to killing Angela that I don't know what to believe anymore."

Glancing around the candlelit room, I suddenly realize William and I are not alone. In the shadows stands Andrew Novak with his arms crossed over his chest. Wearing a long, black wool coat, black leather gloves, and a severe scowl on his face, the man looks as menacing as the rabid dog I remember him to be. Behind him stands Felix Jager, his frowning face no friendlier than Andrew's.

The four of us are the only people in the mausoleum, at least of those who are still alive. My chances of staying that way don't amount to much, given the obvious malice in Novak's grimacing face. Accusing William of murder in front of his attack dogs wasn't a brilliant move on my part. I need to watch what I say and do going forward, or risk winding up dead and buried with my sister without anyone on the outside being the wiser.

"You can believe everything I told you, Amy. I know that you've been having some memory issues, so maybe I should explain it again," William says, shifting nervously from one foot to the other. When I don't respond, he starts. "That night in Raleigh when we learned Maddy was dead, Angela and I got into a horrible fight in our hotel suite. She confronted me about my affair with Maddy and her pregnancy."

A memory from that night flashes in my mind.

I'm in my hotel room, lying on my bed trying to come to grips with the news of Maddy's death. I answer a knock at the door. It's Angela. The sorrow I see on her face can't match what I feel inside—unrelenting remorse. Behind the closed door, we hug each other and cry. Wracked with shame, I confess to my sin of omission—not revealing Maddy's pregnancy when I first learned of her disappearance.

The fire I see in Angela's eyes tells me she's angry. She pulls a tissue from her pocket and hands it to me. "It's your fault. You should have come forward, reported Maddy's pregnancy to the authorities when she went missing. But you didn't. Why?"

"You're mad at me. I can't blame you," I reply, sniffling. "I'm upset and angry with myself, too. I should have never promised Maddy that I'd keep her secret, but she begged me. She was afraid if anyone else knew, it would leak to the media and mire the campaign in a scandal. She didn't want her family to know, either. So, when she disappeared, I didn't see anything sinister behind it. I just thought she'd gone somewhere to hide, wait out her pregnancy and give the baby up for adoption. If I'd thought there was a chance Maddy was in danger, I'd have told someone immediately."

Angela jumps from the bed. "That asshole!" With a wild look in her eye, she storms out of my room mumbling William's name.

William casts his gaze downward, as if truly repentant, and continues. "Angela accused me of being involved in the poor girl's disappearance and murder. I confessed to the affair to her but told her I didn't know Maddy was carrying my child, that I didn't know anything about her disappearance or death. Your sister wouldn't believe me. She got violent. She started throwing things, then came at me with her fists. I pushed her away and she fell, hit her head on the marble table and—"

William chokes on his last words. Tears well up in his eyes. The man is either sincere or missed his calling in the theater. "I know I haven't been the best husband, that I cheated on Angela, treated her more like a lowly staffer than a wife at times, but not once in all the years we were married, did I ever raise my hand against her. When she fell . . . it really was an accident."

I say nothing in response. I can't. The horrors underlying William's words, spoken finally out in the open, are just too much.

"When I couldn't rouse her, I called Andrew. He came right away and ordered me out of the room. A couple minutes later, he came out and told me Angela was dead." William's eyes grow wide with panic, as if reliving that night. "I was in shock. I . . . I couldn't believe what I'd done. I didn't know what to do. Andrew took over, said he'd take care of everything. He told me to go back to my room and take a sleeping pill, so that's what I did."

Out of the corner of my eye, I spy Andrew and Felix whispering. I strain to hear what they are saying but can't make out a word. Angela had confided her fears to me about William's chief of staff last spring, terrified about what he might do to win the election. I should have listened to her. As the mastermind of such a horrific cover-up, I don't doubt but that he is the most dangerous of the three men in the stone-cold room with me.

The memory of Andrew barging into my hotel that night now haunts me.

"Your sister collapsed, Amy. She had a nervous breakdown, and it's your fault. You told her Maddy was pregnant with William's baby. She went off the deep end, accused William of having the girl killed, when nothing could be further from the truth."

My gut clenches with anguish. "I'm sorry. I didn't know William was the father. Maddy refused to name him."

"Well, it's too late now. Angela is on her way to a private clinic. No one can know about this, no one can know what's happened, or we can all kiss the White House good-bye."

My heart is breaking. "I'm sorry. Truly I am. If there is anything I can do—"

"There is. You need to take Angela's place. You're identical twins. You can easily impersonate her. All you need is her wig. I can arrange for you, as Amy, to disappear. It'll be temporary, just until Angela is recovered and able to resume her life, her duties at William's side. But you can't tell anyone what is going on, who you really are. No one. Understand?"

The horror of the plan stuns me. My heart is in my throat. I can't speak.

"If you don't do this, William will lose the election, and all the hard work and sacrifice everyone put into this campaign—your sister's, especially— will be for nothing. If you won't do it for William, do it for her. Do it for your country."

My mind races with fear, fear of losing Nick if I put him through this heart-wrenching deception.

"Do it for the girls. They need their mother."

My shoulders slump as I heave a sigh. I have no choice. I must protect Olivia and Sophia.

CHAPTER 63

Reeling from the pain of the recollection, I cast my gaze from Andrew and back to William.

With his shoulders slumped, his head bowed, he seems burdened by his own words, as if the heft of his confession bears heavily on his mind.

"Andrew told me everything the next morning," William continues. "By then, he'd set everything in motion. The staging of your disappearance. The disposal of—" He stumbles over his words. "—the body. The switching of records in your dentist's office. You remember this now, don't you?"

I close my eyes, nod, and sigh, then return my gaze to William.

"I did kill Angela. But it was an accident. I didn't mean to hurt her. Please, Amy, you must believe me."

Even though I heard William's confession before—on the day I fled my life—I feel the immensity of his words—and the memories they elicit—more heavily now. I remember the frustration of having every request to see Angela returned with a dire warning against it, that the intrusion of family or friends would thwart her progress. I remember the heartache I felt knowing I couldn't reveal myself to Nick, the guilt I felt seeing him so broken about my disappearance, and the fear I had of him walking away from me when I was finally free to confess my deception. I remember, too, the pain of knowing that I could never make Nick happy while the guilt I felt for Angela's condition dragged down my own spirit. I remember the only pleasure I took from impersonating my sister came from playing mother to her daughters, Olivia and Sophia, the two bright spots in my life who I couldn't have loved more if I'd carried them in my own womb.

I remember playing my part through the election and the months that followed, feeling the ever-present yoke of these dark emotions upon my soul. They drove me to pour myself into my public role and my private duties as Angela, hoping that by taking on her burdens, I could ease my sister's reentry when she was well enough to resume her own life. More than anything, I remember the shock wave that rolled through my body that afternoon when William confessed to killing Angela, the shame of knowing I'd been manipulated into covering up my sister's death, and the anger I felt at myself for being so naïve. With all that was burdening my mind and my heart, I snapped, just as Dr. Malone said could happen, when the news of Angela's death and William's confession became the one last, unbearable straw to break in what had become my soul-crushing life.

Now, though, I'm not sure what to believe. William's confession seems heartfelt, even credible. I still don't buy it. A powerful man like William—harsh, controlling, manipulative— would say anything to have me continue to do his bidding. He did it once—coached by Andrew—the day after he killed Angela, then lied about it as he begged me to cover up her absence from the campaign. How my sister hid the dark side of her relationship with William from me, I can't even fathom, but he hid his abusive side, too.

Standing across from me, I stare at William shivering in the cold, wringing his gloved hands to help keep them warm, and contemplate my own next move. Then it hits me. *Hands—William's hands!* In the heat of William's confession, he'd apparently mesmerized me, lying to me once again, leading me to overlook Angela's real cause of the death. My sister didn't die from the head injury she sustained after William knocked her down. No. Angela was strangled to death. *Like Maddy.* William did it, just as Dr. Malone pointed out when she said abusers often resort to violence when they feel threatened. My goal now must be to extract a murder confession from William. I just hope it doesn't cost me my life.

CHAPTER 64

"**A**my, please. Say something."

William's voice jars me from my thoughts. I turn toward him and stare into his eyes. Feeling colder than I have all night, I pull my coat close around my body but know it won't be enough. The chill I feel has nothing to do with the frigid weather.

The next few minutes, I'm certain, will offer the opening I need, sealing my fate one way or the other. But in order to gauge my chances against Andrew, I have to know what role William played into the conspiracy to kill me.

"Aren't you even curious where I've been, William? Why I'm here, and how I got locked inside Angela's casket?"

"I'm sorry, Amy. When you disappeared, Andrew put his man, Felix, on the job to find you. He learned you'd been in a car accident and were suffering from amnesia. When he finally discovered your location, you'd disappeared again. Felix told us you weren't alone. Someone, we don't know who yet, was helping you, hiding you from me and the girls—your family."

In the next moment, William is by my side on the bench. The frown on his face is more sad than angry. "We suspected you knew your real identity by then and needed to draw you into the open. So, Andrew arranged for Angela's body to be returned to Bulloch Hall, then had the media broadcast news of Amy's pending interment. He guessed you couldn't stay away, wouldn't remain in the shadows while your sister was buried, and he was right. Andrew and I drove down this morning. I was prepared to spend the next few days here, waiting for you to show up, but thankfully you made it a short wait."

William rises from the bench, crosses the room, and lays a hand on Angela's casket. "I'm sorry you got locked inside. I don't know how that happened." He turns to face me with a weak smile on his face. "But it doesn't matter now. You're safe. We're here to bring you back home where you belong. I need you now more than ever. The girls, too."

I stare at William's face. His eyes remain apologetic, his smile sympathetic. Could he really be completely in the dark about the attempts on my life? I can't trust him.

"Really? I had no idea . . ." are the only words I can muster.

I'm desperate for a glimpse of Andrew, his reaction to my words, but I don't dare turn my head for fear that the moment our eyes meet, it will be all over. He will see that I know the truth, the whole of it. Angela's death wasn't an accident. She died with William's hands at her throat. My best bet is to downplay the conspiracy between the three men and get the hell out of their clutches before it's too late.

"Well, thank god you arrived when you did, William. A few more minutes, and I would've suffocated. Now, if you don't mind, I've been locked in here all night, and I could really use a bathroom and a hot breakfast."

I make a break for the door, but before I can take two steps, Felix moves to block my path.

Behind me, Andrew speaks, his words slow and deliberate. "You're going nowhere. We still have a few matters to discuss. Matters that need to be settled before the world discovers that you, or rather Angela Lockhart, has returned to her family safe and sound."

CHAPTER 65

"**W**hat matters?" I ask, turning toward William. "What is he talking about?" Inside, I feel a glimmer of hope. My death is not a done deal.

"Before I explain, Amy, let me say this. You believed in me once, enough to dedicate yourself to supporting me, my work, my campaigns for office. If I haven't destroyed your faith in me and the good that we've done together on the behalf of Virginia, and now, what we could do for our country, I think you owe it to yourself to listen to what I have to say."

William steps forward, takes my hands in his, and looks into my eyes. His touch, his gaze is more than I care to bear. I jerk my hands back and turn away.

"All right, I understand. You hate my guts right now. Just hear me out, then decide. First off, I want you to know that I never meant to hurt anyone. Not you, not Maddy, and certainly not Angela. Truth be known, she was a better wife to me than I was a husband. I already admitted that. But politics and power do strange, awful things to people. I'm not trying to excuse the way I treated Angela, just explain it. Deep down, I still cared for Angela. If I could change the past, or at least change places with Angela, I would. But I can't."

I know where William is going with this. I heard a similar line of bull from him days ago, when he first confessed to covering up

Angela's death, sending me running from my life. The horror behind his words is just as palpable now as it was the first time. But I can't let on how I feel. To have any chance at staying alive, William and his henchmen must think I am willing to accept what is about to be offered.

"That leads us to where we are today, Amy. Flawed individuals, all of us, unable to undo our mistakes, but with an obligation to the future. We, that is, Andrew and I, we need to know what your intentions are now that you know that Angela is, well, not coming back."

"My intentions?" I ask, doing my best to feign surprise at the question.

"Yes, Amy."

With his head held low and shoulders slumped forward, William looks far less like the alpha male I'm used to and more like a whipped dog.

"I know it's asking a lot for you to continue impersonating Angela," he continues. "It's a lifetime commitment. I get that, but I'm not expecting you to stay with me forever. You can divorce me after I'm out of office. You can live your life anyway you please after that."

William's despicable proposition, though I'd heard it before, still stuns me. But it's not my reaction, I'm interested in. It's Andrew's.

I spin around to face William and steal a glance at his chief of staff. He looks wound tighter than a guitar string, ready to snap at the next turn of a tuning peg. His eyes, filled with malevolence, telegraph *his* intentions. He wants me dead.

"Please, Amy. I implore you."

I hear desperation in William's voice, see fear in his eyes. He knows I hold his fate in my hands.

"Try to understand. Coming out with the truth will not bring Angela back. It will only hurt more people, especially Sophia and Olivia. Think of them, Amy. Think about how living with the public knowledge and disgrace that I accidentally killed their mother and covered it up will affect them for the rest of their lives. I know how much you love the girls. Are you willing to sentence them to a lifetime of shame and humiliation just to see me in jail for an unfortunate, horrible accident on my part?"

I can't hold back my anger. I slap him across the face, hard enough to sting my own hand. "Are you insane?!" I shout. "It's bad enough that you're asking me to completely overlook the fact that you murdered my sister. And you did, William, you did. Angela's autopsy proves it. She didn't die from a fall. She was strangled. But now, you're asking me to cover it all up, give up my own life, just so your daughters don't have to know what a manipulative, evil bastard you are."

William's eyes flare with panic. "It was an accident. I swear," he shouts back. "I didn't strangle Angela. I didn't lay a hand on her. Why don't you believe me?"

Suddenly, the mausoleum is filled with frantic echoes, someone pounding on the door. "This is your security detail, sir." The words are muffled by the thick oak door. "Open up. Let us in."

I lurch for the door only to have Felix block my path. Turning away, I stumble into Andrew's arms. My chest tightens as our gazes meet, and I see the fury in his eyes. Frightened, I pull away, tripping over my feet as I do, until William catches me mid-fall, and helps me to my feet.

"I texted your detail to stand down," Andrew says. "Told them you are fine." His tone is calm, collected, but his face and body language seethe with rage. He appears ready to blow. If I'm right, my fate is in the path of the blast.

Andrew steps forward, stops inches away from my face, and growls. I can feel his hot breath on my face. "Nobody can get in or out of here without breaking down the door." His gaze shifts to William. "It's time to face facts. This bitch knows too much to go along with our plan.

She's a liability, now. We can't let her leave this room." With a quick nod toward Angela's casket, he makes his plan all too clear.

With time running out, I'm left with one course of action. Call in the cavalry.

"Help!" I scream at the top of my lungs. "Help! Nick, where are you?"

William acts before anyone else, grabbing me by the shoulders, pressing me against the cold, stone wall, muzzling me with his hand.

"Please, Amy, he's not kidding here. I can't stop him. Tell him you'll do everything he asks of you. I don't want to see you hurt."

I wrangle out of William's fierce grip, then lunge at him with my fists. He dodges my punch and pushes me aside, causing me to lose my balance and fall backward. A flash of pain on the back of my head is the last thing I remember before everything goes dark.

—

I'm jarred awake by an intense pressure on my throat, a desperate, panicked need for air. Unable to move, seemingly pinned to the cold floor, I open my eyes to find Andrew straddled atop me, his hands clasped around my neck, his face clenched in an obvious battle between control and rage. The room echoes with a frenzied thumping, the cracking of wood, the voices of desperate men demanding someone open the door.

"Stop, Andrew. Don't kill her." The shouts are William's. I see him, out of the corner of my eye, struggling to wrench free of the hold Felix has on him.

I thrash about, hoping to knock Andrew off me, but his body weighs me down.

"Talk, bitch! Tell me about Costa. How much does he know?" Though his face is contorted with anger, Andrew's voice is subdued, cool, and restrained. "Who else knows Angela is dead and that you have taken her place?"

When he suddenly relaxes his grip on my throat, I gasp for air, unsure what to say if I could.

In the next second, he delivers a stinging slap across my face. His hands are back on my throat before I can recover from the shock of the blow. I struggle to wrench his hands from my neck, but his grip tightening around my throat is the only result.

"Look at me, bitch!" Andrew's voice is now agitated, elevated.

In no position to disobey, I follow his order. Staring into his face, I see a different Andrew. With his jaw clenched, his eyes wild with fury, he's clearly lost control.

"Talk now," he screams. "Or I'll strangle the life out of you, like I did your fucking sister."

My heart seems to seize up at Andrew's confession. Before I can process his words, the room erupts with the sound of glass shattering on the stone floor. The noise draws Andrew's attention away from me. His hold on my throat loosens. Despite struggling for air, I somehow manage a weak cry for help.

"This is the Secret Service," a deep voice shouts into the building. "We have reason to suspect that the president-elect and his wife are in danger inside the mausoleum. Unlock the door and exit the building quietly with your hands up."

I recognize the voice. I close my eyes and summon a scream with every ounce of air I can muster. "Nick!"

My plea is punctuated by the blast of a gun. As more shots ring out and bullets seem to bounce off the walls, Andrew ducks for cover, like the coward he is, throwing his arms over his head.

With renewed energy, I seize the opportunity before me and claw my fingernails into his eyes. He screams and bolts upright, clutching his face. Adrenaline pours through me as I ram my clenched fist into his crotch. He doubles over, his face contorted with pain. I shove him aside, scramble across the floor, and take cover behind the bier where my sister's casket rests.

"Hold your fire and keep your distance," Felix shouts. "Or I'll plug your precious president-elect."

Hoping to get a clearer picture of what is happening, I inch my way to the front of the bier, then pull back the drape and sneak a peek. Across the room, pressed against the wall, Felix stands next to the shattered remains of a stained-glass window. William is with him, bound by Felix in a one-arm chokehold, and frozen in fear by the large, black pistol pressed to his head.

"He means what says," William yells, his voice fragile and hoarse. "Stand down."

Beyond the growing ringing in my ears and the thumping of my heart inside my chest, the room is now eerily quiet except for Andrew's low groans and William's weak whimpers.

"What are your terms?" Nick's voice booms through the broken window.

Andrew, struggling to stand, appears to catch Felix's attention. With a sneer of disgust, the big man turns his malignant frown in my direction. Our eyes lock on each other. My blood runs cold as he narrows his eyes and smiles. At that moment, I know his plan. With no hope of escape, Felix intends to kill both William and me, Andrew, too, then go down himself, fighting. From the wide-eyed terror I see on William's face, he knows it, too.

I pull back out of Felix's line of fire as his bullet whizzes past me. The roar of the shot reverberates as two more shots ring out, their blasts ricocheting off the walls. A loud thud peals through the room—*a body hitting the floor.*

Rather than scramble for safety, I hazard another look. I have to know who has been shot, who could be dying. Without a sense of fear to hold me back, I crane my neck and peer past the bier. Inches away, Andrew lies still, his head turned toward me. Blood, seeping from a hole in his forehead, runs into his cold, fixed eyes.

I can't hold my tongue. "Burn in hell, you bastard!"

Out of the corner of my eye, I spot Felix taking aim in my direction. William suddenly comes to life, stomping hard on Felix's foot, elbowing him the gut. The man doesn't so much as flinch, except to throw William to the floor.

"Hah!" Felix sneers. "The man elected to be the most powerful leader in the world is not so powerful after all." He trains his gun on William's head. I clamp my eyes shut and retreat. I can't watch Felix take yet another life.

My body recoils when the shot rings out. I let out a scream louder than I could ever imagine. The ringing in my ears is deafening. I fight back the tears welling up in my eyes, crying for William, who, despite his personal failings, wasn't a murderer and didn't deserve his fate.

Unwilling to sit idly by while Felix puts a bullet in my head, I grab the first defensive object I see. Fixing my tear-filled eyes on the floor at the head of Angela's casket, I cock the thick, brass candlestick in my hands, and wait for Felix's towering shadow to come into view.

A moment later, I come out swinging.

CHAPTER 66

I sit at the kitchen table of my childhood home, drawing warmth from the hot cup of coffee in my hand and the presence of Nick by my side. With my other hand, I hold a cold compress to the back of his head. He winces in pain from the pressure, but like the gentleman I know him to be, he doesn't complain. I'm glad for that small act of courage. I feel guilty enough for whacking him in the face instead of the vile rat I intended to take out.

We are alone, just the two of us. I'd asked for a few minutes with Nick to thank him in private for his heroic actions in thwarting a known assassin's plot to kill me. Nothing more was said to explain what happened inside the mausoleum, no mention of who might have hired Jager or why, or where I had been all this time. That will all come later, after Hayward's chief of staff arrives via Marine helicopter with a throng of federal agency heads in tow, all tasked with the safety and security of the United States.

"You beaned me pretty good, Ma'am," Nick says, gritting out a smile.

I stifle a cringe at the sight of Nick's missing front tooth. After his soft brown eyes, Nick's bright, straight smile has always been my favorite part of his face. And while I know the damage can be easily fixed, it doesn't make me feel any better.

"Actually, my blow caught your chin. That's how you lost that tooth. You got that big bump on your skull from hitting the floor. I'm sorry,

Nick, deeply sorry. That candlestick was meant for Felix. I had no idea he was already dead. When I heard that last gunshot, I was certain Felix had killed William."

"Felix made a fatal mistake when he pushed your husband to the ground," Nick replies. "It gave me a clear shot to take him out." He fingers the bandage on his chin. "I have to say, Ma'am, you pack quite a punch, and that's not just me talking. From what I hear, you single-handedly took out Novak. Disabled him with a poke in the eyes and fat punch to the groin. The creep probably didn't even know what hit him."

I shake my head in response. "I may have disabled him, but I didn't kill him. He died from a gunshot wound to the head."

"Novak stumbled into Felix's line of fire. He was aiming to kill you. But if you ask me, Ma'am, that fiend got just what he deserved. Killed by his own hired gun."

"Divine justice," I add with a weak smile, although I feel far from blessed. While I'm relieved the bloodshed has come to an end with the deaths of Andrew and his henchman, I know my ordeal is far from over. I haven't yet confessed the truth of Angela's fate and my identity to anyone, not even Nick. With Maddy and Angela's killers cold and stiff under a couple of sheets in the Bulloch family mausoleum, the only other person who knows the truth is William, and he hasn't yet said a word to anyone either.

When the Secret Service descended on the scene inside the mausoleum, I'd been too dumbfounded to speak. William and I had been examined for injuries, then whisked to the kitchen for first aid. Once there, William had insisted on a few minutes of privacy after his security crew tended to our minor wounds. When we were alone, he again asked what my intentions were. I didn't know what to tell him, except that I had to think about it. To William's credit, he agreed to abide by whatever choice I made, whenever I made it, no matter how it might affect him and the girls.

Now, my stomach churns with indecision. My heart aches having Nick so near, knowing we are still separated by my lies. I long to tell him the truth, to feel his strong, comforting arms around me. I thirst for his lips on mine, yearn to hear his strong, deep voice say, "I love you."

But I can't do it. Tell him truth. Not yet at least. My subconscious warned me to keep hiding, and for now, that's the only path I see forward. I don't know if I can survive the pain of Nick walking away from me forever over my lies, the anguish I've caused him, as my dream foretold after our first encounter in my fugue-filled world.

My heart, though, says I need to protect the life Nick and I share by giving it the chance it deserves, the opportunity to prove we belong together, that united in love and commitment, we are strong enough to weather whatever life throws at us, no matter how tragic.

At the same time, my heart cries out for me to protect Angela's daughters. The truth could do irreparable harm to my sweet young nieces. During the months in which I took their mother's place, it was clear they felt my absence—the loss of their aunt from their lives. Saddened at the mere mention of my name, they once asked what they did to send their Auntie Amy away, why she didn't love them anymore. As things stand now, I'm not inclined to put them through the truth out of fear of what it will do to their little hearts to learn their mother is never coming home, or that as their beloved aunt, I betrayed their trust by perpetuating such a vicious lie.

Fate has left me with an impossible choice.

Nick's voice pulls me from the dark abyss of my thoughts.

"While I have your ear, allow me to apologize for everything. I failed you in so many ways. I failed to protect you from Felix more than once. I failed those he killed in his twisted search to find you after I hid you away. Worst of all, as we ran for our lives, I failed to earn your trust that I could protect you, me, and others from harm.

If I had, you wouldn't have driven off to take matters into your own hands. Again, I'm sorry."

"Please, Nick, stop. You shouldn't apologize for my actions." I say, shaking my head. "When the news came over the radio that three employees of a Culpepper ambulance service were found tortured and killed, I knew Felix had struck again." My words come out full of fire and conviction. "With five people killed because of me, it was time for me to stop being a coward and come out of hiding. I knew you'd try to stop me from confronting William, or at the very least, insist on coming along. And for the record, I did trust you. I *do* trust you. I knew what I was doing, Nick. I knew the situation was dangerous. I was trying to protect you. I knew I wouldn't be able to live with myself if I survived this horror, but you didn't."

Our gazes meet, and for a moment, I see a flash of hope in Nick's eyes, a fleeting recognition of an emotional connection between us, as if he has finally seen past my false front. But the moment quickly passes. Across from me, shaking his head, Nick is still in the dark.

"I'm sorry, but it's not your job to protect me. It's supposed to be the other way around."

I set the cold compress on the table and take his hand in mine. "But in the end, you did save me, Nick, despite my best efforts to make it impossible for you to do so. I even unplugged the battery from my phone so you couldn't track my movements. So, how did you find me?"

"I recovered your GPS signal."

"That doesn't make sense." I return the compress to the back of Nick's head. "When I got locked inside the mausoleum, I decided to call Mimi even though I knew it might tip you off to my whereabouts. But I dropped my phone trying to plug the battery back in. When it didn't start up after I reinserted the battery, I thought it was broken."

"Well, enough of it worked to get a signal out. I got a general fix on your position in Lynchburg, but the signal died before I could pinpoint your exact location. There was only one place you could be—Bulloch Hall. I tried to call you but never connected."

In the next few minutes, Nick sums up his efforts to track my movements. He arrived at my family's estate just after ten, then checked in with the agents on duty, who reported no unusual activity. He grilled Mimi and learned I'd come and gone hours ago, then stopped by the last place Mimi had seen me—the mausoleum. He never stepped inside, merely scanned the room with his flashlight. Seeing no sign of me, he turned his efforts to searching Lynchburg for the Honda.

"If only I'd done a more thorough job. I should have searched the mausoleum, but I couldn't," Nick says, flustered, stammering to speak. "I couldn't bring myself to even shine my light on Amy's casket. I screwed up. I almost got you killed."

"Excuse me, Ma'am."

I turn my head toward the firm, female voice. It belongs to Rachel Keller, a tall, lean Black woman on Angela's security detail, one of the many agents who moved in and out of my life during the months in which I impersonated my sister. I know their names, recognize their faces, but know little about the men and women who protected me over the last three months. Working in shifts, these tireless public servants remained part of the background, quietly watching over me whether I was on the campaign trail or in a hotel conference room. In my role as Angela Lockhart, wife of a presidential nominee, and later, wife of the president-elect, they'd never left me alone, except when William or I asked for privacy.

"I'm sorry for the interruption, Ma'am," Agent Keller continues. "President-elect Lockhart was just informed that the helicopters carrying President Hayward's chief of staff and the heads of national security are thirty minutes out. He wants to speak with you before meeting with them. If you'd accompany me, Ma'am, I'll take you to him. He's in the study."

I nod my assent without saying a word. I have a good idea what William wants to talk about. With the grilling that likely awaits us, we need to have our stories straight. And I need to deliver him my decision.

As I rise from my chair to leave, I turn and grab a last peek of Nick. Sadness wells up in my heart knowing the torture that awaits me if I decide to remain with William as his wife. With his heroics, Nick will be asked to stay on with the Presidential Protective Division of the Secret Service. I'll never be able to get him out of my sight, out of my mind, out of my heart. I'll wake each morning longing for a glimpse of his smile. In his presence, I'll yearn for his gentle touch, hope for a tender word, some recognition that he loves me, as I love him. And I'll live in agony knowing he won't, knowing he can't, because to him, Amy is dead and gone.

"I'll be back to check on you, Nick." I offer a weak smile, steal a caress of his shoulder, then turn to leave, uncertain about who I'll be the next time I see the only man I have ever loved, and likely, always will.

CHAPTER 67

When the thick, oak doors to the study open, William is waiting for me, sitting behind my father's desk, an ornate, mahogany monster, an antique reportedly from Napoleon's summer palace. According to the estate's property inventory, my father paid a small fortune for the imposing piece of furniture that made his visitors feel small and powerless in his presence. At least, that's how I always felt whenever my father summoned me.

Now, with William sitting in my father's chair, the events of my life are all too clear, and I feel small once again, like a little girl waiting for her father to deliver his latest edict. That was my life growing up sheltered at Bulloch Hall. Angela's life, too. As the daughters of a powerful U.S. Senator and his equally ambitious wife, we'd been raised to serve one purpose—to advance my father's career and those of the men he would choose for us to marry. And up until that fateful afternoon when I learned my sister was dead, that's how my life had been lived, to unceasingly support the political agenda of my father and his apprentices. No resistance, no questions allowed.

Not that Angela had it any better. Her marriage to William was arranged, at least where Angela was concerned. Her choice of a mate was of little interest to my father. At the time, William was a fast-rising star in my father's small, tightly controlled circle of hand-picked political protégés. He seemed more than happy to marry Angela. Whether he did so out of love for my sister, or for our father's powerful political and financial connections, I never knew.

Even after our parents' deaths, neither Angela nor I broke from our parents' mold. The two of us served as faithful servants in William's political career. Everything I did came through Andrew, who had thrust himself into the role of William's chief of staff and closest adviser after my father's death.

Now, as William stands behind that imposing desk, his attitude reminds me so much of my father. Stepping toward me, he pulls me into a tight hug, pinning my arms to my sides, a controlling move my father frequently used with me and my sister.

"Please, sit," William says, when he finally releases me, directing me to the small, narrow chair that sits in front of the desk.

Once we are both seated, our relative positions leave me feeling uneasy, like I'm back in time, sitting across from my father, trying to explain away some behavior on my part that displeased him. Across from me, William looks different from the beaten down man I sat with earlier in the kitchen. The despair I saw then in his eyes is gone, replaced with arrogance. His downtrodden frown is now a cocky grin, his slumped shoulders are now straight and tall. It's obvious my father's study has cast a spell over William, renewing his sense of invincibility and omnipotence. I know now that his expectations of me have changed.

When the door clicks shut behind me, I want nothing more than to grab Nick by the hand and make a run for our lives without ever looking back. But I don't. I need to decide who I'll be when I walk out of the room. There's too much at stake to let my emotions, my fears, rule my fate.

"Thank you for coming," William says, with a firm, authoritative tone. "I don't know if you've decided what to do going forward, but so much has happened in the past week, so much that I didn't know, that I thought we'd better talk, get on the same page before we debrief everyone."

"Yes. That would be a good idea," I reply, relieved William didn't press me to announce my decision.

"I can understand why you fled the hotel suite after I told you Angela was dead," William continues from his perch. "You were angry. You felt betrayed. What happened after that?"

Over the course of the next several minutes, I detail all that had happened to me, including Felix's attempt to stage my death as a car accident, Nick's heroic efforts to rescue me and hide me from my would-be assassin, and the trail of bodies Felix left behind in his murderous pursuit to finish the job he started. That I'm able to relate my story in a calm, just-the-facts manner surprises me. I chalk it up to knowing that the worst is over. I'm no longer forced to fear for my life and the lives of other innocents. William, to his credit, listens attentively throughout my narrative and seems genuinely horrified of all that I've suffered.

"Andrew was behind it all," I say, after finishing my tale.

"Yes. It has his mark all over it. I knew he was ruthless and ambitious. I turned a blind eye to the awful things he did to people over the years in my name. I had no idea he'd kill to keep me in power, although there were a few fatal accidents involving my political opponents early in my career that I always wondered about. He even hinted on more than one occasion that your parents' plane going down over the Atlantic wasn't an accident."

I'm not surprised at the news, just angry. "It was worse than that, William. You heard Andrew when he had his hands around my neck. You didn't kill Angela. She didn't die from a fall. Andrew strangled her. He was behind the conspiracy, Maddy's murder, too, I suspect."

The scowl on William's face suggests he's as angry as I am, so I continue. "Andrew's confession needs to come out. The whole cover-up needs to see the light of day. The families of those killed as part of Andrew's horrific effort to silence Maddy, Angela, and me need to know the truth. They deserve closure, to see that justice has been served with the deaths of those who murdered their loved ones. Too many people have died to protect the dark secrets we share. I think it's time to let the truth of Andrew and Felix's ruthlessness, their crimes, come to light."

With those words, William bolts to a stance, plants his hands on the desk, then leans forward and glares at me. "Are you saying you're through, you won't continue in your role as Angela? Why would you do something so selfish? Do you know what that will mean?"

I'm taken aback by William's aggressiveness, his hostility, but inside, I seethe at his words, his accusatory tone, his effort to intimidate me. I've seen him go ballistic when backed into a corner or otherwise challenged. My father pulled the same act on me on the few occasions I dared to question his decisions or otherwise stand up for myself. I always backed down. This time, I'm determined to stand my ground—for me as much as for Angela, Maddy, and the five other innocent souls wrenched so cruelly from their families.

Determined to make William defend his indefensible position, my answer is short and simple. "What does it mean? You tell me."

With a sour look on his face, William pulls back his shoulders and thrusts out his chin. He couldn't look more indignant and self-important if he tried.

"It means everything you, Angela, and I have worked so hard for will be for nothing. I'll be forced to resign the presidency before I'm even inaugurated. I'll be thrown in prison for my role in Angela's death, maybe even some of the illegal acts Andrew committed in my name over the years. A political neophyte of a vice president will take over the most powerful job in the world. Olivia and Sophia will live under a cloud of ignominy and disgrace. Is that what you want, Amy? Chaos for our country and shame thrust upon our family?"

When I don't respond immediately, William slams his hands down on the desk and leans toward me. I meet his angry gaze with a blank stare, daring him to continue. In the next moment, he does.

"Listen to reason, Amy. The men responsible for all these deaths are dead. Andrew Novak and Felix Jager will never hurt anyone again. Nothing we say or do now can bring back anyone they murdered. Justice has been served without forcing a trial that would hurt you, me, the country, and the girls."

He pauses for a moment, then narrows his eyes and stares at me, as if trying to read my mind. "Or are you just trying to punish me for being unfaithful to your sister?"

I'm stunned by William's words, his righteous tone, implying that I'm to blame for the awful situation we share, not him. His entire speech, I realize, is an attempt to manipulate me, just as he did the day he confessed to Angela's death. This time, however, I know too much for William to sway me. He may not have killed Angela with his own bare hands, but his lack of integrity, his poor judgment, and misplaced trust in Andrew set into motion a series of events that led to the deaths of so many innocent people. How could I trust William after all he's done? Would I ever feel safe harboring this vile secret William and I share?

At the same time, William's words prove to me that he isn't worthy of the American people's confidence or trust. Nor do I agree that all my time and energy helping to elect William to the presidency will go to waste if he is forced to resign before taking office. Congress must have ratified the Electoral College vote by now, so the country will be in good hands. During my time with the campaign, I got to know William's running mate, now Vice President-elect, Maria Gonzales, and found the former Navy fighter pilot and two-term Governor of Ohio to be intelligent, well-versed on a range of domestic and international issues, and dedicated to working across the aisle for the good of the country.

The only point of William's I agree with is the need to protect Olivia and Sophia. It's the only argument of importance to me, although from William's impassioned speech, the girls are clearly an afterthought. Angela's daughters must come first. They are family, my blood. Too young to lose their mother so tragically, and too innocent to have their father torn from them for falling for the same lies Andrew told me. Olivia and Sophia have their whole lives ahead of them. They deserve a normal life with an intact, loving family. They deserve the carefree, happy childhood their mother and I never had, the childhood I now want to give them.

Ready to face down William, I stand up and hold my ground. "I do know what is at stake, William, more than you could know. But this time, I'm calling the shots."

EPILOGUE

Upstairs, at the window of my childhood bedroom, I look out on the mausoleum, grieving for Angela, Maddy, and the others killed in my stead at the hands of Andrew Novak and Felix Jager. Their lives have been cut short, but I'm left to live mine. Whether or not my future has a chance at happiness, I don't know. It's not up to me.

I close my eyes, trying to envision Nick, me—*us*—that we'll have a life together, something we both wanted before that awful night when I made the biggest mistake of my life—falling for Andrew's murderous deceptions. But I can't seem to picture it in my head. Too much has happened to expect my nightmare to end so easily.

In the darkness of my own mind, I see it again. I recognize the scene. *I'm at Bulloch Hall, in the dimly lit hallway outside my bedroom. Watching Nick walk away, his dogged gait, his unwavering silence revealing his intention. He is never coming back.*

I shudder at the vision, unsure whether it's a premonition or my imagination running wild from anxiety. It doesn't matter either way. I have no choice. I must tell Nick everything. He deserves to know the truth. I deserve to have my life back. If Nick shuns me and walks away forever, I'll accept his decision and live with it without looking back—no sorrow, no regret. I refuse to let guilt rule my life one more minute.

I jump at the rap on the door. With my heart ready to leap out of my chest, I drop onto the settee beneath the window and breathe. *Inhale . . . exhale . . . inhale . . . exhale.*

"Ma'am? Are you okay?" Nick urgent words pass through the door. He knocks again, this time more fiercely.

"Yes. Please, come in."

When the door opens wide, Nick steps inside and closes the door behind him. He looks tired, weary. His clothes, the same jeans and shirt he wore yesterday, are rumpled. I want nothing more than to run to him, throw my arms around his broad shoulders, and kiss away his pain, but I can't. Not until I know if he will have me—again.

"This room is just as I pictured it would be," Nick remarks, crossing toward me. "A bedroom fit for royalty."

The room, blanketed in deep reds and filled with heavy, baroque furniture, turns my stomach. "I assure you this is not my style. I didn't have a lot of say in decorating my own room, neither did, ah, my sister." I spin away to hide the blood draining from my face, a reaction to a near-miss. I can't say Angela's name until I'm ready to reveal myself to Nick.

"My mother had the best decorators from Washington do the whole house. She and my father wanted Bulloch Hall in all the top-tier home magazines. My parents thought it would boost their standing with the D.C. crowd."

I turn to Nick and gaze into his eyes. "But that's all history, Nick. I'm tired of living in the past with its demands, its secrets. I feel as though I've lived these last few months, no, my whole life, with my eyes closed, running from my cowardice, running from my mistakes. I'm ready to own up to everything I've done, ask myself and others for forgiveness, and never look back again. I want a future where I'm the boss of myself, not someone else's minion. I want to make my own choices based on what I want, not what others insist I must do for the good of the country or their own selfish purposes. I'm going to take back my life, my future, and live it *my* way."

My words stun me. Going into this meeting, I didn't prepare a speech. I didn't have time, nor did I have the courage to think about what I might say. But now, as I reflect on what I've just said, I'm proud of my words, the mettle behind them. Though I've never expressed them inwardly to myself, or outwardly to anyone else, they convey exactly what I've felt for most of my life. The words, and the conviction behind them, are the one good thing to come of this harrowing ordeal.

"After what I'm about to confess, I hope you and I, well, I hope you'll still want to be part of my life."

"I don't understand, Ma'am," he replies, as his smile disappears.

I rise from the settee. This is a speech I can't deliver sitting down but standing on my own two feet. "I have something to say. Something very difficult. Please, have a seat and let me finish."

Clearly confused, Nick shakes his head, and perches himself on the edge of the bed.

"There's a lot more to this conspiracy than you or I ever suspected, and it did start with an affair, with Maddy getting pregnant by William. Maddy confessed her pregnancy to Amy. And that night in Raleigh, when the FBI informed us of Maddy's death, Amy told Angela."

Across from me, Nick is restless, clearly confused and eager to jump in and say something.

"Please, let me get through this." I avoid his gaze. "It will all make sense very soon."

Fraught with nervous energy, I start pacing to room.

"Angela confronted William with the news, angrily accused him of being the baby's father and having Maddy killed. They had an awful argument. A physical one. And he accidentally knocked her down."

I stop at the window and gaze at my own reflection and wonder if Nick is seeing what I'm trying to say. "When Angela hit her head on a marble table, she lost consciousness. William panicked and called in Andrew to deal with the situation. Unfortunately, Andrew's solution was to strangle Angela to death and let William think he had accidentally killed her."

"I don't understand," he says. "None of this make sense unless..."

The moment of truth has come, one I must face with Nick head-on. I need to see the look in his eyes when I tell him. I turn around.

"Yes, Nick," I say, holding my breath. "I'm Amy."

Sitting a few steps away, with his brow furrowed, his eyes pinched and staring into mine, I can't tell if he's confused or angry. He begins to say something, then stops, shakes his head. His silence speaks volumes. I have lost him.

Slowly, Nick stands up. I close my eyes, afraid that I'll burst into tears when I see him walk away. Suddenly, his arms are around me, his hold desperate. My heart leaps at his embrace, one I return with all the strength I can muster and crying tears of joy.

"I'm never going to let you out of my sight again," Nick says, whispering in my ear. "Never."

"I don't understand, Nick. After what I put you through, how could..."

He pulls away. I open my eyes as he wipes a tear from my cheek.

"I still love you? That's easy. I never stopped. When you disappeared, I swore if I ever got you back, I would never let you go. Even when I thought you were dead, I couldn't do it. So, that's what I'm doing now."

Our lips meet, a long soft kiss of tender love. When we come up for air, we hold each other once more, then sit together on the settee. With Nick's arm around me, my head resting upon his shoulder, our free hands clasped together, I feel liberated and happier than I have in months, perhaps even, my entire life.

"I never stopped loving you, Nick, even when I couldn't remember. As Kay, as Angela, I felt your pull every time you were near."

"I have to admit, I felt the same way," Nick says with a sigh. "You can't imagine how guilty I felt being attracted to you, as Angela, with Amy gone."

"Yes, I can." Without saying a word, Nick appears to understand and goes no further down that path.

I spend the next minutes detailing the chain of events as I now remember them, from the moment I discovered Maddy's pregnancy to the moment Felix ran me off the road. I leave nothing out.

"That's quite a story," Nick says, when I finish. "I'm sorry I was so oblivious. I should have—"

I press my finger to his lips. "Shh. We've both said and done things we're sorry about. Let's not look back at our mistakes, and instead, make a commitment to the future. Right here and now, let's promise each other one thing—no more secrets, no more lies, no more apologies."

"Agreed." He seals the deal with long gentle kiss.

"As far as no more secrets or lies, that applies to William, as well. We came to an agreement when we were alone in my father's study. That is, I told him what the plan was going forward. He argued for continuing the charade, but I wouldn't back down. I told William I was prepared to confess everything—what he said and did, Andrew and Felix, me, too—so he really didn't have a choice. When we finally debriefed the president's chief of staff and the other department heads, we gave them the whole unvarnished truth, detailed everything, all the who, what, when, where, why, and how's of everything that transpired, from Maddy's confessed pregnancy the day she went missing to this morning's showdown in the mausoleum. We made clear that Andrew was the mastermind behind all the evil and Felix his hired tool."

"What happens now? Will William be charged?" Nick's face freezes with fear. "Are you exposed in any way?"

"The directors didn't come right out and say it, but I could tell they were stunned by the revelations. They left the room for a good while to discuss the situation."

Over the next few minutes, I summarize the thoughts and recommendations the directors offered after they returned to discuss them with William and me. Their first assessment was to exonerate me. As an unwitting player in the conspiracy, and the target of Andrew's hit man myself, they saw me clearly as a victim, and it would be their recommendation that I not face indictment by any state or federal court.

Their assessment of William's culpability was not so hopeful. Too many crimes had been committed to ignore his role in them. In the matter of Angela's death, he would likely face serious charges in North Carolina, aiding and abetting murder, conspiracy after-the-fact, among them, and serve prison time for those crimes. William's exposure in Maddy's death was uncertain. An investigation by the Virginia authorities would determine his fate in the case. William, in response, took up pen and paper, wrote a letter of resignation, and handed it to the Attorney General with a request that he be allowed to hire a lawyer and put his affairs in order before turning himself in.

"After all the mistakes he made," I continue, "William finally did the right thing. He told the truth and is preparing to live with the consequences of his actions."

Nick leans in and kisses me. "Best of all, we get to resume our lives. We get our happy ending after all. I can't wait any longer to ask you this."

A quick moment later, Nick is on one knee, holding my hands in his. Looking up at me, I see love in his eyes, joy in his smile. "Amelia Marie Bulloch, will you marry me?"

I want to jump up and cry "Yes!" But my answer can't be so simple. There's something I still must confess to Nick.

"I love you, more than you could ever know, Nick. But William's confession has consequences for me, for us. I'd like to marry you, if you'll still have me, but I'm a package deal. William is facing serious prison time. He could be behind bars for years. What I'm trying to say is that Olivia and Sophia are coming to live with me. If we're married, you'll need to love them, raise them as your own, just as I will. I want them to have a loving family with two parents at home, the kind of family I never had. But if you're not ready for a family—"

Nick bolts upright, pulls me to him, and wraps me in his arms. "That package sounds perfect to me. You know I'm crazy about those girls—or did you forget?" He pulls away, and with an impish grin on his face, gives me a playful wink. "Maybe we could give them a houseful of brothers and sisters to sweeten the deal."

"Now, that's an offer I can't refuse." Laughing, kissing, we enjoy the moment, its meaning—our future together has already begun.

When the laughter stops, my thoughts turn to Angela. "You know, Nick, I agreed to Andrew's crazy scheme mostly to protect my nieces. They needed their mother, not their aunt. So, I played the role, put my heart and my soul into being Angela, mothering them as if they were my own flesh and blood. It was a labor of love. I enjoyed every minute of it."

My eyes start to mist over as the joy in my heart melts into sorrow. "At some point, I'll have to explain their mother's death, their father's role, as well as mine. With Olivia going off to school, she'll be around people who might talk, so I will have to address this issue sooner than I'd like. I'm not so worried about their reactions now. But when the girls are older, and they more fully understand all that happened and why, I can't help wondering if they'll be able to forgive me for betraying both their mother's trust and theirs."

"I can't see that happening. Those girls love their Aunt Amy. They'll understand and forgive you, just as I did."

I flush with gratitude at Nick's words, as he gently kisses my cheek.

"But you're right. It's a delicate issue, one we need to be prepared to discuss with the girls before someone else does."

I take his hand in mine and lay it on my heart. "At the same time, I feel a huge sense of loss, not just for me, but for Olivia and Sophia.

As young as they both are now, I'm the only mother they'll likely ever remember. Little by little, they'll forget Angela's voice, her smile, her warm, loving hugs. Forgetting those you love is the worst thing that can happen to anyone." I squeeze Nick's hand. "Believe me. I know."

As Nick engulfs me in his arms, he kisses away my tears. "We won't let that happen. We'll work together, with Mimi, Ed, perhaps William, too, to keep the memory of Angela alive for the girls."

I nod. "Yes, it will be a good lesson to for them, for everyone—that family, and the love we share for them, never dies as long as we hold their memories near in both our minds and our hearts.

THE END

ACKNOWLEDGMENTS

est She Forget has been a labor of love for ten years, a story that started with a twinkle of an idea while watching an identity theft commercial as I huffed and puffed away on the treadmill at my gym. I spent the rest of my workout bouncing the basic premise around in my head, following one "what-if" question with another, until I had a dark, twist-filled story to tell and a first scene to write. I jumped off the treadmill, bolted home, and started typing away.

Like most authors, my first draft was awful, but through subsequent revisions, both major and minor (too many to count), and two title changes, *Lest She Forget* has finally made its way into your hands. So, first off, thank you, dear reader, for making the leap of faith in treasure and time, to buy (or borrow) and read my debut novel. I hope you found Amy's story a thrilling tale, one worth recommending to your friends, as well as online to the greater reading public via social media and book review sites, such as *GoodReads* or *BookBub*.

But neither you nor I would have the thrill of this book without the advice, expertise, support, and friendship of hundreds of people who inspired my efforts. Space does not permit even a simple list, but I'll do my best to name those whose contributions were especially significant. So, here we go—

First off, thank you to the amazing CamCat family:

- Sue Arroyo, my publisher, for believing in me and my story. I'm in awe of your entrepreneurial spirit, business acumen, and drive in creating CamCat Books, a dynamic, cohesive, and inspiring community of staff and authors working together to share great stories with the world.

- Helga Schier, CamCat's editor extraordinaire, for your keen insights, honest feedback, and most off all, enthusiasm for *Lest She Forget*, driving me to write the best story possible. My copyeditor, Christine Van Zandt, for catching my typos, grammatical errors, repetitive words, inconsistencies, and more.

- Bill Lehto, CamCat's hugely-patient business manager, for loving *Lest She Forget* and recommending it for publication.

- Maryann Appel, CamCat's Art Director, and Olivia Hammerman, book designer, for working with my ideas to create a stunning cover design for *Lest She Forget*.

- CamCat's staff for your amazing efforts to produce a beautiful book and promote me and all my fellow CamCat authors: Laura Wooffitt, Abigail Miles, Gabe Schier, Meredith Lyons, Elana Gibson, Kayla Webb, Jessica Homami, Nicole Delise, and Camryn Flowers.

- My fellow CamCat authors, too many to name here, for your friendship, support, and cross-promotion.

A huge thank you to Anne Brewer, my amazing developmental editor. Your keen insights guided my first major revision, leading to a tighter, more suspenseful story. Thank you also to Terri Bischoff, editor, Crooked Lane books, for your feedback that led me to revise my first two chapters.

Thank you to my Sisters in Crime nationally and across two chapters (SinC Atlanta, Florida Gulf Coast SinC) with special thanks for invaluable advice, counsel, support, and friendship over the years: Hank Phillippi Ryan, Chris Goff, Martha Reed, Debra Goldstein, Beth Terrell, Sharon Marchisello, Shirley Garret, Maggie Toussaint, Teresa Michael, along with too many others to name here.

International Thriller Writers, especially Dawn Ius, former editor of *The Big Thrill,* for giving me the opportunity to interview, write, and learn from so many talented authors and share my thoughts with the thriller-reading public. A big thank you also to ITW's wonderfully supportive Debut Writers Program: Tori Eldridge, program coordinator, and Elena Hartwell Taylor, Facebook community administrator, and all its debut authors, both past and present.

Clay Stafford and the great team behind Killer Nashville, the crime writers conference that launched my journey into crime-writing in 2013 and, in 2022, my publishing career, when I received my offer in-person from Sue. In the nine years I've attended Killer Nashville, I've had the pleasure of meeting hundreds of people—authors, editors, agents, marketing gurus—who helped me: hone my story-telling skills; pitch my books; learn about crime, forensics, and the business side of writing; meet and talk with some of the biggest authors in the business; and most importantly, connect and reconnect year after year with great friends who have contributed to my success.

I also want to thank all my friends and family scattered cross Minnesota, Iowa, Georgia, and Florida for their love and encouragement as I travelled this road to publication. I need to give a big shout-out (or perhaps, an apology) to three generous people, my cousins Tony and Deb Wand, and my Chi Omega sister, Laurie Blessum—thank you for reading a very early version of *Lest She Forget* and politely encouraging me, nevertheless.

A big shout-out also to my big sister, Teri Wuebker—thank you for being one of my biggest fans, for sharing your enthusiasm for me and my book in-person and via Facebook with your friends.

Thank you to my amazing kids, Olivia and Frank, for bringing so much joy to my life and sharing this adventure with me.

Last, but not least, my eternal love and gratitude to my husband, Lou, for our wonderful life together, as well as the unwavering support you've given me in pursuing my every interest and dream from the moment we met.

ABOUT THE AUTHOR

Lisa Malice is a psychologist-turned-writer. *Lest She Forget*, her debut novel, earned finalist honors in several unpublished writing contests, including the Chanticleer Clue (Thriller) Contest. She is an active member in Sisters in Crime (SinC), International Thriller Writers (ITW), Mystery Writers of America (MWA), and the Authors Guild. A native of suburban Minneapolis (Edina), Lisa earned her B.S. in Psychology from the University of Minnesota and her M.S. and Ph.D. from The Georgia Institute of Technology. After more than three decades in Atlanta, Lisa now lives in the Tampa area with her husband, a business start-up consultant, with whom she raised two wonderful young adults, Olivia and Frank. When she's not writing or reading, Lisa loves to spend her time hiking, sailing, fishing, kayaking, and snorkeling. She also enjoys golf, travel, entertaining friends and family, and playing fetch with her granddoggy, Pepper.

Learn more and connect with Lisa:
www.LisaMalice.com
www.Facebook.com/LisaMaliceAuthor
www.Instragram.com/LisaMaliceAuthor

If you enjoyed Lisa Malice's
Lest She Forget,
consider leaving us a review
to help our authors.

And check out Kate Michaelson's
Hidden Rooms

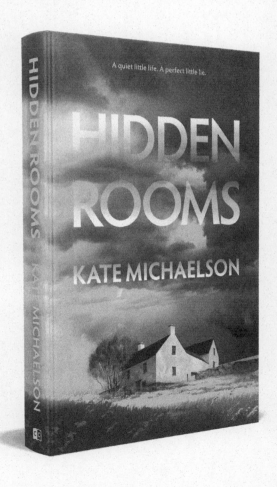

Chapter 1

ate September 2022

L I grew up inside a lightning bolt, in a family of pure momentum. My siblings and I were young, stupid, and fearless in our white gingerbread house, surrounded by dark earth, green shoots, and wild woods—untamed beasts running loose from morning to night. We snarled and bucked, more a pack than a family.

Born less than a year apart, my brother Ethan and I spent most of our lives scrapping after the same few things, pinching each other where we knew it would hurt the most. But we also protected each other. When Trevor Paltree shoved Ethan off the tall metal slide the first day of preschool, I kicked Trevor's little ass, and I'd do it again.

Only, now, I didn't know what protecting my brother looked like, though I felt fairly certain that kicking his fiancée's ass was not it. Besides, I couldn't even say what exactly his fiancée Beth was up to, which (admittedly) undermined my argument. Putting my head down and going along with the wedding might feel cowardly, but it also seemed like the least destructive path forward.

So, that's how I found myself pulling up to Ethan and Beth's house to pick up my puce monstrosity of a bridesmaid's dress with Beth's recent words still replaying in my mind. "Riley, you know I'd never do anything to hurt Ethan." The problem was that she also once said with a wink and a smile that what Ethan didn't know couldn't hurt him.

I got out of my car and lifted my hair off my neck to catch the breeze. The autumn sun had built throughout the afternoon into the kind of fleetingly gorgeous day that makes up for Ohio's multitude of weather sins: one last warm postscript to summer. Rain loomed in the low shelf of clouds to the north. I crossed my fingers that it would hold off until I could get home to walk Bruno. Maybe I could even get a run in if my energy held out.

My phone buzzed, and I knew without looking it would be my sister Audra. She called most days and knew that just the previous night, I'd finally worked up the nerve to have a conversation with Ethan about Beth. She would want the details. I was amazed she had waited this long.

"How'd it go with Ethan?" Her melodious voice skipped along briskly. People usually went with what she said simply because they were so swept with how she said it. As her sister, I was an exception.

"Hello to you too." I continued toward the house but slowed my pace. "I'll give you one guess how it went."

"Hello, *dearest* Riley. I'd guess he got mad."

"Not just mad. He guilt-tripped me. I asked him if he'd noticed anything wrong with Beth and he acted all injured about it. He told me, 'she thinks you're her friend.'" I mimicked Ethan's self-righteous tone. The jab still stung. "I told him I think of her as a friend too, which is how I know she's hiding something." Admittedly, I couldn't untangle what it was.

"Yeah, but what kind of friends can you be with someone like her? It's like being friends with a mannequin. I don't know how you can tell if she's hiding something when she never shares anything about herself—"

"Look, I can't talk about it now." I lowered my voice as I neared the house. "I'm at their place getting my dress. I'll call you later."

"Call me on your way home. Good luck."

"It'll be fine," I responded, but the line was already dead.

As I climbed the porch steps, the front of their house looked so Instagram-perfect that I wondered whether I'd been seeing problems that weren't there. The afternoon light slanted across pumpkins and mums that Beth had arranged just so. Dried bundles of corn rattled in the breeze. Beth had set out a blue ceramic bowl full of kibble for Bibbs, the half-feral cat that had adopted her and Ethan.

The only thing amiss was the open door of the cast-iron mailbox nestled amidst the pumpkins and mums. Beth would kill the mail carrier for ruining the ambiance. I grabbed the few pieces of mail in the box and shut the little door obligingly, like a good future sister-in-law.

Careful not to disturb a precarious wreath of orange berries, I knocked on the screen door and tapped my foot, ready to grab my puffy dress and go. I had been a whirl of motion all day, zipping through work and crossing items off my to-do list. I worked for Wicks, an oversized candle company that sold overpriced candles. Today was my last day in the office before a trip to England to transfer systems for a new distribution center.

I'd been fighting some kind of long-term bug for months, but today I felt a glimmer of my former self, twitchy with energy and moving at a clip to get everything done. Deep down, I sensed that rather than a sudden return to health, my energy was more of a fizz of nerves, arising from the uneasy note I'd ended on with Ethan the night before. Our squabble had nagged at me throughout the day, like an ache that couldn't settle in my joints as long as I kept moving.

I rapped once more on the door and when no one answered, I tried the handle. Unlocked. This was not unusual in a town where nobody locked their doors, but Beth wasn't from here. At least she hadn't lived here long enough for people to think she's from here, which was typically a person's whole life.

I plastered a smile on my face and stepped into the house—immaculate as usual and smelling faintly of cinnamon. I couldn't tell if the homey scent came from something baking or wafted from a candle. A friend from Wicks and I played a game of trading terrible ideas for candle taglines. Still in work mode, my brain began composing a homespun blurb about the charms of cinnamon. *Nothing welcomes 'em in like cinnamon!*

Appalling. I'd write it down later.

"Beth?" I called out. The only reply came from the ticking of the grandfather clock down the hall. I peeked into the small kitchen, where the pale blue vintage-style fridge rattled and groaned inefficiently in the corner. My mom once described it as, much like Beth, looking cute and sucking up energy. I had snorted, mostly relieved my mom had directed her acidity somewhere other than me.

I poked my head into each room downstairs: each as spotless and Bethless as the last. Checking my phone, I sighed. Nothing. I replied to her last text with *At the house to get my dress. Where are you?*

It seemed fair to look in the backyard and then leave in good conscience. As I passed through the small kitchen again, I noticed that the door out to the backyard stood open a few inches. I pushed it open fully and descended the steps off the back porch.

Ethan and Beth lived on ten acres, and the smells of sweet, smoky autumn air and sun-warmed fields hit me as I walked into the yard. Unlike the front of the house, the back was still a work in progress, with a freshly rinsed, cracked concrete patio jutting up unevenly and half-finished projects littering the yard, but the view of the fields and, beyond that, the forest ramping up for fall lent the mess a pastoral charm.

Laundry billowed on the clothesline, the edge of a sheet skimming the top of the soft green grass. I imagined Beth reveling in her home-maker image as she hung the laundry out to dry and taking pictures of the bedding wafting in the breeze to post. The clouds to the north had bloomed from gray into a more ominous purple while I'd been inside, and a cooler breeze had picked up. With the serene blue on one side and clouds heavy with rain on the other, the sky seemed to be of two minds. But I may have been projecting.

As I looked at the coming rain and the clothes on the line, something about Beth's absence struck me as wrong. She had been odd lately, but disappearing in the middle of the day didn't really fit her brand of odd. If anything, she was the opposite—staying close to home and fastidious about her routine and the wedding plans. The hairs on my arms prickled in the breeze.

Passing the clothesline, I had just decided to text Ethan when a sheet caught a gust of wind and billowed into my face. As I struggled to grab its fluttering edges, I felt a wet stickiness. Finally grasping it, I pulled the fabric taut. A pattern of little, yellow fleur-de-lis dotted the white cotton, but it was the irregular dark red splotches that caught my attention. The marks trailed across the lower corner where they became more saturated and coalesced into the shape of a hand. My scalp tingled, and my ears began to ring. A dozen scenarios flashed through my mind, all ending in fresh blood and a missing Beth.

"Well . . ." I tried to slow my breath. "That doesn't seem good." My head swam and my vision tunneled as I reached for my phone.

More Thrilling Reads from CamCat Books

CamCat
Books

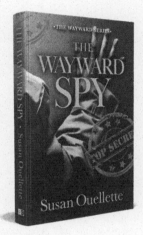

Available now, wherever books are sold.

CamCat
Books

VISIT US ONLINE FOR MORE BOOKS TO LIVE IN:
CAMCATBOOKS.COM

SIGN UP FOR CAMCAT'S FICTION NEWSLETTER FOR
COVER REVEALS, EBOOK DEALS, AND MORE EXCLUSIVE CONTENT.

CamCatBooks   @CamCatBooks   @CamCat_Books   @CamCatBooks